THE TRUTH ABOUT THE DEVLINS

ALSO BY LISA SCOTTOLINE

FICTION

Loyalty

What Happened to the Bennetts

Eternal

Someone Knows

After Anna

One Perfect Lie

Most Wanted

Every Fifteen Minutes

Keep Quiet

Don't Go

Come Home

Save Me

Look Again

Daddy's Girl

Dirty Blonde

Devil's Corner

Running from the Law

Final Appeal

ROSATO & DINUNZIO SERIES

Feared

Exposed

Damaged

Corrupted

Betrayed

Accused

ROSATO & ASSOCIATES SERIES

Think Twice

Lady Killer

Killer Smile

Dead Ringer

Courting Trouble

The Vendetta Defense

Moment of Truth

Mistaken Identity

Rough Justice

Legal Tender

Everywhere That Mary Went

NONFICTION (WITH FRANCESCA SERRITELLA)

I See Life Through Rosé-Colored Glasses

I Need a Lifeguard Everywhere but the Pool

I've Got Sand in All the Wrong Places

Does This Beach Make Me Look Fat?

Have a Nice Guilt Trip

Meet Me at Emotional Baggage Claim

Best Friends, Occasional Enemies

My Nest Isn't Empty, It Just Has More Closet Space

Why My Third Husband Will Be a Dog

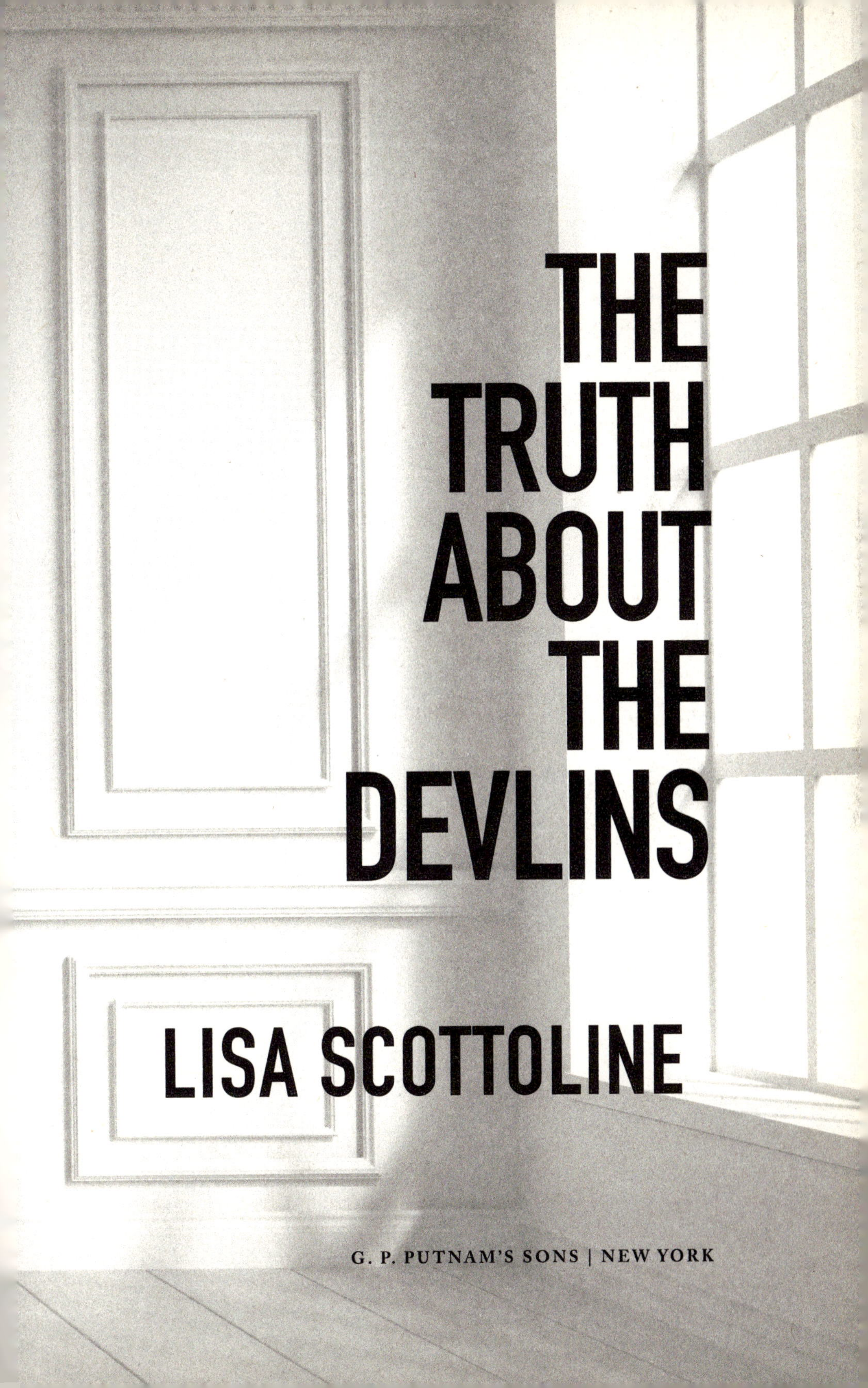

THE TRUTH ABOUT THE DEVLINS

LISA SCOTTOLINE

G. P. PUTNAM'S SONS | NEW YORK

PUTNAM
— EST. 1838 —

G. P. PUTNAM'S SONS
Publishers Since 1838
An imprint of Penguin Random House LLC
penguinrandomhouse.com

The Library of Congress has catalogued the hardcover edition of this book as follows:

Names: Scottoline, Lisa, author.
Title: The truth about the Devlins / Lisa Scottoline.
Description: New York : G. P. Putnam's Sons, 2024. |
Identifiers: LCCN 2023056487 (print) | LCCN 2023056488 (ebook) |
ISBN 9780525539704 (hardcover) | ISBN 9780525539711 (ebook)
Subjects: LCSH: Murder—Investigation—Fiction. |
LCGFT: Thrillers (Fiction) | Detective and mystery fiction. | Novels.
Classification: LCC PS3569.C725 T78 2024 (print) |
LCC PS3569.C725 (ebook) | DDC 813/.54—dc23/eng/20231208
LC record available at https://lccn.loc.gov/2023056487
LC ebook record available at https://lccn.loc.gov/2023056488

ISBN 9780593719824

Printed in the United States of America
10 9 8 7 6 5 4 3 2 1

Book design by Lorie Pagnozzi

With love for Francesca, my wonder of a daughter

THE MAIN THING IS
TO BE MOVED,
TO LOVE,
TO HOPE,
TO TREMBLE,
TO LIVE.

—AUGUSTE RODIN

CHAPTER ONE

At first I thought I heard him wrong. It was impossible coming from John, my older brother, the firstborn son, the Most Valuable Devlin. Me, I'm the black sheep, the baby of the family, the charming disappointment. John was Class President, and I was Class Clown. He was Most Likely to Succeed, I was Most Likely to Get a Speeding Ticket. That's why I never expected him to confess to murder.

"What?" My mouth dropped open. "Did you just say you *killed* somebody?"

"Yes." My brother nodded, jittery. His blue eyes looked unfocused, which never happened. Lasers have nothing on John Devlin.

"That can't be. Not *you*. You're, like, the best—"

"I did it," John said, panicky. "I *killed* a man. TJ, what should I do?"

"How do I know? You're the lawyer." I didn't get it. John and everyone else in my family were lawyers in our family firm, Devlin & Devlin. I'm a convicted criminal. On second thought, maybe I would've asked me, too.

"God, no, I can't believe this." Tears filmed John's eyes, which surprised me. I didn't know he had any emotions except disapproval.

We stood on the large flagstone patio overlooking the pool and pool house. When he'd taken me outside tonight, I thought he wanted the two grand I owed him.

"John, who did you . . . kill?"

"A client."

Yikes. I'm an investigator at the law firm. My family keeps me behind the scenes, but I don't need applause, just a paycheck. Being an ex-con doesn't pay as well as it should. "Tell me what happened."

"I don't know where to start. Oh God, this is awful." John grimaced, stricken. He ran his tongue over his lips. "Okay, well, we were at the corporate center, Knickerbocker Quarry. I hit him with a rock—"

"A rock?" *What is this, summer camp?* "Why? When?"

"Less than an hour ago. I came directly here."

Meanwhile there was no blood on him. Only my brother could kill somebody with a rock and not get dirty. His silk tie was spotless and his Brioni suit fit him like Batman. "How did you beat him with a rock and—"

"I didn't beat him. I threw the rock and it hit him in the head. I heard a crack . . ." John's upper lip curled with disgust. "Then he *dropped*."

I figured it was his fastball. John pitched for Villanova, where every Devlin but me went to college. "Then what happened?"

"I came here. I knew Nancy and everybody would be waiting. I panicked." John raked a hand through thinning brown hair. He was forty years old but looked fifty and usually acted eighty, but not tonight.

"Okay, let's go. We have to do something with the body."

John recoiled. "Like what?"

"Bury it?" *Isn't that why you're telling me?*

"TJ, no, we can't. I don't know what to do." John rubbed his face. "We can't leave now. You know how Dad is about his birthday."

I glanced through the window to the dining room, where dinner was just getting underway. My mother was setting an antipasto platter on the table, and my father stood talking with my sister, Gabby, and her husband, Martin. John's wife, Nancy, sat with my little nephew, Connor, who was playing with a Matchbox Jaguar I'd brought him. My father's birthday was a national holiday in our house. Christmas never had it so good.

John straightened, blinking. "TJ, I can't live with this. I'm coming clean. I'm going to tell—"

"No, stop." I grabbed him by his hand-stitched lapel. "You'll go to prison."

"I deserve to."

"You can't handle it."

"*You* did."

"That's how I know you can't."

"I can if you can."

My brother is crazy competitive. If he'd been in the Donner party, he would've pigged out. "John, let's go—"

"Here's Mom now." John turned, and my mother opened the French doors to the patio, making a chic silhouette in a dark Chanel pantsuit, backlit by the chandelier. Marie Spano Devlin had the only brown eyes and strong nose in our family, and her olive skin was spared our regulation-Irish freckles. Silvery strands gleamed in her onyx-black chignon and lines bracketed her mouth, but to me, she'd only gotten lovelier with age. I adore my mother, and she always has my back. She calls me her little devil, which fits.

"Boys, time for dinner."

"Mom, sorry, we have to go." I detected Lambrusco on her breath, sipped out of sight because of my sobriety. The scent wasn't strong, but I'm McGruff for booze.

"Go where?" My mother blinked, puzzled. "We're about to eat."

"I know, sorry." I tugged John into the dining room, and my mother stepped aside, her lips parting in dismay.

"TJ, what's going on? You can't miss dinner."

"Please, eat without us." I hustled past the table as everyone looked at us in surprise, especially my father. Paul Francis Devlin had graying light brown hair, and we looked a lot alike. We had the same blue eyes, round and set far apart with thick eyebrows, a longish nose, and a mouth that was on the big side. Every time I looked at my father, I saw a successful version of myself. I can only guess what he saw when he looked at me.

"TJ, where do you think you're going? You'll miss dinner."

"I know, I'm really sorry but it can't be helped." I kept moving but my father was already out of his chair. He'd taken off his tie, and his white oxford shirt was wrinkled from the workday. He was a big guy, six three and in decent shape. He'd played basketball at Villanova before they were Final Four good, a former power forward who still exuded power.

John added, "I'm sorry, too. We'll be back as soon as we can."

"John, what did TJ do *now*?" my father snapped, assuming that I was in trouble and John was helping me, which even I had to admit made sense. I was the Bad Son and John was the Good Son. Our roles in our family are like our seats at the kitchen table. Forever.

I dragged John out of the house and down the flagstone steps to the circular driveway. My parents lived in a McMansion that reeked of curb appeal, on six acres of perfect landscaping in Philly's exclusive Main Line. Automatic sprinklers whirred in the garden, and the air smelled like ChemLawn. I never felt at home here because we grew up in the Devlin starter house, and our problems started after we got rich. Not that I have anything against money. Money has something against me.

We walked to my car, which was parked behind John's and my sister's black Range Rovers. My father and mother both have black Range Rovers, too. Sometimes I'm surprised they didn't name the firm Devlin & Devlin & Devlin & Devlin.

"I'll drive, let's go." I opened the door and jumped in my car, and John followed suit, frowning.

"New car? You've owed me two grand since forever."

"You'll get it back, I needed new calipers." I'm a car guy. I buy cars at seized-asset auctions, fix them up, and flip them. This one was a 2020 Maserati Quattroporte, formerly owned by a drug kingpin. Basically, I put the car in cartel.

"Don't drive crazy."

"Have we met?" I pressed a button, igniting one of the most distinctive engines on the planet.

We took off.

CHAPTER TWO

We whizzed past big stone houses, townhome developments, and strip malls. John let his anxiety show now that we were alone, raking his hand through his hair again. I gave him time to calm down, but I had questions.

"So, John, tell me what happened."

"It's horrible, it all happened so fast, I just reacted."

"What happened? Break it down."

"I don't know where to start." John rubbed his face. "There was so much blood. I didn't mean to kill him. I wasn't aiming for his head. I was aiming for the gun."

"Who's the client? Do I know him?"

"No. His name's Neil Lemaire. He's the accountant at Runstan Electronics."

"Why were you meeting with him?"

"Okay, well." John tried to rally. "The company's being acquired, and I was doing due diligence. I found irregularities in the accounting."

"Like money missing?" My brother has an accounting degree *and* a law degree, but I can juggle.

"Yes."

"How much?"

"About a hundred grand."

Wow. "So he was embezzling?"

"Ya think? It had to be him because he's the only accountant at the company. I told him we needed to talk and he asked me to meet him, so I agreed."

"Alone?"

"Yes."

I realized my brother was a dumb smart person. I myself am a smart dumb person. If I were accusing somebody of embezzling a hundred grand, I'd bring an army. "So then what happened?"

"I confronted him, and he denied it. Then he offered to pay me to cover it up."

I brightened. "How much?"

John shot me a disapproving look. "I didn't ask, TJ. I'm in a fiduciary relationship to Runstan. I can't countenance criminal acts by its employees."

"Weren't you curious?"

"Of course not."

"Me, neither," I said, but I wasn't kidding anybody. "Then what happened?"

"I said no, and Lemaire started pacing back and forth. Then all of a sudden, he pulled a gun on me and told me to get on my knees."

Holy shit. "So that's self-defense. He threatened your life."

"Right, I know, but still . . . I killed him."

"It's not murder, though."

"Technically, self-defense is a defense to murder. Don't play lawyer, TJ."

"Don't play criminal, John."

"Anyway, I knelt down and saw a rock on the ground, so I grabbed it and winged it at him. I hit him in the forehead. He dropped and fell on his back. He didn't move. It was awful. There was blood all over his face, and his legs were bent under him. He was dead."

"Then what did you do?"

"Like I said, I got scared, I panicked, I ran." John shook his head, and I could see he was getting nervous again, a sight I would have otherwise enjoyed.

"Okay, don't worry, just calm down."

"How can I?" John threw up his hands. "I killed the guy!"

"Deep breath. Relax."

"Oh, shut up." John fell silent, looking out the window.

I gripped the wheel, driving fast. We'd be there in no time, and my emotions were catching up with me. I've done terrible things, but I'd never kill anybody. My destruction is aimed at myself, where it belongs.

I realized that once we got there, we'd have to decide what to do. I knew what I'd do, but I didn't know what John would do.

I focused on the road, and we hurtled ahead.

CHAPTER THREE

It was dusk by the time we reached a deserted stretch near an underpass to the Pennsylvania Turnpike. There was nothing around, no lights or security cameras, only a rusted cyclone fence collapsed in sections around a grassy area, accessed by a service road of gravel, dirt, and stones that were bad for my undercarriage. I drove the Maserati only on dry asphalt and never to a murder scene.

"John, *this* is the place? You said it was a corporate center."

"This is Phase Two of Knickerbocker Quarry Center. They start construction next month. Phase One is on the other side of the quarry."

"So how'd you end up here?"

"We met at the corporate center, and Lemaire told me to follow him, so I did. I didn't know it was like this until I got here. Park ahead, near the opening in the fence."

I drove up, cut the ignition, and we got out of the car. John bolted ahead through the fence opening, and I hurried after him on a deer path of weeds and overgrown grass. I was almost through when I heard John's shocked voice.

"TJ!"

I reached him, standing in a clearing. There was no dead body, only dirt, grass, and brush. "Where is he?"

"I don't know," John answered, astonished. "He was right here. He was on his back. He was dead, I know it. Blood *poured* onto the ground."

We both looked down. Blackness glimmered underneath the grass, rubble, and stones. I crouched and swiped the spot with my fingers, which came away gritty with blood. "Okay, so he was here. I don't see the gun or the rock, do you?"

"No. He must've taken them."

"Hmm. Odd. That would be thinking straight, for somebody who had his clock cleaned."

"What do you mean?"

"You know, he'd be woozy, like you feel after a brawl."

John snorted. "I've never been in one."

"You're Irish, bro. You should be ashamed."

"That's a stereotype."

"It's a virtue."

"Whatever, clearly he's alive." John threw up his arms. "Which means I didn't kill him! Thank God!"

"Wait." I realized something. "Where's his car? There was no car out front."

"My God, yes!" John shot back, elated. "His car's gone! He really is alive!"

"It's the likeliest explanation."

"It's the *only* explanation." John broke into a grin. "He's alive, he drove away. What else could have happened?"

"I'm thinking."

"Of what?"

"What else could have happened. I'm trying to analyze—"

"You? *Analyze?*"

That stung, but I stuffed it. I'm good at stuffing my feelings, though apparently it's a bad thing to be good at. "How do you know he was alone?"

"There were no other cars."

"He could have had somebody already in place, hiding."

John's smile faded. "Why would he?"

"In case something went sideways, which it did. Someone could be watching us, even now." I scanned the scene but saw nothing suspicious. The corporate center and apartment complex were on the far side of the quarry. Beyond that was the Pennsylvania Turnpike, and the whooshing of traffic was background noise.

John grimaced. "You really think someone's watching?"

"It's possible. What kind of car did he drive?"

"I don't know, a Volvo?"

"A sedan?"

"Yes."

"What color?"

"Maroon. TJ, is *everything* about cars?"

I let it go. "Let's look around, just in case. You go right and I'll go left." I took off, searching for a body. There was none, only more weeds, underbrush, and thornbushes. The wind picked up, and brownish reeds rustled with a dry sound. Shards of beer bottles glinted in the grass, and I expected to find a used condom, but didn't. Kids today disappoint me. Always on TikTok.

I walked through a section of cyclone fence that had been torn down, then stepped on a metal sign. DANGER—CLIFF EDGE, it read in big red letters. NO TRESPASSING BEYOND THIS POINT. Below that was a stick figure in cartoon waves. DEEP COLD WATER. DO NOT SWIM. I got the gist.

I reached the quarry, a massive chasm of about eighty acres excavated into the earth. Its drop was steep and lethal, and its stone walls striated with gray, black, and dark brown veins and ledges of vegetation. There was water at the bottom, its greenish chop glimmering in the waning light. I squinted for a floating body but didn't see one.

My gaze stayed on the water, and the notion that John could have been killed was sinking in. I grew up idolizing my brother and following him everywhere, even worming my way into the dugout of his Little League All-Star team. A snippet of memory took me back to playing catch with him in the backyard after dinner, when dusk would shade to darkness so gradually I didn't realize day had become night. Fireflies would fill the air like fallen constellations.

John would call out, *TJ, time to go in!*

Not yet! I never wanted to go in. It was the only time I had my big brother to myself. He was my own personal All-Star.

We have to go in, the fireflies are here! You'll catch fire!

What? I looked around, panicky. *You catch fire from fireflies?*

Yes! You burn to death if one touches you. Like hell!

"TJ!" John called out, jolting me into the present.

"John, what do you know about Lemaire? Is he married or what?"

"He's gay, single, that's all I know. Why?"

"I'm wondering if somebody else knew he was embezzling. Or if he was working with anybody else."

"You mean a co-conspirator."

Okay, Perry Mason. "Yes."

"He's the only accountant in the department. The bookkeeper's an old lady."

"Maybe it wasn't someone who worked with him, maybe it was a friend of his. My point is, someone else could know what he was up to."

"I don't know anything else about him."

"We're assuming he's not dead because his car's gone, but what if he was part of a conspiracy? His co-conspirators could have come here and taken his body and the gun. That could be true whether he was dead or alive. They wouldn't want this to come to light any more than we do."

"So he could be dead, after all?" John groaned. "I could have killed him?"

"I don't know what happened. We can't know on these facts."

"Should I call him?" John raised his phone. "See if he picks up?"

"No. I don't want it in your phone records. When did you arrange this meeting?"

"Today. On the phone around three."

"Did you call him or did he call you?"

"I called him."

"Did you confirm in an email or text?"

"No." John started shaking his head, upset again. "Oh man, oh man—"

"Did anybody know you were meeting him? Like Sabrina?" Sabrina was our receptionist, who was also my brother's work wife, but it was a bad marriage.

"No, I didn't tell her, I just said I was leaving for the day."

"Did she make a note on the calendar, like she usually does?"

"I don't know. How the hell would I know?"

"Were there any messages for you when you got back?"

"I didn't go back. I went straight to Mom and Dad's. Sabrina knew it was Dad's birthday. We had the cake at the office, remember? She probably assumed I was going out for a gift or a card."

I thought it made sense. The thing about a family business is that there's no line between work and home, or between your business and your *business*. Employees at Devlin & Devlin had watched me grow from childhood to incarceration, and if I could monetize my entertainment value, I'd be rich.

"John, so nobody knows you were meeting Lemaire here today?"

"Correct. You think somebody took his body, the gun, and the car?"

"It's a possibility. Or he bounced. I'm thinking the Caymans."

"So what do I tell Stan?"

"Who's Stan?"

"Stan Malinowski. He owns Runstan. Remember, we met him when we were little. Dad took us to see him."

"Oh, right."

"Whatever, I owe Stan an opinion letter on the acquisition next week."

"John, if this gets out, there's not gonna be an acquisition. When a company's accountant goes missing, that's not a company I'd acquire. And I buy drug-dealer cars."

"No, don't say that. The acquisition has to go through. It's a massive deal."

"Look, right now we have bigger problems, and if we're gone longer, it'll look suspicious. I say we go home and have cake." Since I quit drinking, I'm addicted to sugar like everybody else.

"What about Lemaire?"

"We'll figure it out. I got this."

"*You?* What're *you* gonna do?"

"Investigate. It's my job, remember?"

"You're not a real investigator. Your job's a sinecure."

"A what?" I didn't even know the definition of the insult.

"TJ, be real. Mom makes work for you. It's a do-nothing job."

I felt my temper flare. "Bro, try not insulting me while I'm helping you. You came to me, so listen to me. We're going home, and you're not going to say anything."

"What about Nancy?"

"What about her?" My brother's wife, Nancy, was like my brother, only with ovaries. I never liked her, and she never liked me, especially after my nephew, Connor, was born. Moms worry when alcoholic ex-cons are around their babies. Go figure.

"She'll ask."

"Make something up."

"She's not stupid, TJ. She'll grill me as soon as we get in the car."

"So think of something. Didn't you ever keep a secret?"

John grimaced. "Not one *this* big."

"Follow my lead."

CHAPTER FOUR

We entered my parents' magnificent dining room, which was dominated by a glistening walnut table and high-back carved chairs. Oil landscapes hung on forest-green walls that matched a malachite surround on the fireplace. A glowing crystal chandelier shed expensive light on my parents, Nancy, and Connor at the table, where fancy dessert plates with gold rims were filled with cake remains. I could hear Gabby and her husband, Martin, in the kitchen, talking and laughing. We'd missed the blowing-out-the-candles, but plenty of cake was left, so things were looking up.

I composed myself. "Honey, we're home!"

My father frowned. "TJ, where were you?"

"Dad, I'm sorry. It couldn't be helped—"

"On my birthday? Explain yourself."

"John, is everything okay?" Nancy cocked her head, and her sleek blond hair fell to one side. She was head-cheerleader pretty in a flowery dress, but her blue eyes glinted and her lips formed a sour pout.

"Sorry, Nance." John kissed her on the cheek, sat down, and ruffled up Connor's hair. "How's my buddy?"

"Daddy, I ate Brussels sprouts."

"Good for you!"

"Big mistake, Connor." I sat down. "You're gonna fart up a storm."

Connor burst into giggles, and I cut myself a piece of vanilla cake with buttercream icing. It was my father's and my favorite, the only thing we have in common except DNA.

Meanwhile he kept frowning. "TJ, where the hell did you go?"

My mother placed a hand on his arm. "Paul, not now. Boys, look what I got your father. It's vintage, an Oyster Cosmograph Daytona, the same watch that Paul Newman had." She gestured to a stainless-steel Rolex with a white face, gleaming in an open green box. My father collected watches, a hobby I never understood. At least cars are fun. Watches only tell you how late you are.

"Wow, nice, Mom," I told her.

"Paul Newman *wishes* he were Paul Devlin," John added.

My father remained undeterred. "Marie, I have a right to know where the boys were."

"Humor me, dear. Put on your watch. Show it off."

My father slipped on the watch, its heavy bracelet glinting in the light. "I love it, honey. Thank you."

My gaze fell on the Rolex and I got a bad feeling, flashing on my senior year at Penn State. I wasn't graduating because I had to take a statistics final and owed a Spanish paper, but the school let me walk in the graduation ceremony. My family arrived that day with my gift, a stainless-steel Rolex Submariner.

My mother beamed. *We're very proud of you, son.*

My father forced a smile. *Take care of that watch. It should last a lifetime.*

Thanks, you guys. I slipped on the watch, but I didn't feel Rolex-worthy. I had doubts I'd get my degree after a college career of terrible grades and excellent partying. I ended up wearing the watch to graduation, feeling like a fraud. I didn't earn a diploma, so I never wore the Rolex again.

My father eyed me hard. "TJ, have you been drinking?"

"No, I'm sober."

"You *swear*?"

"Yes, I swear I'm sober." I met his eye evenly. I felt solid in my sobriety, 708 days and counting, almost two years now, but I was only five months out of prison and court-mandated rehab. My father loathed that I was an alcoholic because his own father had been. I had to train him to trust me again, a problem reserved for excellent liars.

"You're not back with bad actors, are you?"

"No, Dad." I'd cut off my old drinking buddies, a tenet of AA, and I'd never see those friends again. One of them, nobody would ever see again. I felt an anguished twinge but stuffed it down.

"I won't pay for another rehab, son."

"You won't have to, and I'm paying you back for the first one."

"Are you *using*? Because if you—"

"No, I'm not," I interrupted, since I can't stand to hear him say *using* like he's in-the-know. I was a beer guy, not a drug addict. A heroin user I met in rehab joked that beer was a pussy addiction, but listen, beer was everywhere, with beer goggles, beer bellies, and *Hold my beer.* Every sport ran beer commercials. When was the last time you saw a heroin ad?

My mother interjected, "TJ, it was about Carrie, wasn't it? Are you trying to get her back?"

"Mom, no." I missed Carrie every minute, but she'd never have me back. I forked some cake into my mouth, eating my feelings. Luckily, they were delicious.

Gabby called from the kitchen, "Dad, lay off TJ! He was working on something for me!"

My father lifted a skeptical eyebrow. "Why didn't you say so before, Gab?"

"Because it's on that pro bono case you hate!"

"Which one?"

"What's the difference? You hate them all!"

I smiled inwardly. I love my sister, the family peacemaker, our own Swiss Miss.

My father turned to me. "TJ, if you were working on Gabby's case, why did John go with you?"

I stalled to think of an answer, finishing my cake. "I needed to borrow money, okay? I didn't want to ask in front of everybody, then we ran into traffic."

"What did you need the money for?"

"New brake calipers."

"Ta-da!" Gabby grinned, entering the dining room with a gift wrapped in tartan paper. My sister was cute, with amused green eyes set close together, a turned-up nose, and a smile like on an Amazon box. She wore her hair in a practical short cut and was dressed in a simple cotton sweater and jeans. She was followed by her husband, Dr. Martin Ngobe, a Nigerian-born surgeon who'd been repairing cleft palates in Kenya when he met Gabby, who was also volunteering there. Martin was a warm and bulky six foot two, also dressed casually in a sweater and jeans. Gabby and Martin wanted to save the world, but I told them to get busy in the bedroom. It's always the wrong people who reproduce.

My mother clapped at the gift. "How exciting! Happy birthday, dear! Tick tock . . ."

My father chuckled. "That's dark, Marie."

"You know what I mean." My mother shoved him playfully, since it was a running joke that she wanted him to retire next year. Unfortunately, the king was in no hurry to give up the throne.

"Happy birthday, Dad." Gabby set the gift down and my father smiled, shaking off his bad mood. He loves presents, which is something I love about him. And I *do* love him, even though he's a hard man to love. He's an even harder man to disappoint.

My father turned to Connor. "Which should I open first, the card or the present? I think the card, don't you?"

"No, Pop! The present!"

"Don't you want to see the card?"

"The present! The present!" Connor giggled. He was an adorable four-year-old with a scattering of freckles and a mop of blond hair. He loves my father, who's great with kids. I still don't know why he wasn't great with me.

"Let's see." My father took off the wrapping paper and handed it to my mother, who folded it by force of habit. When we were growing up, she used to save wrapping paper and give us blank birthday cards so they could be reused. The first time she signed my birthday card, I knew we were rich.

"My God, will you look at these!" My father ran a hand over the gift, a set of Winston Churchill's *A History of the English-Speaking Peoples* with old-fashioned red leather covers and gold-embossed spines. "These are beautiful, just beautiful."

Gabby smiled. "They're first editions, printed in England."

"Where did you find them?"

"John did, at a rare-book dealer."

"Wonderful." My father opened the front cover, marveling. "They're not books, they're *artifacts*. Really splendid *artifacts*. Churchill was an excellent writer, you know."

"We know, Dad," Gabby said, since, thanks to my father, we knew more about Winston Churchill than most Americans. Or Brits. Or historians.

"Great gift, kids. Thank you all." My father beamed at us, even me, and a childish sort of happiness came over me. I flashed randomly on one of our best times as a family, maybe when we were little, on vacation down the Jersey Shore. We'd go on the rides at night at the boardwalk, and our favorite was the bumper cars, with their weird odor of burning rubber.

Come on, TJ! My father would dare me to crash into him, and I would hit the gas and plow into him, giving us both whiplash and sending us into gales of laughter.

Gabby, watch out! My brother would bump into my sister, and my mother would chase us across the dark floor of mysterious metal. We'd all bomb around and bang into each other, with electrical sparks showering us.

When the ride stopped, my father would wipe tears of laughter from his eyes and we'd climb out of the cars, shaky and wobbly, then chatter all the way home, reliving every collision. We were such a young family back then, when joy could be bought for a booklet of tickets that my mother used to say were expensive, but were, in fact, invaluable.

I remembered it now, swallowing hard and watching my father hug Gabby and shake Martin's hand, all of us beaming—even John, his smile masking his secret.

I felt a sudden rush of love for him and my family, imperfect though we were. My brother had gotten himself into trouble, and I'd help him, for his sake and for all of us. My family had rallied for me not long ago, and it was time to do the same for them.

I would start tonight.

CHAPTER FIVE

We said our goodbyes in the driveway, with my mother giving me a warm hug and whispering in my ear that I deserved a better woman than Carrie, when I knew the opposite was true. My father waved goodbye from the doorway, his large figure filling its frame. His remoteness told me he suspected I was *using*.

I went to my car, opened the door, and waved. "Happy birthday, Dad!" I called, but he didn't reply.

I told myself he hadn't heard me.

That's quality stuffing, right there.

I pulled into the parking lot of the emergency department at the hospital nearest the corporate center. If John had injured Neil Lemaire, the accountant might have driven himself here. I'd found a photo of Lemaire on the Runstan website and he looked about my age, thirty-five, with clipped red hair and a face like the Keebler Elf, if the Keebler Elf embezzled cookies.

I jumped out of the car and headed toward the hospital's entrance.

Its glass doors slid aside, and I made a beeline for a reception desk. There was a large waiting room to the right, and I scanned the occupants for Lemaire, but he wasn't there. It was mostly families and a young girl in a lacrosse uniform with a bloody knee. Oddly, the sight of the girl made me wonder if I'd ever have a daughter.

You'd be a great father, Carrie used to say, in the beginning.

I put on a worried expression for the receptionist behind a plastic divider. "Excuse me, I'm hoping you can help me. I think my brother might have come in with a head injury. He called me earlier tonight and said he was hit in the forehead with a rock." I didn't supply any name because I didn't know if Lemaire would have used his real one. "He looks like this." I held my phone up to the glass, showing Lemaire's photo.

The nurse shook her head. "No adult's been in with an injury like that."

"Have you been here all evening?"

"Yes, since four o'clock."

"Thank you." I turned away, glancing at the lacrosse girl.

I could still hear Carrie, at the end.

I'll never have a child with you! Ever!

I checked two other hospitals in the area, but Lemaire hadn't gone to either. A real investigator would have a police scanner, but I was a nepotism hire with common sense. I surveilled housewives on nooners at the Courtyard Marriott. Adultery was still worth money at settlement.

Your job's a sinecure.

I shook it off and drove away. I wasn't sure of my next move and felt my energy ebbing, so I pulled into a Dunkin' drive-thru, got a coffee, and scrolled back to Runstan's website and checked Lemaire's bio: "A Pennsylvania native, Neil Lemaire graduated from La Salle with a degree in accounting and worked as a financial advisor at PNC, bringing a wealth of business experience to Runstan. He lives in Phoenixville and volunteers at a local cat rescue."

I sipped my coffee, scrolled to Facebook, and plugged in Lemaire's name. A slew of entries popped up, but one of the thumbnails was a ginger cat. I clicked it on a hunch; Lemaire had red hair, so maybe he rescued a ginger cat. Sure enough, it was Lemaire's Facebook page. You don't have to be a detective to connect the dots.

I scanned his Facebook timeline. There was no personal information, only photos of skinny tabbies, Persians with clumpy fur, calicos missing parts of their ears, and a blind cat. I skimmed the captions: "Walter is a purrbaby AND a furbaby!!" "Mr. Fluff is going to his furever home!" "Bring double the love home! Benny and the Jet must be adopted together!"

I scrolled to Instagram, and Lemaire had an account there, too. He posted the same cats and kittens, but no personal information. I scrolled to the white pages, scanned the addresses that popped up, and picked the only one in Phoenixville, where his bio said he lived.

I'm basically a detective.

It's not rocket science.

I parked down the street from Lemaire's house, though a Maserati was too conspicuous for a stakeout vehicle. I had a black Toyota RAV4 and a blue Subaru Forester for that purpose, but I didn't know I'd be doing this today. At least the Maserati was dark. Actually its exterior color was *blu nobile*, a metallic blue that twinkled like a starry night over Florence.

The street was quiet, and the houses dark. I eyed Lemaire's modest brick house, which had a plain front door, a bay window, and two bedrooms on the second floor. There were no lights on inside, and no car in the driveway.

On impulse, I got out of my car, crossed the street, and hurried to the house. I sprinted up the driveway, steering clear of the front door in case he had a Ring camera or the like. Home technology made my job harder. Thanks for nothing, progress.

I went up to a window on the side of the house. Suddenly a motion detector clicked on, blasting the area with light.

I froze, flattening against the window. I stayed still, waiting for the light to flick off. I hoped the neighbors wouldn't think it was suspicious, since there were deer and other wildlife in Chester County.

The motion detector clicked off. My eyes adjusted to the darkness, and I couldn't see anything inside the house. I spotted something sitting in the driveway. It was the ginger cat, and I figured Lemaire had a pet door because his cat was outside, seemingly waiting for him to come home.

Aw.

I couldn't learn much else without breaking in, so I bolted from the house. The motion detector light went on again, but I cut into the shadows on the lawn. I reached my car and slipped inside.

Then I realized something. If Lemaire had co-conspirators, then they would know that John had discovered there was money missing. That meant my brother was in danger.

I hit the ignition, grabbed my phone, and pressed John's number in Favorites. He was Number Five, dead last. "John?" I said when he picked up. "Are you alone?"

"No, what's up?" he asked, his tone guarded.

"So Nancy's there?"

"Yes."

"Listen." I lowered my voice. "I'm worried these guys'll come after you. Can you go to her parents' in Jersey for a few days?"

"No."

"Why not?"

"I have to work."

"Can you send her and Connor there?"

"Probably."

"Do you have a gun?"

"No. Do you?"

"No, I can't, on parole. How about a baseball bat? Your old one?"

"I think so."

"Keep it under the bed. Put on the burglar alarm, too. Maybe don't go to meetings for a few days. Stay at the office."

"Okay. Thanks."

Thanks? I felt touched, since John wasn't big on please-and-thank-you. "You're never getting that two grand now, bro. You made me an accessory-after-the-fact."

"Oh yeah? I'll sue you for it."

Ouch.

"See you tomorrow, TJ."

"Okay, bye." I hung up.

I exhaled, blowing off steam. I loved my brother and wished it weren't so hard with us. I knew he was angry at me because I'd done so many stupid things when we were growing up, mostly when I was drinking. I'd started in middle school, sneaking Miller Lite from my father's supply in the basement, delivered by the distributor as a standing order. We had the biggest house on the street, and my parents loved to entertain, so everybody knew the Devlins' was the party house. Nobody kept track of the basement beer supply.

Except me.

I remembered being down there before John's high school graduation, drinking in the dark while they all ran around upstairs getting ready. I was drunk by the time we left for the ceremony, held outside on the school's football field.

You did what, TJ?

It was my mother, furious because I'd called Bravo Pizza on my flip phone and ordered five pies to be delivered to the stands—during the ceremony. The other families had burst into laughter at the remarkable sight of a pizza deliveryman climbing the metal bleachers with a stack of aromatic boxes. The bleachers erupted in an impromptu pizza party just as the valedictorian began to speak.

John was the valedictorian.

Thinking back, I felt a wave of guilt. I owed my brother whatever I could do for him now.

I headed for the next stop.

CHAPTER SIX

I pulled into the Brandywine Corporate Center, a complex of octagon-shaped buildings, one of which contained Devlin & Devlin, a medical supply company, an insurance company, and a reinsurance company. I didn't know what reinsurance was, but I guessed it was another layer of people who deny payment on valid claims.

I got out of the car and hurried past a mulched bed of corporate flowers to the entrance. I card-swiped at the door and went inside. The building had smoked glass windows, and the only lights on were in the hallway, which meant the cleaning crew was here somewhere. The walls were white and the carpet gray, a generic entrance that neither appealed nor offended, like décor for capitalists.

I made a beeline for our office, with its plaque in fake-Gothic font. Devlin & Devlin referred to my father and mother, and my mother claimed that first Devlin was her. They started the firm together, my father practicing business law and my mother family law, though she mostly represented husbands, a reverse-psychology switcheroo that proved surprisingly lucrative.

I unlocked the office door and entered the Merrie Olde England of my father's dreams, since no one could constrain his Anglophilia.

The walls were painted a Farrow & Ball color called Incarnadine, which I'm pretty sure meant Blood. The couches and side chairs were covered with shiny red tartan, and the reception desk was polished mahogany, matching the end tables. Gilt frames encased fox-hunting scenes next to laminated articles about every Devlin but me. Nobody was framing a mug shot.

I went to the reception desk and checked Sabrina's calendar, where she made all her notations. She hadn't made one for John today. I went down the hall to see if she had left him any phone messages.

I turned on the light and went into my brother's office. The opposite wall had a window and shelves that held two TV monitors wedged between casebooks and business journals. There was a brown leather couch, its seat cushions occupied with neat stacks of papers, and a Thomas Moser cherrywood desk, on which were more stacks, a Mac desktop, and a Phillies mug. John was a sports fanatic, forever taking clients to games. At least a sports addiction was tax-deductible.

John practiced business law, and my father had transitioned his clients to him as retirement neared. My mother sent him clients, too, since many were self-employed. There were more family businesses than most people realized, and plenty of us born into a job description, like me.

I crossed to the desk and looked around for phone messages, but there were none. I was about to leave, but my gaze fell on a baseball in a plastic cube with a plaque that read CONNOR'S FIRST GAME BALL.

I picked it up on impulse, and it jarred loose a memory. My brother and I grew up playing baseball, my father coached, and Devlin & Devlin sponsored the team, predictably named the Devils. I was a better player than my brother, but I never got a game ball.

Dad, I deserve it, I have the best batting average on the team.

I'm the coach. I have to avoid the appearance of impropriety.

The what?

I can't look like I'm playing favorites. Your shirt says Devlin & Devlin. That's my business.

But it's my team.

No, it's my *team, and you're not getting a game ball.*

I set down the ball with a sudden ache. Everyone says women have biological clocks, but I was starting to feel like I had one, too. I wanted kids, I *loved* kids. I'd set myself behind in my life, a fact that I was realizing in recovery. I didn't want to be an old-man father, but I was aging into the category.

I shook it off, left the office, and turned out the light.

I'd done all the investigating I could for one night, but I couldn't stop thinking about John and Lemaire. My heart eased as I drove up to the Episcopalian church with its fieldstone façade, arched windows, and graceful white spire that soared into the night sky. The church hosted twelve AA meetings a week, with names like Good Talk & Bad Coffee, Sobriety & Serenity, and ODAAT, for One Day at a Time. Tonight's meeting was Hang In There, which was my home group. I pulled into the lot and parked with the other cars.

I crossed to the back door and descended stone stairs to the basement. Fluorescent lighting illuminated a hallway of painted white cinder block with a gray tile floor. I passed meeting rooms and bulletin boards with construction-paper letters that read KIDS CAN BE PEACEMAKERS and a hand-painted mural, YOU ARE FEARFULLY AND WONDERFULLY MADE, PSALM 139:14. I didn't feel that way, but that's what the meeting was for.

The hall ended in propped-open doors, and I went inside to a small room with a cheerful flowery rug that cozied up a cheap gray carpet. Against the wall was a polished wooden pew next to an old upright piano with a book of sheet music on its stand. Multicolored lights wound around a pillar, and next to it, a red-and-green sign that read JOY.

"Hey, everybody." I grabbed a folding chair while everyone said their hellos, getting cups of lukewarm coffee and flimsy plates of store-brand sugar cookies.

"Hi, TJ." Jake looked up from his seat, his legs crossed. He chaired this meeting and was also my sponsor, and I loved the guy. He was fiftysomething with salt-and-pepper hair and grayish eyes matching his grayish beard. Designer glasses perched on his thin nose, and a half smile was etched into his lined face. He always dressed classy for our cargo-pants crowd, tonight in a navy-blue V-neck sweater, khakis, and loafers.

I sat down, taking in the familiar faces. I used to try to suss out everyone's occupations, but in time I realized none of that mattered here. It was Facebook-inspo obvious but I had to experience it a few times to get it through my head. That's why I'm a smart dumb person.

It was an open meeting, and the usual talkers were Cheryl, a middle-aged white woman in a Cavalier King Charles spaniel T-shirt, Melissa, a young Asian woman whose sense of humor I adored, and Phyllis, a Black woman who loved purple, down to her painted fingernails. Antonio was a construction worker who reeked of cigar smoke, Samuel, a poetry fan who regaled us with old-timey snippets, and Brian, a big Iraq vet who brought new members like Chris, the small, wiry man next to him in a camo T-shirt and jeans.

We were about to start when Greg entered the room, an octogenarian who used a cane because of a bad hip. He'd been sober for forty-two years, but he came to meetings off and on, proof that lifetime sobriety was possible. He went to his chair, which Samuel opened for him.

Jake crossed his legs. "Hello, folks. I'm Jake and I'm an alcoholic and a drug addict."

"Hi, Jake," we all said in unison.

"Let's start with the Serenity Prayer, shall we? 'God grant me the serenity to . . . '" he began, and everybody recited together, then we read the AA Preamble and the Promises. When we were finished, Jake looked around the circle. "Cheryl, glad to see you healthy again."

"Thanks." Cheryl grinned. "No more scooter. My knee's better. Yay!"

"Good." Jake smiled back. "Tonight, let's talk about compassion, not only for others but for yourself. All of us who struggle with the disease of addiction and alcoholism know that we were selfish when we were drinking and using drugs. I've shared my own experiences, and it's cringeworthy to look back and realize that was me. One way to come to terms with our past is to live in the present. Another way is to view our past through a more compassionate lens. Who would like to get us started? Anyone have an experience they'd like to share?"

Melissa raised her hand. "My name is Melissa and I'm an alcoholic."

"Hi, Melissa," I said, with everyone else.

"It's hard to see it that way because I'm so sick of this pattern I have, like I keep sabotaging myself over and over and I don't know how to stop it. I'm sober a year next week and I'm not picking up, but I'm still sabotaging."

"How so?" Jake asked gently.

"Okay, so I see this therapist I can barely afford. I like going, but at the same time, I don't. You know what I mean?"

Antonio nodded. "I go to a marriage counselor, and I love and hate it."

Brian muttered, "Same with Planet Fitness."

Everybody laughed, and Jake motioned to Melissa. "You were saying. Folks, let's keep the cross talk to a minimum."

"So I'm always late for our session, and it makes him mad, and the last session we ended up talking about why I'm late. So now I'm spending money on therapy *about* therapy." Melissa broke into a hapless smile. "And it's on me, it's a me problem. I don't have compassion for myself."

Greg interjected, "Keep coming back, Melissa. We all have bad habits. I have bad habits older than *you*."

Everybody chuckled again, and Phyllis looked at her with sympathy. "Don't beat yourself up, honey. We're trying to break our worst habit right now. You can only break so many habits at once."

I thought of Carrie. "Right, I self-sabotage in a million ways. I have a suitcase of self-sabotage, like Felix's bag of tricks."

Phyllis grinned. "Felix the Cat? I remember that cartoon. I loved it."

"Me, too." I felt a happy surge. "Remember the song? 'Felix the Cat, the wonderful, wonderful cat—'"

"—whenever he gets in a fix—"

"—he reaches into his bag of tricks!"

Everybody laughed, and Jake waved his hands, trying to restore order. An AA meeting had a structure and he'd get us back on track, but our fellowship created a cheery bond. This meeting had already accomplished a purpose, for me. It made me realize I wasn't alone.

It was my home group.

And I was home.

But that didn't mean I wasn't missing something.

An hour later, I was sitting in the car across the street from Carrie's house. I knew a heart could ache because mine did from time to time, and all of those times were about her. I'd been in love before her, but she got *through*, and I was still in love with her now.

Her townhouse was in a cluster, each house with its own driveway. All of the townhouses were dark, and the only car in her driveway was her white Camry, thank God. I checked her social media all the time to see if she was dating anyone, and it was still just old photos of her with fellow teachers. She didn't like social media and wanted to set a good example for Emily.

My gaze strayed to her bedroom, then to her daughter Emily's, who'd be four now. We'd met in Wegmans, where I'd been buying beer, when a little girl came giggling around the corner, then a mother chasing after her, also laughing. I caught the little girl before she ran into me, and that got me talking to her grateful mother, then something told me I wanted to be in their lives. Carrie and I started seeing each other, and my feelings for her were bound up in a tangle of mother-daughter curls, the two of them the best package deal ever, like a car loaded with every feature you wanted and some you didn't know you needed.

We used to pile into Carrie's bed at night and read to Emily before bedtime. Carrie loved me too much to see that I was a functioning alcoholic. She believed me when I told her my hangovers were migraines. She didn't deceive herself; I deceived her. She believed my lies, until one night.

June 7.

I was about to start the ignition when I spotted a plush purple rabbit on the driveway behind Carrie's car. Tomorrow morning, she would be rushing to school and run it over.

I'm not good at reversing, she always said.

I got out of the car, hurried across the street, and plucked the rabbit from the driveway. Then I went to the front step, set it down, and went back to the car.

I loved Carrie and Emily.

So I drove away.

CHAPTER SEVEN

The next morning I took the Subaru for my stakeout at Runstan's, where Lemaire worked. I wanted to see if he showed up, so I parked in the lot, sipped coffee, and fake-scrolled my phone. I had on a ball cap and sunglasses, the closest I come to Detective Wear. There'd been no news of him online, dead or alive, and I'd driven by his house again this morning. No maroon Volvo.

Runstan's brick façade spanned three storefronts at the end of a generic strip mall that held a Chinese restaurant, a pizza place, and a dry cleaner's. The Runstan entrance was a glass door flanked by squarish windows, and it didn't look like a multimillion-dollar business, but you don't have to be an alcoholic to know that appearances are deceiving.

It was 7:27 A.M. when cars started appearing, turning into the strip mall and parking lot. I kept an eye out for Lemaire in his maroon Volvo. So far, no luck. There were designated spaces for the president, vice president, and sales manager, but not accounting.

The designated spaces filled up, and I got a look at Stan Malinowski, the owner, when he got out of an old Explorer. I remembered him from years ago. He'd grown bald and round, but still had a port-wine stain on his forehead. John nicknamed him Stain, which was the one time I remember my father yelling at my brother.

I prayed Lemaire would show up. Car after car came in until the lot was full and the Runstan employees had gone inside.

No maroon Volvo and no Lemaire.

I drove to the office and parked in the farthest corner of the lot, next to a gray Porsche Carrera and a white Mercedes S-Class that belonged to the owners of the insurance and reinsurance agencies. Whoever said crime doesn't pay never worked in insurance. Or reinsurance.

I chirped the Subaru locked and headed toward the entrance with a box of donuts. I opened the door into Merrie Olde England and a waiting area with a well-dressed man and an attractive woman, a mix of my parents' clients. More than one soon-to-be ex met their next soon-to-be ex in our waiting room, which made my parents as proud as billable pimps.

"Good morning, Sabrina," I said to the receptionist, who looked up from her desktop over black reading glasses. She was an older friend of my mother's, and her sweet face was framed by clipped gray hair and omnipresent pearl earrings.

"TJ, how are you?"

"Great, thanks." I set the box of donuts on the table. "You?"

"Fine. Gabby wants to see you on her pro bono case. It's some type of prisoner litigation for Holmesburg inmates."

"Will do. I'll see her after John." I left the reception area and headed down the hallway toward his office. His door was closed as usual, so I knocked and opened it to find my father standing in front of John's desk, which surprised me. We usually went to my father's office, not the other way around.

"Dad, John, good morning."

"Bright and early, I see," my father said curtly, folding his arms in his dark suit.

"Good morning, TJ." John looked strangely grim in a European fit shirt with a shiny Hermès tie, regarding business casual as Straight-up Communism.

"Is everything okay?" I asked, keeping it light. I hoped that John hadn't told my father about Lemaire, which would only complicate the situation.

"You tell me," my father shot back.

John answered, "TJ, I told Dad about last night. I told him everything."

Dumb smart person. "Why?"

"I had to. It was the right thing to do. We can't hide a secret that big." John met my eye directly. "I told him you fell off the wagon."

"What?" I recoiled, shocked. It felt like a gut punch. I couldn't collect my thoughts. I'd be sober for two years on June 7, and my sobriety meant everything to me. It was the one thing I prayed over every night.

"TJ, I had to. I don't think we should keep it secret. I told Dad I smelled alcohol on your breath before his birthday dinner and how you admitted you had a few beers. We left the house so Mom didn't find out. I'm sorry, I promised not to tell, but it's the truth."

No. It was a lie, the worst lie ever. I'd worked so hard to stay sober. I changed everything about my life and followed the program like a religion. I hadn't relapsed, not once, which was crazy. My home group even called me Relapse Virgin.

My father scowled. "TJ, you think this is my first rodeo? You and

John disappearing last night? I knew it wasn't on a case of Gabby's. She covered for you, too. You think I don't know what's going on?"

No, no, no. I didn't know what to say. It killed me that he thought I was drinking again. I struggled every day to stay sober. Some even struggled to stay alive. Others didn't succeed. Jesse, for one. But I couldn't think about him now.

John interjected, "I told Dad that we called your sponsor, and he got you back on track. It's okay, TJ. You can admit it. Dad understands, and so do I."

My chest tightened with anger. I was too furious to say anything. I couldn't support the lie but I couldn't bust John. I'd never call my sponsor with my brother anyway. That wasn't even how it worked.

My father sighed, unfolding his arms. "TJ, listen to me. Hear me. You cannot start drinking again. You have to stop drinking for good. If you drink again, you're fired."

"Fired?" It panicked me. "Dad, no, I need this job, you know that—"

"Then change. You never change. You never will."

"I am, I have, I've changed—"

"Bullshit. Prove it." My father glared at me. "I haven't spoken to your mother about this. I'll keep it between us. Get to a meeting today. Call your sponsor again. Do whatever it takes. Straighten up and fly right—or we're done."

"No, Dad, okay." I reeled, not knowing what to say.

John added, "TJ, it's for your own good. We're both behind you."

My father headed toward the door. "It's about damn time you take responsibility for yourself, TJ. That's all I have to say. Understood?"

"Yes," I told him as he left the office, closing the door behind him, and I could barely wait to vent my anger at my brother. *John, what the hell?* I wanted to yell at him, but I'd be overheard. "You told Dad I *relapsed*? How could you do that? That's the worst possible thing—"

"I had to."

"No, you didn't!"

"Yes, I did. He came in first thing. It caught me unawares. He said he was up all night. You know how he gets, a dog with a bone." John spread his arms, his starchy shirt wrinkled at the elbow. "I had no choice, TJ. He wasn't going to let it go. I had to come up with something."

"You couldn't think of another lie? My sobriety, it's a big thing. It's *everything*."

"I didn't start it, Dad did. He suspected it and asked me if you were drinking again, so I went with it."

"Still, you don't get it. There's nothing more important to me, I changed my life—"

"I get it—"

"No, you *don't*. I'm sober almost two years. It's a word-of-honor thing."

John scoffed. "Come on, I'm sure people lie—"

"How dare you," I interrupted, getting angrier. "Why are you sure? What do *you* know? You never worked the program. You don't know anything about the program. We don't lie about it. *I* don't lie about it. The whole point is to *stop* lying."

"What was I supposed to do? Wouldn't it be worse if Dad knew about Lemaire and the money?"

"Why? One is a lie about me, and the other is the truth about you. How can you compare?"

John blinked in annoyance. "TJ, you know you're sober. What does it matter what Dad thinks? Isn't all that matters what *you* think, what *you* know?"

"Still, it's a lie. It's wrong. I'm *sober*. And I want him to know it."

"He'll get over it. In a little while, you'll tell him that you're sober again and he'll forget all about it."

"No, he won't. And neither will I." I couldn't let it go. "You're an asshole, John."

"Okay, whatever." John exhaled. "Let's move on."

"I can't!" I said bitterly.

"Well, try. This Lemaire thing is life or death."

"You could apologize, you know."

"I'm sorry," John shot back.

"Act like you mean it."

"I do. I'm sorry."

I tried to move on. "So where's Lemaire? Do you think he's dead?"

"I don't know."

"So what do we do now? Do you think we should tell the cops?"

"No, not yet."

"What about Stan? Not yet?"

"Yes, right." I thought a minute. "If Stan calls, tell him you're working on it."

"What if Lemaire calls?"

"Take it, but be aware he could be recording you. What about Nancy and Connor? Did you send them away?"

"Yes, to her parents. She said she'd stay a week, maybe two."

"Good." I felt a wave of relief. "Did you see anything suspicious on your street?"

"No."

"You should take a picture, morning and night. Make sure no one's tailing you, like if you see a car that doesn't belong to your neighbors."

"I don't know my neighbors' cars. I barely know my neighbors. The lot size is four acres."

"You get your baseball bat?"

"Yes."

"What did you tell Nancy about where we went during dinner?"

John hesitated, and I realized why.

"You told her I relapsed, too, didn't you?"

"TJ, listen—"

"Really?" I felt furious all over again. "It's wrong, John. It's just wrong—"

"Is it *that* big a deal?"

"Yes, plus you just *lied* to me. You told me Dad suspected I relapsed, but *you* thought of it. *You* thought of the lie and told him."

"TJ, it basically happened that way—"

"'Basically' isn't the same thing!" I turned on my heel and headed for the door. "See you later."

"Where are you going?"

I opened the door. "To a meeting, *Dad*."

I got in the Subaru, reeling. I couldn't absorb the fact that my father thought I had relapsed. I couldn't forget the look on his face, his disappointment bone-deep. I knew in my gut that I'd seen that expression before, on the worst day of my life.

Can you read, write, and understand the English language?

It was a judge speaking, the Honorable Deborah Rati-Jio, a former trial lawyer whom my father had helped elect to the bench. She was seated at the dais in the modern courtroom at the Chester County Justice Center. The afternoon sun struggled through the venetian blinds, and despite the air-conditioning, I was drenched in flop sweat.

Are you now under the influence of alcohol, drugs, or any licit or illicit substance that may impair your judgment or decision-making?

No. I was answering the questions as I stood at counsel table, wearing a dark suit with a Tommy Bahama tie, palm trees swaying incongruously down my chest, a poor choice in retrospect. I'd never forget the pattern because it was all I stared at during the colloquy.

Are you now being treated for a mental illness?

No. I remember answering and trying to look at the judge, seated on the dais in front of the seal of the Commonwealth on the paneled wall. Shame prevented me from meeting her eye or anyone else's, in a courtroom full of people who knew the Devlin family, among the most prominent in the county.

Have you been able to consult with your lawyer in responding to the charges?

Yes. My lawyer was Angela Martinez, one of the best criminal lawyers in the state, hired by my parents. Assistant District Attorney Pete Deegan also knew my father, since both were big-time Villanova boosters. The Commonwealth had offered me a plea deal that was more than fair, one year in jail.

Do you understand the charges against you?

Yes, I answered, an eye on the bailiff standing at the side door, a lean, older Black man whom everybody called Mack. He looked down at his polished shoes during the proceeding, as if to save face for my family.

Has anyone used any force or threats against you in order to coerce you to enter this plea?

No. I felt my mother's eyes on my back. I couldn't bring myself to turn around, and I knew exactly what she would look like in the gallery behind me. I could always read her expressions; the lifting of her right eyebrow, the wrinkling of her nose, the pursing of her lipsticked lips. Today, she would feel mortification for her, and pain for me.

Has anyone made any promises of benefit to you in order to entice you to enter this plea?

No. The pews were packed with lawyers carrying boxy trial bags and cumbersome exhibits mounted on foamcore. They were about to continue a weeks-long negligence trial over an Amtrak train crash, and I'd heard them greeting my father, surprised to find that his younger son was the defendant today.

Do you understand that you need not enter a plea of guilty, but may plead not guilty and go to trial?

Yes. The negligence trial had attracted the press, and a sketch artist set up wide pastel chalks and a pad of brown paper. Later, my parents would pressure the media not to run a story about my charges, and they would agree. It would be as if my wrongdoing never existed, the blessing-and-curse of privilege.

Do you understand that if you proceed to trial, you would have to be proven guilty beyond a reasonable doubt and if the Commonwealth cannot prove you guilty beyond a reasonable doubt, you must be set free on these charges?

I answered, *Yes*, then Judge Rati-Jio came to the main question:

How do you plead, guilty or not guilty?

Guilty, I answered, but I spoke too softly for the court reporter, her manicured hands halted over the stenography machine.

Mr. Devlin, could you repeat that for the record? How do you plead? Guilty or not guilty?

Guilty! I called out, my own judgment against myself echoing in the courtroom. The jury condemns you in a trial, but when you enter a guilty plea, you condemn yourself, in public. It was utterly the way I felt inside. I was *guilty* to the core of my very being.

Judge Rati-Jio asked a few more questions, and I answered on autopilot. I thought I might faint from guilt, if such a thing were possible. I was wrong, I was guilty, and I would pay for my crime. I entered the plea because I wanted to take responsibility in front of my family, even in front of my God. I hadn't had a drink since it happened and I was going to prison, where I belonged.

A uniformed cop came toward me and clamped steel handcuffs on my wrists, which locked with a grim click, and I turned to meet my father's eye.

My father looked back at me, so deeply agonized that his expression seared into my brain, to be recalled this very moment. It was the exact same expression I'd seen on his face this morning, when he thought I'd relapsed.

Tears came to my eyes. My sobriety was the only thing I was proud of, and I wanted my father to know I stayed sober. John might think it didn't matter, but nothing mattered more to me.

I knew that whatever trust my father had in me was gone forever.

CHAPTER EIGHT

I pulled out of the Runstan lot, hit the road, and got my head back in the game. I was guessing that if Lemaire was dead, whoever he was working with would've abandoned his maroon Volvo, and sooner or later, the car would find its way to an auction lot. Meanwhile I knew a guy who got a heads-up on new inventory coming to the auctions, since I went to him for my own cars.

I called him, and he picked up after one ring. "Hey, Patrick."

"Yo, TJ," Patrick said, in his gravelly voice. "How's the Maserati?"

"Beyond."

"Don't fall in love."

"Too late." I smiled, cruising ahead.

"You'll never get rich that way, kid." Patrick chuckled. "You gotta sell it."

"Not yet." I headed down Route 29 past a Chick-fil-A, Wegmans, Target, and Panera. Traffic was busy, midmorning in the suburbs.

"I'm getting in a Lambo next week."

"Whoa. DOJ bustin' up those cartels."

"No, a hedge funder."

"Same thing."

Patrick chuckled again. "You interested?"

"No, thanks, I'm tapped out."

"It's only a year old, four thousand miles. Mint condition, wrapped."

"Who wraps a Lambo?"

"A hedge funder?"

We both laughed, then I got down to business. "I'm calling because I need a Volvo sedan for my sister. Newish. Will you keep an eye out?"

"Hold on, let me look." Patrick hit a few keys, a clacking sound. "I see two comin' in, a wagon and an SUV, both older."

"It has to be a sedan." I didn't like lying, but I had to.

"What about a nice Lexus SUV, only a year old, five thousand miles? She'll like it if she likes Volvo."

"No, thanks. If a Volvo sedan turns up, let me know."

"Sure. Yo, you're single, aren't you?"

"Yeah . . ." I didn't add that I'd sat in front of my ex's last night.

"Listen, my niece is on the market. Her name's Maya. My wife told me to fix her up, and here you call. It's like a sign. Her husband died last year. She's sick of the apps. I don't know what that means, but you prolly do."

"I do." I'd lurked on Hinge but had yet to make an official profile. I'd have nothing to list but Prison and Rehab. *Line up, ladies!*

"She's beautiful, no joke. You'd love her. No kids."

"I like kids."

"That's because you don't have any. What do you say? You want that Volvo, don't you?"

"Your niece for a car? There's a name for that. I think it's a felony."

Patrick laughed. "Come on. She's a knockout. You don't have to take my word. I'm sending you a picture and her number."

My phone chimed with an incoming text.

"TJ, did you get it?"

I stopped at the traffic light, debating what to do. I'd known Patrick only three months, so he didn't know about my past. I didn't want to tell him because I knew he would see me differently. Rehab was one thing, but prison another. He wouldn't fix me up if he knew the truth.

I said, "Patrick, I gotta go. Let me know about the Volvo."

"Okay, but don't wait on Maya. I'm telling you, this girl's gonna *go*."

I hung up, my chest tight. I couldn't think about another woman, my heart was full of Carrie. I could still remember the moment I fell in love with her, in IKEA of all places. We'd drive to the Plymouth Meeting store to see what was on sale and take Emily to lunch at its cafeteria, where we'd have Swedish meatballs and crackers like hardtack, proof that Swedes have better teeth or better dental insurance.

One time we needed a chest of drawers and we passed a display furnished with a puffy couch in off-white fabric. Emily ran into the fake family room, and I went after her and sat down on the couch, sinking in.

Wow, Carrie, this feels great. Sit down a sec, honey.

Carrie eyed the laminated price tag. *Backsälen. It's too expensive.*

They don't charge you to sit. Come on.

Carrie flopped down on the other side of Emily. *Why is everything so expensive?*

Because the world doesn't pay teachers enough. How great is this couch?

I can't afford it.

You can if we split it.

Carrie cocked her head, her ponytail flopping over. *You want to buy a couch with me? You're playing house.*

No, I said, realizing something. *I'm not playing.*

• • •

I drove to Lemaire's house listening to news radio, but there was no mention of him. His driveway was still empty, and the house looked still. I didn't park because it was too risky in the daytime. I assumed he hadn't been home and that he hadn't gone to work today, unless I'd missed him. I thought of his ginger cat and hoped it had food and water.

I drove back to the quarry, parked, and got out of the car. I wanted to make sure Lemaire's body wasn't dumped there. I could see the service road and its surroundings better now, and the entire area was deserted. I trudged through the underbrush to the spot where John had hit Lemaire. Dried blood had soaked into the dirt. Still no sign of the gun or the rock. I thought about taking some pictures but didn't want them on my phone.

I left the spot and walked to the left, where I'd looked around last night. I found the NO TRESPASSING sign and continued beyond to the edge of the quarry, which seemed a likely place to dump a dead body.

I looked all the way down, and it was quite a drop, maybe three hundred feet to the water. The sun shone on its surface, which wasn't as choppy as last night. Its color was a murky green, and I scanned the water in quadrants. I didn't see a body.

I turned away and walked back, trying to imagine where another car, or a person, could have hidden. I didn't have any more answers than last night.

I went back to the car and drove around looking for the Volvo, in case it had been abandoned nearby. No luck. I kept the radio on, but still no news of Lemaire. It occurred to me that the co-conspirators, if they existed, would want to get out of town. If they had driven, I couldn't track them, but they could have flown. They could have gone to the airport and abandoned his car there.

I headed toward Route 252 to the airport.

I approached the Philadelphia International Airport, which sprawled southwest of the city, surrounded by its oil refineries and trucking terminals. Traffic was congested on I-95, with trucks and cars heading to Delaware and Jersey. An orange haze hung in the sky, and carcinogens made my nose twitch.

I reached the airport, where its massive terminals sat in a curved line, designated A through F. Each had a dedicated parking lot situated on one side of a street that ran through the airport, with the ticketing and airplane gates on the other. All I needed today was the parking lots.

I started with the Terminal A lot, taking a ticket at the turnstile at short-term parking, then drove around looking for the maroon Volvo. I drove past car after car, but no luck, then went to long-term parking. By the third level, I'd seen every type of vehicle in existence, but only a few Volvos, none maroon.

I was on the fifth level of Terminal C when my phone rang. I answered it without checking the screen, assuming it was John. "Yes?"

"TJ?" said a woman. "My uncle Patrick gave me your number."

CHAPTER NINE

I braked in the aisle. "Uh—"

"It's Maya Vitelli. Am I catching you at a bad time?"

"No, I'm in the car." I scrolled to my texts and checked her picture. Maya was a beautiful Indian-American woman with large dark eyes, the most remarkable feature on her delicate face. Her nose was slim, and her chin came to a point like a heart. Gold hoops peeked from her thick hair, glistening black to her shoulders.

"Oh, then let's hang up. It's not safe."

"No, it's fine, I'm in a parking lot, don't worry about it, we can talk now, it's fine." Words raced from my lips. My mouth was a Ferrari, but my brain was a tricycle.

"I was wondering if you wanted to go out."

My mouth went dry. Her voice sounded so nice, with a trace of a Philly accent that I liked. Only Philadelphians like Philly accents.

"TJ, hello? Did I lose you?"

"Yes, no, sorry, I was . . . thinking."

"Okay, this is embarrassing." Maya laughed awkwardly. "Forget it. I thought I'd give it a shot."

"No, that's okay." I cringed. "I, uh, was just in the middle of something."

"I'm calling because my uncle gave you the wrong number. I got a new phone. He also sent me your picture."

I blinked. "I didn't know he had a picture of me."

"He got it off a law firm website?"

"Oh, right." I was drunk when that picture was taken. It's the best picture of me ever. I'm a hot drunk.

"He thinks you hung the moon."

"He doesn't know me," I shot back, and Maya chuckled, assuming I was being self-deprecating.

"I'm a widow, I don't know if he told you."

"He did. I'm sorry about your loss. What, uh, do you do?"

"I work for a reinsurance company."

"What a coincidence!" I blurted out, unthinking.

"You're in reinsurance? I thought you worked in a law firm."

TJ, you idiot. "No, there's a reinsurance company in my office complex. I always wondered what reinsurance was. It sounds complicated."

"It's not. It's just insurance for insurers."

"That sounds complicated to me. Basically, it's calculus."

I realized I was trying to flirt, like a chick flapping its wings. "So, Maya, do you like calculus?"

"Yes, I love it."

"And you sell calculus policies?"

Maya chuckled. "Yes, and I'm the office administrator."

"You boss people around."

"You got a problem with that?"

"No, I like bossy women." I worried that sounded politically incorrect, so I shut up. I looked at her picture again and couldn't deny a little thrill. It felt like hope, maybe even a glimpse of a future.

"So when do you want to have dinner? Tonight works for me, and so does Saturday night. I don't play games. I hate games."

"Me, too."

"So tonight or Saturday?"

"I can't tonight." *I have to find a dead accountant.*

"How about Saturday?"

I started to choke, without knowing why. Maybe I wasn't ready for a future. "I, uh, don't know if Saturday's good for me."

"Next weekend then?"

"I don't know yet—"

"Tell you what, TJ, your name's TJ, right? What's it stand for?"

"Total Jerk," I answered. It was either funny or messed up, maybe both.

"Look," Maya said flatly. "You have my number. Call me if you want to go out."

"I'll do that."

Maya snorted. "I'll hold my breath."

"No, I'll call—"

"Yeah, right. Bye."

"Bye," I said, but Maya had already hung up.

My heart sank. I hated being The Guy Who Disappointed Women. I talked about it all the time, in my home group and back in rehab. I talked about how I disappointed women, but I never did anything about it.

You never change, my father had said.

I called Maya back.

It took most of the day, but I scanned the cars in the A through F lots and didn't find a maroon Volvo. I didn't check remote parking because nobody takes a shuttle to skip town. I left the airport and headed home on I-95 in heavy traffic, deciding to call my brother.

My anger at him resurfaced when I saw his thumbnail photo on my phone, but I tried to stuff my resentment while the call connected.

"John," I said, after he picked up, "did you hear anything from Lemaire? There's no sign of his car at the airport. I checked the quarry again, but nothing new."

"No, he hasn't called." John sounded tense. "I don't know if he went to work today."

"I didn't see his car, so I assume he didn't. My guess is he won't. If he hasn't skipped town, he'd have to explain the head injury."

"I thought about calling there, but it would be risky in terms of the record."

"Agree. He hasn't posted anything new on his social."

John groaned. "So he just disappeared?"

"Evidently. You stayed in the office today?"

"Yes, I canceled outside meetings until we know more."

"Good."

"What are you going to do?"

"Probably drive by the house again. See what I can see."

"I'm worried."

"You should be."

John paused. "You're still pissed at me, about the relapse thing?"

"Of course. You threw me under the bus. Now I'm running around trying to save your ass." I tried to let it go, only because he was in trouble.

"I said I was sorry."

"Whatever."

John fell silent. "Gabby's looking for you on that pro bono case. You should call her. We have to act like everything's normal."

"I gotta go," I said, not wanting to talk to him anymore.

"Stay in touch. Bye."

"Bye." *Bro.*

Traffic was light, and I called my sister. "Gabby, hi. Sorry, I know you wanted to see me, but I got busy."

"Where are you?"

"On the road."

"Remember we have dinner with the client tonight. I mentioned it last week."

Oops. I had forgotten. I would drive by Lemaire's after dark. It would be less risky then anyway. "Who's dinner with again?"

"Our client's Chuck Whitman. He's lead plaintiff in the Holmesburg Prison lawsuit. I want to double-check the Complaint with him before I file."

"Okay, what time's dinner?"

"Six o'clock. But can you come over early, so we can talk?"

"I can't, I'm running late."

"Too bad." Gabby sounded disappointed. "Martin and I thought it would be good to spend some time together. You know, just us."

I didn't get it. "Why? Is something going on?"

Gabby paused. "TJ, I heard you relapsed."

I drove to Gabby's on autopilot, my thoughts elsewhere. I hated that she thought I'd relapsed, too. Growing up, she was always so great to me, almost like my mother even though she was only two years older.

I found myself thinking of her Sweet Sixteen, held in our backyard with the Devlin party-machine in high gear. My parents loved to entertain, throwing big bashes for the holidays and inviting their friends, clients, and the parents of our teammates. Everybody got to know each other over the years, combining friendship with business like a capitalistic hairball.

Ours was the best party house, spacious and designed for entertaining, and our friends loved to come because there were so many places we could get away from the adults. Cases of beer and soda got delivered and stacked behind the pool house, with nobody keeping track. Top-shelf booze was everywhere. Coolers outside were filled with beer, chardonnay, and rosé.

The party would start, and the adults helped themselves to drinks, looking the other way while we did, too. Most of the parents felt the way mine did, that kids were going to drink, so they might as well drink at home. I was borderline drunk at Gabby's Sweet Sixteen, a pool party with my father grilling filets and my mother making Devlin Eggs. Afterward it was time for cake and candle-lighting, but I was behind the garage making out with Amy Gallagher. I was trying to unfasten her bathing suit top when I heard Gabby talking on the microphone we used for karaoke.

Thank you all for coming. I light the first candle for the people most important to me, my mom and dad. I love you, guys.

The crowd reacted with awws, and my parents said in unison, *We love you, Gabby! Happy birthday!*

Amy shifted, pushing me away. *TJ, the ceremony's starting. We have to go.*

Gabby was saying, *I'm lighting this candle for my big brother, John. He's the best brother anyone could ever have. He's King of French Vocab and always takes great care of me.*

More awws followed, and John saying, *Love you, Gabby! Happy birthday!*

Amy wriggled out of my grasp. *I don't want to get in trouble, TJ! Get up!*

Gabby was saying, *I light this candle for my brother TJ. He's the most fun ever. TJ? TJ, where are you?*

Amy dragged me out from behind the garage and tugged me to the pool, where heads began to turn. Everyone burst into laughter, putting two and two together.

Gabby laughed. *TJ! Where were you?*

Sorry birthday, Gabby! I called out drunkenly, to uproarious laughter.

I love you, TJ!

I love you, too! I told her, and I remember feeling grateful. Gabby didn't blame me, she never blamed me. She only worried about me.

My father blamed me, though, and that night after everyone had gone home, he took me by the arm and walked me out to the garage with a six-pack. *You wanna drink, TJ? You're gonna drink.*

No, Dad, really?

You think it's funny? You think everything's a joke?

We reached the garage, and my father pushed me against the wall, shoved me to the ground, and handed me a can of beer, popping the tab. *You're gonna learn this lesson. You're never gonna embarrass me again. Drink it, TJ.*

Dad, I didn't mean to—

Drink! My father jammed the can against my lips and poured beer down my throat. I tried to swallow while he ranted, angrier than I'd ever seen him. *You take everything for granted! You think this business came from nothing? It didn't! I built it from the ground up, and so did your mother! It has our family name on it, do you know what that means?*

I swallowed gulp after gulp, gagging and sputtering beer everywhere.

I run a business, TJ! Our name is our brand! When you embarrass me like that, you ruin our family name! You ruin our business! You're a selfish, spoiled brat!

I started to choke, my gorge rose, and I vomited.

Don't tell your mother! my father said, throwing down the can.

CHAPTER TEN

Aw, TJ, how are you?" Gabby met me at the front door, her short brown hair framing her pretty face, soft with sympathy.

"I'm fine," I said, but it was a lie.

"Come here." Gabby hugged me, and I hugged her back, smelling her faint vanilla perfume. She still had on her work clothes, a blue turtleneck and khakis. "Were you at a meeting?"

"Yes," I lied again.

"Good. People relapse, TJ. I read online that it's part of recovery and there's no shame in it. We all know that now." Gabby's loving gaze met mine. "I give you credit for the work you've done so far. You were sober for almost two years."

"I was, I really was." It drove me crazy to tell her I'd relapsed. I used to lie about being sober when I was drunk, now I was lying about being drunk when I was sober.

"I know you can get sober again. I'm *so* proud of you, and everything's going to be okay."

"Thanks."

"Come on in." Gabby led me into their living room, decorated with art and statuary from all over the world. Red-and-black kilim rugs in geometric patterns hung on the wall, and large wooden masks stood in the corner with pottery painted orange, yellow, and green. A sectional couch was heaped with Ecuadorian blankets under walls lined with photos from their trips. Travel guides and trip scrapbooks stuffed their bookshelves.

"TJ!" Martin came from the kitchen, throwing open his arms. His eyes were a warm brown, as dark as his skin, and he was in his beloved Spurs sweatshirt with jeans. "Bring it in, mate."

"Hey, bro." I hugged him back, touched.

"You know there's no shame in relapse, don't you? It's very common."

"Thanks." I didn't know how much more of this I could take.

"Alcoholism is a disease like any other. You'll get back on track with the program. I saw an article published by researchers at Stanford, attesting to AA's efficacy. I'll email it to you."

"Thanks." I turned to Gabby. "So Dad told you?"

"Yes." Her face fell. "I ran into him around noon and I could tell something was bugging him. He told me John smelled beer on your breath and you left his birthday dinner so Mom wouldn't find out."

"She doesn't know, does she?"

"No, and I don't think Dad will tell her."

"I hope not," I said, cringing. The person I hurt most with my drinking was my mother, which killed me.

Martin rested a hand on my shoulder. "I have many friends who could help you, addiction specialists and the like. Therapists, too. I'd be happy to call any of them."

"No, that's okay."

"Don't be too proud, man."

"I'm not."

"Family therapy can be helpful, too."

"Right." Gabby rubbed my back. "I would go with you if you wanted, TJ. I remember our family meeting in rehab. Do you?"

"Yes, of course." I flashed on our session, which had been painful. My family had driven up to Evergreen Recovery in the Poconos, which had more rehabs than trees. They'd dressed like they were going to Mass and we sat in a circle with a counselor. My family was supposed to say how my alcoholism affected them, a belated intervention that opened my eyes. Gabby cried even more than my mother, sharing memories I didn't remember.

I guess when we were younger, like in high school, that's when I started to worry about him. Gabby's voice was choked with emotion. *We learned about alcoholism in Health, but I thought you had to be a grown-up to be alcoholic. I just thought TJ partied, like all the boys I knew on the baseball team.*

Gabby shook her head. *Anyway, I never asked him, but he would say, just tell Mom I've been with you, or tell Dad I'm at practice, and I realized we had to hide his drinking from my parents. He never asked me to, so don't blame him, I don't blame him.* Gabby looked at me, wiping her eyes with a balled-up Kleenex. *I don't blame you, TJ. I blame me.*

Gabby, please, I blurted out, though I wasn't supposed to interrupt. *I'm to blame for what I did, not you.*

The facilitator interjected, *Gabby, go ahead.*

I just wanted to help him. When I opened the recycling, there were so many cans, just so many cans. Taking out the recycling was my chore, and the cans took up too much space and so I would take them out at night and crush them. Then I got the idea to put them in the neighbor's recycling, in case my parents looked in.

Sweet Jesus. I'd had no idea.

I think that was the hardest thing for me. Gabby wiped her eyes again. *He was keeping a secret and I wanted to help him. I used to worry at night that somebody would look in the recycling and find out. And I didn't know what to do.* Gabby turned to the facilitator. *Does that mean I was an enabler?*

No, it means you were too young to deal with this situation and you love your brother.

Gabby sniffled, with finality. *Just so I didn't make it worse. I never want to make it worse. I only wanted to help. I love my brother.*

I tried to shake the memory as Gabby led me into a foodie's kitchen, filled with delicious aromas. Copper pans hung over a brown-flecked granite island, where she and Martin were always making a dish I'd never heard of. "What's for dinner?"

"Goat."

"What?" I asked, aghast.

Gabby burst into laughter. "We had you going, didn't we?"

Martin snorted. "TJ, every time you come for dinner, you act like you enter a new dimension."

I chuckled. "It is, okay? Like that spice, what is it?"

Gabby rolled her eyes. "Coriander? We get it at Whole Foods."

"TJ, sit down and relax." Martin crossed to the stove and began stirring a stew that bubbled in an orange cast-iron pot. I took a seat at a rustic farm table set with simple white plates, surrounded by four pine chairs.

"Here." Gabby brought me a glass of water. "Are you up for meeting a client?"

"I'm fine." I felt touched. "Don't worry."

Martin looked over. "We're a family, TJ. We love you."

"Thanks." I sipped my water, hoping to dislodge the lump in my throat.

CHAPTER ELEVEN

Chuck Whitman arrived, and we shared a delicious meal and conversation that flowed freely. Chuck was seventy-six but in poor health. His hair was a sparse white, contrasting with his brown scalp, and his face was lined with deep wrinkles draping his mouth and his lips, which turned slightly down. Frail with a hunched posture, he had on a flannel shirt and baggy jeans. We cleared the table, then Martin went upstairs to his study, leaving Gabby to open her laptop and start our meeting.

"Chuck, I still remember when you called me about the case. It seems like yesterday, doesn't it?"

Chuck smiled. "I'd say you put it together pretty quick."

"Thanks." Gabby tapped a few laptop keys. "Begin at the beginning, would you? I want to double-check my facts before I finalize the Complaint."

Chuck nodded, sipping his coffee. "I guess around 1966, when I got sent to Holmesburg. I did two years for possession of marijuana."

Damn. I shuddered at the harshness of the sentence. Now weed was practically legal in Pennsylvania. I felt a kinship with him, though I didn't tell him that I had served time, too. He would have asked why, and I couldn't begin to compare my bid in a suburban county jail with Holmesburg, one of Philadelphia County's worst jails, notorious for overcrowding and bad conditions, especially in that era. It had since been shut down.

Chuck continued, "Anyway one day a doctor came, and he told me I was picked to be in a test for some kinda product they was working on."

"And you don't remember the doctor's name, do you?"

"No."

Gabby looked up from her laptop. "What makes you say it was a doctor?"

Chuck paused. "He had a white coat."

"He wasn't the prison doctor from the infirmary?"

"No."

"And the coat said University of Pennsylvania, is that correct?"

"Yes, that's right."

Gabby hit a key. "Did he tell you which product they were testing on you?"

"No, it was something with your skin is all. Everybody wanted to be in the tests."

"And you earned three dollars per test?"

"Yes. The money was better than the other jobs you could get. You worked in the shoe shop, you earned fifteen cents a day." Chuck scratched his head. "So many other guys were doing it, you could see in the shower, they had squares on the back. Patch test, we called them."

"Like a skin-patch test," Gabby said, tapping away.

"Right. Anyway, I said yes because you got three dollars in your commissary. So you could get cigarettes, whatever you wanted. It was a good deal."

"And you underwent approximately thirty-two skin-patch tests in a year and a half, is that right?"

"Yes. We'd get in line in the morning, like three times a week, and we'd go see the doctor."

"Can you describe the process?"

"The doctor would listen to my heart and all, ask me how I was doin', then he tell me to turn around, and tape up my back. Then he put the stuff on and put me under the lamp, a bunch of times."

Gabby turned to me. "They would create a grid, then apply the lotion and expose each square to a sunlamp for a different time period, up to half an hour. They were trying to see blistering, burning, bleeding, and any other adverse effects of the ointment. It was essentially a Phase I test, which answers the question, is it safe?"

I recoiled, horrified. "And they were testing it *on* him?"

"And others." Gabby returned her attention to Chuck. "Did he give you any pain medicine?"

"No, it didn't hurt in the beginning, but then it started to bleed in between. All of us had scabs and patches and scars on our backs, like one of them patchwork quilts." Chuck gestured at his back. "That's what mine still look like."

"Do you mind if I see and take a picture?"

"Fine with me." Chuck rose and unbuttoned the top of his flannel shirt, then turned around, easing his shirt off his shoulders. His back was entirely scarred with small squares placed willy-nilly from his shoulders to his waist, the pinkish bumps standing out against his dark skin, hideously haphazard.

"Gabby, was this *legal*?" I asked, outraged.

"Yes, back then. More correctly, there wasn't anything making it unlawful." Gabby took a few pictures, then set down her phone. "Thanks, Chuck." She turned to me again, by way of explanation.

"This case begins with Dr. Albert Kligman, a dermatology professor at Penn's medical school. He saw the inmates as subjects to be exploited, like a big controlled experiment. As he told the newspaper, 'All I saw before me were acres of skin. It was like a farmer seeing a fertile field for the first time.' He said he saw the place as 'an anthropoid colony, mainly healthy under perfect control conditions.'" Gabby cocked her head, her expression grim. "Do you know what 'anthropoid' means?"

"No, honestly."

"Apelike." Gabby and Chuck exchanged disgusted looks. "Kligman was considered a genius, but he was a racist with no moral compass. He turned Holmesburg and seven other county jails in Philadelphia into a massive moneymaking enterprise based on human medical experimentation."

I recoiled. "How did he do it?"

"He set up three private businesses, primarily one named Ivy Labs, trading on Penn's Ivy League prestige. He ran paid research programs for major companies like Johnson & Johnson, Dow Chemical, and R.J. Reynolds, who wanted to test new products on the inmates. There were roughly twelve hundred inmates at Holmesburg and most of them participated in product testing. Minority inmates were given the most dangerous tests. It lasted until the mid-seventies, and if you ask me, this is Philadelphia's version of what happened to Henrietta Lacks at Johns Hopkins and the syphilis studies at Tuskegee."

"What products did they test?" I asked, appalled.

"Hundreds. They started with creams, toothpaste, deodorant, dandruff shampoos, hair dye, detergents, soaps, and ointments for poison ivy and ringworm. Their hair and teeth fell out. Their eyes were irritated by shampoos rubbed into them three times a day. They inoculated prisoners with staph infections, wart virus, herpes simplex, and herpes zoster. The men were used like guinea pigs." Gabby gestured at a thick file on her desk. "Most of the records were destroyed by the prison or Kligman."

I felt shocked. "What was the product in the skin-patch test on Chuck?"

"Tretinoin, an acne medication that Kligman was developing, which works by exfoliating the skin. It irritates, burns, and blisters when exposed to sunlight. It turns out that tretinoin becomes Retin-A and its sister drug Renova, which helps with wrinkles." Gabby's sharp eyes flashed with anger. "Retin-A, Renova, and its progeny are used in anti-aging and anti-wrinkle creams now. You've probably seen the commercials. Our lawsuit is the horrifying origin story of one of the most lucrative products on the market today."

I couldn't get over it. "So they experimented on human beings for a *cosmetic*?"

Gabby nodded. "Their lawyers would say, 'Not a cosmetic, a drug with cosmetic applications.'"

Chuck snorted. "Their lawyers are full of *shit*."

My God. "So we're suing the doctor, right, Gabby?"

"Unfortunately, no, he passed away in 2010. We're suing those responsible for the testing and those that benefit from it currently." Gabby counted off on her fingers. "Bausch Health currently manufactures Retin-A, and Kligman assigned the original patent to Johnson & Johnson. Rhone Pharma is the parent company of Fournette Labs, which makes poison ivy medication. Chuck and the other defendants tested their products after they were given poison ivy. I've sent the defendants demand letters with draft complaints for the past two months, and nobody has made a settlement offer."

"How much are you asking for in the lawsuit?"

"Fifteen million for seven plaintiffs."

Wow. "That's real money."

"Sure as hell is," Chuck interjected with a smile.

Gabby added, "A plaintiff's personal injury lawyer could ask for more, but we know there's a legal issue and we want to settle and fast."

Chuck shook his head. "I'm not getting any younger, and I got bills on account of the cancer."

"Cancer?" I repeated, my heart sinking.

"Yeah, I got skin cancer, melanoma, and my doc says it's on account of those tests. I had chemo, and I don't know if it's going to do any good or not."

"I'm sorry to hear that." I felt sickened for him.

"Thanks." Chuck straightened. "When the doc told me, I said to myself, I have to do something about this. So I went to your sister. We found six other guys in Philly and Jersey in the skin-patch and other poison ivy tests. They got melanoma, too. They moved away after they got out."

Gabby turned to him. "Did you bring your new medical bills?"

"Yes, here." Chuck slid a wrinkled manila envelope across the table. "You think we'll be able to get them to pay up?"

"I'm hoping so, but we do have one major legal problem, the statute of limitations. The testing took place in the sixties and seventies, and the time for filing a lawsuit passed long ago."

I interjected, "That's a technicality, isn't it?"

"Yes, but technicalities matter in the law."

"So what are you going to do?"

Gabby perked up. "Bottom line, there is some precedent that helps us. A group of Holmesburg inmates brought suit decades ago, but it was thrown out on the statute of limitations. The judge said that those plaintiffs couldn't prove that there was a reason they couldn't have brought the lawsuit sooner." Her tone turned professorial. "That leaves an opening for our litigation. Our plaintiffs *can* make such a showing. Chuck and other plaintiffs weren't in the state after their release. That's our lawsuit, in a nutshell."

Chuck turned to me. "I been in the Dominican Republic with my daughter and her husband. I only got back last year."

Gabby nodded. "All I have to do is get to a jury, and I know I'll get a verdict. When the facts are this outrageous, they'll find a way to give punitive damages. It's a different world now. At least I hope it is."

Please God. "How can I help, Gab?"

"I need you to check on our other plaintiffs, update them, and see if we have any new bills or info before we file. I've spoken with all but a handful."

"Okay." Just then, my phone rang. I slid it from my back pocket and glanced at the screen. *John.* "Excuse me," I said, rising. "Okay to take this? It's John."

"Sure."

I raised the phone to my ear, leaving the room. "Yes?"

"Lemaire's dead. I just saw on TV. They found him shot in the head in his car. They didn't say if it's murder or suicide. The cops are at Dutton Run Park right now."

Jesus. "On it."

CHAPTER TWELVE

My windshield wipers beat rhythmically, and I could see cops in raincoats directing traffic past Dutton Run Park. Lemaire was dead, and my mind raced with possibilities. Something, or someone, had happened to the accountant since last night, after John had left him at the quarry. If Lemaire had been murdered, then I assumed there was a conspiracy in the embezzlement scheme.

I craned my neck to see ahead. Smoky flares and sawhorses blocked the entrance to the park, which had equestrian trails and a soccer field. A makeshift screen had been set up in the parking lot and blocked the view from the road. Calcium-white klieg lights shone behind the screen, next to a black Chester County Coroner van and gray-and-blue West Chester Police cruisers, their red-and-white light bars flashing in the rain.

Traffic moved forward, and I stopped when I reached the first cop and slid down my passenger side window. "Officer, what happened?"

"Keep moving," he answered, waving an orange flashlight. I obeyed, then spotted another parking lot ahead on the opposite side of the street. It was filled with TV news vans, their white microwave towers spiking into the rain.

I reached the second parking lot and pulled in among the media, which seemed to be leaving. Techs packed generators and collected black electrical cables. Cameramen disassembled makeshift canopies and folded up klieg lights on tall metal stalks. Shiny SUVs bearing station logos reversed with drivers on phones, their faces obscured by condensation on the windows.

I cut the ignition, got out of the car, and hurried to a shiny white SUV with a station logo, flagging it down as it pulled out of the space. I dug my office ID out of my pocket and flashed it when the window lowered.

"Hey, I'm a freelancer, can you help me out?" I asked the driver, blinking against the rain. "Do they know if it's murder or suicide?"

"They're not saying."

"Have you heard anything else, unofficially?"

"Just that time of death was tonight. Otherwise they're keeping it tight."

"Were there any witnesses? Did you guys interview anybody?"

"No."

"Is next of kin down there? They must have been notified or the cops wouldn't have made it public."

"Nobody's there from the family. We gotta go, buddy. Good luck." The cameraman slid up the window.

The rain was driving, drenching me, but I hustled from the lot, hurried across the street between cars, and jogged down to Dutton Run Park. There was nobody protecting the perimeter from the side, only from the front along the road, and I angled down to the parking lot to see around the screen.

Klieg lights were everywhere, and the coroner and crime techs clustered around the car in question, but it wasn't a maroon Volvo. It was a white Mercedes sedan, C-Class.

What?

I shielded my eyes against the rain, my mind racing. I knew it was a Mercedes because its grille was distinctive.

I didn't get it. Lemaire was found dead in a car that wasn't his—or the Mercedes was his and the maroon Volvo hadn't been. Or he owned both cars for some reason. I myself owned three, but then again, I was nuts.

Suddenly a cop came over, grim-faced under a cap covered with plastic. "Sir, I need you to—"

"Officer, I'm a freelancer." I flashed him my office ID, its lanyard hanging. "I heard that the victim was identified as a Neil Lemaire. Can you confirm that?"

"Sir, please contact our media office. I'm going to need you to leave now."

"Do you know if it was murder or suicide?"

"Sir, I need you to leave—"

"Who's his next of kin? Who did they notify?" I looked around but didn't see any civilians.

"Now go!"

I jogged back to my car in the downpour and climbed into the driver's seat. I fished around for some Dunkin' Donuts napkins and wiped my face and head. I kept an eye on Dutton Run Park. Bright flashes of light came from the screen, so I knew they were photographing the body.

In time the flashes stopped, so I knew they were finished. The coroner's van moved closer to the screen, and shadowy figures in windbreakers unloaded a gurney, barely visible in the gloom. They must have been putting the body into the van, and in the next few minutes, they closed its doors.

My stomach churned, and so did my thoughts. I felt sad, regardless if it was murder or suicide. It made me sick to remember that I'd thought about suicide myself, at my lowest point. It had been in prison, and it was the first time after my parents visited.

I knew something was wrong the moment they entered the visiting room, noisy with families talking and laughing. My mother was in a dark pantsuit with her hair pulled back, but something was off about her expression. My father guided her by the elbow, which was strange.

Mom, you okay? I went to hug her, but the guard waved me off.

No contact, Devlin!

I stepped back, mortified. *Ma? Are you okay?*

My mother nodded but didn't answer. Tears filmed her eyes, which darted around the visiting room.

Dad, what's going on? What's the matter with Mom?

She's fine, TJ, but she can't talk. My father eased her onto the bench and sat down. *She has lockjaw.*

What's that? I asked, shocked.

A jaw disorder. She has to use a straw to eat. She can only take liquids. She has a special mouth guard.

My God! When did this start?

A few weeks ago. She wanted to see you, but she wasn't well enough.

Is it painful?

Yes, she's in massage therapy to ease the inflammation.

How do you get lockjaw?

Stress, my father answered matter-of-factly.

Looking back, I wasn't sure I remembered anything after that answer. I'd given my mother lockjaw, a brilliant woman who loved nothing better than conversation. She could convince any client of anything. She won moot court in law school. She loved oral arguments in court. I would hear her talking nonstop in her book club, and she'd spend hours yakking on the phone with her friends. She and I would talk in the kitchen late at night, over tea and toast.

I remembered that night, sitting in my cell, the lowest I've ever been. I couldn't stop crying. I didn't see any way out. I didn't know if I could change, I didn't know if I deserved to. All I wanted to do was die, and I thought I deserved to die. It was the first time in my life I considered suicide, so I understood something about what Lemaire might have gone through tonight.

I sent up a prayer for him. I didn't know who was mourning him—or who had conspired with him.

I only knew about the cat.

I parked on Lemaire's street, relieved to find that the lights in his house were on. There was a yellow VW Beetle in his driveway, and a silhouette in the living room going back and forth. It was either a friend or a conspirator, or both. I took a photo of the VW's license plate, so I could run it down.

Whoever it was, I hoped they fed the cat and took care of him.

My phone pinged with a text, and I picked up the phone.

It was from John: **COME OVER ASAP NO MATTER HOW LATE**

CHAPTER THIRTEEN

We met in John's home office in his basement, a square room with one wall of law books, accordion files, and black binders of business regs, opposite another wall with glass cases displaying his sports memorabilia like signed footballs and a baseball card collection. A Thomas Moser radius desk dominated the space, with two desktop computers, oversize monitors, and a laptop. The desk chair was the requisite Herman Miller, with blue webbing to match a navy rug.

I faced John. "I don't know if it was murder or suicide, they're not saying yet. They think it happened tonight. The only thing is, they found him in a white Mercedes."

"What about the Volvo?" John's eyes flared in confusion. He was still in his work clothes, but tieless.

"I don't know. I'm guessing the Mercedes was his. The cops released that name and I don't think they'd get that wrong, since you have to keep the registration with the car. So I think it's more likely his than not."

"So the Volvo wasn't his?"

"Unsure. I doubt he had two cars. If he knew he was going to meet you, he might have used another car, especially if he was going to kill you. It could have been stolen or maybe it belonged to one of his co-conspirators, who could have killed Lemaire to avoid being exposed."

"Oh no." John sank into his desk chair. I would have sat down, but there wasn't another chair.

"I spent all day looking for the maroon Volvo, but we still need to find it. Whoever drives it could be a co-conspirator." I met John's eye. "In the meantime, you should buy a gun."

John nodded. "Man, oh man."

"That said, I don't think we should go to the police. It's not like Lemaire was found dead after you met with him. I doubt you were the last person to see him alive. There's been a whole day in between, and like I say, the time of death was sometime tonight." I was thinking aloud. "He had to have done something today, and he could have gone to work. When I staked out Runstan, I was looking for a Volvo, not a Mercedes. Anyway, whoever lent him the Volvo doesn't work at Runstan or wasn't there."

"This is driving me crazy." John shook his head. "I should go to Stan tomorrow and tell him what happened at the quarry. I like the guy. I have a fiduciary duty to his company. I'm not going to keep it from him."

"What if he wants to go to the cops?"

"I thought about it, and I doubt he will." John's eyes flickered knowingly. "It would throw a monkey wrench in the acquisition, and he stands to make a fortune when it goes through. He'll sweep this under the rug."

"A loss of a hundred grand? Won't it show?"

John snorted. "It's easy to hide that money. This way if it comes out later, we told the truth. Honesty is the best policy."

Starting now. "Okay, what about Dad? Are we going to tell him?"

"No, why?"

"I'd like him to know I didn't relapse. We can tell him we left dinner because you thought you killed Lemaire."

John's lips parted. "Are you serious?"

"Totally. You just said, honesty is the best policy. He told Gabby, too. I want them both to know the truth."

John rose, frowning. "That's not the same thing. Your relapsing is personal, what happened at the quarry is business."

"So? What's the difference?"

"Business matters, this doesn't."

Huh? "My sobriety matters. How did you not get that message?"

"Oh, believe me, I got that message." John chuckled without mirth. "Your sobriety, your sobriety. The whole damn family has to talk about your sobriety twenty-four seven, the same way we used to talk about your drinking twenty-four seven. We don't drink on a single holiday because of you. Whether you're a good boy or a bad boy, somehow it's always about you. You have to be the center of attention, since the day you were born."

I felt taken aback. "You jealous that Mommy and Daddy brought home a new baby?"

John laughed. "How could I be jealous of you?"

Thanks. "Then why can't we tell them I didn't relapse? Why does the truth matter when it comes to you, but not when it comes to me?"

"I don't want to tell Dad because it will make things worse."

"How?"

"Game it out, TJ. You and me, we go into his office and tell him that we lied. What's his reaction?"

"Anger."

"And what would that make him do?"

"Yell. What else is new?"

"Ask yourself, if this whole thing blows up, do you think Dad retires next year? I don't." John's eyes burned, his intensity plain. "Dad and me, we're in a power struggle, and if I slip, he takes the advantage. Nobody exploits weakness like Dad. I don't want to be under his thumb anymore."

Yikes. "Still, that affects you more than me. You want to run the firm. You want him to hand it over to you."

"*Hand* it to me? He's selling it to me."

"Whatever, the argument's the same."

John shook his head. "It affects you, too. What if Dad finds out we lied to him? He'll never trust you again."

"He doesn't trust me now."

"He's going to fire you if you relapse again. What do you think he'll do when he finds out you lied to him about his own client? He'll fire you for sure, TJ. He can't fire me. I have my own clients, and it would destroy the firm."

I knew it was true.

"When I run the firm, your job is safe. I wouldn't fire you, TJ. I'd never fire you."

"Is this a bribe?" I almost laughed.

"No, I'm assuming I don't have to bribe you." John frowned. "You're not going to Dad on your own without me, are you?"

"No, I'm . . . not." I hadn't thought that far ahead. "I'm just trying to understand why you don't want to tell him."

"TJ, listen." John took my arm. "If we tell him, he'll never retire, so I'll have to leave the firm and start my own."

"Then that's what should happen."

"You think that would be a friendly parting of the ways? Knowing Dad? Knowing me? It wouldn't be pretty."

"So be it."

"What about *Mom*?" John's gaze connected with mine, and I knew instantly what he meant, even if he was bluffing. If he left the firm, it would kill my mother. She saw the business as a future for us. She believed in Keeping The Family Together.

I sighed, giving in.

CHAPTER FOURTEEN

I got home, dropped my keys on the counter, and crossed reflexively to the refrigerator, following a route as fixed as a flight path, a habit of coming home and getting a beer. I opened the door and stood in its cool rhomboid of light.

This was The Moment.

Rehab teaches you to watch your behavior and interrupt your triggers, and this was my moment of truth, especially in my current mood. For most people, refrigerators don't qualify as the enemy, but mine was out to get me.

Feel bad? Have a beer.

Feel good? Have a beer.

I didn't buy beer anymore, only green bottles of San Pellegrino water, but that didn't matter in The Moment. I could turn around, go out again, and ruin everything. I breathed through The Moment, letting it pass over and somehow through me.

I grabbed a bottle of water, cracked the cap, and took a swig, feeling like I saved my own life, which I had in a way. Churchill said, *When you're going through hell, keep going.* He was referring to World War II, but it also applied to Miller Lite.

I eyed the refrigerator shelves, stocked with healthy foods. There were leafy heads of romaine, strawberry yogurts, broccoli, wrapped wild-caught salmon, and fresh dill. I'd learned that I like to cook, plus it gave me something to do in the kitchen other than drink. I grabbed a yogurt, then closed the door, found a spoon, and made a point of sitting down at the table. It seemed silly, but mindfulness meant the difference between order and chaos, sobriety and drinking. The world may think I'd relapsed, but I knew I hadn't.

I drank my water at the table and looked out the window. The lights were off in the houses across the street, all an older tract design with clapboard siding and a brick foundation. I lived on the first floor of the house, and the apartment upstairs was a pied-à-terre for a couple who visited their grandkids in town.

I ate my yogurt and hoped the sugar would improve my mood. I worried John could be in danger and I was still mad at him for the relapse story, but now I had to buy in. My mother didn't need more heartache from me.

I looked out the window idly, then spotted something odd. There was a dark sedan parked down the street in front of my neighbors, the DeGennaros, but it wasn't theirs. I'd never seen the car before and I knew my neighbors' cars because everybody parked in the driveway, and if they had a second car, they parked it in front of their house. Nobody ever parked in front of somebody else's house.

I scanned the car, maybe a Hyundai. It was parked facing me, but I couldn't identify the model. I couldn't see if anyone was sitting in the car because there were no streetlights or ambient lighting. I tried to remember if it had been there when I'd come home, but I didn't know. I wondered if it had followed me home from John's.

I slid my phone from my pocket and pretended to make a call. I faked a laugh, then started taking pictures of the Hyundai. I pretended to hang up and set the phone down, then rose with my phone and yogurt, crossed to the kitchen, and turned off the light.

I sneaked back to the window in darkness, out of sight. If the Hyundai stayed, I was paranoid. If it didn't, I was in trouble.

I waited, watching. Five minutes passed, and I was about to shrug it off when the Hyundai started its engine and cruised down the street in my direction.

I ducked aside so its driver couldn't see me. The Hyundai passed my house, and I started taking pictures.

It was a black Hyundai Elantra, two-door, older.

The Hyundai reached the corner and turned left, vanishing.

I hurried to my laptop to download the pictures, so I could see them better.

I hoped for a license plate.

CHAPTER FIFTEEN

The next morning dawned sunny, and I parked up the street from my brother's house. I was in the black Toyota RAV4, plus I had on my ball cap and sunglasses. I'm professional that way.

John's Range Rover was still in his driveway, and I had to know if the Hyundai would follow him. Last night I'd enlarged its photo, but it had been too dark to see the license plate. The Hyundai was nowhere in sight now, and I hadn't seen it on my street this morning.

John's street was lined with fake French châteaux, mock English Tudors, and modern glass boxes landscaped with specimen plantings, mulched beds, and solar-powered lighting. The quiet peace of the privileged was interrupted only by dog walkers and joggers checking Apple Watches on the run.

I sipped my coffee and checked my phone. It was seven-thirty A.M. John had told me he was going to see Stan first thing in the morning, so he'd be leaving soon. I hadn't phoned or texted him because it would raise questions if we had a flurry of communications around the time of Lemaire's death. I couldn't convince anybody that I liked John all of a sudden. I wasn't *that* good a liar.

John emerged from his house in a dark suit, his stride to his Range Rover characteristically purposeful. I'd never walked that way a day in my life, even on my way out of prison.

He climbed into his car and took a right turn out of the driveway, and I kept my head down just in case, though I knew he wouldn't recognize my stakeout car because he'd never seen it before.

The Range Rover reached the end of the street, and I took off after it. We wound through the neighborhood, and I followed the Range Rover at a safe distance. We reached Lancaster Avenue, four lanes lined with shops, restaurants, and businesses. Traffic was congested, and I kept an eye out for the Hyundai. It felt odd to stalk my own brother, though I was still pissed at him. I fought the temptation to rear-end him.

Suddenly I spotted a black Hyundai following John from two cars back, in the slow lane. It looked like the same one as outside my house last night, but I couldn't be sure. If it was, it had to be somebody connected to Lemaire, whether to his embezzlement or death.

I shifted forward, keeping an eye on the car. BLUE ROUTE, read the big green sign, and I watched the black Hyundai follow John onto the on-ramp to the highway. I followed, maneuvering to the far right lane. Traffic was congested, but it was easy to separate at this speed. Sooner or later, I'd get a glimpse of the Hyundai's license plate.

We zoomed up the highway together as an unwitting caravan, and the notion put me on edge. Seeing John stalked made the threat so real, and I couldn't help but flash on the black coroner's van last night. Whoever these people were, they weren't playing games.

I switched lanes and got a clear view of the Hyundai license plate.

"HOK6253," I said aloud. I grabbed a pen and wrote it on my hand.

Half an hour later, John pulled into the Runstan parking lot, which was beginning to fill up. He drove directly to the visitor spaces and took the first one.

The Hyundai trailed him, heading to the right and parking in the outermost space, which was exactly what I would have done. I pulled into the first open space near the entrance, giving me a clear view of my brother and the Hyundai to the right.

I turned off the engine, pushed up my sunglasses, and waited to see what would happen. John left his car and headed into the building. Cars began pulling into the parking lot, and I scanned them for the maroon Volvo, but no luck. Runstan employees emerged from their cars and headed into the office.

I lowered the brim of my cap and kept an eye on the Hyundai. Nobody got out. It was too far away to get a good look at the driver. I took a few pictures anyway, keeping an eye out for the maroon Volvo.

I set my phone down, hoping the Hyundai driver would get out, maybe get a coffee at the pizza place, so I could see what he looked like.

BOOM! Suddenly someone pounded on my window.

I startled, looking over.

CHAPTER SIXTEEN

Dad?" I said, my mouth going dry. My father was standing next to the car in a sharp gray suit and silk tie. Oddly, he held a white pastry box.

"TJ, what are you doing here?" he demanded through the window.

I started the engine to lower the window, but he was already storming around the car. He tore open the passenger door and climbed into the car, ending up so close I caught a minty whiff of his aftershave.

"TJ, why are you here?" My father met my eye directly. "And why are you wearing that getup? Are you hungover?"

"God, no," I blurted out, getting my bearings.

"Tell me you're not meeting a *connection*. Do you know this is Runstan's parking lot?"

"Yes, Dad, I'm with John, I was going to meet him here—"

"*John's* here?" My father blinked, surprised. "What's he doing here?"

I thought fast. "Did you hear on the news? About Runstan's accountant?"

"Of course. Why do you think I'm here? I came to pay my respects to Stan." My father turned to look at the entrance. "John's inside *already*?"

"I think so. He's here to see Stan, too. That's his car." I pointed at the Range Rover, and my father's ire shifted from me to John.

"What the *hell*? What time did he get here?"

"I don't know."

"Why didn't he call me and tell me he was going?"

"Isn't Stan his client?"

"No, Stan's *my* client," my father shot back, knitting his brow. "I brought Runstan in when John was just a kid, for God's sake."

"But he's doing their work now, isn't he?" I asked, making trouble for a good cause. I needed to stall him so John could talk to Stan. I glanced at the Hyundai over my father's padded shoulder.

"So? Runstan wouldn't *be* a business but for me. I know Stan from day one." My father pursed his lips. "You remember? I used to bring you here. You met Stan, with the birthmark? You used to call him Stain."

"No, *John* called him Stain."

"The point is, that's how long ago I represented him. He was an electrician in Philly back then. I even helped him name the company. He liked to run, so I said, 'Why don't you call it "Run, Stan,"' and that's where he got the name."

"I didn't know that." I still thought it was a dumb name.

"Your mother got him a terrific post-nup. He didn't even know what that was."

"I don't, either." I knew it would trigger a Dad-lecture, like flipping a switch.

"A post-nup? You need a post-nup when you didn't get a prenup. It's essentially a negotiation of a divorce that takes place when the marriage is on solid ground. Financial circumstances change, and high-wealth clients need to protect themselves. For example, when Runstan took off, it constituted a material change in Stan's circumstances. I told him he needed a post-nup right away. Follow?"

"Yes." I doubted I'd ever need a prenup *or* a post-nup. I didn't know if I'd ever nup. Meanwhile I checked the Hyundai, and the driver was still inside.

"You know what happened? We began to negotiate the post-nup, and Stan's ex, Janine, starts asking for half of the business. Mind you, she hadn't shown interest before, at all. So that tells you something, doesn't it?"

I nodded, but all it told me was that she wanted a fair share.

"She even asked for a percentage of future revenues. It would have required audits, accounting, reporting out the wazoo. A slow-motion nightmare, right?"

"Yes." *No, a slow-motion nightmare is an accountant dead in a car.*

"I saved Stan a fortune, and they got divorced a year later. I *saved* Runstan for him." My father returned his attention to the Range Rover. "John should have called me and told me he was coming."

"It probably slipped his mind." I knew if I criticized John, then my father would defend him, so I was employing Devlin-double-reverse-psychology.

"That's the problem. He should have remembered. We could have gone together. Why didn't he call me?"

"Did you call him?"

"No, he's supposed to call me."

"Maybe he didn't get a chance. It happened so late."

"So what? He knows your mother and I get up early. How long does it take to call? Or text? He's always on that phone."

"Did you know the accountant?"

"No, but what difference does that make? Stan's in the lurch, with the acquisition and all. Hell, I called him as soon as I saw it online this morning. I told him I'd stop by on my way in." My father frowned, in thought. "I wonder if John didn't call me on purpose. What if he got here early to beat me to the punch?"

"He would never do that." *He would totally do that. But he didn't this time.*

"I know, but still. Sometimes I think he's pushing me out the door."

"No, he's not." *Churchill felt the same way. Maybe you're both right.*

"He thinks it's easy to run the firm, but it's a lot of responsibility. The ultimate responsibility. It's about leadership."

"I'm sure."

"Did he bring pastry? It's a condolence call."

I masked my smile, knowing it was my mother's influence. She thought carbohydrates cured everything.

"Hmph." My father reached for the door handle. "Well, anyway, let's go. Come on."

No. I had to watch the Hyundai. "Dad, you go. I'll wait here."

"No, you're not sitting in a car like a vagrant. Come in and say hi to Stan. It's good client relations."

"He's not my client."

"He's a client of the firm, smart-ass. Let's go." My father stepped out of the car, brushed down his suit, and stood at the open door. "He'd like to see you."

"He doesn't remember me."

"He asks after you."

"I don't remember him."

"Then how'd you know you didn't call him Stain? Get out. Now." My father slammed the car door, then stood outside waiting for me. There are mountains that move more easily than my father, so I got out of the car.

"I'll stop in but then I—"

"And take off that ball cap. It's juvenile."

"I'll take it off inside." I didn't want the Hyundai driver to see my face.

My father shook his head, walking to the building. "TJ, when are you gonna grow up?"

I assumed it was a rhetorical question. I kept my head down as I trailed my father, watching the Hyundai under my brim. My father reached the building and opened Runstan's door, but before I went inside, I took one last look at the Hyundai.

Whoa.

Its door was opening. The driver would be out in a minute. I could finally get a look at his face.

I stopped, stalling in the threshold.

"Gimme that hat," my father said, yanking off my cap.

Yikes. I was exposed, just like that. The Hyundai driver was getting out.

"TJ, come in!" My father pulled me inside.

CHAPTER SEVENTEEN

A teary clutch of Runstan employees filled the reception area comforting each other, and among them were Stan and John, who masked his surprise at seeing me. Meanwhile all I could think about was the Hyundai driver. I glanced outside, hoping for a glimpse. The window didn't afford me a view.

"Stan, I'm sorry." My father bear-hugged Stan. "What a tragedy."

"Thanks, Paul." Stan had a faintly rough-hewn presence, successful in an operations-guy way. His short-sleeve shirt and khakis lacked the corporate polish favored by my father and John, who were more at home in a conference room than on a plant floor.

My father gestured to me. "TJ wanted to come to pay his respects."

"Stan, I'm so sorry," I said, cued.

Stan nodded sadly. "Good to see you, TJ. Thanks for coming." He gestured to John. "Looks like I got the whole family, huh?"

"Absolutely." John nodded. "We're here for you."

"*All* of us." My father forced a smile. "I would've come earlier, but I stopped for pastry. Marie sends her sympathy, too."

"Give her my love." Stan smiled back, completely unaware that World War III was erupting between my father and brother.

Stan's face fell. "Poor Neil. I knew something was wrong when he didn't come into work yesterday. He was really a sweetheart, wasn't he, gang?"

"He sure was," answered a young woman sitting in one of the reception chairs. "It's so sad."

"*So* sad," chimed in an older woman, and the rest added, "I feel awful." "I wish he had called me." "He seemed fine, like he was doing better." "He called in sick yesterday, but he never got sick."

I realized they thought Lemaire died by suicide. "I'm sorry, I didn't know the police had an official cause of death."

"They don't." Stan shook his head. "They're going to investigate and come talk to us tomorrow."

"I worried it was murder," I said, fishing. "There's so much violent crime these days."

"I doubt it," Stan said somberly. "We all knew Neil was down, emotionally. He broke up with his boyfriend before he came here."

"Did he have family?" I glanced out the window, but still had no view of the Hyundai.

"Not here. His mom lives in North Dakota, and his dad passed away. Our bookkeeper, Lillian, was his emergency contact. They worked together, thick as thieves. She's in his office now, packing his things." Stan gestured behind to a hall beyond the cubicles. "Anyhow, TJ, you look good. Say hi to the gang. These folks are the best." He motioned to the employees. "I'd introduce you, but you'd forget the names."

"I'm sure. Hi, everybody, I'm sorry about your loss."

"Thank you," said a young woman, then they all chimed in. "Nice to meet you." "You look just like your father." "Exactly, father-and-son."

Stan pointed at a skinny, older Black man with a lined face, rising from a chair on the end. "TJ, remember Mike Dedham? He worked here when you used to come with your father."

"Yes, hi, Mike." I called to him, remembering.

"Hey." Mike wagged a knobby finger. "You used to yap about cars."

"I still do," I glanced out the window. No luck.

My father clapped me on the back. "TJ and I were just talking about the good old days, Stan. I was telling TJ how I named the company."

John interjected, "But the company's grown so much since then. Stan, you've done an incredible job."

Stan beamed. "Thanks. We started with one plant and now we have three. In this office, it used to be me and my ex. Now we have an admin *department*."

"You sure do!" my brother and father said in unfortunate unison.

A young woman sniffled. "But without Neil."

Stan let the awkward moment pass. "I'm sorry he won't be here for the acquisition. I couldn't have done it without him and you, John."

My father interjected. "Don't forget me and Mike. We're pioneers."

Stan chuckled. "'Pioneers,' I like that. Right, Mike?"

"*Damn* right," Mike shot back. Everybody smiled, and I peeked out the window.

My father shot me a dirty look. "TJ, why so jumpy? You owe somebody money?"

John answered, "Me, for one."

Everyone chuckled, and my father put his arm around Stan. "You and I need to sit down and talk over the acquisition. The show must go on."

John frowned. "Dad, we discussed it already."

My father interjected again. "Stan might want my thoughts, too, son."

I had to check out the Hyundai driver. "I'll let you lawyers talk. Stan, good seeing you again."

"You too, TJ."

"Fine, TJ," my father called back.

"Catch you later, TJ," John added, and they walked Stan into his office like a kid in a custody battle.

I crossed to the door, but felt a hand on my arm. I turned around to see Mike, fixing his rich brown eyes on mine.

"TJ, hold on," he said, his voice low. "Not everybody thinks it was suicide."

CHAPTER EIGHTEEN

One look at Lillian Duvall told me she was in mourning. A petite woman in her sixties, she sat crestfallen at the desk behind a large monitor. Her graying hair slipped out of its ponytail, and she had on a black sweater and pants. The office had a modest desk, but there was a tall plant with large green leaves in one corner and, across the way, a shelf with lush ferns, bluish-purple African violets, and verdant English ivy. Framed close-ups of tropical birds covered the walls.

"Excuse me," I said softly, interrupting her reverie.

"Oh!" Lillian peered around the monitor, blinking puffy blue eyes. She straightened, trying to rally. "I'm sorry, can I help you?"

I introduced myself, entering the office. "You probably know my father and brother, who represent Runstan."

"Of course. You look like your father."

"I'm younger," I shot back, and Lillian smiled. I realized I wanted to cheer her up, a wish I hadn't known I had before this very moment. "Do you mind if I sit down? I wanted to speak with you."

"Go ahead." Lillian gestured to a chair.

"I'm sorry about your loss." I took a seat. "I came with my dad this morning, to see how you all were doing."

"Thank you." Lillian sighed heavily. "It's so hard to believe that Neil's gone. He was a great boss and a wonderful friend. He called in and told me he was sick, but even that worried me. He never got sick. I worried about him all day." She paused, swallowing hard. "He's only been here a year, but he left a mark on you. He wanted to make things better. Do you know what I mean?"

"Yes. Judging from this office, I do. He's made it special, with the plants."

"He used to say he liked oxygen, not plants."

I smiled, liking Lemaire's sense of humor. It was hard to remember he was an embezzler.

"He was a kind man in a world that's not very kind."

I sensed Lillian hadn't had an easy life. She had an aura of someone who'd lived alone for a long time. Or maybe that was me.

"He was a dream to work for, really. He treated everybody with respect and he worked hard. He took ownership of everything. He even did the grunt work. He didn't leave it for me."

I wondered if it freed him to embezzle without her knowing. "That's nice, considering the acquisition. That must have been a lot more work."

"Yes, it was, but as soon as Stan told us he was selling the company, Neil kicked it into gear. He handled the books, and that was fine with me. I even got a vacation this year, two weeks with my sister and her kids in the Outer Banks. I never could take that much time off when I worked for the old accountant."

"So Neil was really dedicated."

"Yes, he really wanted to do well here and he put in for a CFO position after the acquisition. I'm sure Stan would have given it to him."

I decided to be direct. "I don't mean to be intrusive, but Mike told me you don't think Neil died by suicide."

"I don't." Lillian's heartbroken gaze met mine. "Neil was depressed, it's true, and he was lonely after he and Daniel broke up. Neil wanted to get married, but Daniel didn't, and it ended before he came to Runstan. But Neil wasn't down enough to . . . Well, you know. He wanted to travel more, see the world. We even talked about taking a trip together, to Scandinavia."

I nodded, and she didn't need encouragement to continue.

"They all think I'm in denial. Maybe I am, I don't know." Lillian stopped abruptly, and her eyes filmed with tears. "I just don't think he would do that to himself or Mango. He loved that cat."

I flashed on the ginger cat, sitting on the driveway.

"He lived for that cat." Lillian reached inside a cardboard box and showed me a few cat pictures. "She was everything to Neil. I was at his house last night, and I swear, she knew he was gone."

I realized Lillian must have been the person in Lemaire's living room, with the yellow VW Beetle.

"She wouldn't stop meowing, and she was walking all over the house, howling. That's why I say that no matter how low Neil got last night, he would never leave her."

"Maybe he thought someone would take care of her."

"No, he knew better." Lillian shook her head firmly. "Mango is unadoptable. She has to get insulin shots twice a day, under the skin. It's hard and expensive. He would never leave her, risking she'd be put down. And now, what am I going to do? I can't take her, I have an older cat and he's very territorial. Nobody wants her."

"I'll take her," I said, surprising even myself.

Lillian blinked. "Are you serious?"

"Yes." Meanwhile I didn't know if I could, I only knew I wanted to try. Maybe I wanted a cat to wait at the end of the driveway for me.

Lillian's lips parted with hope. "Do you have pets? Mango doesn't like other pets."

"No other pets."

"Kids? She doesn't like kids, either."

"No kids. I have a yoga mat. Is she okay with yoga mats?"

Lillian laughed, happy and relieved, and I felt my heart ease, so I kept going.

"How does she feel about yoga blocks? Also those weird straps."

"I have to warn you, the injections are expensive."

"I have money."

"You have to inject her yourself. Do you know how?"

I heard about it in rehab, does that count? "Yes."

"She's at Neil's. I fed her there this morning. When do you want her? I can bring her to you."

"I'll get her from Neil's house," I told her, realizing I'd stumbled into a golden investigative opportunity.

"How wonderful!" Lillian jumped up, came around the desk, and threw open her arms. "Thank you so much!"

"You're welcome." I rose and gave her a hug, but Lillian clung to me and began to cry, her head against my jean jacket.

"I miss him . . . so much. I wish he were alive . . . he should be alive. I wish I knew . . . what happened . . . if somebody did this to him."

"I understand," I told her, feeling oddly the same way.

"I'm sorry, I'll be right back. I'm going to the ladies' room." Lillian let me go and hustled from the office, wiping her eyes.

I realized she'd left me alone with Neil's computer, which could contain evidence of his embezzlement or whoever he was working with. She had just been on it, so I might not need to reenter a passcode.

I closed the door, hurried to the desk, and got busy.

CHAPTER NINETEEN

I left Runstan ahead of my father and brother, who were still in with Stan. I looked around the lot and the Hyundai was gone. I scanned the surrounding area, but it was nowhere in sight.

I went to my car, my thoughts churning. Inside the pocket of my jean jacket was a thumb drive filled with Lemaire's email and as many of his files as I could copy. I hadn't had time to read them, but they had to help me get to the bottom of his murder, if it *was* murder.

I reached my car, got in, and headed out of the parking lot, making a call. "Patrick?"

"Yo, I heard you're seeing Maya tonight. Can I be best man?"

I smiled, having forgotten. "No, but I got a license plate I need you to look up."

"Okay, but we love that girl. You better treat her right. Wait, my wife wants to talk to you. I'm going to give her the phone."

Argh. "No, Patrick—"

"TJ, this is Teresa," said a woman, her voice even more gravelly than Patrick's. "You're taking out my favorite niece. She's my baby girl, this one. You better treat her right."

"I will."

"I don't want her reaching for her wallet. She's gonna say she's a feminist, but you better don't let her pay."

"I won't."

"You hurt this girl, you answer to me. Goodbye." I heard some muffled talking, then Patrick said, "Okay, you heard from the boss."

"I sure did. Now can I tell you the plate number?" I read it off my hand. "It's a black Hyundai Elantra, maybe three years old."

"You in the market?"

"No, it's for a case."

"Another wife foolin' around?"

"It's confidential."

"Lemme get back to you. I have to talk to my buddy."

"I need it ASAP."

"On it. And you better pick up that tab."

"I'm not a monster," I told him, and we both hung up.

I headed to the Devlin & Devlin office, checking the rearview mirror for the Hyundai. In time, I decided that I wasn't being followed. I worried that John might have been, but there was nothing I could do about that until he got back to the office. I kept the radio on for any update on Lemaire, but it was all national politics. The death of a random accountant had become yesterday's news. Seeing Lillian's anguish this morning had put a face on the loss for me. I tried to shake it but couldn't.

I snapped off the radio.

I entered the office to find Gabby in reception, fresh and crisp in her navy blazer with jeans. "Hey, lady."

"TJ, how are you?" Gabby asked, her eyes concerned, and I remembered she thought I had relapsed.

"I'm fine. Really."

"Come with me. I want to talk about the Holmesburg case." Gabby walked me down the hall to her office. "I was worried, since you're in late."

"I was with John and Dad at Runstan."

"Oh boy." Gabby rolled her eyes.

"You don't know the half of it."

"Nor do I want to." Gabby chuckled.

We entered her office, which was as sunny and eclectic as her house, decorated with woven kilims, wooden sculptures, and photos of her and Martin taken around the world. They reminded me of Neil, who had wanderlust, too, and I wondered why I didn't. Maybe I had to get it right at home first.

"I have a list for you." Gabby crossed to a cluttered desk, tore a page off a legal pad, and handed it to me. "These are the plaintiffs I want you to check in with."

"Okay, thanks." I scanned the sheet, which had four names and addresses.

"Start with Joe Ferguson. Chuck has been in touch with him, and Joe agreed to see you. I emailed him a Complaint and tell him I'm going to file ASAP. Get any new medical bills or any new health news. If he has questions, I'm happy to call or meet with him. Make sure he knows the lawsuit won't cost him a dime. He's going to think there's a catch, but just tell him."

"We're fighting for justice."

"Exactly." Gabby smiled. "Can you get started right away?"

"I gotta check in with John, then I'm on it."

"Okay. Let me know if you need *anything*." Gabby looked at me with concern, and I hated deceiving her.

"You're a great sister, you know that?"

"Yes," Gabby answered, and we both laughed.

• • •

I handed the thumb drive to John. "Take a look at this. I copied Lemaire's spreadsheets and documents from his computer at Runstan."

"Really? How?" John's eyes lit up, and I filled him in about Lillian while he inserted the thumb drive into his laptop. His office was quiet, and the TVs on the shelves played Italian soccer on mute. John loved sports regardless of country, like Doctors Without Borders, only a selfish lawyer.

"Lemaire must have kept a record of where he got the money from or which banks he deposited it to."

"Right, let's see." John started hitting keys, and the screen filled with spreadsheets. "This could be a treasure trove, but it will take time to go through."

"Don't copy the files. We don't want them on your laptop."

"I know," John said irritably. His attention returned to the screen. "I don't see the accounts that looked suspicious to me. I bet the real books are hidden or encrypted. We need our IT guy. What's his name again?"

"Andre."

"Can you call him?" John kept reading, his eyes racing back and forth. "Get him over here ASAP?"

"Okay, but—"

"TJ, what were you doing at Runstan anyway?" John took out the thumb drive and handed it to me. I updated him about the Hyundai, and he recoiled. "I'm being followed? Why didn't you call and tell me?"

"Again, we need to keep the record clear. I had your back, literally. I was there the whole time. I'm running the Hyundai's license plate now."

"Why are they following us? What do they want?" John glanced worriedly at the laptop. "We can't go to the cops now, Stan doesn't want to. I told him everything this morning, about the missing money and Lemaire pulling a gun on me."

"How did he react?"

"He was shocked, but he wants to keep it quiet. If it comes out, it'll jeopardize the acquisition. Vuarnex is a public company, and if there's any impropriety, the deal goes south. Stan really believes it was suicide anyway."

"But what if it was murder? Lillian thinks it was."

"Who does she think did it?"

"She doesn't know."

"Do you think she knew about the embezzlement? She's the bookkeeper. Was she in cahoots with him?"

"No, not at all. Tonight I have a chance to get inside Neil's house." I told him about adopting the cat.

"TJ, what are *you* gonna do with a cat?"

"Love it?" Then I remembered something. "Did Stan tell you that Lemaire was angling for CFO after the acquisition?"

John frowned. "No. Stan doesn't even have a CFO. He runs the company like a mom-and-pop shop."

"So what happens with the missing money?"

"Stan's going to cover it up, so it won't raise any questions."

"Isn't that illegal?"

"Yes, and I told him so, but it's his books and his deal."

I knew it was lawyerspeak for looking the other way. "So if we don't go to the cops, we're helping him cover it up."

"As his lawyer, I can only advise him. The rest is up to him. Welcome to the real world." John shrugged. "By the way, you wouldn't believe that meeting with me, Dad, and Stan. It was like we were fighting over a woman."

"Dad thinks you're trying to push him out of the firm."

"I *am*," John shot back.

I actually felt bad for my father. "Can't you just let him be? Humor him on Runstan?"

"Why should I?"

"Because your last name rhymes?"

"So?" John fumed. "The fact that he knew Stan from before doesn't mean anything."

"What's the difference to you?"

"Money." John leaned on the desk, warming to the topic. "Mom and Dad bill by the hour, at five hundred bucks. Billing per hour is a typical fee structure for lawyers who practice family law, litigation, trusts and estates, and the like." John glanced at the laptop. "But mergers and acquisitions can work differently, and I'm charging Runstan a premium tied to the sale price of the company."

Whoa. "You mean a commission, like a realtor? Why did Stan agree to that, if it costs him more?"

"Good question." John nodded, clearly pleased. "Because I set up the acquisition. I was representing Vuarnex on a minor matter, and I could see it made sense for them to acquire Runstan. I pitched both sides and put the deal together."

"Like a matchmaker." I thought of Patrick and his wife, Teresa, but John's eye roll told me it was a dopey analogy.

"Vuarnex uses Morgan Lewis, and I represent Stan. I don't make a big thing about it vis-à-vis Dad. I preserve the fiction he's the head of the firm, I save his own face *for* him. But it's coming back to bite me."

"So what's your fee for Runstan?"

"A million bucks."

I gasped, astounded. "So you're gonna be a millionaire?"

John didn't reply except for a spreading smile.

"John, are you *already* a millionaire?"

"Duh, what do you think?"

Wow. "How much is Runstan selling for?"

"Stan's about to come into twenty million dollars."

"What? Stan, who drives an old Explorer? If I were coming into twenty mil I'd drive . . ." I fantasy-shopped. "A Maserati I didn't have to sell for rent."

John chuckled. "Vuarnex is going to pay him a nice salary, and he's going to run the company at the same office. That's why he doesn't want to go to the cops."

"Because it would cost him twenty mil."

"Yes, and the Runstan acquisition is my deal. That's why it's ridiculous that Dad's fighting me. He thinks Runstan is his client and he wants *half* of my fee. Five hundred grand."

Ouch. "Can't you negotiate with him?"

"With my own father?" John's face flushed with anger. "He should be happy for me, not trying to take money I earned."

"If you go by your hourly rate, what would your fee in Runstan be?"

"Thirty grand. I told him I would give him my entire fee as if I had worked on an hourly-rate basis. We all keep our own fees, after we throw in for fixed costs."

"So you're at thirty grand and Dad's at five hundred grand." I groaned. "That's pretty far apart."

I hadn't known how they handled billing. I hadn't thought of it as my business, but in a way, it *was* my business. At least it was my family. Anyway it was my family business, which was confusing.

"We pay fixed costs off the top."

I realized I myself was one of the fixed costs, like ballpoint pens. I made $80,000 a year as an investigator, and I thanked my lucky stars every day. There are worse things than being a Bic.

"Gabby does her pro bono work on her own dime. It's her choice to save the world." John glanced at the TV, watching a player score.

John folded his arms over his tie. "I'm not giving in."

"He's not, either."

"He's greedy."

"I don't think it's about money."

"TJ, everything's about money."

"I mean, it's about ego. It's hard for him that you bring in so much more."

"That's not my problem."

"Yes, it is or you wouldn't be fighting with him."

John waved me off. "I don't care, he doesn't need the money. They're set for life."

"Mom and Dad?" I realized I didn't know anything about my parents' finances. I knew they were comfortable and everybody was more comfortable than I was. Basically, I was uncomfortable. "Tell me."

"They have fifteen million invested with the same people I do."

Wow! "Wow!"

John checked his phone. "Anyway, I have work to do. Can you take that thumb drive and call Andre?"

"Sure, but I have to do something for Gabby. You're here for the rest of the day, aren't you?"

"Yes."

"Good. Don't go anywhere." I didn't want to worry about John being followed, but he was already typing into his phone.

"What are you doing for Gabby?"

"She's suing on behalf of inmates at Holmesburg during the sixties. They were used for medical experimentation."

"That's a loser," John said absently, reading his phone.

CHAPTER TWENTY

I left the office and hurried out to the parking lot, scanning for the Volvo or the Hyundai. I got in the car and took off, troubled. Now that I knew how much Runstan stood to gain with the acquisition, it made sense that Stan didn't want to go to the police about Lemaire. But if Lemaire had been murdered, John and I were obstructing justice and putting ourselves in the crosshairs.

I satisfied myself that I wasn't being followed, so I focused on driving to meet Joe Ferguson, the first person on the list for Gabby's lawsuit. Cars and tractor-trailers clogged the road, and I entered Marcus Hook, a small town at the southernmost border of Delaware County, birthplace of the Philadelphia Accent. We had grown up in nearby Norwood and still had its bona fide flat *o*'s and dropped *g*'s, to my parents' consternation.

I passed a Wawa and a Fireworks Supercenter, then turned onto a street lined with modest two-story brick homes, their low-profile roofs dotted with satellite dishes. The front yards were small, and American flags flapped in the sunshine with Flyers banners. None of the houses had driveways, so along the curb were a lineup of older cars. I could have made a fortune flipping them, but today I was on a mission.

I parked in front of the Ferguson house, got my messenger bag, and knocked on the door. Its wood trim alligatored in grimy patches and its brickwork needed repointing. White shades covered the windows. The door was opened by a middle-aged Black woman in maroon scrubs with a pin-on tag that read DELCO HOMECARE above her name, Pam.

"Can I help you?" she asked from over the chain lock.

"My name is TJ Devlin, and I'm here to see Joe Ferguson about a lawsuit over Holmesburg. My sister, Gabby, called about our contacting you?"

"I remember, but this isn't the best time—"

"Let him in!" a man yelled behind her, presumably Ferguson.

"Come in." Pam smiled, unlocked the chain, and I entered the small living room, surprised to see that Joe Ferguson was a very sick man. He lay in a pleather recliner with a crocheted afghan covering his short, thin body. Cigarette smoke wreathed his grizzled head, and his dark skin had a grayish pallor. His eyes and cheeks were sunken, but his aspect was sharp as he fixed a frown on me.

"What are you lookin' at, son?"

I felt like I was intruding. "Are you sure this is an okay time? I can come back—"

"There's no other time!"

"Okay, Mr. Ferguson."

"Call me Joe!"

Pam shot him a look, picking up a handbag and keys from a side table. "I have to go to the store, and I'll leave you two alone. See you later."

"Siddown." Joe motioned to the plaid chair beside him, which faced an old television on a wooden cart. A tray table held a box of Kleenex, brown medicine bottles, and a crowded ashtray.

"Thank you." I took a seat, setting the messenger bag on the floor. "My name is TJ—"

"I'm dyin', not deaf." Joe sucked on his cigarette, drawing his cheeks. "You didn't know, did you?"

My mouth went dry. "No."

Joe snorted. "Don't worry. You're dyin', too."

"I know."

"At least I know when. You don't."

I laughed. "That's true."

"I'm goin' before you."

"You'd better," I shot back on impulse, and Joe burst into laughter, emitting cigarette smoke. "I'm joking, I didn't mean to—"

"It was funny!" Joe crushed out his cigarette, eyeing me with new regard. "I like you, son! My daughter and son-in-law come by, they got long faces. They act like I'm dead already."

I felt a pang for him. "They love you, that's why."

"They're comin' tonight. They need to loosen up. This cancer, it's all over now."

"You were in the skin-patch test?"

"Yeah, and the poison ivy and the ringworm, too. My back got so many scars, it look like a *map*. I didn't think there was nothin' wrong with it. They were doctors." Joe shook his head. "Now there's nothin' anybody can do. They gave me chemo, it didn't work. They only expected me to last two months. I made it to three yesterday."

"Thank God."

"I got to see the Eagles in the Super Bowl again."

"Sorry they lost."

"Okay, but they were *there*." Joe grinned back, and I felt amazed that I was talking with a man facing his own demise with bravery, even humor. He was about my father's age, and I wondered how I'd feel if my dad were dying. The thought tore me in two, my love and anger a one-two punch.

"Now, for the lawsuit, do you have any new medical records?"

"Yeah." Joe waved at the counter. "I got 'em ready, like she asked."

"Good." I reached in my bag and got the Complaint. "I can take you through this and make sure we have the facts right."

"Don't bother. Read it to me or ask me. I'm not in school no more."

I flipped to his section of the Complaint. "What do you remember about the skin-patch tests? What did they do?"

"We went into the room and they cut up our backs and put the medicine on. Then we went under a lamp. It was like an assembly line. I got three bucks a shot." Joe shrugged. "I didn't think much about it till Chuck and the lady called, what's her name?"

"Gabby Devlin, my sister."

"She talked to Pam, too. She's a nurse so she understood. Got the scars on my back. On my shoulders, too."

"Did they explain what product they were testing?"

"No."

"And you were in Holmesburg in 1966, for only one year?"

"Yeah, I was there before my trial. They charged me with aggravated assault, but I didn't do it and I couldn't make bail. That was the reason I did the test, to make bail. The judge set five grand, so I needed five hundred bucks. I couldn't get it."

My God. "So you were only there awaiting trial? You were innocent?"

"Yes." Joe blinked matter-of-factly. "They picked up the wrong guy. I tried to tell them, but they didn't believe me."

I felt speechless, struck dumb by the injustice. I looked down at the Complaint, but the words swam before my eyes.

"Son?"

I tried to focus, skimming the lines. "Then you left Pennsylvania from 1967 to about 2021?"

Joe nodded. "Lived with my son in North Carolina. Moved back last year, after he remarried."

"Did you read anything about any controversy over the testing? It was in the paper after 1972 or thereabouts?"

"Never saw a thing. I was down there."

"Didn't hear it from anybody up here?"

"No. So when are you gonna file this lawsuit?"

"As soon as possible. This week or next." My chest tightened, wondering how much time he had left.

"You know it ain't gonna do no good, don't you? They'll never pay a dime. They got too much money to have to pay. The only folks who pay are the ones who *don't* have money."

"I hope that's not true. We're going for a nice, big settlement."

"I'll hold my breath," Joe shot back wryly.

Marcus Hook wasn't far from where we'd grown up, and I found myself driving through our old neighborhood, in Norwood. The streets that had once seemed so wide were only a single lane, lined by houses smaller than I remembered. Lawns were patches of grass dotted with hummingbird feeders, concrete statuary, and ceramic statues of the Virgin Mary. I hadn't been back here since we'd moved away, and on impulse, I turned onto our old street.

I cruised past the tract houses, the family names flooding back to me; the McGlaughlins, the Russos, and the Morskis. Our parish was Saint Gabriel's, where I went to school and memorized the question-and-answers in the Catechism for my First Holy Communion.

Who made you?

God made me.

I reached our old house and stopped out front, overwhelmed by a sense of coming *home*. The house was a modest two-story with a brick façade and a white front door, and my father had paid $60,000 for it, which had sounded astronomical to my little-kid sense of numbers. There was a mountain laurel by the door that was the only thing bigger than I remembered. It used to reach midway up the doorjamb but now formed a verdant bower on a trellis over the door. I used to look at its blossoms, shaped like wondrous pink parachutes, and I could picture them now, marveling that God could make something so perfect, far better than me.

I remembered John, big and tall, and I remembered Gabby, too, curly-haired and giggling, drawing hopscotch on the sidewalk. She didn't matter the way John did, neither of us did. I didn't remember how I knew, but John was almost as important as my father in my family, a father-in-the-making.

The more I sat in front of the house, the more I remembered about him. I wanted to wear a striped rugby shirt like him and ride a black BMX Stingray like him. He was always doing cool things with his friends. Once on the Fourth of July, we were on the front lawn under the big tree after we had come home from fireworks in the park. John and his friend Tooey were huddled together in the dark, their backs to me.

John, what are you guys doing?

Get lost, TJ! John said over his shoulder.

Can I see?

Catch! John said, turning, and reflexively I put up my hands, then a ball of hot light exploded in my palm.

I found myself coming into the present, looking down at my right hand, then turning it over. One of my three lifelines was puckered in a patch, a burn scar. I hadn't remembered it until this moment, but now all of it came back, my parents taking me to the emergency room, and me coming home with a bandaged hand.

I closed my eyes, trying to think of what had happened next. I thought hard, but I couldn't remember anybody asking me what happened. I don't remember John ever getting yelled at or punished. I don't even know where Gabby was that night, in retrospect. I only remembered something my mother said, which she said all the time.

Boys will be boys.

It was so strange to think of it now, to try to understand. They had looked the other way. I flashed on fights, bloody noses, swollen eyes, and a broken tooth I didn't remember until this moment. John used to beat me up and I never fought back, never stood up for myself. I just took it.

I realized I was still taking it. I couldn't knuckle under to John like a permanent little brother. I had to figure out how Lemaire died and decide what to do about it, even if it meant going to the cops, blowing up John's million-dollar fee, and halting Runstan's acquisition.

Grow up, TJ.

My father was right.

I hated that.

I took off, heading for Lemaire's.

CHAPTER TWENTY-ONE

I got to Lemaire's house and parked at the curb just as Lillian was pulling into the driveway in her yellow VW Beetle. The street was coming to life at the end of the day, neighbors returning from work, walking dogs and bringing in the mail.

"Hey, Lillian!" I got out of my car and crossed the lawn as she emerged from the VW in her black sweater and knit pants.

"TJ! I worried you'd change your mind. I asked around about you . . ." Lillian didn't finish the sentence, and I knew that my reputation had preceded me.

"Of course I'd come. I want my cat." I felt guilty deceiving her, but I needed to see what I could see in Lemaire's house, which could lead to whoever killed him. We turned together toward the paved path to the door.

"You'll give her a good home, won't you?"

"Yes, absolutely."

"Good." Lillian extracted a set of jingling keys from her purse. "I stopped by Petco and got the canned food she likes."

"Thanks. How much do I owe you?"

"Nothing, it's the least I can do. She's very picky. For example, she likes tuna, but it has to be flaked. I made a list." Lillian slid a key in the lock and opened the door, and I followed her inside while she kept talking. "She gets one can a day in the morning. You have to put it in the fridge if she doesn't eat it. You can't leave it out."

"Okay," I said, looking around. The living room was furnished with a royal blue couch and chair on a patterned rug. A walnut entertainment center contained a newish TV, books, and a turntable with a vinyl collection.

"She gets dehydrated, with her condition. You have to change the water every day."

"I will." I noticed a kitchen to the right and stairs to the left. "What a nice house. Is it two bedrooms or three?"

"Two." Lillian set her bag and keys on an end table. "Neil used the second one for an office."

Bingo. My heartbeat quickened at the prospect of getting into Lemaire's office. "I wish my place were this neat."

"He kept the litter box immaculate. You will, too, won't you?"

"Of course."

"But you just said your apartment wasn't clean."

Argh. "The litter box will be the cleanest thing in the place. I'll leave no turd behind."

"Good." Lillian smiled, looking around. "Mango's probably hiding. She used to hide from me in the beginning."

"You check downstairs, and I'll check upstairs." I headed for the staircase, but Lillian turned, puzzled.

"But I thought we'd go over the list first. Maybe she'll come out—"

"Why wait?" I hit the steps. "Mango!"

"Mango!" Lillian left for the kitchen, and I reached the top of the stairway and made a beeline for the office, a small room with shelves full of books, a file cabinet, and a dark wood workstation with a desktop Mac.

"Mango!" I called out, for show. I crossed to the file cabinet, hoping for bank accounts or the like. I tried to open a drawer but it was locked. I tried the other two drawers, also locked. I looked around for keys and didn't see any.

I hurried to the computer and moved the mouse. The screen sprang to life, requesting a password under a close-up of Mango, her green eyes glowing. On impulse, I typed in *Mango1*, but it didn't work. I typed in *Mango123*, but that didn't work, either. I probably had one more strike.

My gaze fell on two drawers below. I opened the top one, which contained pencils, pens, Runstan thumb drives, and Post-its. I didn't see any keys for the file cabinets.

I opened the second drawer, and it held a few manila folders. I pulled them out and thumbed through them quickly. They were labeled *Comcast*, *PECO*, and *Mercedes Financial.* Oddly, there were no bank statements.

"Mango!" I went to the last folder and got a lucky break. It was labeled *Passwords*, and I tore it open. Inside were sheets of passwords, incomprehensible combinations of capital and lowercase letters, numbers, and weird signs. Lemaire was a Suggested-Strong-Password kind of guy. I, on the other hand, always went with Carrie's birthday.

I scanned the list, located Lemaire's desktop password, and typed it in. The screen came to life with an email account, and the sidebar showed two accounts, Neil.Lemaire@Runstan.com and 03jdso@gmail.com, which must have been personal.

I clicked the personal account, and the screen opened to reveal recent emails, all of which were from the same person, one Daniel Rocha.

His boyfriend, Daniel, I remembered Lillian saying.

I scanned the list, and the display excerpted the first line of each email:

I miss you and can't wait to see you . . .
I thought of you today when I saw a copy of . . .
I can't believe you're working so hard and I really hope Stan appreciates . . .
I love you and you are always in my thoughts. It amazes me . . .

I scanned the dates of the emails, and they were from last week and the week before. Lillian said that Lemaire had broken up with his boyfriend, but that didn't seem to be the case. I scrolled down to sample Lemaire's responses, and they were equally affectionate, so I wasn't buying the theory of suicidal depression.

"Mango!" I called out, again for effect. I got out a Runstan thumb drive from the drawer, plugged it in, then opened the files on the desktop and scanned them. There were Excel spreadsheets of financial information, and I selected as many as I could for copying.

Suddenly I heard footsteps on the stairs. I hurried out of the office and down the hall to find Lillian at the top of the staircase, shaking her head. I asked her, "Did you find her?"

"No, she must be hiding."

"Let's go." I took Lillian's arm and led her down the hall. "Maybe she's under the bed."

"I was just going to say that."

"We can get her together." I led her into the bedroom, turning on the light. "You take the far side, and I'll take the near side."

"Okay." Lillian went around the bed, and we both bent down. It was dark underneath the bed, and I saw a stray sock, but no cat.

"Let's check the closet. Maybe she got stuck inside. You never know." I got up and crossed to the closet, opened it, and scanned the contents. It held a bunch of clothes hanging neatly and shoes in a line on the floor, but no cat.

"Hmm, maybe she's in the office."

"I just saw her!" I faked a cat-spotting, hustled out of the bedroom, and ran ahead of Lillian to the office. The computer files had been copied, and I took out the thumb drive and stuck it in my pocket just as Lillian was coming down the hall. I was fake-scratching my head when she appeared in the threshold.

"TJ, did you get her?"

"No. I swear I just saw her."

"There she is!" Lillian whipped her head to the right. "She just went downstairs, that little stinker!"

"I'm right behind you!" I said, giving chase.

It took us over an hour to find Mango, who had burrowed into the seat cushion of a chair from underneath, which I hadn't even known was possible. It took doing to extract her, but eventually I knelt on the rug and held her in my lap.

"Hey, Mango, it's going to be okay," I told her, stroking her soft head while she struggled to get away.

"She likes you already."

"Don't oversell it, Lillian."

"I think you should feed her, so she knows to look to you for food. I also have to show you how to give her an injection."

"Okay." I rose with Mango, who kept struggling, and Lillian scratched her behind the ear.

"Mango, meet your new daddy."

New daddy? Me?

Mango looked up at me, blinking big green eyes. I could swear I felt a connection between us, but then again, I have an active imagination.

Lillian smiled. "TJ, you're going to be a great father."

I'll never have children with you, ever!

• • •

It was dark by the time Lillian walked me to the door, the thumb drive in my pocket and the cat carrier over my shoulder. Lillian and I said our goodbyes, barely audible over Mango's screeching, a noise I didn't know cats could produce.

"Lillian, why is she crying? It's so loud, like an owl, or a fox, or something in the woods—"

"Cats can be really loud. Hold the carrier level."

I adjusted the strap. "Should I give her treats?"

"No, she's just not used to the carrier. Get going. Goodbye!" Lillian pushed me out the door, and I sensed she was worried I'd change my mind.

"Okay, bye." I reached the car and put the cat carrier on the passenger seat. Mango screeched and screeched, the noise reverberating in the car. I'd already loaded the back seat with a bag of kibble, canned Fancy Feast, medication, dishes, toys, and something called a Furminator.

"It's okay, sweetheart," I said, but Mango caterwauled. I peeked through the carrier's black mesh, but all I could see was her open mouth and pointy white teeth.

I put the seat belt around the carrier and drove off.

She was my furbaby now.

It took me ten minutes to realize I was being followed.

CHAPTER TWENTY-TWO

I checked the outside mirror. A black compact car was two cars behind me, and it looked like a Hyundai, but I wasn't sure. There was a Tesla on my bumper and a boxy dark van between me and the black compact. I felt as if it had been back there awhile, but I wasn't sure when I had picked it up. The cat was screeching, and I'd been too distracted to keep watch.

I took a right turn, then a left, driving through random streets. The Tesla peeled off, but the van remained and so did the black compact, at a distance. There were no streetlights, and it was too dark to see if the car was a Hyundai. I still had the Hyundai license plate written on my hand, but the mystery car's license plate was on its back bumper.

I headed home, and the Hyundai driver would expect me to go in that direction. A few twists and turns gave me a chance to see if it would keep following me. It did, and so did the van. I steered onto Route 100, a major artery lined with big stores, streetlights, and plenty of ambient light. Meanwhile the cat continued to screech.

I stopped at a red light, peering at the rearview. Cars lined up behind me, their headlights cutting the darkness. Exhaust wreathed the cars in chalky clouds. The black compact was still back there. Under the streetlights, I could see my fears confirmed. It was the Hyundai.

My mouth went dry. The cat kept screeching, and I couldn't take it anymore. I unzipped the carrier and Mango scooted out, then scrambled under the passenger seat. She didn't stop screeching, but the seat muffled the sound.

The light turned green, and I fed the car gas, keeping an eye on the Hyundai. Traffic was stop-and-go to the next light, then the one after that, and I drove tense, with the cat wailing.

The light turned red, and I braked with the other traffic. My fingers clenched the steering wheel. My chest tightened.

I stared at the traffic light's burning red circle, literally seeing red. I didn't like being followed. I didn't even like that John was being followed. But I wanted to know who killed Lemaire. It was time to see who the hell was driving that Hyundai.

I put my car in park, got out, closed the door, and stalked down the line of traffic. Startled drivers looked up at me. I passed a Lexus, then a Toyota truck. I made a beeline for the Hyundai, but I couldn't see inside because it was too dark.

The stoplight changed. Cars started to drive past me. Exhaust filled my nostrils. The Hyundai idled, facing off against me. I realized the driver could be armed. I put my hand in my pocket like I had a gun.

Cars whooshed around me, and I advanced on the Hyundai, which veered into the right lane to avoid me. I lunged for its front door, grabbed its handle, and came eye to eye with its driver.

No. Behind the wheel was a young Black woman, plainly terrified. She raised her hands like she was being carjacked.

"I'm sorry, miss!" I called through the window. "Go ahead, please!"

The woman hit the gas and took off. I headed back to my car, traffic streaming past me, giving me wide berth.

Suddenly out of the corner of my eye I saw the blur of a black Hyundai, *the* black Hyundai. It sped away, but I got a clear view of its license plate.

HOK6253. I didn't have to check my hand to know it was a match.

"Hey!" I took off, chasing the Hyundai in traffic. Cars swerved to avoid me. Horns blared. Drivers flashed me the finger. I kept running, but the Hyundai disappeared up ahead.

I stopped, breathing hard while cars moved around me. I turned, walked between the lanes, and went back to my car. I pulled on the handle, but the door didn't open.

Mango was propped up on the door, screeching and screeching. The button on the door was down. I was locked out.

I reached for my phone to call for help, but it wasn't in my pocket.

Then I heard it ringing.

Inside the car.

I tried to flag down a driver who would let me use his phone to call for help, except even if I did, my phone knew my numbers but I didn't. I didn't know anybody's number except my sponsor's. I had AA, but not AAA.

Mango was freaking out inside the car. My phone was ringing, undoubtedly with a call from Maya. I was never going to make our date on time.

I kept waving my arms, but car after car passed me. I considered blocking traffic with my body, but people carried concealed these days.

Finally a Lexus driven by an older man stopped, and he lowered his window. "Is that a *cat* making that noise?"

"I know, right?" I answered, validated. I noticed a garment bag hanging in his back seat. "Can I borrow a coat hanger?"

I slipped into my driver's seat, put Mango back inside the carrier, and zipped it closed. She kept howling, but I picked up my phone and saw two calls from Maya. I braced myself and called her back. "Maya, I'm sorry, but—"

"You stood me up."

"I'm sorry, I can explain—"

"I sat there like a smacked ass."

"I'm really sorry. What happened was—"

"Did you ever hear the saying 'When someone shows you who they are, believe them?' Well, you showed me."

"I have a good reason—"

"Are you bleeding from the head?"

"No, I got held up—"

"Why didn't you call?"

"My phone was in the car."

"So?"

"The cat locked me out."

"Yeah, right." Maya hung up.

Argh. I hung up and was about to set the phone down when I saw that Patrick had called, too, so I called him back. "Patrick—"

"TJ, you stood her up? Why?"

"I got locked out of the car, it's a long story. I'm really sorry."

"You got me in trouble with my wife."

"Please tell her I'm sorry."

"Oh, *that'll* be fun." Patrick snorted. "Anyway my buddy ran that plate for the Hyundai. It's registered to a Barry Rigel in Exton. I got the address."

Finally, a break. "Rigel is the legit owner?"

"Yep."

"Thank you. Can you text me his address?"

"You owe me big-time."

"I know. Again, I'm sorry."

I hung up, my heart beginning to pound.

Got you, Barry Rigel.

CHAPTER TWENTY-THREE

"We're home, Mango!" I unlocked my front door, went inside, and set the carrier down on the living room rug. I unzipped the flap and the cat darted out, scooting under the couch. Mercifully, she stopped meowing.

"Good girl!" I crossed to the kitchen, filled a bowl with water, and hurried back to set it in front of the couch. I knelt down and peeked underneath to see her crouching in the darkness, blinking with distrust.

"You can count on me," I told her, a vow. Just then my phone rang, and I slid it from my back pocket to see it was my mother. "Hi, Mom. What's up?"

"Honey, can you come to the office? We were burglarized. They turned the place upside down."

I gasped. "Are you okay?"

"Yes," my mother answered, but she sounded upset. "We weren't here."

"Thank God." My gut told me it was connected to Lemaire and whatever the hell was going on. "When did this happen?"

"Just come. The cops are on the way."

"So am I."

• • •

Police cruisers were parked in front of the building entrance, and I hurried into the office. Chairs in the waiting room had been knocked over, and crystal lamps were shattered on the hardwood floor. There was no computer on Sabrina's desk, and wires strayed from the surge protector like frayed nerves.

I heard voices and the crackle of police radios emanating from down the hall, so I hurried to the conference room, where my father, mother, Gabby, and John sat at the table. Two uniformed cops stood against the wall.

I stiffened reflexively, acutely aware that I was hiding evidence of embezzlement and murder in my pocket. My prison days came back to me at the sight of dark uniforms, gleaming badges, and holstered Glocks.

"Hi, everyone," I said, masking my reaction.

"TJ, come in." My father gestured to me. "Officers Dembek and Pastona, this is my son TJ. He's our firm's investigator."

"Nice to meet you, TJ." Officer Dembek shook my hand with a professional smile. He was tall with strong features and in decent shape, like me if I'd followed the straight and narrow.

"So, we were burglarized?" I took an empty seat and grabbed a water bottle from the table.

"Yes. We're just about finished here."

"Do you have any suspects?" I cracked the water bottle and took a sip. "I'm sorry if you've already gone through this, but I'm curious."

"Not a problem. If you're an investigator, it's an occupational hazard." Officer Dembek nodded. "It's too soon to have a suspect. We'll let you know as the investigation develops. I can tell you that the insurance company was burglarized here last month. Same MO. Crowbar the entrance, take the electronics, vandalize."

"What about surveillance footage? We have security cameras, don't we?"

"There's a camera at the corner of every building, but not at every entrance. Your entrance is out of range."

"What about the lot? What were they driving?"

"They parked out of range. They knew what they were doing."

My father shook his head, angry. "I already have a call in to the management company. They should have informed us about the other burglary and upgraded the security system. It's gross negligence."

I needed information. "Officer, what time do you think the burglary took place?"

"We estimate around eight-thirty P.M."

"It seems early, doesn't it?"

"No, not really. It's after dark, and the other burglary was early evening, too. They come after business hours but before the cleaning crew. The last time, they walked out with the computers like they were moving them."

I wondered if one of the burglars had driven a maroon Volvo. It couldn't have been Barry Rigel because he'd been after me in the Hyundai. Or at least, it was likely he'd been driving his own car. "Were there any witnesses?"

"We didn't get a report from anyone. Nobody called anything in. We'll canvass tomorrow."

"What about the cleaning crew?"

"They're the ones who called us. They found the doors broken."

My mother looked upset. "They took my laptop and my coral earrings from my top drawer. I can't wear them on the phone because they click against the glass. I never should have left them here."

My father touched her shoulder. "Don't blame yourself. They took anything they could sell. They took my old Bose radio."

"And my new laptop," Gabby said, her lower lip buckling. "It figures, the one night I don't bring it home."

John met my eye, meaningfully. "They took my desktop, monitors, laptop, and my sports memorabilia, even Connor's baseball."

"Oh man, I'm sorry." I flashed on the thumb drive of the files I'd copied from Lemaire's office computer. I'd left it in my desk. "I wonder what they took from my office."

Officer Pastona looked at me. "Is yours the one behind the file room?"

"Yes, my laptop was there."

"They took it."

My father straightened. "Officers, you had a question before TJ arrived. You asked whether we thought this crime could have been intentional. I told you no, but that answer was incomplete." He turned to me. "TJ, do you know anybody who would do this?"

"No." I suspected the burglary was related to Lemaire but couldn't say so.

"But you know bad actors, from prison. Maybe one of them wanted easy money. Did you tell them about the firm?"

I felt my face go red. The cops turned to me with new eyes, since I'd been demoted from privileged son to certified dirtbag. My mother looked stricken, and Gabby flushed with embarrassment. Only John sat composed, as if he hadn't gotten us into this mess in the first place.

I bit my tongue. "Dad, no, that's not possible. If you mean that I know ex-cons, I do, but I don't contact them. It's a condition of my parole, and I follow the rules."

"What about the people from your meetings?"

"No. Alcoholics don't break into—"

"Drug addicts, then. You know some, don't you?"

"Dad, seriously? I do, and you do, too. You just don't know you do. I can tell you who in our waiting room is on Valium, Percocet—"

"Do you owe them money? Would they be trying self-help? Taking electronics to sell them—"

"No, absolutely not."

"—because they *vandalized* us, like they're angry."

"I don't owe anybody money."

"You owe your brother."

"Dad, I don't owe money to anybody else. I didn't have anything to do with this, so enough with the cross-examination."

My father didn't reply, but turned to the cops. "Officers, I have another possibility. My wife practices family law, involving divorce and custody disputes. Her cases are unusually emotional, and it's possible that an unhappy spouse took out their anger on us. I know stories of disgruntled litigants attacking or even shooting divorce counsel."

My mother frowned. "I don't know of any clients who would be that angry at me, but I guess it's not impossible."

"Thanks." Officer Dembek slipped his pad in his back pocket. "Mrs. Devlin, if there are some clients that concern you, perhaps you could generate a list of them and send it to me. I believe I left you my card."

"I will."

"Thank you. As I said, we'll stay in touch." The two officers headed for the door. "Goodbye, folks."

"Goodbye, thanks," my father said, and we all followed suit.

"I'll check my office," I said as soon as they left, already on my feet.

CHAPTER TWENTY-FOUR

I hurried down the hall, angry at my father and worried about the mess we were in, which was getting worse. I reached my office and crossed to the drawer, which hung open. The thumb drive was gone, and so was the petty cash I kept there. Pencils and pens lay scattered on the floor.

John appeared in the doorway. "TJ, do you think—"

"I think this burglary has to do with Lemaire. They took the thumb drive. I don't know why. They couldn't have known about it, but it was marked Runstan."

"Maybe they want to keep quiet whatever was on it." John's mouth tightened. "I think this was a warning, too. There's too much destruction, and they knew Connor's baseball wasn't a collectible. They're telling me they can get to him. They want us to shut up about Lemaire. Message received."

My gut wrenched. "So what are you saying?"

"I'm saying we shut it down. No more investigation. We're in over our heads. It's not our business, it never was."

"But I just got a lead. Barry Rigel is the man who's been following us in the Hyundai. I have his address and I'm going to investigate."

"No, don't."

"Rigel could have killed Lemaire, or know why he was murdered."

"You don't know he was murdered."

"Yes, I do. I found emails from his boyfriend on his home computer."

"You got into his home computer, too?" John blinked, surprised. I brought him up to date and dug the thumb drive from my pocket.

"Here's the files from his house."

John put up his hand like a traffic cop. "You keep the thumb drive. I don't want anything to do with it."

"I copied everything I could. If there are financial files, they could be hidden, too. I could call Andre—"

"No, I don't think you should. I say we end this now. To be real, I'm afraid." John grimaced. "This is the time to get out. Lemaire's dead and everybody thinks it's suicide, so that's going away. The acquisition's on track. Stan will shut up. We need to forget the whole thing."

"We can't—"

"Why not? They took Connor's *baseball*, TJ. That makes it personal. Thank God I sent him out of town." John shook his head. "This stops now."

"But we can't just let it go," I said, feeling it inside. "A man's dead and I just got the name of the guy who probably killed him. I can't pretend that didn't happen."

"*I* can. If we keep digging, we pay the price. And for what?"

"Justice. You're supposed to care. You're a lawyer."

John frowned. "When my family's in jeopardy, I'm a dad. You'd understand if you were, too."

Ouch. "I understand, John. I love Connor, too."

"If we shut up, my family stays safe. The only guy who gets hurt if we're quiet is already dead. Anyway what are you going to do, TJ? You're going to run it down like a cop?"

"No, like an investigator."

"You're not a real investigator."

"I am now," I said, feeling it for the first time.

"Don't be ridiculous."

"Then we should tell the cops," I said, even though it was the last thing I wanted to do.

"No, never. That's why I didn't say anything to them just now."

"We're obstructing justice, John."

"Not if they don't find out."

I almost laughed. "I thought I was the only criminal in the family."

"TJ, come on. If we tell the cops, we don't drop out. It's not like you make a statement and it's one-and-done. We get questioned multiple times. We go back and forth. We're already being followed. It'll be obvious we're cooperating. We have to testify. You'll put a target on our backs."

My heart sank. "What if we go into witness protection or something like that?"

"Enough. I'm not going to the cops, and you're not, either." John pointed in my face. "If you do, I'll deny everything. I'll say you're lying."

"Are you serious?" I asked, shocked. Then I realized I shouldn't be, since he'd betrayed me before. At this point, betraying me was his hobby. I felt angry and didn't try to stuff it. "You came to me, remember? I wouldn't be *in* this but for you—none of us would!"

John blinked, softening. "TJ, I have to protect my family."

"I'm your family, too, asshole."

"Look, let's start over." John took my arm. "I know you love Connor and Nancy. Let's play it safe, for their sakes. Drop the investigation. Go back to your regular work."

Suddenly the door opened and Gabby came in, fixing a worried gaze on me.

"TJ, are you okay? I told Dad that he was inappropriate to talk to you that way in front of the cops. He's just stressed about the break-in."

"Right. Usually he's a barrel of laughs."

"What are you guys up to anyway?" Gabby looked from John to me, arching an eyebrow. "All of a sudden you're hanging?"

"I'm running down some things for my beloved brother." I wanted to change the subject. "Gab, I visited Joe Ferguson today and I'm worried he's ill."

"I'll call him tomorrow, thanks."

"I even went back to our old house."

Gabby's eyes lit up. "Aw, what was it like?"

John looked over. "Still a dump?"

Gabby winced. "John, that house was nice. I loved it there."

"I loved it, too." I felt a warmth return. "It looks the same, but you should see the mountain laurel beside the doorway. They trained it to go over the door like a trellis."

Gabby smiled. "That must look pretty."

John rolled his eyes. "It was just an azalea."

I looked over. "No, it was a mountain laurel. I remember Mom telling me, it's the state flower."

"Oh please."

"It was," I said, sounding like a kid, even to myself. I didn't know why I cared.

Gabby started to go. "TJ, come with me. I want to put my office back together."

John turned to the door. "Me, too."

"Me, three," I said, an old joke. They walked ahead and I followed them down the hall, looking at their backs. It felt horribly comfortable, tagging along.

It really was time to grow up.

"I'm sorry, Gab." I put an arm around her as we surveyed the damage. All the sculptures she loved had been broken, and her kachina dolls were torn to pieces. Her books were strewn on her kilim rug, and photos broken on the hardwood.

"Really, who would do this?"

"I don't know." I hated lying to her.

"It's definitely malicious." Gabby gestured to her broken ceramic vases on her windowsill. "I got them from Greece. I mean, why destroy them?"

"It's terrible." I wondered what she would do if she knew the truth. She wouldn't want Connor or anybody to get hurt, but she wouldn't keep her mouth shut, either.

"TJ, I know my Holmesburg case doesn't generate fees, like whatever John has you doing, but I want to file the Complaint this week. Can you put it on the front burner?"

"Sure."

"I called the other three plaintiffs on your list, and they can see you tomorrow morning. Can you do that?"

"Yes, absolutely."

"Don't ditch me for John."

"I won't." *Or at least, not anymore.* "I'm on it."

"Thanks, let's clean up." Gabby headed for the door. "I'll go get Fantastik and paper towels."

"Why?"

"You wouldn't put things back on a dirty shelf, would you?"

I gathered it was rhetorical.

I peeked in John's office when I walked by, and he was on the phone, his outline an indistinct reflection in the dark window. The office looked hollowed out without its screens and computers, since he had more electronics than all of us put together.

I kept going down the hall to my mother's office, surprised to find her alone, picking up the crystal awards, legal treatises, and framed photos dumped from her bookshelves onto the floor. The burglars had made a mess of her office, which had always been my favorite, with its Danish-modern desk and chairs, vintage Norwegian rya rug in orange and blue, and framed Helen Frankenthaler posters, alive with bold colors.

"Ma, let me help." I hustled to her, picked up some books, and set them on the low-slung couch. "I would've come earlier, I thought Dad was with you."

"He's outside checking the cameras." My mother straightened, tucking a strand of hair behind her earlobe, where a diamond stud sparkled. Her eyebrows sloped unhappily, and up close, I could see the pencil lines underneath had worn off. She seemed unraveled, standing in the detritus of the office.

"You okay?" I asked, feeling guilty. Now my parents were the victims of a conspiracy they had nothing to do with, and I couldn't even tell them why.

"I never realized how much I loved this office until I saw it in this state. This is *my* place, even more than the house. It's *mine*." She surveyed the damage, clucking. "You know Virginia Woolf, *A Room of One's Own*?"

"No," I admitted.

"Well, the title says it all. *This* is the room that's mine. Everything else I share, every single room in the house. But not this."

"I understand. We'll put it back together. I'll help."

"But first things first." My mother met my eye, pursing her lips. "I'm sorry for the way your father acted with the police. He's going to say he's sorry."

"You brokered that?"

"Yes."

"Thanks, but I don't need him to apologize."

"I want him to." My mother sighed, putting her hands on her hips. "It gets old, cleaning up after him. Sometimes I feel more like a janitor than a wife."

I felt as if my mother were letting her guard down, since she rarely talked negatively about my father. "So don't do it anymore. You don't have to."

"Yes, I do. He has to know when he crosses the line."

"But, why?" I never had a frank talk with her about my father, so I went with the flow. "He won't change."

"I'm not trying to change him, God knows. If he hasn't changed yet, he's not changing."

"Then what's the point?"

"It's a check on misconduct, that's all. There has to be rules. That's why we have laws." My mother gestured at the lawbooks on the couch. "You know the husbands I represent, they're angry. The wives, too. The emotionality is off the charts in my practice. You see people at the worst times in their lives. Try to stop a father from seeing his kid, or a mother. Everybody loses their minds, even the worst parents, *especially* the worst parents. They'll fight over the cost, the alternating Tuesday/Thursday, or the 'my weekend'/'her weekend.' They'll fight over the extra day of vacation. Or whether the kid should play soccer or lacrosse. *Everyone* is at their worst. But you know what keeps them in line? The law. *Me.*" My mother pointed to a little framed motto she kept on her bookshelf, DIVORCE IS BETTER THAN MURDER. "It's true. That's why it's funny."

"Yikes."

"So don't tell me that your father shouldn't apologize. He should."

I couldn't let it go. "A forced apology isn't an apology."

"Oh, you want *mens rea*, too? You want the proper intent, not just the words?" My mother smiled crookedly. "Be realistic. This isn't criminal law, it's civil. The standard is lower. Take the settlement you can and get out of court. It may not be a real apology to you, but it is to him, believe me. You know he doesn't like to apologize. You have to force it out of him. Every time, it's like you're asking for a *kidney*, for God's sake." My mother made a ball of her fist and shook it. "He has to think about someone other than himself. He has to think about you and the effect of his words on you. Because it's *right.*"

That, I got. "Justice."

"Exactly." Her expression softened. "You know he loves you, TJ, and he knows this is a difficult time for you. We both do."

I swallowed hard, wondering if she knew about my alleged relapse. I wanted to ask her, but I couldn't bring myself to confirm the lie and I couldn't tell her the truth, either. I didn't know what to say, and my mother patted my arm.

"Don't worry about it, honey. Anyway, I can't stand my office this way. You know me."

"You like to clean."

"No woman likes to clean. What she likes is to restore order. There's a difference." My mother smiled again. "Maybe that's what I do with your father, too." She shrugged it off, eyeing the mess. "'Into each life some rain must fall.'"

I didn't have the heart to tell her it was monsoon season. "Guess what? I stopped by the old house today."

"In Norwood?" My mother brightened. "I miss that place. How does it look?"

"Great, but let me ask you, was it a mountain laurel or an azalea beside the door?"

"A mountain laurel."

"I knew it. The state flower."

"Remember the state bird?"

"The ruffed grouse." I laughed. "Still got it."

My mother laughed, too. "You were such a funny kid. I remember you memorized the state capitals, too."

"I'm a font of useless information."

"Stop putting yourself down." My mother waved me off. "Now let's clean this up. I don't want to be here all night."

"You want me to wipe the shelves down?"

"I already did. Lucky for you."

I started picking up the books, her Dante collection. "Just tell me where these go."

"Over there." My mother pointed, then started picking up photographs from the rug while I shelved the books and squared them up.

"Push them to the back or lined up in the front?"

"The perennial question. To the back."

"Agree." I pushed the books back, then kept going while she put the photos back on the shelf, which was when I realized that they weren't the typical pictures of her and my father at various Pennsylvania Bar Association events, but family photos.

"How did I not know about these?"

"They're usually on the bottom shelf."

"I haven't seen them in ages."

"Look at this one." My mother showed me the photo and I leaned over, feeling a rush of emotion. It was a faded old photo of her and me when I was little, sitting on the bench in front of the Baskin-Robbins on Lancaster Avenue, grinning at each other while we ate ice cream cones. I was in my T-ball uniform, and she was in a sweatshirt and jeans.

I smiled, touched. "I remember you used to take me for ice cream after baseball. What did you use to call it?"

"The Rum Raisin Run," my mother answered, and we both laughed.

"We were the only ones who liked rum raisin." I thought for a second. "Wait, do you think it had rum in it? Real rum?"

"I don't know." My mother lifted an eyebrow, surprised. "Whoops."

"That was fun, that we did that." I thought about it now, looking at the photo. It was unusual that the two of us spent time alone like that. We always did things as a family. "Did you do that on purpose, being alone with me?"

My mother nodded. "Yes."

I met her eye. "You thought I needed it?"

"Maybe." My mother shrugged. "It was hard for you, all of you kids so close in age. It was nice to have something special for you." Her smile faded. "I should have done more with you alone, truly. I worked too hard, I took on too many cases. Back then, I had eighty actives. I should have referred more out, been home more."

My heart wrenched. "I would have started drinking no matter what, Mom."

"That's not true."

"Yes, it is." I kissed her on the cheek, getting a fading whiff of her rose perfume. "You're a great mother."

"I could have been better."

"Now *you* stop putting yourself down."

A new concern flickered across her lovely features. "TJ, I have something I really want to say. You're not going to like it."

Uh-oh. "Go ahead, what?"

"I think you know something about this burglary tonight. I don't want you to answer me or say anything. I just want you to listen." Her forehead wrinkled deeply, as if she were aging on the spot. "I don't know whether you're back with your old gang, or people you thought were your friends—"

"Mom, no."

"Shh." My mother held up an index finger. "Don't say anything."

"Why not?"

"Because I don't want you to lie to me."

Ouch. "I'm not lying," I shot back, but I was. Just not the way she thought.

"You have to listen to me. Will you?"

"Yes." I sensed something happening, as if the air between us was getting heavy.

"Whatever you're involved in, TJ, I want you to be careful. Nothing matters to me the way you matter to me, and the people who did this tonight, they're dangerous. You have to be careful, for me. You know why?"

"Because you love me."

"No," my mother answered flatly. "Because I'm tired of being afraid for you."

We put her office back in order, talking idly to get back to normal. Afterward I headed for the door, exhausted, heartsick, and jonesing for a beer.

When I got to the car, I made a call.

CHAPTER TWENTY-FIVE

I entered the diner and approached the booth where my sponsor, Jake, awaited me behind a cup of coffee. He had on a black sweater, dark slacks, and his loafers.

"Thanks for coming," I said, sliding into the booth. "You know you're the classiest thing in this place."

"Thanks."

I glanced around at the other customers, a rough crew of haggard men. "Everybody here at this hour is in AA or should be."

Jake looked at me with concern. "Can we finish deflecting?"

"I'm just trying to make you laugh."

"That's my point." Jake motioned to the waitress, an older woman who nodded back.

"Okay." I settled in. "You want to know why I put up the bat signal?"

"TJ, I'm not Batman. I'm an alcoholic like you."

"Well, you didn't call me, I called you."

"We help each other, TJ. It's the truth of the fellowship. So how are you doing?"

"I've been better." I paused while the waitress came over, set a mug in front of me and filled it with fresh coffee, which smelled good even though it wasn't Dunkin' Donuts.

"Sir, can I get you anything to eat?" she asked pleasantly.

"Cake, please. Any kind is fine, just so it's cakey."

"Be right back."

Jake looked at me expectantly, since he morphs into the Sphinx when he wants me to talk. I love the guy, and I'm learning more about him. Like I know that he has nine years of sobriety and that his wife once tried to push him off a balcony, but I don't know what he does for a living. My fantasy is that he's a psychiatrist with a weakness for Gucci.

"I don't know where to start," I said, meaning it. I couldn't tell him about the murder or embezzlement because I didn't want to involve him.

"Were you thinking about picking up?"

"I guess so, underneath." I tried to organize my thoughts. "I'm in over my head on a lot of fronts. I'm messing up. I know those feelings are triggers, and when I started to feel that way in the old days, I would pick up."

"Good for you, catching it." Jake paused. "What's going on in the friend department? Are you making sober friends?"

"No." I was supposed to make Sober Friends, but I missed the days when I could just make Friends.

"You need a support network, TJ." Jake's tone was trademark no-judgment. "You can't isolate."

"I'm not, I'm just trying to deal."

"Friends help you deal, you know that. Especially after Jesse."

I felt a twinge. His name triggered me, a term I had to admit applied too much lately. Maybe I was trigger-happy. "I know, but there's a lot going on now. I've got trouble with my brother. He turned on me. Plus I screwed up my date, the first one since Carrie. I stood her up because the cat locked me out of the car."

Jake blinked. "Pardon?"

I told him the story, editing out embezzlement and murder, and he listened as the waitress brought over a thick wedge of chocolate cake with a fork and a napkin.

"Thank you," I told her, my mood improving.

"You were saying."

"So I called my date to apologize and I got that feeling, that sick feeling because I hurt her." I stopped, realizing something as I spoke. "Before, all the thoughts would have been about me. But I thought about her. That I hurt her."

Jake nodded, looking pleased. "Good."

"It's a low bar."

"Progress, not perfection."

"The question is what to *do*. I'm done feeling this way. I'm *done* with this, I couldn't be more *done* with this." I felt my own disgust, the more I gave it voice. "I want to change this, I *have* to change this. I'm *tired* of being this guy."

Jake shrugged. "Is there something that comes to mind, that you could do? Maybe make amends?"

"You mean like in the program?"

"The principles can be applied to anything."

"I'll send flowers, thanks." I picked up my fork and dug into my cake, delicious because chocolate is perfect.

"Did you eat dinner?"

"No." I'd forgotten, with everything that went on.

"You know to watch that. Remember HALT."

"Right." HALT was our acronym for hungry, angry, lonely, and tired, which were the times that we were likely to drink. But for days, my routine had been thrown off. "It's been crazy at work."

"What's going on at work, apart from fighting with your brother?"

I realized I couldn't be specific about my fake-relapse, so I forked another hunk of cake into my mouth. "I feel the lowest since I got out of rehab."

"Can you say why?"

"I'm investigating a hard case, and I was face-to-face with somebody dying of cancer, like, could die *tomorrow*. He's part of a lawsuit that even if we win, won't come in time for him."

"That's serious."

I tried to shake it off. "But then, this is how people live, normal people who don't drink. They do this every day and they don't drink. They do it and they don't whine. They *handle* it. This plaintiff I'm telling you about, his name is Joe, *he's* handling it. He's handling *death*. He doesn't have to call somebody to come hold his hand."

Jake's face fell. "You're doing fine."

"I don't feel like I'm doing fine. I feel like I'm screwing up." I wolfed down the rest of the cake.

"Maybe you should think of it this way." Jake linked his fingers in front of him. "You said you made a date, right?"

"Yes."

"You got a cat, though you never had one before?"

"Yes."

"It sounds as if things are getting harder at work. You met someone at the end of his life. That's a special time that you shared with someone—that's special."

"You're pushing it with the *special*."

"My point is, this is *why* you got sober, TJ. To have these difficulties. To straighten things out at work. To get a woman to go out with you. To get a cat. To make your own choices. This is the goal, TJ. You're living for the first time ever. Do you follow me?"

I blinked. "Honestly, yes."

"You didn't do any of these things before. All you did was drink. This is new to you, isn't it?"

"Yes."

"So you're going to make mistakes. You're a beginner."

"At *life*?"

"Exactly." Jake smiled. "Normalize that doing hard things can make you feel good, but it's difficult. Credit yourself for dealing with challenges you never did before. Be patient with yourself. Time takes time. Welcome to life."

"Thanks," I told him. I did feel better.

Jake seemed to relax. "I have faith in you. Keep coming to meetings. You don't have to do it alone. The program is there for you, all of us are. It's the way to stay sober, one day at a time."

"How do you know?" I asked, surprised to find myself burning for the answer.

"I believe it from my own experience. If you told me I'd never drink or do drugs again, I couldn't take it. But I can get through one day." Jake pursed his lips. "You know, lately I study Buddhism. I find it helpful in my meditations and the like. There's a monk named Milarepa, and he says, 'At the beginning, nothing comes, in the middle, nothing stays, and in the end, nothing goes.'"

"What does that mean?"

"He was talking about his spiritual practice but it applies to my sobriety. In the very beginning, in that first month or so, I had a hard time. I skipped meetings, I didn't commit to the program. For me, every *minute* was hard." Jake rolled his eyes. "And in the middle, I relapsed, I picked up again. But now I'm sober and I think I'll stay, one day at a time. Be here now. It's very Zen. Now I know inside that *nothing goes*." Jake leaned back, with finality. "Again, only one day at a time."

"One day at a time, Batman."

CHAPTER TWENTY-SIX

The next morning, I couldn't get Mango from under the couch for her fix. Meanwhile I'd barely slept, thinking about Barry Rigel in the Hyundai, Jake, the burglary, my mother, and all that was going on. I hated not following the lead on Rigel but I had to give in to John, and I needed to follow up on the appointments that Gabby had made for me.

"Here's your bribe," I told her, setting a dish of flaked tuna in front of the couch.

Mango blinked.

"Come on, honey, please." Mango didn't budge, so I reached underneath, pulled her out, and set her on the rug. I held her in place, then pulled two folds of the skin behind her neck together to form a tent, the way Lillian had taught me. I picked up the needle filled with insulin, stuck the needle into the tent, and depressed the plunger. I gave junkies an A for effort. It was so much easier to open a can.

Mango meowed, then scurried away.

"I'm sorry," I called after her.

I don't think she believed me.

But I was surprised at how much I meant it.

• • •

I was back in the Subaru, trying not to think about Rigel. I'd looked out for the Hyundai or Volvo, but I didn't see them. Either Rigel had switched cars or I wasn't being followed.

I hit the Schuylkill Expressway and headed into Philly, following directions through the hardscrabble neighborhoods north of the city. Run-down brick rowhouses lined the blocks among vacant lots, check-cashing agencies, dollar stores, and bodegas. Bars covered the windows of the houses, porches sagged, and potholes were everywhere.

I pulled up in front of Tony Bales's rowhouse, got out of the car, and knocked on the door.

Tony was eighty-two, Black, and bald with sunken cheeks. His neck was so thin that the collar of his Phillies T-shirt gapped and his sweatpants bagged on him. His weight loss was due to skin cancer, now in remission, and congestive heart failure. He hosted me at a round wood table in a small, clean kitchen with a wooden cross over the entrance. A church calendar hung on the wall and bulletins for women's choir practice were stuck to the refrigerator under a Phillies magnet.

"So you're gonna sue those bastards?" Tony asked with a smile. His eyes were rimmed with cataracts, but his aspect was remarkably sharp behind his trifocals.

"Yes, my sister is. I'm helping."

"Like a paralegal? My granddaughter does that, in Center City. She likes it."

"I do, too." I slid the Complaint from my messenger bag, turned to his section, and skimmed it quickly. "Let me confirm a few facts, if I can."

"Fine." Tony shrugged. "I got nowhere to go. Game's not on till the afternoon."

"So you were in Holmesburg from 1963 to 1965."

Tony thought a minute. "Yes."

"Then you left Pennsylvania from 1966 to 2021?"

Tony thought again. "Sounds about right. Met my wife, she was from Athens, Georgia, so we went down there and got married. She wanted to be near family. My boys are still down there. My daughter, this is her house. She's at work."

"I understand. And you didn't know anything about the controversy over the testing, that came out in the newspapers later?"

"Never heard a thing. I was down there."

"Do you remember the skin-patch tests, where they tested Retin-A?"

Tony nodded. "Right, I did those tests. I needed the money. My cellmate made out like a bandit. He was in the army tests."

"What army test?" I asked, confused.

"Those were the tests where they tested those drugs. They gave him LSD. It made him see things, like big cockroaches on the walls and birds flying around. It made him crazy."

Wait, what? "Are you sure about that?" I didn't remember Gabby telling me about any such tests.

"Sure I'm sure. They put two trailers behind Cellblock H, and my cellie moved in there and he told me the cells were padded, like for crazy people. They watched him through a camera and they took pictures of him when he was on the drug. He said it was a bad trip."

"Oh my God," I said, shocked. "The army did this? Was it like MK-Ultra? The government's mind-control experiments?"

"*That's* what it was." Tony snapped his fingers. "I remember now."

"Does my sister, Gabby, know about this?"

"Yes, I told her. I just keep forgetting that MK name. It was for the army or for the CIA, something like that. Guys got in those tests because they paid three hundred dollars a shot."

"And these were administered by Dr. Kligman and his group?"

"Right, they did it all. They ran all the tests." Tony shook his head. "When my cellie came back after those tests, he'd be acting a fool. He had to wear a badge."

"What kind of badge?"

"A badge we called the pay-me-no-never-mind badge. Because those boys be acting so crazy the only explanation was the drugs the army gave him, or the CIA or whoever." Tony clucked. "The army gave him dioxin, too."

"*Dioxin?* Dioxin is toxic."

"I know, they were trying to make Agent Orange. You know, like they sprayed all over the place. That's a damn *poison*. I looked it up. And another guy I know, he got *radiation* injected into him in those trailers."

"Are you serious?" I had no idea what Tony was talking about. None of this was in our Complaint. "What kind of radiation?"

"Isotope, I think your sister told me. The army injected him."

"My God. I didn't know there were other tests. I thought it was only the skin-patch."

"No, they tested a lot of things. You think this case will get me help with my doctor bills?"

"I hope so," I answered, still trying to process what he just told me. "I'm betting on my sister. She'll fight to make this right."

"She your big sister?"

"Yes."

Tony's expression softened. "My big sister, she passed. They're all the same, though. Bossy."

"Yes, but in a good way."

"Hundred percent," Tony said, smiling.

I called Gabby as soon as I got in the car, filling her in as I made my way through the city streets. "Is what he's saying true, about the army and the CIA?"

"Yes, totally. Unfortunately."

"This happened under Kligman?"

"Yes."

"So why isn't it in our Complaint? Why aren't we suing for that, too?"

"We can't."

"Why not? It could have altered people's brain chemistry for the rest of their lives."

"I know, but I don't have any of those clients. Chuck's the one who came to me, and he tested Retin-A and poison ivy meds. So did the other guys, and they were all out of the state afterward. It's a narrow class, and I can't make a lawsuit out of thin air."

"Can you find anybody who went through those other tests?"

"Not easily. Like I told you, they destroyed the records. You can barely find anybody alive anymore."

"Tony told me that his cellmate was also injected with some kind of radioactive isotope. Is that true, too?"

"Yes, the Atomic Energy Commission authorized testing at Holmesburg, under Kligman."

"Oh my God, Gabby." I felt too shocked to concentrate on traffic.

"What if I could find you a plaintiff, somebody who had gone through that?"

"Thanks, but it wouldn't help." Gabby clucked. "Suing the government, the army, the CIA, and whoever runs the Atomic Energy Commission now, that's next-level litigation. They have governmental immunity, and they'll fight you to the end. Believe me, there's a case in Canada trying to do it over MK-Ultra."

"How does the government get immunity for crap like that?"

"Because it's the government."

"So where's the justice?"

Gabby sighed. "The law has its limits, TJ."

"Because it's made by the government to protect the government and made by companies to protect the companies."

"You sound like a public-interest lawyer." Gabby chuckled grimly.

"It's just wrong," I said, feeling my gut twist. For once, I couldn't find the humor.

"I know it is, but I do what I can do, and I do *everything* I can do. When Chuck came to me, I knew that I could help him and the other men in his position. I can't bring the big-ass case against the government, but I can file a discrete, highly provable Complaint that will enrage a jury enough for punitive damages. I can get justice for Chuck and the guys who got skin cancer, and you can, too. So feel good."

"I don't. I can't." I tried to shake it off, but couldn't. "Joe Ferguson told me they'll get away with it, and they are."

"Not this time."

I spent the afternoon driving north, where I met with Joaquin Hernandez and Walter Melendez. The men were older, Puerto Rican, and in poor health, and their experiences in the skin-patch tests were consistent with Tony's and Joe's. Both had been in Puerto Rico and hadn't heard about the previous lawsuit, and they had no new medical problems.

I headed home on Torresdale Avenue, which ran through an industrial section of Philly, and the route took me past Holmesburg Prison, which was still standing, though it had been closed for years. The sky was getting dark, but on impulse, I pulled over and parked at the curb.

The prison itself wasn't visible from the street, only a massive stone wall topped with boxy security lights that no longer worked. Old-fashioned Victorian turrets anchored its corners, with panels of cracked windows and peaked verdigris roofs. To its left was a padlocked parking lot encircled by a rusted cyclone fence topped with barbed wire. On it a sign read CITY OF PHILADELPHIA.

I took it in, thinking. I knew there were crimes that needed punishment. I myself had committed one and I'd punish myself forever. But what turned my stomach was that crimes would go unpunished because of proof problems, statutes of limitations, or the fact that the people wronged didn't have means.

I eyed the prison. It struck me that I was trying to get justice with Gabby but obstruct justice with John. Lemaire's murder weighed on my mind, and I had the address of the man who might have killed him. Barry Rigel.

In this mood, I was tempted to pick up. I knew it, I could feel it. Down the street was a bar with an old-fashioned neon sign blinking through the night. I imagined myself ordering a beer, or six. Once I started drinking, I wouldn't stop, and I'd lose everything I gained so far.

Get to a meeting.

I picked up my phone, scrolled to the Meeting Guide app, and pressed a blue icon with the white folding chair. I thumbed through the list of meetings, both in person and on Zoom, a sign of the times. There were meetings at every hour and three at seven P.M. The closest was only two miles away at Clubhouse 29, whatever that was.

I pulled into the parking lot and cut the engine. Clubhouse 29 turned out to be an old house repurposed for events, and a handful of cars were parking on the street. I watched everybody get out, collect in the entrance, and go in together, talking and laughing, like I did in my home group.

It struck me again how we all looked different, of every skin color and body type, shape and size, professional and working-class, driving expensive or cheap cars, connected only by the fact that we were powerless over alcohol.

Powerless.

I started to get out of the car but stopped myself, experiencing an epiphany. It wasn't wanting to drink that had driven me to the meeting. It was a feeling of *powerlessness.* I'd had it since last night, when John told me to forget about the investigation. I wasn't in prison anymore and I was no longer a baby brother, but I was still acting powerless, doing what I was told.

I closed the car door and started the engine.

I didn't need to go to a meeting.

I had something else to do.

CHAPTER TWENTY-SEVEN

Barry Rigel lived in the Glen Meade Apartments, a complex of two-story townhouses with brick façades and builder-grade front doors. Rigel's house was at the corner of Block C, with an air-conditioner unit in the front wall. The lights were on inside, and the black Hyundai was in the reserved lot.

I parked in the guest lot and mulled over my next move. Neighbors were rolling out trash bins and leaving them at the curb, so it must've been the night before trash day. I checked Rigel's house, and he hadn't put out his trash yet. Sooner or later, he'd have to. Even bad guys had trash.

I sipped my coffee and waited, looking around. An older man smoked a cigar on his doorstep. Runners in reflective sneakers jogged by in the dark. A burst of laughter came from an outdoor party two doors down. A string of pink and blue lights ringed the front yard, likely a gender-reveal party.

I'll never have children with you, ever!

I thought about Carrie, then Maya. I'd sent Maya flowers to make up for standing her up, but she hadn't called or texted. I'd have to find somebody else to marry and divorce me. I couldn't wait to meet my first ex-wife.

Suddenly a light went on in Rigel's backyard, and I watched, riveted. Rigel emerged from the door in his fence, rolling his trash bin behind him. He walked with his head down, a wiry guy in jeans and a camo T-shirt that looked vaguely familiar.

Wait.

My heart began to pound. I'd seen Rigel somewhere before. Then I recognized him, with a start. He'd come to my home group with Brian, the Iraq vet. He'd told us his name was Chris, but that must've been a lie.

"You, Rigel!" I jumped out of the car. "You were in my *meeting*?"

Rigel took off, running down the sidewalk away from me.

"Stop! Wait!" I ran after him. "Stop!"

Rigel accelerated. I ran harder, gaining on him. People looked over from the party. Silhouettes appeared in lighted windows. Front doors opened.

Rigel raced toward the end of the street. I closed the gap between us. Ten feet apart, then seven, then five. I reached out to grab him. We were almost at the end, then everything happened at once.

Rigel jumped off the sidewalk and veered into the street just as a black pickup truck barreled around the corner. Its massive grille crashed into Rigel.

"No!" I screamed, leaping aside. Rigel catapulted into the air. The pickup truck missed me by inches. I felt the heat of its engine as it lurched to a stop, its tires squealing.

I reeled, horrified. Rigel lay on a lawn across the street.

A female driver jumped out of the pickup, phone in hand. "Oh my God! I didn't see him!"

I raced to Rigel's side, kneeling down. "Rigel, Rigel!"

Rigel's agonized gaze shifted to mine. He was alive, his breath ragged. I fought tears of horror and confusion. I had to call 911. I fumbled in my pocket and got my phone.

"Rigel, hold on, I'm calling 911. Stay calm." I pressed 911 into my phone.

Rigel struggled to breathe, his chest shuddering. His body trembled. Blood foamed at his mouth.

"Oh my God!" The pickup driver ran over, sobbing. "Barry? Barry! Is he . . . okay? Is he okay? Please let him be okay! I shouldn't have been on my phone!"

Rigel moaned in agony. A dark stain appeared on his T-shirt. Blood from his crushed chest.

The 911 call connected, and I said, "Emergency, please send an ambulance! Glen Meade Apartments in Goshen! A man was hit by a pickup truck!"

The dispatcher asked, "Sir, what is your name?"

I told her. "But please, hurry!"

"I've dispatched an ambulance. Is he breathing?"

"Yes, yes, but hurry!"

Neighbors began to gather behind me, talking. "Did you see that?" "He went flying!" "That guy was chasing Barry!" "Who hit him?" "Terry! She was on the phone!" "It was her fault!" "No, he ran in front of the truck!" "I missed the whole thing!" "Who *is* this guy?" "Does he live here?"

I rose, stepping away to hear the dispatcher.

"Sir, what is his condition—"

"Who *are* you?" an old man asked, pointing at me. The neighbors formed a shocked half circle, pointing and talking. "You, who are you?" "What's your name?" "Where do you live?" "What are you doing here?"

"I . . . I'm on with 911." I edged away, phone to my ear, trying to hear the dispatcher. "Hurry, please," I told her, but the old man dogged me.

"I *said*, what's your name?" Two other neighbors followed him, taking videos.

"Excuse me." I walked away, listening to the dispatcher and texting John.

COME QUICK GLEN MEADE APTS

The next half hour was a nightmarish blur. The ambulance took Rigel, and the police escorted the pickup driver to her house, only a few doors away. Cops erected a makeshift perimeter with flares. Cruisers blocked the scene around the pickup truck, which stood askew with its door open. Accident reconstruction techs arrived in logo SUVs.

I felt shaken and horrified. I didn't know if Rigel would survive. I didn't know what would happen to me. My thoughts raced over one another. The cops would ask questions. They'd arrest me. I'd go back to prison. Neighbors collected on the sidewalk and lawns, pointing, talking, and taking videos of me and the scene. A cop told me to stay inside the perimeter, center stage in the worst show ever.

I looked over to see John hustling through the perimeter, his white shirt bright in the darkness, his tie flying. "TJ!" he called out, motioning.

"John!" I hurried to him, panicky. "John, I think Rigel could die, I didn't—"

"It's okay." John took my arm calmly. "Come with me. Where's your car?"

"Ahead." I pointed, my hand shaking. John led me from the scene.

Cops hurried by, but none stopped us. "I recognized him from my home group and—"

"Shh. We'll talk later." John squeezed my arm, walking briskly, face forward.

"But the cops are going to ask, I have to explain, I was chasing him and—"

"Quiet." John shot me a look. "This isn't the time or place."

"But what do I do? What do I say? I think we tell them everything. I think it all comes out—"

"Shut *up*." We reached my car, and John opened the door and pushed me into the driver's seat. "Get inside. Wait here. They're going to take you in for questioning—"

"Oh no." A bolt of fear raced through me.

"Don't worry. We're going to get you out of this."

"We should tell them—"

"TJ, listen." John put a hand on my shoulder. "Remember when this all started? You said I should know what to do? That I'm the lawyer?"

"Yes," I answered, looking up at him.

"I do. So this time, follow *my* lead."

I wrung my hands in the back seat of the police cruiser, which felt horribly familiar. The hard vinyl bench. The scratchy bulletproof divider. The greenish glow of the laptop screen on the console. The stolid expressions of the cops. The long guns between them in the rack, held vertically. The loud crackle of the radio with incomprehensible codes.

I looked out the window, fighting for self-control. I told myself this was now and that was then. It wasn't the same night, but it *felt* the same, and my body went back in time, dragging with it my thoughts, my feelings, my memories.

It was a cool night like this one. I was driving home and I really meant to go home, where Carrie was waiting for me. But all I could think about was a cold beer, so I stopped in the first bar I saw. I hadn't meant to have more than one, but before I knew it, I had six.

I was feeling great until the cops showed up and dragged me outside—where Emily, Carrie's daughter, only two years old, was crying in her car seat. She'd been asleep, and I'd forgotten she was in the back seat. Tears streaked her perfect cheeks.

I felt myself die from shame, even drunk as I was. I'd left Emily alone in an unlocked car. It was a cool night, but I was lucky. She could have died. She could have been kidnapped. Anything could have happened.

Bystanders shouted and pointed at me. The cops shoved me into the cruiser and I broke down, knowing I was a guy who would leave a kid in a car to go drinking.

Guilty!

They say that drunks have to hit rock bottom to change, and I'd experienced plenty of rock bottoms, but that night was the lowest I would go, the deepest depth I could fall. The date was June 7, and I would never forget it because it became my sobriety date. I never drank after that, not one drop. I went to jail, then rehab, but there would never be enough amends or apologies. Carrie would never have me back, and I didn't deserve her or Emily.

Guilty!

I tried to shed the memory now as we drove up to the Justice Center in West Chester, a seven-story brick edifice that held offices of the sheriff, detectives, district attorneys, and courtrooms. Its imposing Greek columns supported a triangular portico over the entrance, and there were detention cells in the basement of the building, where I'd been held when I was arrested before.

American and Pennsylvania flags flapped in front of the building, and I shuddered as we pulled up under the sign PARKING FOR WEST CHESTER POLICE ONLY.

Standing at the curb was John.

With my father.

CHAPTER TWENTY-EIGHT

The cops led us to Interview Room Four, a sterile cubicle with black plastic chairs around a smooth fake-wood table. There was a large video camera on a tripod next to the table, but I didn't know if it was running.

I sat down next to John, trying to get my emotional bearings. I kept thinking about Rigel getting hit by the truck. The horrifying thud. His scream. The heat of the truck engine.

Meanwhile my father stood in the doorway with the two cops, greeting them like a host and shaking their hands. "Officer Mullen, any relation to Jimmy Mullen? Owns a PVC pipe company? We're on the Chamber together."

"Jimmy's my uncle." The cop grinned. "He speaks highly of you."

"As well he should," my father shot back. "Send my regards, will you? Jimmy's a great guy. Helluva golfer."

"He cheats."

"Who doesn't?" my father said, and they both laughed.

"Please, sit down." The other officer gestured my father into a chair next to me, but he sat down at the head of the table, then took over.

"Officers, I think we need to talk about the press. I expect you will not be releasing the details of this incident."

Officer Mullen nodded. "We release the minimum, as per procedure."

"Good." My father smiled. "I don't know if there will be civil litigation, but you know how people are. When they find a deep pocket, they call 1-800-Fund-My-Retirement."

Officer Mullen chuckled. "I hear that."

"So you won't speak to any plaintiff's lawyers who happen to call, will you?"

"No, we always refer them to Courtney, in Comms."

"Good, thanks."

"By the way, sorry about that burglary at your office. One of my buddies met you last night. Jason Dembek."

"Right, good guy. Any leads yet?"

"No, but they're working on it."

"Good. The management company agreed to put up some lights, now that the horse is out of the barn." My father snorted. "Anyway, how can we help you? We're happy to cooperate—"

"Dad?" John interrupted him. "I'll take it from here. I'm representing TJ."

My father blinked. "John, we're not here in any professional capacity. We're here as family, and we're happy to help—"

"No, we're not."

"Of course we are." My father frowned. "There's no need to come out swinging."

"It's the law," John snapped.

Gulp. I knew why my brother was going on the offensive, but my father didn't.

John turned to the cops. "Officers, a pickup truck struck a man. The driver of the pickup is the one you should be questioning, not my brother."

"We *are* questioning her, too."

"Then why wasn't she brought here for questioning? She was interviewed at her home."

"I assume it was a courtesy."

"That's my point. Why wasn't my brother afforded the same courtesy? I don't think she was even breathalyzed." John shrugged pointedly. "Do you know if she was?"

Officer Mullen hesitated. "Uh, no, I don't."

"My brother hasn't broken any laws, so I'm at a loss to explain why we're here. I think it's aggressive and discriminatory."

My father recoiled, grimacing. "John, really?"

"Yes, Dad."

My father turned to the cops. "Officers, I'm sorry, my son John is protective—"

"Dad." John looked over. "Please, don't apologize for me. I'm doing my job."

My father glared at him. "You don't need to be adversarial."

"This is custodial interrogation." John turned to the cops. "I'm surprised you didn't Mirandize him."

Officer Mullen straightened. "We consider this an informal interview."

"Until it's not. But by then, it's too late for my brother."

Officer Mullen met John's eye, his demeanor cooling. "Your brother's on parole. He served a year for endangering the welfare of a child."

"Is that why you hauled him in here, but not the driver? That's discrimination. My brother served his time. He pleaded guilty and accepted responsibility. His crime was a misdemeanor, induced by alcohol. He made a mistake and was punished. Evidently, he's still being punished."

I swallowed hard. I'd never heard John defend what I'd done, even when I couldn't.

Officer Mullen shook his head. "We didn't bring him here because of his record. We brought him here because we needed to complete the investigation. He seemed ready, willing, and able to answer our questions. We're entitled to investigate whether he's in violation of his parole."

"He's sober and doesn't possess a firearm. The only possible parole violation would be if you suspect him of commission of another crime. And I can't imagine the facts on which you would base such a belief."

Officer Mullen frowned. "That's what we're here to determine. We can't complete the investigation if he won't answer questions."

"The accident tonight happened in front of eyewitnesses. I know, I was there. Any one of them could help you complete the investigation."

"They weren't involved."

John leaned forward, bearing down. "'Involved' is an imprecise term, irrelevant here. The only person with any criminal culpability is the driver, whom you're treating with kid gloves."

"We'd like to understand your brother's relationship to Mr. Rigel."

John shook his head. "No, you're fishing for a parole violation, and I'm not going to let you. My brother has a Fifth Amendment right against self-incrimination. I'm minutes from concluding this so-called interview."

"Fine, have it your way." Officer Mullen bristled. "It's our understanding that your brother was running after Mr. Rigel. We'd like to know why."

"I'm not going to let him answer."

"Does your brother deny he was chasing Mr. Rigel?"

"I'm instructing him not to answer that."

"Was your brother engaged in an altercation with Mr. Rigel?"

"Instructing him not to answer that, either."

"How do your brother and Mr. Rigel know each other?"

"Officer Mullen, what do *you* know about this Rigel? What's his occupation?"

"I'm not here to answer your questions. You're here to answer ours. Does your brother know the victim?"

"Victim?" John repeated, his eyebrows lifting. "My brother's a victim, too. He had to jump out of the way of the pickup. The driver was speeding *and* she was on her phone. Eyewitnesses told me so, and you would know that, too, if you interviewed them. My brother could have been grievously injured like Mr. Rigel."

Officer Mullen paused. "Mr. Rigel was pronounced dead on arrival at the hospital."

No, no, no. A wave of guilt engulfed me. If only I hadn't chased him. If only I hadn't gone to the apartment. I had so many what-ifs, so many questions. Did Rigel kill Lemaire? Why had Rigel come to my home group? I didn't know if any of the answers mattered now. They wouldn't change the fact that Rigel's life ended because of me.

"This interview is over." John shot up, motioning me to my feet. "Let's go, TJ."

I rose on weak knees.

My father followed, grave.

We walked outside, and as soon as we were alone on the street, my father turned on us, furious. "I swear, I don't know which of you embarrassed me more. TJ, I'll deal with you when we get home. John, what the hell were you thinking?"

John stopped. "Dad, there's a lot you don't—"

"Shut up! Let's go, TJ. I'm in the garage across the street. I'll take you to pick up your car. I don't want a word out of you on the way, not one word. I'm calling your mother. She's worried sick." My father stalked across the street, taking out his phone.

John and I exchanged looks. We both knew we'd have it out at the house.

I dreaded the scene, but it was time.

CHAPTER TWENTY-NINE

I had an out-of-body moment as I entered the family room, a perfect suburban tableau gone horribly wrong. Crystal lamps twinkled and end tables shone, but my parents looked grim, flanking a cold fireplace in red-striped wing chairs. A mantelpiece lined with framed photographs of them with Monsignor Harris, Bishop Agence, and other power Catholics overlooked a teary Gabby and Martin on the couch. John was standing, and he turned when I started talking, bursting with the speech I'd rehearsed on the way over.

"Everybody," I began, "I know there's a lot you don't understand. It's time to explain."

"Agree." John nodded. "TJ, you go ahead, and I'll footnote."

"Yes, go ahead, TJ." My father stood up. "Who's this Rigel and why were you chasing him?"

I braced myself. "It started the night of your birthday, Dad. John was doing due diligence on Runstan for the acquisition and he caught Lemaire embezzling—"

"Wait, what?" My father's eyes flew open. "The accountant? He was *embezzling*?"

"Yes," I answered.

"John?" My father whipped around to my brother. "Why didn't you tell me? I had a right to know. Runstan's my client."

John blinked. "Dad, I have no idea what TJ's talking about."

"John?" I couldn't believe my ears. My chest tightened. "You told me so. You thought you killed Lemaire."

My father gasped. "*Killed* him?"

My mother's eyes filmed. Gabby grimaced, and Martin recoiled.

"TJ, what are you talking about?" John met my gaze, preternaturally calm. "You're drinking again. You need to get back to rehab."

No, no, no. "Don't you dare, John." My face went hot. I couldn't process what was happening. "You just defended me. You can't do an about-face this fast. You told me Lemaire pulled a gun on you—"

"TJ, face it." John glared at me. "You're drinking again and getting mixed up with your old—"

"No!" I launched myself at John, tackling him. He fell backward, and I leapt on top of him, grabbed his tie, and punched him in the face. He grunted, trying to buck me off. I cocked my arm but my father caught one arm and Martin the other. They hoisted me to my feet and dragged me backward.

John scrambled away. "TJ, you're a mess!"

"TJ, out!" My father started walking me out of the room, with Martin behind him.

"Dad, you have to believe me! I'm telling the truth!"

"No more, TJ." My father's skin mottled with emotion. "We're not taking any more of this. You're killing your mother, *killing* her."

"Dad, wait!" I raised my hands. "Call Stan right now! He'll tell you. There's money missing. Ask him!"

"Are you insane?" My father faced me in the entrance hall. "I'll do no such thing."

John got up, brushing himself off. "Dad, don't. You'll embarrass yourself and me."

"Dad, if you don't call Stan, I will—"

"Enough!" Gabby came over. "Get a grip, all of you. Let's see if TJ's telling the truth. Dad, call Stan. Put him on speaker."

My father turned, aghast. "Gabby, TJ's drinking. You can't believe anything he says."

"Call Stan, please." Gabby set her jaw. "Dad?"

"No, John's right, it's embarrassing."

"Dad, TJ's going to call if you don't. It should come from you, don't you think?"

"Okay, fine." My father huffed, slid his phone from his pocket, and scrolled through it, pressing the button. "Not one word, you two."

I shut up, breathing hard.

John fell silent.

"Stan, it's Paul here," my father began, fake-cheery. "Sorry to bother. How are you? Good, glad to hear it. Listen. John and I have been talking. Do you mind if I put you on speaker? Thanks." He pressed the button.

"So, what can I help you with?" Stan asked matter-of-factly.

"It's about the acquisition." My father held up the phone. "Were there any accounting issues that surfaced during John's due diligence?"

"God, no, not that I know of. John tells me we're good to go. I even gave an interview to the *Inquirer* today about the acquisition—"

No. "Dad, he's lying. He doesn't want the embezzlement to come out. He wants to keep the acquisition on track. He stands to make—"

"TJ, quiet!" My father covered the phone, but Stan kept talking.

"What did TJ say? Is John there? John, is there a problem?"

John answered, "Absolutely not. I'm sorry we called—"

"Stan?" I grabbed the phone from my father's hand. "This is TJ. Tell the truth. Lemaire embezzled from you, and you and John are covering it up to keep the acquisition—"

"TJ, yo!" Stan raised his voice, angry. "Are you calling me a liar? What the hell are you—"

"Stan, admit it! Lemaire was murdered—"

"Are you nuts? Neil Lemaire committed suicide! The coroner confirmed it today! Paul? Paul, are you there? Get this drunk off the phone!"

"I'm here." My father grabbed the phone back. "Stan, excuse us. Every family has rough patches, and we're having one now. Sorry we bothered you." He hung up and pushed me back against the door.

"Dad, no, please!"

"Get out, TJ! I'm done with you! Get out of my sight!"

My mother cried out, "Paul, no! Stop!"

"Get out!" My father yanked open the door, pushed me outside, and slammed it closed in my face.

CHAPTER THIRTY

I drove home, numb and empty. It was drizzling, so I turned on the windshield wipers. The rhythm of their flapping matched my heartbeat. Traffic was sparse, and the asphalt streets were a slick black. Humidity formed halos around the streetlights and the bright signs of the passing strip malls and box stores.

I flashed on my mother crying. I hated that I had caused her pain again. I also hated that I couldn't begin to understand John.

I drove on autopilot. I wanted to pick up at every block, but I kept going, trying to outrun my craving, racing myself to get home. I could almost hear the crack of a tab on the can. I could almost taste the first sip. My nostrils filled with the smell of hops. Miller Lite was my go-to, but I drank them all, foreign or domestic, canned or bottled, commercial or artisanal.

I pulled into my driveway, got out of the car, and looked around reflexively, then remembered that no Hyundai would be following me now.

I felt confused. I didn't know what was going on. I didn't know what Rigel's death ended, if anything.

I went to the house, let myself in, and turned on the light. Mango sprinted from the windowsill and bolted to her hiding place under the couch. She needed her shot, so I got her works and went over to get her.

I knelt down and looked under the couch. Mango backed up, and I noticed a strange black line on the rug, coming from the baseboard.

I reached for my phone, turned on the flashlight, and shined it underneath the couch. It was a thin black wire, which the cat must have pulled free.

I went around the back of the couch and shone the light on the wire, then followed it with my fingers. The wire disappeared under the bound edge of the rug, where it had been concealed. I followed it to the corner of the room, then under the windowsill to the table. The wire ended in a small black microphone.

A bug.

I searched the apartment and found another bug along the wall in my bedroom. I left both in place.

I looked around to figure out how somebody could have gotten in. I checked the back door, but it was locked. I checked my bedroom window, and it was unlocked. I never bothered to lock it, so that must have been the answer.

I went out to the car and searched everywhere, including the undercarriage. I found a GPS tracker under the back bumper. I left it there, too, and went back inside, my thoughts churning.

I didn't know when the bugs and tracker had been planted. I didn't know who, if anybody, was left to surveil me. I had to find out, but not at this hour.

I went to catch Mango.

My hero cat.

CHAPTER THIRTY-ONE

My phone pinged at seven A.M. with an incoming text from Gabby: **IF YOU DON'T CALL ME BACK I'M COMING OVER THIS MINUTE.**

I scrolled to Favorites and called her. "Gab, don't come over. I'm fine."

"I was worried. Why didn't you call?"

"I should have." *I was finding bugs.*

"I'm on the way to work. I can stop by. We can talk."

"No, don't." I didn't want her here. I didn't know if it was safe. "I need some time alone."

"Last night was awful. Dad lost his mind, so did John. Frankly, so did you. TJ, what were you talking about, the accountant was murdered? And do you really know that Rigel guy?"

I couldn't tell her. "Gabby, it's between me and John—"

"Why? What's going on with you two?"

"It's my business. Let me handle it."

"I'm trying to help," Gabby said, her tone softer.

"Thanks, and I'll let you know if I need you."

Gabby sighed. "Are you going back to rehab?"

"No, I don't need to."

"TJ, you're in denial—"

"I'm not. Let it go. It's my business."

"I can't, TJ. Too much weird stuff is going on. You're with a guy who gets hit by a truck? Our office gets burglarized? John says it's all connected to you."

"He's lying." I sat up, rubbing my eyes. "I can't explain, and you won't believe it anyway."

"Well, if you can get sober—"

"I'm sober." I wished she believed me.

"Well, whatever, there's bad news and I can't sugarcoat it. Joe Ferguson died last night. It was peaceful, and his family was with him."

"Oh no." I flashed on Joe and our interview in Marcus Hook. My chest felt heavy at the loss, and the injustice. "I'm sorry."

"So I'm not waiting any longer, I can't. I'm going to open settlement negotiations and I scheduled a meeting with the defendants, pre-Complaint. I need you to work the case full-time."

"Dad fired me, remember?"

"I'll pay you as a consultant."

"How? You're not getting paid."

"I don't take a fee for my time, but litigation expenses like paper, pens, or expert and consultant fees come out of the settlement. I can't pick up the tab for costs. I'm forbidden by the Code."

"I'm not sure the plaintiffs understood that, and I don't want to take their money."

"Okay then, I'll pay you."

"Out of your pocket? No way. I'll work for free until I get a job."

"What are you going to live on?"

"Rolex-and-Maserati sandwiches."

Gabby chuckled. "Okay, fine. The meeting is today at two o'clock. I'll text you the address. Be on time. Wear a suit."

"Yes, boss."

"Hey, you're your own boss now. See you later. Love you."

"Love you, too." I hung up and rolled over, surprised to see Mango near my feet, curled into a ball.

Aw. I went to pet her, but she jumped off the bed. I'd left my jeans at the foot, and they were covered with cat hair. Oddly, I didn't mind.

I flashed with an idea, and I got up. I suddenly had something important to do this morning, before my neighbors left for work.

I hustled up the flagstone walk to the Hennesseys' house next door. It was well-maintained, with a Ring doorbell on the jamb of the front door. I knocked.

After a minute the door was opened by Morris Hennessey, an older mortgage banker who still wore a tie to work. "Good morning, TJ."

"Morrie, I'm sorry to bother you so early."

"That's okay, we're up. What is it?"

"Do you have a Ring doorbell on the back door?"

"No, why?"

Damn. "My watch is missing and I was wondering if somebody got in through the bedroom window. I don't lock it."

Morrie frowned. "I'm sorry to hear that. We don't lock the back window, either. Maybe we should start."

"Have you noticed any unusual cars on the street lately?" I was thinking of the maroon Volvo, but didn't want to suggest it.

"No." Morrie's eyes flared in alarm. "Do you think that somebody's . . . What's it called, *casing* the street?"

"I don't know but keep an eye out."

"Will do. Thanks, TJ."

"You're welcome." I left, crossed the driveway and my own front lawn, then went to my other neighbors, the Wax-Gormans. Susanne was a librarian, and her husband, Jim, worked as a graphic designer. Their cars were in the driveway, and I hurried up the path to the front door, a lacquered black with no Ring doorbell. My hopes sank but I knocked anyway.

Susanne answered, her blue eyes sharply intelligent. "TJ, good morning."

"Hi, sorry to bother you. I'm wondering if you have a Ring camera on your back door, by any chance?"

"No, we don't." Susanne shook her head, and her silver earrings swung back and forth. "I keep thinking we should get one. The Hennesseys have one."

"Only out front."

"Why do you ask? Is there a problem?"

I told Susanne the same story, and she arched an eyebrow.

"TJ, you think the burglar went in through your back window?"

"Yes."

"So he climbed your back fence?"

"He must have."

"Come in."

I stood with Susanne under a magnolia tree, next to the fence that divided our backyards. The magnolia sprouted white buds and its branches also hosted a white plastic birdhouse, with a camera inside. Good news for me, but bad news for birds who don't want their picture taken.

"There's a camera in the *birdhouse*?" I asked, amazed. "Why?"

"To watch the birds remotely." Susanne scrolled through her phone. "See the little tray? I put birdseed there and I love to watch them. I use safflower seeds because squirrels don't like them."

"You watch it on your phone?"

"Yes, when I can. There's an app." Susanne showed me her phone, then thumbed through pictures of blue jays and robins. The focus was excellent, and in the background was a section of my backyard fence.

Bingo. "It could show someone climbing into my backyard."

"Yes, it could."

"Please tell me it takes pictures."

"Yes, videos, too." Susanne pointed to a gray line on the phone screen. "This shows there was activity I missed. I don't watch it all the time, obviously."

"So if we go to those gray lines, we'll see if it detected a bird or anything else?"

"Yes. It even has night vision. When do you think you were broken into?"

"I don't know. Within the past few days? Maybe a week?"

Susanne checked her watch. "Hmmm. It would take a long time to go through that much video, and I have to get to work."

"Can you send the video to me, so I can look myself?"

CHAPTER THIRTY-TWO

I sat at my laptop, staring at the screen. The video from the birdhouse camera gave me an excellent view of a man climbing over my fence. It was Barry Rigel.

I rewound the video and played it again. It was daytime, and Rigel's arm and leg came over the fence, his head toward the camera. He looked up, and I could see his face. He'd broken into my house while I was at work.

I eyed the image, mulling over what could have happened to Lemaire. Rigel could have killed him, but I didn't know why. If Rigel hadn't killed him, it could have been someone else in the conspiracy. *Somebody* owned the maroon Volvo that Lemaire had been driving that first night.

TJ, is everything about cars?

I remembered what my brother said, but now it gave me pause. I realized that I didn't really know if there ever had been a maroon Volvo at the quarry at all. John had told me so, but now I didn't know if I could believe anything he said. Still I didn't know why he would lie or why he'd pick a maroon Volvo.

I shifted forward and googled *Barry Rigel* and *Exton*. Onto the screen popped a headline, LOCAL MAN, 45, HIT BY VEHICLE AND KILLED. I clicked the link:

> **EXTON—Barry Rigel, 45, died last night after he was struck by a pickup truck at the Glen Meade Apartments in West Goshen. The pickup truck was driven by Terry Pantolo and the incident occurred around 10:00 P.M. The pickup was traveling west on Pickering Valley Road approaching Brinton Avenue. Rigel was walking in a northerly direction and not in a crosswalk when he was struck. Rigel was rushed to Paoli Hospital, where he was pronounced dead from his injuries. Pantolo was not injured and remained at the scene after the victim was struck. The matter remains under investigation.**

I flashed on last night. The horrific crash. The sickening *thud*, the heat of the pickup's engine.

I shook it off, rereading the article. I realized it didn't mention me, so my father had worked his Chamber of Commerce magic. Devlin & Devlin would suffer no consequences, and neither would I. Privilege was an awful, beautiful thing.

I sat back, wishing to God I had a beer. I used to start every day with a breakfast beer, or three. I went through three thirty-packs a week, and if you want to drink that much, you have to start early.

I got my thoughts back on track and kept researching Barry Rigel, but there wasn't much more to learn. He didn't have any social media, and the white pages showed that he was the only person who lived at his address. An ad came up, *Want to Run a Criminal Background Check on Barry Rigel?* and I clicked *yes*, putting $250 I didn't have on my credit card. It turned out that Barry Rigel didn't have a criminal record, unlike me.

I sat back, rethinking Barry Rigel. I knew he was linked to Lemaire but I couldn't figure out how. I decided to work it from the other direction and start with Lemaire. There had to be a funeral scheduled, so I searched for his obituary. The first link that came up was from a funeral home, and his wake was tomorrow.

I eyed the obit, realizing that Stan would be at the wake. I wondered now if he was covering up Lemaire's embezzlement, if John had really told him that Lemaire was embezzling, or whether Lemaire was embezzling at all.

I mulled it over. It felt like a puzzle with too many missing pieces, and I couldn't put it together. One important piece could be Lemaire's boyfriend, Daniel Rocha, who wasn't mentioned in the obituary. He must have found out by now Lemaire was gone. I still had the thumb drive with his and Lemaire's emails in my jean jacket.

I jumped up, got the jacket, and dug inside the pocket for the thumb drive. I brought it back to the kitchen table, sat down, and plugged it into the laptop, opening Lemaire's private email account.

The first emails from Rocha flooded onto the laptop, with his email address. I sorted them and started going through them for a cell number. I hit pay dirt near the end, when one had an automatic signature and cell number.

I picked up my phone.

CHAPTER THIRTY-THREE

Malvern was a quaint town in Chester County, its main drag lined with antiques dealers, hip little restaurants, and a saddlery that catered to the horsey set. There wasn't a strip mall or chain store, not counting the Wawa, which was a necessity. There was on-street parking, which I took advantage of, having left the GPS tracker hidden at home.

I waited for Daniel at a sidewalk table outside the Buttery, a bakery restaurant with a funky chalkboard menu. He'd chosen the spot, and I recognized him walking toward me because I'd looked him up on Instagram. He was tall and lanky as a male model, with a lean face and thick brown hair, and he had on a gray sweater with jeans and Blundstones.

I stood up when he reached me and shook his hand. "Daniel, I'm TJ. Thanks for coming. I'm sorry about your loss."

"Thanks." Daniel managed a smile, his greenish eyes narrowing in the sunlight. "It's devasting that he's gone."

"I know, I'm sure." I sat down. "I appreciate you coming."

"I wasn't sure when you called, but when you said you took Mango, you were in."

"Thanks. She's not a big fan of mine, but I assume she misses Neil."

"No, she's just bitchy."

I smiled. "You can see her if you want to."

"Thanks. Just take good care of her. I would have taken her but my apartment doesn't allow pets." Daniel paused. "I'm still trying to get used to the idea that he's gone. It's weird because we were off and on, then long distance. I keep thinking I'll see him this weekend."

"Let me get you something to eat. The scones here are great." I motioned to the waitress, who came over and cocked her head.

"Can I help you?"

"Yes," Daniel answered. "Tea, please. Lipton is fine, and a raisin scone with butter."

"Be right back," the waitress said, taking off.

Daniel sighed. "Now, what was it you wanted to know about Neil? It's nice to talk about him to somebody who isn't crying. Our friends are a mess."

"Well, I'll pick up on that. I noticed you weren't mentioned in the obituary."

"Neil's mother Stalinized his obit. She never accepted that he was gay. I was the one who encouraged him to come out, and she never forgave me."

"I'm sorry." I'd heard similar stories in rehab.

"Neil took care of her, he even paid for full-time nursing. She had MS. He wanted to be there himself, but she threw him out and he moved here." Daniel paused, with a sigh. "We were talking about getting married, but he thought it would upset her too much. She still can't decide if she's letting me and our friends go to the funeral. I'm going to respect her wishes. We all feel the same way. Neil would have wanted that."

I felt for him, and the waitress came back with his tea, scone, and a ramekin of salted butter.

"Thanks," Daniel said to the waitress, then returned his attention to me. "Anyway, we were seeing each other, but I got a job offer in Orlando and gave him an ultimatum. We broke up, and I took the job. I work as a designer for a woman who's in commercial real estate all over the country, headquartered in Atlanta. We got a gig in Philly about two weeks ago, so I took it, and Neil and I started back up. We were talking about a trip, then . . . this happened." Daniel took the tea bag out of the cup and set it on the saucer. "He started going downhill a week or two ago. He wasn't sure he wanted to go on the trip. He did get depressed from time to time, then I found out he . . . passed."

"How did you find out?"

"I saw it on social. I can't say I was surprised."

"You mean about the way he died?"

"Yes." Daniel's eyes filmed. "You can say 'suicide.' It's okay."

"Do you have any doubt he died by suicide?"

"No." Daniel blinked. "Why, do you?"

"I've spoken with Lillian, the bookkeeper. You know her, right?"

"Of course, love her."

"She thinks he was murdered."

"What?" Daniel recoiled, grimacing, and I decided to tell him everything. I started with what happened with John on my father's birthday and went all the way through to finding the bugs in my apartment. He listened through a second cup of tea, asking questions from time to time.

"Quite a story," Daniel said, lifting an eyebrow when I was finished. "Okay, I have thoughts. First, I low-key hate your brother."

I smiled. "I hear you."

"But I still think Neil died by suicide. Now that I know that he was embezzling, it makes sense. It answers, Why now?" Daniel swallowed hard. "I just wish he'd told me, or called me. I wish we'd gone out to dinner that night. We were supposed to. We even had reservations, but I had to work late. It'll haunt me forever."

I felt for him. "But what about the embezzlement? Was he that kind of guy?"

"He needed money, and I wouldn't put it past him to skim." Daniel smiled sadly. "Like I said, his mother was sick, and he was her sole support except for Social Security. He had a good salary at Runstan but it wasn't enough to cover her needs and his own."

"Lillian told me he was trying to become CFO."

"Yes, that's true. Money mattered to him. When we talked about the trip, he was worried about the cost."

"Would he pull a gun on my brother?"

"Possibly. He had a handgun. He grew up hunting." Daniel leaned over the table. "But I think you're looking in the wrong direction. How well do you know Stan?"

"Not that well."

"I've heard my share. If Neil was embezzling, I guarantee Stan was in on it."

I shifted forward, intrigued. "Stan's trying to cover it up."

"Of course he is." Daniel's eyes flashed. "Neil and I were together when the acquisition started to happen. Stan never *dreamed* he'd be acquired. You have to understand, it's like winning the lottery. You know how much they're buying him for?"

"Yes."

"So imagine that. Stan thought he died and went to heaven. I mean, Runstan makes money, but it's basic, if you know what I mean, and Stan is all about money. I wouldn't be surprised if *he* was stealing, from the jump."

"But he'd be stealing from himself."

"Please." Daniel snorted. "You know a business and a CEO are two different things, right? Plenty of CEOs steal from their own company. I think my boss skims, too. Bosses steal legally, and the books lie. Stan's family drives company cars, and they go on trips paid for by the company, Neil told me."

"Really? But he drives an old Explorer."

"To work, he does. He has a Corvette at home and his wife drives a Benz. They have a motorboat, too." Daniel rolled his eyes. "I'll tell you something else you don't know about Stan. He's a tough guy, for a CEO. He came up through the ranks and he's got a lot of union pals in Philly. I wouldn't be surprised if one was Barry Rigel. Stan could have had Rigel bug your apartment and follow you and your brother."

I tensed, hearing it said aloud. "I wondered about that, too. Do you think Stan would kill Neil?"

"No." Daniel met my eye, directly. "I think Stan would kill *you*."

I felt a chill. "Why?"

"To shut you up. You're asking questions. You could blow up the acquisition. Your brother's willing to shut it down and play along. He stands to gain financially, just like Stan. You know who doesn't? You. You went rogue when you went to Rigel's house. They don't know how to control you, and you won't let it go. *You're* the loose end."

"Oh man." My mind reeled. "I've been wanting to go to the police. If I do, I'll be safer."

"No, you won't. They take care of the powers that be. Runstan employs a lot of people, and the acquisition is major business news. Your father erased your involvement with Barry Rigel's death, didn't he?"

"Yes," I answered, cringing.

"Well, Stan's got more clout than your dad. If you start making dangerous allegations about him, it's your word against his, and you'll be even more exposed."

I knew he was right, since ex-cons generally didn't win credibility contests. "I could try to make a federal case out of it. Get to the FBI."

"Bad idea. You'd have the same problems, and it will take longer."

"So I can't go to the cops, but I can't let it go. What do I do?"

"You're an investigator. So, investigate." Daniel leaned over. "But on the down-low."

"Right."

"One last thing." Daniel paused. "I know who owns the maroon Volvo."

I walked Daniel to the garage, where he'd parked his maroon Volvo. I'd been imagining the car for so long that it was impossible to believe it was in front of me, and that its owner wasn't homicidal.

"Nice car," I told him.

Daniel shrugged. "It runs great."

"And you lent it to Neil that night?"

"Yes, his car was in the shop. He told me he had a meeting to go to, I assume with your brother. And by the way, he had a bandage on his forehead and told me he hit it on the countertop when he bent over. So we had a quick lunch, and I followed him to the shop and he dropped off his car. It wouldn't start from time to time. Then he drove me to the station, and I took the train back to Philly."

"And the next day?"

"We swapped. I took the train, we went to the shop, he got his car, and I drove back to the city. We were going to have dinner in town, but I was busy."

"And that night, he drove to the park."

"Yes." Daniel's lower lip began to buckle. "He was scared, alone, and desperate."

"Come here, pal," I said, giving him a hug.

• • •

I drove home with one eye on the rearview mirror, but now I didn't know what kind of car I was looking for. It scared me to think that I'd become a loose end, but Daniel was right. I didn't know if I agreed that Lemaire had died by suicide, but my theory he'd been murdered was shaken. Still, Lemaire could have died by suicide, and I could still be in danger. So could John.

I gripped the wheel tighter, my thoughts churning. It occurred to me that whoever worked with Rigel would want revenge for his death. The media wasn't revealing my involvement, but plenty of people at the apartment complex saw what had happened. Stan and anybody who worked for him could start asking questions and find out about me.

When I reached my street, I turned the corner, scanning for cars that didn't belong to my neighbors. My heart stopped when I spotted one parked in front of my house. But this car, I recognized.

A black Range Rover, the official car of Devlin & Devlin & Devlin & Devlin.

I had no idea which Devlin was inside.

CHAPTER THIRTY-FOUR

My mother had no makeup on, and her eyes were puffy. Her mouth drooped, and deep lines bracketed her lips. She wasn't as put together as usual, wearing a beige quilted jacket over a black sweater, sweatpants, and her gardening clogs. She carried her big black Birkin, the Range Rover of handbags.

I let her in. "How long have you been sitting out there?"

"Not long."

I shuddered to think the house was being watched. "You should've called."

"I wanted to ambush you."

I closed the door behind us. "You're sneaky."

"No, I'm sly. Sneaky people are dumb. Sly people are smart." My mother entered the living room, set down her handbag, and turned to me. "Have you been drinking?"

"Absolutely not." I remembered that the microphone was under the table, if anybody was still listening. "Let's go sit outside. It's a nice day."

"I'm fine inside. Let me smell your breath."

"No."

"Yes." My mother took a step toward me. "I'll go outside if you let me smell your breath."

I gave her a whiff. "See?"

"You drink too much coffee."

"Come on." I led her through the apartment to the back door, and we went into the backyard, where I had a round white table with matching white-wire chairs.

"What a nice set," she said, surprised. "Where'd you get it?"

"A thrift shop in Frazer."

My mother ran a manicured finger over the table. "Fermob."

"What's that?"

"A nice French make."

"I was raised right." I pulled out a chair for her, and she sat down, linking her hands on the table.

"Where were you, TJ? I've been looking for you in every bar in a five-mile radius."

"Just now?" I felt a guilty pang. "Mom, you didn't have to do that."

"I'm worried, after last night." Her expression was tender, if strained. "I love you, honey."

"I love you, too."

"You *have* to go back to rehab. I know it will work this time."

"I don't need to—"

"Please, I'll pay for it. You don't have to ask your father."

"I thought you had joint accounts."

"So does he." My mother lifted an eyebrow.

I smiled. "I didn't know you were so gangster."

"Keep up."

I laughed, but she was deadly serious. Something about her manner was different, as if she was stripped down, almost raw.

"TJ, no more excuses. You're going to rehab."

"Mom, I'm not drinking."

"I don't believe you." My mother folded her arms, her lovely features stony. "You need to go back to rehab. Otherwise, we can't even talk. Your father wants to start tough love."

"The only love he has is tough."

"I'm here to talk about you, not him. You attacked John. You *punched* him in the face." My mother softened. "You don't know what it's like to see your sons at each other's throats. You're brothers. We're a *family*."

"Mom, John and I are not close."

"You used to adore him."

"The question is, did he adore me? No."

"Why, because he used to tell you to get lost?" My mother scoffed. "That's normal."

I remembered the other day, in Norwood. "He beat me up when I was little. I got stitches over—"

"Whatever happened doesn't matter now."

"I think it does." My chest went tight. "When you tell me how close we are, that's not my lived experience, as they say."

"Still, it doesn't justify hitting him last night." My mother's dark eyes widened, incredulous. "You turned on him, your own brother!"

"Mom, he turned on *me*—"

"Tell me, then, what did he do? How? You said he caught Runstan's accountant stealing. He said that's crazy talk." My mother leaned over, placing her palms on the table. "If he's lying, then tell me how. Explain it to me. You've been keeping something and it's time to get it out."

"Okay, I'll tell you." I'd already broken the seal telling Daniel, and she deserved to know as much as he did. So I launched into the story from the beginning, telling her everything except that I was a loose end. She listened quietly, taking a break only when I got her a glass of water, and by the end, she seemed terribly sad and, oddly, lost.

My mother sighed. "So John . . . made it all up?"

"Yes." I felt validated, but I hardly felt good. It just made the awfulness real.

"I believe you. It makes more sense. And it jibes with what I've been seeing lately in him. Something's come over your brother." My mother looked away, her gaze unfocused. "Now I know why he's been so excited about the Runstan acquisition. Nobody told me about the premium billing. Your father kept it to himself." My mother slumped. "None of this justifies what he's doing, what he's become, to keep the acquisition on track. This is obstruction of justice. This is *criminal*."

"Should we go to the police?"

"Turn him in? Your *brother*, my son?" My mother's eyes filled with tears. "Honestly, I don't know if I can do that."

"What if he can make a deal?"

"Still, if Stan's involved, they'll charge him . . ." My mother's voice trailed off, and she wiped her eyes. "I mean, how long do you think a law firm lasts, when they start turning in their clients?"

"If the clients have done wrong—"

"It would be a scandal, and the press would be terrible. It could ruin us, everything we've done, all our hard work—it would be wasted. It would kill your father. Oh no." My mother covered her face, and I put an arm around her. Her back felt frail, and I had a horrible sense she was breaking.

"Everything's going to be okay."

"How?" My mother lifted her face from her hands. Emotion mottled the skin on her face and neck. "I don't know what to do for you."

"You don't have to do anything for me. You shouldn't do anything."

"Of course I should. I'm your mother, and John's. I can't let him get away with this. I'll have to figure this out. Get things back in order." My mother kept shaking her head, looking away. "I want to have a talk with John, but he'll deny it, and your father will believe him. The family will split in two."

I came to the same realization, and the notion left me unmoored, tethered to nothing. "Listen, don't do anything yet. Sleep on it. Remember you always used to say that?"

"Yes." My mother nodded slowly.

I glanced at my watch. "I have to get changed to meet Gabby. She has a big meeting in her pro bono case. She told me not to be late."

"Right, that's important," my mother said vacantly. "Go get dressed."

"You all right?" I stood up, my hand on her shoulder.

"Do I have a choice?" my mother answered matter-of-factly.

CHAPTER THIRTY-FIVE

The conference room held more lawyers than I'd seen in my lifetime, attorneys for the City of Philadelphia, the College of Physicians of Philadelphia, the University of Pennsylvania, Johnson & Johnson, Bausch Health, Rhone Pharma, and Fournette Laboratories, with a few counterparts listening on Zoom.

Gabby was holding the meeting in a space-for-rent in Hessian Post Plaza, a corporate park off Route 202, since Devlin & Devlin was a shambles. The requisite prints of city hall, Eakins Oval, and Boathouse Row covered three walls, and the fourth was smoked glass overlooking the parking lot. A long conference table dominated the room, and everyone found their swivel chair.

Gabby and I sat on one side, facing a corporate wall of lawyers behind laptops. She looked professional in a trim blue dress, and I had on the suit I'd worn for my guilty plea, which looked better without the handcuffs.

I kept an eye on the window for anything suspicious. I had to be on the lookout, but I didn't know what I was on the lookout for. With Rigel dead, it wouldn't be a Hyundai, but I didn't know which car it would be. I didn't have a face, either. It made me tense, on edge.

"Let's get started, shall we?" Gabby motioned to me, so I reached into our boxy trial bag, extracted a bunch of thick Complaints, and handed them out before returning to my seat.

Gabby cleared her throat. "Thank you all for coming. I've already emailed you the Complaint I intend to file in this matter, and my colleague has just distributed hard copies. I'll begin with the facts, explain why I think I'll prevail, and end with the rationale for our damages claim of fifteen million dollars. I'll take this case to trial if need be, but I'm hoping that we can settle as soon as possible."

I watched the lawyers skim the Complaint, their expressions varying between professional interest and boredom, then returned my attention to the parking lot.

"The facts in this lawsuit are undisputed. The late Dr. Albert Kligman was a professor of dermatology at Penn's medical school, and in the 1950s through the early seventies, he used thousands of inmates at Holmesburg as human subjects in medical experimentation, specifically in tests for hundreds of cosmetics, drugs, and other commercial products."

Suddenly my gaze was drawn to something outside. A group of three women was leaving the building, and one of them looked familiar.

Gabby continued, "Our Complaint concerns the skin-patch tests and other dermatological testing that Dr. Kligman conducted on inmates at Holmesburg. I represent seven former inmates who now have melanoma and have experienced untold pain, suffering, and financial losses over decades as a result of the testing. As you know, among other drugs, the testing supported the research and development of Retin-A and Renova, which have proven incredibly lucrative for your corporate defendants. Simply put, it's time to pay my clients for the heinous damage your clients caused them."

I realized I recognized one of the women outside. It was Patrick's niece Maya, whom I'd stood up the other night. She and her friends stopped to talk between the cars in the parking lot.

Meanwhile the young female assistant general counsel for the University of Pennsylvania was speaking up. "Gabby, I hope you're aware that the current dean of Penn's medical school issued a formal apology for what Dr. Kligman did, in August 2021."

The assistant city solicitor chimed in, "Yes, the City apologized, too, in October 2022, via Mayor Kenney himself."

An older lawyer nodded, representing the College of Physicians of Philadelphia. "The College of Physicians made an apology of its own, though we had *nothing* to do with such experiments."

Gabby leaned forward. "Frankly, none of these apologies constitute justice for my clients. Let me address each of you in turn." She faced the lawyer for the College of Physicians. "Your client may have apologized, but before it did, the College of Physicians honored Dr. Kligman with a Distinguished Achievement Award." Next she turned to the assistant city solicitor. "My research reveals that tests were conducted not only at Holmesburg, but at seven other county prisons. The City can never apologize enough for its utter dereliction of duty in opening up the county prison system to the most heinous commercial exploitation of its citizens, whom the City had a duty to protect." Finally Gabby faced Penn's assistant general counsel. "The University of Pennsylvania allowed Dr. Kligman to operate under its auspices, and its Ivy League imprimatur attracted major corporations like Johnson & Johnson, as well as smaller companies like Rhone Pharma and Fournette Laboratories. This is where I tell you that I'm a graduate of Penn's law school, and I recall its Latin motto, *Leges sine Moribus vanae*, which means 'Laws without morals are useless.' It's time to make that motto true and compensate these plaintiffs. So many of the men who were so grievously injured have passed away or are impossible to locate, especially given the apparently willful destruction of their records. One of the plaintiffs, Joe Ferguson, just passed away yesterday, and I won't allow further delay to enable your clients to escape responsibility." Gabby leaned back in her chair, addressing the group. "Folks, your clients have wronged my clients, and justice is long overdue. So apologies just don't cut it. They're simply too little, too late."

"Excuse me." The female local counsel for Johnson & Johnson didn't blink. "I don't see how your suit survives the statute of limitations. You must know that a similar suit was dismissed on that basis in 2002."

Gabby nodded. "Of course I know that. The case you're referring to is *Yusuf Abdulaziz v. City of Philadelphia, Dr. Kligman, & the University of Pennsylvania*, and it was dismissed on statute of limitations grounds. However, Judge Weis made clear that those plaintiffs lived in the Philadelphia area, so they knew or should have known of the controversy following the testing and could have brought it earlier. The judge left open the possibility of a different result if a plaintiff could show they were *not* within the jurisdiction and could not have known. Our Complaint meets that requirement, and I represent only plaintiffs who were outside the state for decades after their incarceration."

I wondered how long Maya would be outside. I wished I could go out and apologize for standing her up.

A scoff came from the lawyer at Rhone Pharma. "But you have only a handful of plaintiffs. I can't believe I came from the city on such a minor matter."

"It's hardly minor, and it takes only one plaintiff to bring this matter to court and to the public eye."

"Now wait one minute," interrupted an older lawyer, outside counsel from Fournette Laboratories. "What do you mean by 'the public eye'? Are you going to try this matter in court or online? Are you attempting to get us canceled? Twitter boycotts? Social media castigation?"

Gabby bore down. "I'm simply going to inform the public of the truth. There's no colorable argument that these plaintiffs have suffered the devastating effects of cancer caused by your clients. Your clients know they did wrong, yet refuse to compensate these men or their families, and they can't have it both ways. You need to go back to them and tell them that if I can get to a jury—and I can under my theory—the sky's the limit on punitive damages. What happened at Holmesburg will shock the conscience of any jury. If your clients won't settle because it's the right thing to do, they should settle because it makes excellent business sense."

I could tell the important part of the meeting was over, and Maya was getting ready to go, too, pulling her key fob from her purse.

Gabby turned to the Complaint. "Now let me take you briefly through the allegations and I'll end with the rationale for our settlement demand, so you can take the figure back to your clients."

I touched Gabby's arm. "Can I go for a minute?"

She nodded.

I mouthed my thanks and took off.

CHAPTER THIRTY-SIX

I jogged through the parking lot, scanning quickly to make sure I wasn't being watched or followed. As I got closer to her, I could see that Maya was a knockout in person. Her eyes were large and wide-set, and her smile dazzled me. Thick black hair spilled over her shoulders, and she looked incredible in a black knit top, jeans, and black heels. I smoothed down my guilty-plea tie.

"Maya, hi," I said, when I reached her and her friends. "I'm TJ, Patrick's friend."

"You stood me up." Maya's eyes went flinty, and her friends exchanged looks, evidently having heard about the Total Jerk Nicknamed TJ. The friend on Maya's left was also Indian-American, with a bright blue streak in her dark hair, and the one on her right was a freckle-faced strawberry blonde.

"I'm so sorry. Did you get my flowers?"

"Yes." Maya remained unsmiling. "What are you doing here?"

"I was in a meeting." I hoped that sounded corporate. "Do you work here? Is this where you sell calculus?"

"What do you want?"

"Well, uh . . ." I met her eye, trying to block out the strawberry blonde looking daggers at me. "I wanted to say I'm sorry."

"You did already, in the card with the bouquet."

"I saw you out the window and wanted to do it face-to-face." I tried to collect my thoughts but couldn't. "I'm really sorry about what happened. I was running late, and it ended with our office being burglarized."

"Burglarized?" Maya snorted, and I realized she didn't believe me. I wouldn't have believed me, either. I almost wished I were back inside. It's easier to face an army of lawyers than a woman with justified anger.

"Yes, it's really true. They took the computers and ransacked the place. We had to call the police." I hoped specifics would convince her. "It's my family's law firm, and they took statues my sister loved and my mother's coral earrings. She used to take them off because they click on the phone screen."

Maya blinked. "I hate that."

Her friend with the blue streak nodded. "Me, too."

The strawberry blonde didn't reply.

I kept talking. "Anyway, burglars ransacked our office and that's why we're meeting here."

Maya hesitated. "If you were burglarized, why didn't you say so when you called?"

"Because it wasn't the reason I was late." I was repeating myself, but I could see her forehead ease. The friend with the blue streak smiled. The strawberry blonde only folded her arms.

"You should have told me," Maya said after a moment.

"Anyway I would love to have dinner with you. I never stood anybody up before and I would never stand you up again. I hope you give me a second chance." On impulse, I got down on one knee. "Will you have dinner with me if I promise to show up?"

Maya burst into laughter, which made me feel hopeful and happy.

"Please say yes because my knee hurts."

"Get up." Maya motioned me up. "People will think you're proposing."

"I am, I'm proposing a date."

"Get up right now."

The strawberry blonde eyed me hard. "Are you a lawyer?"

"No, an investigator."

"Do you have a PI license?"

"No, but look at my suit. I'm basically James Bond."

The blue streak glanced at Maya. "I like him. He's funny."

The strawberry blonde shook her head. "I don't know, sis."

"You're sisters?" I asked, confused.

"Sorority sisters," Maya corrected. "We were Omega Phi at Penn State."

"I went to Penn State, too," I said, desperate to connect.

"Really?" Maya brightened. "I got my MBA from Smeal."

"Wow, an MBA?" I remembered at that moment that I didn't have a college degree—or a job, for that matter.

Blue Streak said, "Maya wants to own her own company."

Strawberry Blonde added, "Maya wants to own her own *country*."

Maya was smiling at me. "My uncle didn't tell me you went to Penn State, TJ. What class?"

Uh-oh. "Pardon me?"

"When did you graduate?"

"Uh, I didn't," I answered. It was my secret shame, on a list as long as other people's Things to Do. Like I had a list of Things to Be Ashamed Of.

Maya's smile faded. "Why not? The tuition?"

"No." My mouth went dry. "I partied too much, my grades went down, and one thing led to another."

Strawberry Blonde interjected, "Led to what?"

Alcoholism, prison, and rehab? "It's a long story," I answered, like a red flag on steroids.

"Well, I should be going." Maya walked to her car. "It was nice meeting you, TJ."

Blue Streak smiled her regret. "Nice meeting you."

Strawberry Blonde smirked. "Later, dude."

By the time I got back to the conference room, the meeting was over and the lawyers were leaving. I read Gabby's expression, which was grim. I put a hand on her shoulder. "What happened? It was okay that I left, wasn't it?"

"Sure, it didn't matter. Nothing mattered. I could have danced naked and it wouldn't have made a difference."

"How so? You did a great job with the presentation."

"Thanks." Gabby leaned against the conference table.

"So what'd they say? What happened?"

"I can tell you what *didn't* happen. Nobody offered any money."

"Did you expect them to?"

"No, but I had hope. They have the money, they did wrong, and they should pay. It's the right thing to do. Instead they're going to delay, hoping I give up."

"They don't know my sister." I started packing the trial bag.

"No, they don't." Gabby shouldered her purse, flashing a defiant smile. "I won't give up."

"*We* won't give up."

"Damn right."

I picked up the bag and put an arm around her. "Say it with me, Gab. 'We shall fight on the beaches.'"

"'We shall fight on the landing grounds.'"

"'We shall fight . . .'" We walked out of the room finishing Churchill's speech, drummed into us verbatim. Gabby felt buoyed, but I knew better. The other side had money and might. All she had was me, and I wasn't enough.

Strawberry Blonde knew that just by looking.

CHAPTER THIRTY-SEVEN

That night at home, I sat in front of my laptop, wolfing down a cheese-and-pickle sandwich for dinner. I'd spent the day looking over my shoulder, wondering if I was being followed. I felt the presence of the bug underneath the couch and wondered who was listening in, and why. Mango lurked there in her lair, having had her shot and flaked tuna, which reeked. Whoever invented air freshener had a cat.

I couldn't shake off my mood, discouraged after the lawyer meeting and Maya's rejection in the parking lot. I needed a job other than being Gabby's sidekick. I'd never applied for one before, and my only work experience was at Devlin & Devlin, after school and every summer.

I logged on to the website of the Pennsylvania Bar Association, figuring I could be a real paralegal. I clicked *Job Seekers*, plugged in *paralegal*, and clicked *Search*. The screen filled with positions, and I clicked the first one: *legal assistant for the City of Philadelphia*. I skimmed the requirements and stopped at BA/BS/undergraduate. I clicked the next few positions. All required a college degree.

I changed the job title to *executive assistant*, then hit *Search*. Every one required a bachelor's degree. I tried *secretary* and hit *Search*. The jobs didn't require a college degree, but a typing speed of ninety words per minute, which I didn't have.

I went to Monster.com and plugged in *investigator*. A list piled onto the screen: field investigator, pharmaceutical technical investigator, investigator network services, research investigator, employee relations investigator, and fraud investigator. All required a bachelor's degree or "equivalent." There was no listing for sinecure.

I tried *private investigator*, which didn't require a college degree, but a PI license. I navigated to find the requirements and found they were three years of experience as a law enforcement agent or an employee of a detective agency. Plus I was disqualified because of a criminal conviction.

What class?

I couldn't forget Maya's question. The obvious answer for me was to go back to school and get my degree, but it felt strange, at my age. I navigated to the Penn State website and clicked *tuition*. A grid came alive with campus locations and residency. I picked *Brandywine*, then *PA resident*, then got the bad news. The tuition was $15,476, and I didn't have five grand, much less fifteen.

I finished my sandwich, thinking it over. I was a decent mechanic, but not licensed. My days of flipping cars were over because that required buying them. The Rolex and Maserati would bring enough to pay rent, food, phone, electric, and cable, but not forever.

Thud.

I flashed on Rigel, hit by the pickup truck. Then a bereft Daniel. My mother's broken heart. Gabby's meeting with the corporate wall. The death of Joe Ferguson. The bug under the couch. The tracker in the garage. Did whoever was tracking me realize I had found it? Could they have guessed I found the bug, too?

My mood cycled down. A familiar despair descended, and I could feel it taking hold.

I got up, grabbed my phone and keys, and left the house.

I drove with one eye on the rearview.

"Let's start with the Serenity Prayer, shall we?" Jake crossed his legs. "'God grant me the serenity to . . .'" he began, and everybody recited together. When we were finished, he looked around the circle. "How are we feeling?"

"Not bad," Phyllis answered, and everybody chimed in. "Decent." "Better than last meeting." "Well, thanks." "Good."

"Good. There's no topic tonight, and I thought we'd share what was on our minds." Jake smiled, then eyed me. "TJ, would you like to get us started?"

"Okay," I answered, shamed into it. "My name is TJ and I'm an alcoholic."

"Hi, TJ." Everyone turned their attention to me.

"Bottom line, I got fired and I don't know if I can get another job. Tonight, it got too much for me. I started to feel like I was going to pick up, so I came to a meeting."

Greg smiled kindly. "Keep coming back, TJ."

Cheryl clucked. "I've been there, TJ. It sucks to get fired. I'm glad you came."

Antonio met my eye. "You did the right thing, buddy. Nighttimes are tough. They put me on my damn *heels*."

"They're the worst," added Phyllis. "I think to myself, 'One *night* at a time.' So fill us in, TJ. We're all ears."

"Well . . ." I was about to continue when a beefy man entered the room in a Carhartt coat, baggy jeans, and work boots. I'd never seen him at a meeting, and his dark eyes were glassy on a coarse face framed by black hair and muttonchops. He opened his folding chair with a noisy shake and sat down heavily next to me, smelling of cigarettes.

You're the loose end.

Jake asked, "TJ, would you like to continue?"

"Uh, yes," I answered, but suddenly I felt anxious. I wondered if Muttonchops had been working with Rigel. It seemed coincidental, his being here the night after Rigel had been killed. If there was a conspiracy, maybe they would replace Rigel. I hadn't told Jake that our group had been infiltrated because I didn't know what to say without getting him involved. Meanwhile everyone was looking at me except Muttonchops, who averted his gaze.

Jake was saying, "TJ? Go ahead, we're here to—"

"Who are you?" I faced Muttonchops down. "What are you doing here?"

Muttonchops recoiled, blinking. "Uh, well, it's a meeting, right?"

"You're not in this group. I never saw you before. What's your name?"

"TJ?" Jake interrupted. "What's going on?"

"He's new. He's never come before."

"That doesn't matter. It's open. He's welcome. What's going on?"

"Jake, there's a lot you don't know." I stood up. "A man named Barry Rigel came to our home group a while ago with Brian, but he was really a killer, stalking me. He was hit by a pickup last night, right in front of me."

"What?" Jake sat up in his chair, his refined features flushed. Everyone burst into nervous chatter.

"TJ, what?" Brian's eyes flew open. "Who are you talking about, TJ?"

"Brian, the guy in the camo T-shirt. He told us his name was Chris, but it's really Barry Rigel. He's a killer, and I think I know who he killed—"

"For real?" Brian gasped, taken aback.

"Did you know him? You brought him."

"Not really." Brian grimaced. "I only met him, like, a week before at the Y, swimming. He struck up a conversation."

"Yeah, well, he lied to you. He wasn't who he said he was. He wanted to get in the group to get to me." I turned on Muttonchops. "Why are you here? You're with Rigel, aren't you?"

"Whoa, chill." Muttonchops raised meaty hands, rising. "What's your problem? You're outta line, buddy."

Jake rushed over, grabbing my arm. "TJ, stop this—"

"Jake, he's dangerous—"

"Stop. I can't have this. You're being disruptive."

"Listen to me—"

"No, go right now, leave."

"I'm telling you—"

"Go!" Jake pointed, and I fled the meeting.

THE WHIP HAND, read the neon sign, glowing bright red through the rain. It was a neighborhood bar that I used to drink in, among other places. I hadn't been back because avoiding my old drinking holes was part of the program. So was deleting my drinking buddies from my phone, which was how I ended up with no friends.

Rain dotted the windshield, and I sat in the car, fighting with myself. Every single neuron in my brain was telling me I needed a drink, hardwired against my better judgment. I couldn't think of a single reason why I shouldn't go in and have a beer, then ten.

I eyed the sign, imagining myself sitting down at the bar, taking that first cold sip and shooting the breeze with Kevin, a nice-enough guy who owned the place. Nice-enough was my standard, since nobody in bars 24/7 was nice. But when you're drinking, they're nice enough.

I couldn't think of a single reason *not* to go in. My father thought I relapsed, so I might as well make it true. Everything else was going to hell. I hated my brother. I was out of a job. Lemaire and Joe Ferguson were dead, with no hope of justice for either. I'd pissed off Jake, and my home group thought I was nuts. I wondered if AA would throw me out and whether I was right about Muttonchops. Maybe I was paranoid, or crazy.

Thud.

The flashback of Rigel came again. I closed my eyes and opened them again, but this time I spotted Emily in her car seat in the back seat. I just now remembered that we'd been singing Raffi together that fateful night, *a little white whale on the go*, before she'd fallen asleep, loving me, trusting me, and never dreaming that I'd forget she even existed for a Miller Lite.

I wasn't going to drink.

I started the ignition.

Time to go home and go to bed.

CHAPTER THIRTY-EIGHT

I had a sleepless night, feeling like a loose end to whatever conspiracy was out there. I tossed and turned, and I even double-checked the wire under the couch to see that it was still in place, sending Mango scurrying away.

Finally I fell asleep, but the next morning, I had to start over again and face reality.

I needed money.

GREG'S COIN & JEWELRY EXCHANGE, read the sign above a storefront in a strip mall, its entrance flanked by bay windows with closed blinds. The easiest thing to sell was my Rolex, and I'd been to two other shops trying to get a good price. My mother taught me to get three estimates, but I doubt she meant my graduation Rolex, with its sentimental value. My father didn't think a Rolex needed sentiment to have value.

I pressed the button next to the door and was buzzed into a clean, well-lit shop. It was farther away, but the other two shopkeepers had suggested I'd get a better price here. The walls were a bright white, and glistening display cases lined the room, containing gold and silver coins encased in plastic and an array of rings and bracelets. Above them hung a framed certificate that read PRECIOUS METALS DEALER'S LICENSE, so the store had more diplomas than me.

"Good morning, sir," said a man emerging from the back. He was in his fifties, with bristly hair atop a fleshy face and wire-rimmed glasses that sat low on his nose. He had on a neat white polo shirt with khakis and his name tag read GREG. He stepped up to a glass counter that held a large plastic calculator.

"Yes, I'm looking to sell a Rolex Submariner. It's about fifteen years old but I only wore it once. I have the stuff that goes with it." I opened my backpack and took out the padded green case with the watch, the registration, and the instruction manual, since a Rolex was fancy enough to require one.

"Thank you." Greg palmed the boxy green case and opened it up to reveal the glistening watch, still in its suede holder. "You weren't kidding. You have the extra links?"

"They're underneath."

"Good." Greg took out the watch and examined it, nodding. "Let me take this in the back a moment, if you don't mind."

"Go right ahead," I said, and Greg turned away just as a young girl who looked like his daughter emerged from the back, carrying a cardboard box that she set down heavily on the counter.

"Sorry for the mess," she said with an apologetic smile, showing braces. "We've got to get everything out of the office."

Greg glanced over his shoulder. "This is my daughter Lily. She's pitching in. A pipe broke in the back, and the office flooded. The walls are soaked, so are the files. Guys are coming at noon to tear out the carpets and put in humidifiers."

"That's too bad."

"Be right back." Greg went back into the office with Lily, who reemerged a moment later with another cardboard box that she put on the counter.

"Lily, if those boxes are heavy, I'm happy to help."

"No, thanks, it's only jewelry, see?" Lily opened the top flap, and inside were transparent baggies of jewelry with receipts. I peeked inside, startled at something orange that caught my eye—my mother's coral earrings.

Whoa. "Those are pretty," I said, pointing.

"These?" Lily plucked them out. "They're old, but I like them, too. You can't buy them yet. This is the hold box. We have to hold everything in here for seven days, in case it was stolen. We can't sell any of this until then."

"Can I take a look at them?"

"Sure." Lily handed me the baggie. "My dad will give you a good price if you come back later. He's very fair."

"Thanks." I handed her the bag, my mind racing. Whoever stole the coral earrings was our office burglar, either Rigel or his coconspirator.

Lily went in the back, and Greg reemerged with my Rolex. "This is in mint condition. Do you want to sell it or pawn it?"

"Sell it, but let me ask you about those coral earrings."

"Like Lily said, we have to hold them, in case the cops come in asking for them."

"Do they, usually?"

"No. They call looking for super-high-end jewelry like diamonds. Otherwise, nothing."

"Who brought them in? Do you remember?"

"No, but I scanned his driver's license. Anybody who sells me anything has to show a driver's license or a state ID. If we make a deal for your Rolex, you will, too."

"I'm curious, could I see the driver's license?"

Greg hesitated. "I don't do that."

"It's not against the law, is it?"

"No, but I don't do it."

"Does anybody ever ask?"

"No," Greg admitted.

"How much for my Rolex?"

"Ten grand. That's better than you'll do online, too."

Wow. "Tell you what. I won't haggle if you let me see that driver's license. And I'll come back to buy the earrings."

Lily returned with another box, and a smile. "Say yes, Dad. Three customers came in today, and he's the only one who offered to help me."

I hustled back to the car and looked at the driver's license on my phone. The photo showed a dark-haired man with a beefy face, large brown eyes, and thick lips. It wasn't Barry Rigel, and so it had to be one of his co-conspirators. It wasn't Muttonchops, either, so I might've wrongly accused him at the meeting.

I felt a shiver of excitement. The license identified the man as Elliott Thompson, 785 Moore Road, Exton, PA. I knew it was probably a fake name and address, but the picture had to be real. These thugs couldn't fake the photo because Greg would have checked it when they left the earrings, like he checked mine. So at least I knew what the mystery co-conspirator looked like. If I spotted him driving anywhere around me, at least I would know I was in trouble.

Still, I'd have to double-check.

I started the engine.

I had ten grand and a tank full of gas.

I was back in business.

I kept an eye on the rearview as I reached Moore Road, a suburban street abuzz with activity. Families piled into SUVs with kids in uniforms and cleats, unloaded reusable bags of groceries from hatchbacks, and mowed sun-dappled lawns. The leaf blowers were out in deafening force, which I hated. Leaf blowers are the only thing impervious to the Serenity Prayer.

I drove ahead, checking house numbers with ADT and Vector Security placards, looking for 785. I was in the low seven hundreds, so the Thompsons must have been at the end of the street on the left.

I continued down the block and spotted the Thompsons' up ahead, a white clapboard colonial with yellow shutters and a fieldstone addition. A dump truck with a red GOT MULCH? sign was blocking the street in front of the house, about to reverse into their driveway.

I braked for the truck, but also watched as a man and a woman emerged from the house, presumably Elliott Thompson and his wife. One look confirmed my theory that the driver's license had been fake. The Thompsons were Black, so definitely not the white thug who fenced my mother's earrings. The man in the photo was Fake Elliott Thompson, but he was still a real co-conspirator.

The dump truck pulled into the driveway, and Thompson gave me a friendly wave, acknowledging my waiting. I wished I could tell him his identity had been stolen, but I'd have to let it lie.

I cruised ahead, getting an idea. There was a way to test my theory that Fake Elliott Thompson was Rigel's co-conspirator, who could have been working for Stan, if Stan had been embezzling with

Lemaire. It struck me that conspiracies were like phone tag for criminals.

And this criminal had their number.

"Lillian?" I said when she picked up. "How are you?"

"Okay. How's Mango?"

"Wonderful, but that's not what I'm calling about. I just texted you a photo of somebody." I had sent her an enlarged picture of Fake Elliott Thompson, editing out the driver's license. "Tell me if you recognize him, like maybe you've seen him around the office?"

"No, I don't know who that is. Why?"

"I'm wondering if he might be one of Stan's friends, from the old days." I hadn't filled Lillian in on my meeting with Daniel, nor did I want to. If Stan was involved in the conspiracy, the less she knew the better. "I know from my dad that a lot of his old friends visit the office."

"They might, but I've only been there five years, and I sit in the back anyway. You'd have to ask somebody who's been there awhile."

"Like Mike Dedham?"

"Yes, he might know. He sits out front."

"Do you have his number?"

"No. We don't keep an office directory, and I never have a reason to call him."

"Do you know where he lives?"

"No." Lillian paused. "But he'll be at Neil's wake this afternoon. We're all going. It's open to the public."

CHAPTER THIRTY-NINE

Jacobson's Funeral Home was a modern octagonal building with smoked glass windows recessed in a brick façade and a pitched gray roof. A boxwood hedge lined its front on busy West Chester Pike, and its parking lot wrapped around the back of the building, for employees and hearses.

I slipped on my ball cap and sunglasses and parked in the back but was still able to see the main lot. Nobody goes around the back of a funeral home, so I assumed I wouldn't be spotted here, either by Fake Elliott Thompson, or my family, whom I expected to be here today.

The wake started at four o'clock, and I checked my watch. Three-twenty. My plan was to intercept Mike Dedham and find out if he could identify Fake Elliott Thompson in the photo. But I'd have to avoid being seen by my father and brother, who would show up in their never-ending custody battle over Stan.

I shifted lower in the seat, pulled down the brim of my ball cap, and waited. The first car to arrive contained three older women, and when they emerged in their black dresses, I assumed that one of them was Neil's mother because she had graying red hair and used a walker.

She looked grief-stricken, and my heart went out to her, though I remembered she had asked Daniel not to come. I couldn't help but think that he would have been a comfort to her now.

There were no cars until closer to four o'clock, then came a flurry of arrivals in a few cars I recognized. Lillian in her yellow VW, then Stan and his wife in his Ford Explorer. Other Runstan employees got out of their cars, and I shifted upward, waiting for Mike. Guests to a wake could come at any time, so I had no idea when he'd be getting here.

Two black Range Rovers pulled into the lot, and I could see my father alone in the first one. John followed him, and then I lost sight of them both after they parked around the front of the building.

Cars continued to pull into the lot afterward, but none were suspicious or had Fake Elliott Thompson behind the wheel. I recognized more employees from the office, but there were some I didn't know, whom I gathered were plant employees because they all seemed to know each other.

Then I noticed a red Prius parking near the entrance, and when the driver got out, I saw it was Mike. I grabbed my phone, got out of the car, and made a beeline for him. He was moving quickly, his head down in a dark suit. He looked up as I approached, but didn't say anything, and I realized he didn't recognize me.

"Mike, it's TJ." I took off the cap and sunglasses.

"TJ, how you been?" Mike broke into a smile. Cars pulled in around us, parking.

"Good, thanks. Can I ask you something before you go inside?"

"Sure." Mike stopped, and I showed him the picture of Fake Elliott Thompson on my phone.

"Do you recognize this guy?"

"It's hard to see in the sun." Mike squinted at the photo. People getting out of their cars looked over, then went inside the funeral home. "Hmm, why, yes, he looks familiar."

"Do you know him?"

"I don't know," Mike answered vaguely, then looked up. "Why?"

"I'm wondering if he's an old friend of Stan's, if he's been around the office? Like from the early days?"

"He *does* look kind of familiar." Mike looked at the picture again. "I don't remember. But you know, I have some pictures at home from back in the day."

"Would they jar your memory?"

"Possibly, and sometimes I write the names on the backs."

Yes. "Could I see them? Maybe come over after the wake, if you're free?"

"Sure, that's fine. I live just down the road, in Broomall. But why?"

Suddenly I heard someone shout my name, and Mike and I looked over to see John hustling in our direction. I didn't know when he'd spotted me, but my father was standing at the entrance to the funeral home. Soon Stan appeared beside him.

"TJ, what are you doing here?" John grabbed my arm, panicky. "You're not welcome here. You have to go, *now*."

"Get your hands off of me." I wrenched my arm free in time to see Stan charging down the steps toward me, with my father on his heels.

"TJ!" John pushed me back. "Go, get out of here!"

"Get outta here, you drunk!" Stan stalked toward me, pointing. "Get outta here!"

"TJ, where's your car?" John asked, wild-eyed, but just then Stan shoved him aside, grabbed me by my shirt, and threw me against Mike's car.

"You junkie!"

"Whoa!" I put my hands up, fending him off. John and Mike pulled Stan off me, and my father stood behind them. People stopped, horrified at the scene, and one tall man in a well-tailored suit jogged over.

"Stan?" the man said, incredulous behind designer glasses. "What's going on?"

"I'm throwing out the trash," Stan answered, hastily smoothing down his tie, suddenly on his best behavior.

"See you later, TJ. I'm in the book." Mike met my eye meaningfully, then headed toward the funeral home.

"Okay, Mike." Shaky, I started to walk back to my car as my brother greeted the tall man.

"Good to see you again, Asit," John was saying. "Dad, meet Asit Shah, in-house counsel at Vuarnex. Of course you know, they're Runstan's acquirer."

"TJ, what was *that* all about earlier?" Mike sat across the table from me. We were in his small kitchen, under an amber fixture that cast a warm glow. His dark tie was loosened, and his shoulders looked bony in his thin shirt.

"Do you really want to know?"

"Good point." Mike lifted an eyebrow. "No. You don't have to tell me more. I don't want to get in the middle. So we never met tonight and we never had the conversation we're about to have. You follow me?"

"Yes."

"But I'll tell *you* something: That fight in front of Asit was *not* good."

"Because he's from Vuarnex?"

"Yes. He's running the acquisition for them. We call him the Shah.

We're on strict instructions to kiss his ass, and we do. We pucker up *good*."

"So he's who my brother found to make the deal with Runstan?"

"Yes. We never see any of the principals, just him. He comes into the office from time to time to meet with Stan and your brother. Sometimes Neil. That tussle in the parking lot could cause repercussions."

"How so?"

"How can I put this?" Mike paused. "Vuarnex is big league. Runstan is bush league. We're not even a fish getting swallowed by a whale. We're more like a fish getting swallowed by the *sea*."

"Okay."

"I was surprised to see the Shah at the wake. He's a busy man. He knew Neil, but not *that* well. Now some people might think his coming was classy, like a gesture of respect."

"Right, that's what I thought."

"On the other hand, he's a cool customer and he plays it close to the vest. He has to be having doubts, now that we're coming down to the short strokes. Neil dies by suicide during the acquisition? The Shah might have a question or two about the way the company's run, about its stability, overall health, *corporate culture*." Mike snorted. "You know Stan never met anything with culture his whole damn life."

I smiled.

"So the Shah comes to the wake, he's got his doubts, and what does he see? Stan attacks his lawyer's *brother*? With his other lawyer, your *father*, in the mix? You know the Shah's gonna start asking questions about the Devlins and a lot else. He's gonna want to know what's up."

I realized I'd given my father and brother some credit for getting Stan off me, but now I saw it in a different light. They weren't worried about me, they were worried about the acquisition.

"So who knows what the Shah thinks?" Mike shrugged. "Whether

Neil died by suicide or was murdered, neither makes Runstan look good. Now Stan looks *nuts.* This is *not* how they play at Vuarnex."

It rang true. "Mike, what do you do at Runstan again?"

"I'm HR. I was the first Black professional hired in the eighties after the first wave of Title VII cases. You're too young to know what it was like back then. Racism, sexism, everything was tolerated in the workplace. You could call somebody the N-word, you could touch a woman's behind. It was all laughed off as a joke."

"The bad old days."

"Yes. Stan hired me because he had to. He thinks HR is a necessary evil, and I'm the entire department. He won't spend another dime."

"I understand." I went for it. "Mike, did you ever get wind of any financial improprieties at the company? Like Neil embezzling, with or without Stan?"

Mike blinked. "My job is to mind the people, not the money. If there's shenanigans with the books, I don't know about it."

"Would you be shocked?"

Mike smiled slightly. "Do I look shocked?"

Duly noted. "Here's what I don't get. Vuarnex is doing their own due diligence, and if there are any financial improprieties, they're going to find them, right?"

"True."

"So are they willing to overlook them? They have to be, or they wouldn't have gone this far."

"You want my take? It depends on what the improprieties are. The problem isn't when you steal from the company, the problem is when you steal from the *government.* Unreported income, tax evasion." Mike clucked, folding his arms. "Vuarnex can't overlook that. They're *not* going to acquire Runstan if that's what's going on. The rest, maybe they overlook. It's all about the deal, and the acquisition will bring in way more than any embezzlement would take."

"If the acquisition doesn't go through, does that affect you?"

"No, I'm retiring next month. It makes no never-mind to me whether we get acquired or not. I already gave my notice, and my pension will kick in."

"Do the employees stand to gain by the acquisition?"

"No. Only a handful in admin will stay, and their salary remains the same. The only person who benefits from the acquisition is Stan, and he's gonna make a fortune. But only if he keeps the wheels on this thing long enough. Before somebody figures out what's going on. Like you."

I met his eye. "Do you have those pictures?"

I stood at the table with Mike looking down at a photograph, its edges scalloped and colors faded with time. It was taken in Stan's office at Runstan and showed three twentysomething men in T-shirts, with big grins and full heads of hair. A young Stan was in the middle, flanked by a young Mike Dedham and a man whose face was blurry and half out of the frame. He looked like Fake Elliott Thompson in the driver's license, but I couldn't be sure.

I pointed at the blurry face. "Who's this guy?"

"Hold on." Mike turned the picture over, and names were written on the back: *Me, Stan, Ryan*. "I remember him. Ryan Martell. He was a buddy of Stan's from the old days in Philly. I think he was a union steward, Local 98, IBEW."

"The electrical union."

"Yes. You know its business manager? Johnny Doc?"

"No. Who's he?"

"John Dougherty. He was Local 98's business manager since 1993. He's been indicted for embezzlement of union assets, wire fraud, mail fraud, honest services fraud. A conspiracy between him and a few others." Mike snorted. "If Stan's helping himself to company money, he learned from the best."

"Wow." I made a mental note, then returned to the photo. "Who took the picture?"

"Janine, Stan's then-wife. That's why it's crappy. She was loopy."

"Let's compare." I set my phone down next to the old photo and compared the facial fragment to the picture on my phone. "I see a similarity, but I'm not sure."

"I think it's him." Mike pointed. "See? The way the cheek curves?"

"Right." I wondered if there was another way to identify the man. "Would my dad know Martell?"

"No, this was early on, before we were incorporated. Stan didn't have a pot to piss in back then. He'd just married Janine."

"Where's Martell now?"

Mike shook his head. "I don't know."

I drove home, multitasking at stoplights. I kept checking if I was being followed while I googled Ryan Martell and got a slew of entries. I followed up and searched each picture, but no luck yet. I turned onto my street, surprised to see a black SUV parked in front of my house and two men in suits talking to my neighbor Susanne in her driveway.

I swallowed hard. I didn't know who the men were, but it looked like official business. One man was tall and older with military bearing and he held a plastic folder with a large gold emblem. The other man was short and younger, and they both had an authoritative demeanor that only cops give off. All this time I'd been worrying about the bad guys, but not the allegedly good guys.

I cruised ahead slowly and Susanne pointed at me, then the two men turned in my direction.

The SUV was parked with the grille facing me, so I couldn't see the license plate. I was betting it was a blue municipal one.

I considered driving past my house, but I was still on parole and couldn't play games. My phone rang on the seat next to me, and I looked over to see it was my mother, but I couldn't take the call now.

I pulled into the driveway, got out of the car, and forced a smile. "Hey, Susanne!"

"Hi, TJ!" she called back, then went inside her house as the two suits crossed the driveway toward me, the older one in the lead.

"TJ Devlin?"

"Yes?"

"I'm Bill Willoughby, sergeant detective of the Chester County District Attorney's Office, and this is my partner, Detective Jim Balleu."

Shit. "Nice to meet you, gentlemen." I shook their hands.

"Got a minute?" Detective Willoughby asked.

We all knew it was rhetorical.

CHAPTER FORTY

I showed the detectives to the couch, fighting a case of nerves. I wasn't sure about my rights. I didn't know if I needed a lawyer. Even if I did, I wouldn't call John. I realized the bug under the couch would record our conversation, but I didn't know which way that would cut. There was nothing I could do about it anyway.

"Can I offer you gentlemen a glass of water or anything?" I asked, assuming they knew that no-alcohol was a condition of my parole.

"No, thanks," Detective Willoughby answered, opening his plastic folder, which had a fresh legal pad and a silver Cross pen in a holder. He was in his late fifties with hooded brown eyes and a sunglasses tan on a long face with a small mouth.

"I'm good." Detective Balleu was a young stud with a bump on his nose and his hair slicked back with gel.

"So how can I help you?" I asked, hearing an echo of my father's hail-fellow-well-met. Meanwhile my phone rang again with my mother calling, but I put it on silent.

"We wanted to open up a line of communication. We hear from your PO that you've been checking in when you're supposed to, staying clean."

"Yes."

"And you're employed as an investigator at your family's law firm?" Detective Willoughby looked at me expectantly, and I knew I couldn't lie to him. Any false statements I made could be grounds for revoking my parole and sending me back to prison. Under the law, cops were allowed to lie to me, but I wasn't allowed to lie to them. So much for justice being equal.

"Well, until recently."

"What happened?"

"I got fired, but I have a job with my sister, investigating one of her cases."

"I see." Detective Willoughby made a note. "Did you tell your PO?"

"Not yet, it just happened, and I don't see him for another three weeks."

"I see." Detective Willoughby nodded. "We heard about the burglary at your family's law firm. That's a damn shame."

"Yes, they took the laptops and vandalized the office, including my own stuff."

"Do you know anything about who could have done that?"

"The burglary?" I swallowed hard, entering dangerous territory. "No, we met with the police that night, and I told them what I know."

"That was before the fatal accident at Glen Meade Apartments? A man was killed, Barry Rigel? You were there, at the scene?"

"Yes," I admitted, shifting in the chair.

"Did you tell your PO about that?"

"It just happened. I'll tell him when I see him."

"Okay." Detective Willoughby made another note.

I held my breath, waiting for the follow-up, every muscle tensed.

Detective Willoughby looked up. "Tell me, do you know a Stan Malinowski? He owns a company called Runstan."

I didn't know why the detective was switching gears, but it kept me off-balance. "Yes, he's a client."

"Were you at a wake today for one of Runstan's employees, Neil Lemaire?"

"Yes," I admitted, telling myself to stay calm. I wasn't about to play into their hands, and they didn't necessarily know anything. There were a lot of people who had seen the fight in the parking lot, and any one of them could have said something. Anyway it wasn't a parole violation to get jumped by an irate CEO.

"Did you know Neil Lemaire?"

"No, I never met the man," I answered truthfully. I felt like we were shading custodial interrogation, like John had said the other night, but nobody was reading me any Miranda warnings. I didn't know if I should pull the plug. I didn't want them reporting me to my PO, so I was damned if I did and damned if I didn't.

"If you didn't know Neil Lemaire, why did you go to his wake?"

"I wanted to meet someone who would be there."

Detective Willoughby consulted his notepad. "Were you at Dutton Run Park the night Lemaire died?"

Oh no. I flashed on that rainy night. I'd spoken to a cop and reporters, so I couldn't deny being on the scene. "Detective Willoughby, I don't know why you're asking these questions. Or why you're here."

"We wanted to talk with you informally." Detective Willoughby shrugged. "A lot has been happening around you—a burglary, a traffic fatality, a suicide. You're going to have a lot to tell your PO when you see him."

"I'm not sure you answered my question," I said, and just then, Mango bolted out from under the couch.

Detective Willoughby startled. "Sheesh, that cat is fast."

"Yes, she is."

"My wife loves cats. Me, not so much."

"She's a nice cat," I said, trying to be casual. I didn't know how much they knew. I felt as if we were playing cat and mouse, literally. And I didn't like being the mouse.

"By the way, when did you get a cat?"

"Recently."

"Where?"

"From a friend, named Lillian," I answered, beginning to worry.

"It's Neil Lemaire's cat, isn't it?"

I swallowed hard. "Yes, I heard it needed a home so I took it in."

"We spoke with Lillian Duvall, the bookkeeper at Runstan. She said you went to his house with her. Is that correct?"

Ugh. "Yes."

"That's a lot of interaction about a man that you didn't even know."

"It wasn't about Neil Lemaire, it was about the cat. I was with my brother and father at Runstan, and Lillian told me the cat needed a home."

"So it's about a cat?"

"Yes."

"I see." Detective Willoughby met my gaze with apparent directness. "TJ, I'll be straight with you. We're thinking you've gotten yourself jammed up. If so, your best option is to get ahead of this. You know how it works from the last time around. If we can talk, maybe we can arrive at a deal."

My heart began to pound. "What fix do you think I'm in?"

"Why don't you tell us?"

"There's nothing to tell."

"I see." Detective Willoughby shrugged again. "Lillian said you spent some time in Neil Lemaire's office at home and at work."

Gulp. "Not much. I was at the house with her and we were looking for the cat, who wouldn't come out. She likes to hide, as you just saw. And at the office I was just talking to Lillian, comforting her. She was upset about his death. That's all."

"I see."

I stayed silent.

"Then it won't matter to you, one way or the other, that we're reopening the investigation into Neil Lemaire's death."

"It doesn't," I told him, masking my surprise.

"Our investigation is in the early stages, and we wanted to come to you in an informal way. We want to remind you that if you have any involvement in any type of crime, in *any* criminal conspiracy whatsoever, it's a violation of your parole. For you, that means you go to jail."

I felt a bolt of fear that was almost electrical. "Of course, yes, I know that."

"Let me give you some advice. Windows open but they don't stay open. They close, too. Do you know what I mean?"

"Right, I know." I struggled to look unflustered. He was trying to turn the screws.

"So, last chance, let's talk turkey." Detective Willoughby crossed his legs. "Have you been involved in anything you want to tell us about?"

"No, I haven't." I used to be a good liar, but the stakes had never been this high. Meanwhile my phone rang silently again, my mother's smiling photo flashing on my home screen, incongruous right now.

"Our problem is that the circumstances raise a lot of questions. We were hoping you could answer them."

"What kind of circumstances?"

"The ones we just talked about. Your involvement with Lemaire and Rigel. We thought you could fill in some blanks."

"I don't think I can, I'm sorry."

"You're not going to be the only person we approach, you know. The early bird gets the worm."

"Okay," I said noncommittally. They evidently thought I was working with others. I wondered if they knew about Fake Elliott Thompson.

"We're reexamining the circumstances of Lemaire's death, and Rigel's. The circumstances suggest there's a connection, and the connection goes through you."

Please God. "Circumstances don't mean anything," I said, grasping at straws.

"We have more than circumstances, TJ."

Gulp. "Like what?"

"We have a statement from your brother, John."

Jesus. I couldn't speak. I didn't know what John had told them. I didn't know what he was trying to do. I didn't understand anything. I struggled to remain impassive. Detectives Willoughby and Balleu were watching me carefully, which was undoubtedly why they had sprung this on me out of the blue.

Detective Willoughby paused. "We have a corroborating statement from your father, as well."

Dad? I jumped to my feet, a fight-or-flight reflex. "You need to go. I'm not answering any more questions without a lawyer."

"Have it your way." Detective Willoughby slid his pen into its holder and closed his folder.

I reeled, going to the door and holding it open. The two men got up and walked out, and Detective Willoughby turned to me.

"Don't leave the jurisdiction, TJ."

"Understood," I said, closing the door.

I ran for my phone.

CHAPTER FORTY-ONE

I sank onto the couch, my mind spinning. I couldn't process what I'd been told quickly enough. My brother had given some kind of statement against me, and so had my father.

I couldn't believe what was going on. Somehow they must have suggested I was involved with Lemaire's death, and now the cops were investigating it as a murder. I didn't know what to do next, but I knew what *not* to do, which was call my brother or father. If I called them, they could lie to the detectives about what I'd said. I couldn't trust them, ever again.

Tears came to my eyes, and I didn't know if it was rage, pain, or incredulity. I couldn't begin to parse my emotions. They felt like a fog blinding me, confusing me. The phone rang in my hand, my mother calling again.

"Mom?" I answered, panicky.

"TJ, I've been calling. There's two detectives who want to speak with you—"

"I know. Hold on." I remembered the bug under the couch, got up, and hurried to the back door, going outside.

"TJ, are you there?"

"Yes," I answered, closing the door behind me. "Mom, John and Dad gave statements to the police? What about? What the hell's going on?"

"I know, I know, I just found out about John—"

"What did they say? Where are you? Where's John and Dad? Are they together? The cops are investigating Lemaire's death as a murder. Did John tell them I had something to do with it? And Dad? What did he say? What does he know? What happened? What the hell's going on?"

"TJ, one question at a time—"

"Mom, I could go back to prison. They told me not to leave the jurisdiction. You know what that means. I think they're looking to charge *me* with Lemaire's death."

"Honey, I know," my mother said, and then I heard a sniffle. I couldn't live with myself if she got lockjaw again.

"Okay, I'll calm down." I sat down in the chair at the outside table. "Just tell me what happened."

"Okay, well." My mother cleared her throat. "Your father and I were at the office. We're trying to put everything back together after the burglary. He came back from the wake and he was upset. Evidently you were there and you got into a fight with Stan and—"

"Hold on, I didn't get into a fight with Stan. Stan attacked me."

"Why were you even there?"

"Mom, I have bigger problems right now, like why my brother and father are turning against me."

"No one's turning against you."

"Then what happened?"

My mother sighed. "John went to the police after the wake and gave them a statement."

"About what?" I asked, horrified, as it dawned on me. While I was meeting with Mike, John had gone to the police. "What did he say?"

"We don't know. It has something to do with Lemaire and Runstan. We don't know the particulars. We just know that he went."

"How do you know that?"

"The detectives came to the office while we were there. We thought they came because of the burglary, but they started asking questions about Neil Lemaire. We asked them why, and they told us John gave them a statement. Your father hit the ceiling. We were completely blindsided."

"Of course." I realized the detectives *wanted* to blindside my parents, the way they had blindsided me. They must have gone to the office right away, after John had made his statement. He'd dropped a bomb and wanted to see us scatter, the Devlins in disarray. "So did you ask them what John said in his statement?"

"Yes, but they wouldn't tell us. They said it was official police business and it was confidential. All they would say is that it was about the death of Neil Lemaire."

"Did John say I was involved in his death?"

My mother hesitated. "I don't know for sure, but they asked us if we thought you were involved."

"No!" I tried not to shout. "Mom, did he accuse me? They're reopening the case, so he must have at least suggested I did it."

"No, John would never. Look, TJ, we don't have all the facts right now. We can't jump to conclusions. Your father's calling John, but he's not picking up. Believe me, your father isn't happy he left us in the dark. Runstan's your father's client, and now he looks like an idiot to Stan. So do I, and I'm the one who did his divorce. If John knows something the police need to know, he's handled it in the worst way possible."

"Then why did Dad give the cops a statement, too? What did he say?"

"He didn't give a statement."

"The detectives said he did."

"They're mischaracterizing what he said. He answered their questions. I don't regard that as a statement per se."

"*I* do. More importantly, the cops do. What the hell did Dad say?"

"The only thing he said was that you relapsed."

I felt stricken. "Mom, that's a parole violation. They could pick me up because of that *alone*. They could send me back—"

"They're not going to. He told them you've got it under control and you're back on track."

"Why did he tell them I relapsed in the first place?"

"He had to answer truthfully."

"But I told you I didn't relapse."

"He thinks you did."

"What did he say when they asked him if I was involved with Lemaire's death?"

"He said he didn't know anything about it."

"Are you serious right now?" My heart wrenched. It wasn't anger, it was hurt. "Really, Mom? He doesn't *know*? Does Dad really think I'd *kill* somebody? Couldn't he have said that I'd never commit murder?"

"Honey, please," my mother said, but her voice wavered. "Your father said he doesn't think it was murder. He said he'd been to Runstan and everybody there said it was a suicide, that they should know best and that he has no reason to doubt that. The police haven't retracted the coroner's finding, so let's not get ahead of ourselves."

"But they're investigating whether it was murder. He could have at least vouched for me."

"You know your father. He was defusing the situation, trying not to antagonize them."

"He was trying to suck up to them, and God forbid he go against John." I felt like the family was taking sides, dividing into factions against each other. "Did *you* answer their questions, too?"

"They didn't ask me anything. They thought I was 'the wife,' so I played 'the wife.'"

Ouch. "But, Mom, couldn't you have said, 'There's no way my son had any involvement'? Couldn't you have stood up for me?"

"Honey, I never volunteer information, ever. It goes against every cell in my body." My mother's voice took on an authoritative tone. "All it does is provoke another question. I'm sure your father had the same instinct."

I realized that they had gone into lawyer mode, not parent mode. "Mom, what about Gabby? Does she know what's going on?"

"No, I'm going to call her now. I was trying to get to you first. TJ, I'm doing everything I can to help you. You need a lawyer, and I've already called Angela, but she hasn't called me back yet."

"Angela Martinez, from before?"

"Yes, she's the best, and I'm sure she'll be happy to represent you again. She'll know what to do. She'll get you out of this."

"Nobody can get me out of this, Mom." I didn't think activating the privilege machine would help this time. John and Dad *were* the privilege machine.

"Angela will be aggressive. She'll back them down."

"Do you think she can get a copy of John's statement? I want to know what he said. I swear to God, I think he's pinning Lemaire's murder on me. I think he might be *framing* me."

"That's ridiculous."

"I don't know him anymore, Mom. I wouldn't put it past him. Everything I did for him makes me look guilty. I investigated Lemaire. I talked to reporters. I talked to cops. I got into Lemaire's computers. I went after Barry Rigel. All of it makes me look guilty as sin."

"I'm sure John didn't accuse you. Why would he?"

"I don't know," I answered, then it struck me. "The fight at the wake happened in front of in-house counsel for Vuarnex. We know John wants to save the acquisition and his fee. He can't shut me up, so maybe he's trying to discredit me. Framing me for murder does that effectively, don't you think?"

"No, that is absurd—"

"Stan would have the same motive. They could be in it together." I made myself think through the next logical step. "What if . . . John killed Lemaire?"

My mother gasped.

"John's the one who knows Lemaire, Mom. Maybe John was embezzling with him. Or Stan, or both of them. What if John was embezzling with Stan and Lemaire?"

"What? Why would he? John has money. So does Stan, and after the acquisition—"

"But what if the scheme started before Vuarnex came into the picture? The acquisition offer came in through John, but out of the blue to him. Maybe Lemaire wouldn't stay quiet about the embezzling. Maybe he threatened to tell Vuarnex—"

"TJ, your imagination's running away with you. I'm not going to entertain this conversation. It's wrong, and you're getting yourself all worked up."

"I'm thinking aloud, trying to figure it out." I didn't know where Fake Elliott Thompson fit in, unless Stan had hired him from the old days, but I couldn't be sure of that yet.

"TJ, let's talk later. I have to call Angela again."

"Thanks, Mom, I love you."

"Love you, too. We'll fix this."

I hung up, afraid that I'd be going back to prison. If I did, I knew I'd have one big regret.

There was something I had to do, and it couldn't wait.

Only one thing mattered to me. Everything else be damned.

CHAPTER FORTY-TWO

Carrie opened her door, her hazel eyes rounding with surprise and her pretty mouth flattening when she saw it was me. She started to close the door, but I stopped it with my hand.

"Wait, please, I just want to talk to you. Can't we just talk?"

"Go away, TJ."

"Just for a minute?"

"Are you drunk?"

"No, I'm sober. Really."

"I don't believe you." Carrie folded her arms over a thin white tank top with cutoffs I remembered too well. Her long chestnut hair was in an adorably messy ponytail.

"It's true. I'll be sober two years on June seventh. You know the date."

"Of course." Carrie's eyes flashed with anger. "It's the day you left Emily in the *car*."

"Yes, and I'm sorry, so sorry, and I've been punished for that, and I punish myself for that—"

"Good, you should feel like absolute shit." Carrie scowled. "*Anything* could have happened to her that night. There's a million possibilities and believe me, I know every one. They still keep me up at night."

"I know, it's awful, it's why I pleaded guilty, I am guilty, I was guilty, and I—"

"Forget it." Carrie put her hands up. "I don't wanna get into it."

"But part of you does—you must, because you just did get into it, and I want to hear it, I really do, you'll feel better—"

"Is this you 'making amends'?" Carrie made air quotes.

"No, but it's the same idea. Making amends is so people I did wrong can express how they feel, and I did you the wrongest—"

"You're here for yourself, not me."

"No, I'm here for both of us," I told her, and suddenly I had clarity on something I hadn't before. "Listen, we were together from when she was little. We can't act like that didn't happen. We ended in a horrible way, and we can't act like that didn't happen, either. So can we talk about what needs to be talked about? I've wanted to come by so many times. I've been by the house a million times."

Carrie frowned. "Okay, stalker."

"Well, not a million, and I saved Emily's purple bunny. It was on the driveway, and you would have killed it."

Carrie didn't smile, but she didn't interrupt me, either.

"Look, I know there's nothing more important to you than her, and you guys were my life, and I just can't let go without talking about this. Part of me thinks you can't, either."

"You're wrong. It's done, after all this time." Carrie shifted on her bare feet and the door opened wider, revealing a long IKEA box on the living room floor behind her.

"Let me guess—you went to IKEA and bought something impossible to build? Emily's at Seth's this weekend? And you've been cursing for two hours?"

"No," Carrie answered, but she smiled just the slightest.

"Okay, three hours."

Carrie laughed, a light sound I'd forgotten until now, one that struck such a deep chord in me. I felt the connection between us, as weightless as a musical note but powerful enough to evoke all the love and resurrect all the hope.

"Carrie, please, let me in," I said, my own heart talking. "We can talk, and I'll make the IKEA thing."

"I can make it. I know how."

"I know you know, but you *hate* to. I'll make it for you, and we can talk." I took another peek at the IKEA box. "It looks big, like a bureau. It's not Hemnes, is it? Please tell me you didn't buy another Hemnes."

"It's for Emily, to match mine."

"Let me do it, please. I built the other one, and Hemnes is the Everest of IKEA. I'm gonna summit."

"No."

"Please?"

"Okay, enough." Carrie opened the door and I stepped inside, breathing in the vanilla-scented candles and the fish stick smells from dinner. The family room was just as I remembered, cozy with the white Backsälen couch we bought together that day. The walls were the same rose color, still lined with three floral watercolors we framed at a do-it-yourself place.

"I remember when we framed those," I blurted out, with a pang.

"So do I. You bled on the matte."

"Because X-Acto knives are mean."

"No, because you were drunk. Right?"

It caught me up short. "Yes."

Carrie threw up her hands in frustration. "How did I miss that? How did I miss any of it? I don't understand, really. I don't know how I didn't know."

"I hid it from you."

"But why couldn't I tell?" Carrie pursed her lips. "Was I in that much denial?"

"No, I deceived you. I'm great at it."

"But you seemed fine."

"There's such a thing as a functioning alcoholic, Carrie. It's me. I'm an all-American high-functioner. I pre-gamed every time I saw you, I pre-gamed every *day.* I was hiding in plain sight, and lying, too." I met her eye with difficulty. "Remember when I told you I got migraines in the morning? I was hungover."

Carrie's frowned. "You drove us everywhere, both of us. You endangered us, every single time."

"I know, I know." I felt a deep pang of guilt. "I told myself I wasn't, but I lied to myself, too. I'm sorry."

"My God." Carrie looked away, putting her hands on her hips. "The thing is, the reality I lived wasn't real."

"I understand. I'm sorry about that, I really am."

"Enough. Build the bureau, then maybe we can talk."

"Okay." I sat on the floor, picked up the Hemnes booklet, and flipped through page after page of incomprehensible diagrams. "Look, only three hundred easy steps."

"I suppose I should offer you something to drink. What would you like?"

"Diet Coke."

"You hate Diet Coke."

"I know, it's penance."

Carrie turned on her heel and went to the kitchen, and I tried to accustom myself to the fact that I was really here. I also prayed I could figure out the Hemnes directions. The last time I built one of these I was drunk, which was the only way to make sense of IKEA instructions.

Carrie returned with a glass of Diet Coke and set it on the coffee table. "Done yet?"

"No, because I have to curse. It's step one."

Carrie sat down on the couch, leaning forward on her elbows. "What happened the night you left her in the car?"

I put the directions aside, since the build-first-talk-later plan had changed. "Okay, I can explain—"

"No long intro, please. I want to know what you were thinking, TJ. I want to know how you left my daughter in a car while you got drunk in a dive bar."

"Right." I'd rehearsed this conversation so many times, but I was getting stage fright. The script didn't come back to me, so I spoke from the heart. "I'll tell you the terrible, terrible truth. I just forgot she was there. We were driving home from Sesame Place, and she was exhausted. We sang, then she fell asleep, and I thought about beer. I pulled over at the first bar I saw, and I forgot she was back there."

Carrie blinked, her lips parting. "That's terrible."

"Yes, it's terrible, that's how you know it's true. I'm very, very sorry for it. I'll be sorry for it my whole life."

"It could have been hot out. If it were hot, she'd be dead. It was *June*."

"I know." I shuddered, having thought the same thing myself so many times. "I'm guilty. I really am."

Carrie looked at me evenly. "I'm not going to make you feel good about this."

"You don't have to."

"I don't need your permission."

"Fair enough."

"It's unforgivable."

"I agree, even if you forgive me, I'll never forgive myself." I moved closer to her. "What I did, it was a terrible thing, and it changed everything. It sent me to prison. It ended us."

"I knew you drank, TJ. I just thought you drank a normal amount." Carrie hesitated. "Wait, I take that back. I mean, there were times I thought you drank too much, and we talked about that, remember?"

"Yes." I remembered. It took her a while to get after me, but she did.

"But it was just beer, and I didn't think you were an *alcoholic.* I know it sounds stupid, but *everybody* drinks beer. My father drinks beer. My brother brews beer in his basement. Hell, *I* drink beer."

"I know," I said, watching her try to think aloud.

"I would never *ever* think you'd do that to Emily."

"I know, I understand."

"You were so good with her."

"She was a joy. She *is* a joy."

"I know you loved her, I know you did."

"I did, I do," I said, my chest wrenching. *I love you, too.*

"And she loved you."

I felt my heart thud. I couldn't say anything. I didn't trust myself not to cry, and this wasn't supposed to be about me. Meanwhile Carrie's face was softening, and she eyed me with a characteristic honesty that was the most beautiful thing about her. I could see that she wanted to connect, that her heart was open, and that what I'd done had hurt her so badly.

"It messed me up, I stopped trusting myself. I didn't trust my instincts." Carrie shook her head. "I was a mess, a *mess*, but I went to therapy, and it helped. I figured a lot of things out."

"Me, too."

"I don't know why it took me so long to go. Therapy's a good thing."

"Yes, absolutely, I agree."

"It's, like, everybody should go. I still go, and you should hear me,

I tell everybody. I even went to an Al-Anon meeting. I learned about my own father, and now when I look back, I think his drinking was a problem, too. I understand myself so much better now."

"I agree, it just helps you make changes, right? I mean, everything's do-it-yourself, isn't it?" I gestured at the framed watercolors. "We framed the pictures, do-it-yourself. We built the furniture, do-it-yourself. Maybe we make ourselves, too. We start out like parts in a box, but it's not you until you *build* you."

Carrie blinked. "Did you just think of that?"

"Yes." I smiled, feeling happy and free for the first time in a long while. "Look at me, having insights. Sober insights." I caught myself. "Except there's no such thing as drunk insights."

Carrie smiled tentatively. "You do seem . . . different."

"I am. I think better, I'm clearer. I try to be mindful, grateful. I know it sounds hokey, but it's true."

"It doesn't sound *that* hokey." Carrie seemed to still, her eyes newly glistening and her lower lip beginning to tremble. "All this time, TJ, I was so mad at you. I *hated* you. We lost everything because of you. We lost each other. Emily lost, too."

My throat caught, since it was just how I felt. "I know."

A tear spilled down Carrie's cheek. "I hated you for what you did, but . . . I guess I never stopped loving you."

"I love you, too," I said to her, feeling a wave of relief wash over me, and in the next moment, she was in my arms.

I woke up naked with Carrie sleeping on my chest. We'd made love, and I'd finished the bureau, which now stood in the middle of the dark room. I breathed in, grateful I had her back. I felt like I had a second chance and my life was starting over. I would get to see Emily again, I could get back on track, and I'd make everything up to both of them.

Carrie awoke with a start and propped herself up. "Oh no. What time is it? TJ, you have to go."

"Now, why?" I stretched, enjoying my happy drowsy feeling. "It's the middle of the night."

"You have to go." Carrie scrambled over me and off the couch. "I'm going away."

"Oh, okay, where?"

"Upstate New York." Carrie slipped into her tank top and shorts, then turned on the lamp. "TJ, last night was a mistake. I shouldn't have done it, it was wrong. I'm engaged."

"What?" I asked, confused. "What are you talking about?"

"I'm engaged. I'm getting married."

"No, wait, what are you saying?"

"I'm sorry, please get dressed and go. I have to pack. He's picking me up at seven-thirty."

I felt stunned, incredulous. "But we just—"

"It was a moment of weakness."

"No, it was love. I love you. I thought we were getting back—"

"No, we're not. I didn't say that."

"You said you loved me."

Carrie's eyes glistened, anguished. "I love him, too, and he's better for me and Emily. Please, go."

"Really?" I felt my heart break all over again.

"Go!"

CHAPTER FORTY-THREE

I hit the gas, driving on autopilot. I was reeling. I didn't know what just happened with Carrie. I couldn't understand. I'd gone from happy to miserable so fast it made my head spin. I thought we'd just gotten back together. She hadn't mentioned another guy when we talked. I lost her all over again.

I'm engaged. I'm getting married.

I turned left, heading anywhere. The night was dark and the streets empty. Tears blurred my eyes. My heart hurt with how much I wanted her. We'd been so good together, so happy. Tonight had been all I ever wanted. Her arms, her skin, her hair, her kiss.

I love him, too, and he's better for me and Emily.

I wiped my eyes, realizing something I hadn't before. I'd thought that if I really got sober, Carrie would take me back again. She had, at first. She *wanted* me back sober, and I wanted to be with her sober. Maybe I'd gotten sober *for her*, like she was my reward for giving up drinking. But in the end, it hadn't worked. She didn't want me either way, drinking or sober. We'd never be together. She was marrying someone else. I couldn't even hope for her anymore. It was over.

Go!

I turned right, wiping my eyes again on my sleeve. I had nothing, and my mess of a life came back to me. My brother was framing me for murder. My father thought I was a drunk and a loser. My mother was heartbroken. My sister had to prop me up with a job on a case we'd never win. My family was breaking up, and I didn't know how we would ever be the Devlins again. I wondered what it really meant to be a Devlin in the first place.

I cried as I drove. I felt lost. I felt myself sliding, weakening. I couldn't stay strong anymore. I felt sorry for myself. I'd never felt sorrier for myself.

I turned right, then left. I drove without thinking, trying to get it together. Maybe I really was what everybody thought I was, just a drunk.

I was caving, crumbling, breaking down. I wanted to give up, to give in, to surrender. I'd been battling not to drink every damn day, but I was tired, so tired, *too* tired.

I couldn't go another day, another night, another minute. I was hanging on to sobriety by my fingernails, but they were breaking off. It was the 714th day, and I was giving up.

The car came to a stop as if it had driven itself here.

I knew where I was, but it looked different. Porty's had been my bar, but it was gone. ELLEN'S EATERY, read a lighted sign, the façade made of pink stucco, embedded with several arched windows. The door was a gleaming white, and next to it a menu mounted under glass, nicely framed.

I considered driving away. I knew I *should* drive away. I still had a decision to make. I could just go.

Go!

I wiped my eyes. I blew my nose on an old napkin I found in the car. I smoothed my hair in place and shifted in the driver's seat. I really should go. None of my old friends would be here. I couldn't call them because they weren't in my phone anymore.

It wasn't Porty's, but it still had beer.

I could stay or go.

I could drink or not.

It was The Moment.

I'm engaged. I'm getting married.

I got out of the car. I was worn down.

I didn't have the strength to fight anymore.

And I hated myself for that.

The room was a sideways rectangle, and the bar was still opposite the door, but it was half the size. I didn't see a bartender, and no one was drinking at the bar. The restaurant was empty except for a group of women finishing up desserts. They must have been a book club because they were yakking away and there was a thick hardcover sat at every place setting. The place smelled like artisanal pizza and waning perfume instead of like booze and stale cigarettes.

I crossed to the bar and sat down, feeling out of place and exposed. The bar itself was clean golden pine and glistened with polyurethane, no longer dark pitted wood with matte blotches where the varnish had worn off. Pricey pendant lights with glass shades shed too much light. Oversize photographs of stone farmhouses hung on the wall behind the bar, having replaced the dusty clutter of liquor bottles and softball trophies. Some would have considered these improvements, but not me. It was all too bright and shiny, and there was nowhere to hide.

The bartender emerged from a door behind the bar, forcing a smile that told me he wasn't happy to see a customer at this hour. He looked young, clean-cut and tall, with a sunny handsome face and biceps that showed in his white ELLEN'S EATERY polo. Everything about him made me miss Porty, the chubby Vietnam vet who used to own the place.

"Can I help you, sir?" he asked.

"Miller Lite, please."

"You got it." The bartender set an ELLEN'S EATERY napkin in front of me, and I was already sick of the logo.

"I remember when this place was Porty's."

The bartender picked up a pilsner glass. "I heard it was a dump."

I let it go. "Do you know what happened to Porty?"

"No. I only work here two nights a week."

"Who owns this place?"

"It's a franchise, there's two others." The bartender poured me a Miller Lite on tap, which I watched as if it were liquid gold, then he reached over and set the beer in front of me. "Here ya go. I gotta clean up in the kitchen. Tomorrow's my day off and I wanna get out of here. Call me when you want another."

"Come back in eight minutes."

The bartender chuckled like I was kidding, but I wasn't. He left through the swinging door, leaving me alone.

I picked up the glass and paused, torturing myself. I could smell the hops. My mouth watered. I hated that I was about to drink, but I was weak, and I hated myself for that, too.

So I took a good long pull on the beer, then swallowed, closing my eyes, maybe so I wouldn't see myself. The chilly taste exploded on my tongue, a clean lager flavor, slightly malty but not too heavy, everything in one gulp. It tasted so good and so very, very bad, both at once. I'd just blown almost two years of sobriety. I was drinking again. I'd never felt more disgusted with myself, so I took another sip.

The sensation, the taste, and the toxic mix of emotions brought back the last time I'd been here drinking with Jesse, and the memory ambushed me. I hadn't even been thinking about him. I hadn't allowed him to surface in my consciousness. I'd been pretending he'd never been alive, much less dead.

Jesse, we should go into business together.

We absolutely should.

We won't, but we should.

Okay, but we'll talk about it and that's almost as good.

We'd both laughed, having been friends for nine years. I'd met him when I needed a cheap muffler, and we both loved cars. He could fix anything that ran on gas, and we had the same sense of humor. We always talked about new business ideas, our conversations fueled by beer, dreams, and denial.

Jesse, we could flip cars. You wanna try?

We definitely could. We know cars and we could sell anything.

Totally. My mother says butter melts in my mouth.

My mother says get out of my sight.

That was the last time I saw him. One week later, I left Carrie's daughter, Emily, in the car and deleted Jesse from my phone. I knew I'd drink if I called him, so I didn't call him, and he didn't call me, either. He'd hear about what had happened with Emily, and he'd know I'd want to get sober, but he didn't want to go there himself. Getting clean was the one thing Jesse Fife never talked about, in our pie-in-the-sky future.

Jesse had a body shop, and everybody knew him as the guy who could get you a motorcycle part, a fake license plate, and any pill you wanted, which was where he went wrong. He died while I was in prison so I couldn't go to his funeral, but I'd mourned him in my cell and chipped in for the headstone. His mother didn't have the money, and nobody knew where his father was. I missed him every day and hadn't wanted to know how he died, but then I found out from somebody else inside.

"Jesse, man," I heard myself say, aloud.

I had no one to drink with, so I drank with a ghost.

I woke up on my back, aware that I was outside and wet. I opened my eyes but closed them again. My head pounded, and I wanted to go back to sleep. I didn't know why I was outside. I was going to have the mother of all hangovers when I woke up, which was not yet.

I woke up again sometime later, clammy and wetter. The rain had stopped, and I squinted up into the limbs and branches of a tree. I could hear birds tweeting and the gentle patter of remaining raindrops on leaves.

I closed my eyes and listened. The air smelled earthy and natural. I was in a park. The ground felt hard underneath me. I rolled over on the wet grass.

I wiped my face and looked down at my shirt. It was wet and so were my pants. I had one sneaker on, and one foot was bare. Miller Lite beer cans lay scattered around me, next to a soggy twelve-pack box.

I sat up, resting one hand on the ground. I wiped the rain from my face and head, trying to get myself together. I dug in my pockets and found my wallet and phone, but not my car keys.

My phone flashlight was on, and I turned it off. My battery was low. It was 11:46 A.M. I'd been here all night.

I stood up, looking around. There were rows of monuments and tombstones everywhere. I wasn't in a park, I was in a cemetery.

I took a step, straightening up. My gaze fell on the engraved granite monument nearest me.

JESSE FIFE

DECEMBER 10, 1986–APRIL 4, 2022

"No," I said aloud. I stumbled over to the monument, reading it again. The etched name was black with rain.

"Jesse," I said, stunned, confused, and horrified. I didn't want to imagine Jesse so high and drunk that he fell down the steps, cut his head on the banister, and bled to death in his own living room.

My eyes glazed when I looked at the headstone. I knew I would be next if I kept drinking. I'd be dead in a grave, underground. I'd be a ghost in a bar, like Jesse. People would say they always knew this would happen. My mother would cry, and my father. Gabby, even John—they all would. *We tried everything*, they would say, *but in the end, nothing worked. TJ finally drank himself to death.*

I fell to my knees, and I began to cry.

I stopped crying, then wiped my eyes and face. I was dry-mouthed, headachy, and raw. I came to my senses and remembered what had happened before the cemetery, before I'd come here. I'd drank as much as they'd let me at Ellen's, then the bartender warned me not to drive. I'd gotten in the car, sat in the front seat, and mulled it over drunkenly. I knew that I'd just made the worst decision of my life and I shouldn't compound it by driving.

Thank God.

So I'd started walking, knowing and not knowing where I was

heading. I was so drunk I didn't think about my brother, my father, Neil Lemaire, Fake Elliott Thompson, or whether I was being followed. I stumbled through the dark suburban streets, bought the twelve-pack on the way, then kept walking until I remembered that Jesse had been buried in the neighborhood cemetery, his grave just behind the new chapel under a tree. I found the cemetery and searched for the gravestone engraved with a Celtic cross, knowing it would be there because I'd helped pay for it.

I rose unsteadily, getting my act together. I wiped my hair back, smoothed down my wet jean jacket, and retrieved my sneaker. I picked up the beer cans and stuffed them in their soggy box. The rain had brought up the earthy smells of the ground, the flowers, the trees, and the bodies around me, among them Jesse's.

Goodbye, pal.

I turned and walked away, surprised that leaving Jesse hurt as much as coming, which made no sense. I focused on the exit of the memorial park, at the end of the long paved road. There was a wrought-iron gate, and its doors were propped open among purple rhododendron.

I kept going, putting one foot in front of the other. I threw the box of cans away on my way out, and started to walk out of the memorial park and into civilization. I reached the gates, passed through, and stopped at the road. Cars whizzed back and forth, regular people hurriedly driving themselves to their important jobs and productive errands.

I wasn't one of them anymore. I had zero days of sobriety. I was back to square one, but I couldn't think about that now.

Then I remembered.

Mango needed her shot.

CHAPTER FORTY-FOUR

I paced like a madman in front of the cemetery, waiting for my Uber. I didn't want to be who I was anymore. I couldn't bear to be in my own skin. I hated myself for relapsing and forgetting about a cat I loved.

Mango was all I had. I was all she had. I'd never forgive myself if anything happened to her.

I searched my phone for *how long can a cat with diabetes go without insulin* and clicked the link. A full list popped onto the screen with answers all over the lot. Some read *could cause increased drinking and urination*, others said *could result in a serious medical condition called diabetic ketoacidosis*. If you miss an insulin shot, your pet *may require emergency veterinary treatment*.

I clicked and read that *missing even one insulin shot could cause your pet to slip into a coma and die*.

My mouth went dry. I didn't have a vet. I didn't know any vets near me. I scrolled to search *emergency vets near me* and put in my home address. There was one fifteen minutes from the house. It struck me that I'd left my keys in the car, but I had a spare house key hidden out front.

Traffic passed me on the side street and I watched the cars, praying that one of them was my Uber, a silver Toyota. The app said the driver was five minutes away, but five minutes couldn't pass fast enough.

I looked up and spotted my Uber three cars back. I broke into a jog toward the car and waved when I got close. The driver was young and he waved back, and I ran to the back seat when he pulled over.

"TJ?"

"Yes." I closed the car door behind me. "How fast can you get me home?"

"As fast as you want."

"Go, it's an emergency."

"Mango!" I threw myself on the rug and looked under the couch, and she was lying on her side. Her eyes were closed.

No. I reached my hand under her, but she didn't wake up.

Please God. Frantic, I took her by the scruff of the neck and slid her out from under the couch. She roused slightly.

"Mango, it's okay!" I lay her on my lap, drowsy but alive. I picked up the needle, made the little tent, and injected her, then I jumped up with her and flew outside into the waiting Uber.

"Go, go, go," I told the driver.

At the emergency vet, I washed my face in the bathroom, trying to keep it together. The walls were painted daffodil yellow and lined with framed posters of a dalmatian puppy, a calico kitten, and a lop-eared bunny. I'd never been in a nicer public bathroom; the only dirty thing was me. I'd gone so low that I couldn't compete with a toilet.

I rinsed my face, willing myself back to the land of the living. The vet tech had taken Mango away as soon as I'd brought her in. The shot I'd given her had no effect, and they told me they'd speak with me after they'd examined her.

I turned off the water and dried my face with paper towels, then rubbed my finger on my teeth for a toothbrush. I finger-combed my hair and smoothed down my clothes, dry now.

I met my gaze in the mirror, horrified at the wretch in my reflection. I looked positively haunted, my eyes bloodshot and puffy and my face bloated from the binge.

I'll take care of you, honey.

I had an epiphany, eyeing myself. I hadn't taken care of Mango because when I drank, I wasn't taking care of myself. It was time to change, this time forever and for good.

I left the bathroom to find out whether my cat lived or died.

"Thank you!" I threw my arms around a startled Dr. Schiller, an older veterinarian, who laughed good-naturedly.

"You're welcome, I'm happy we were able to help."

"You have no idea how much this means to me!" I wiped my eyes, trying to get it together. I hadn't cried the whole time I was waiting to hear, but now the waterworks gushed. "I swear to God, this is never going to happen again, I'm going to take better care of her."

"It's important to keep up with the shots. You got her here in the nick of time."

"Thank you, God." I sent up a thankful prayer. I'd prayed more in the last few hours than in my whole life. "I know, I've learned my lesson. I swear to you, you can't even know."

"We have to keep her here tonight. We need to hydrate and observe her. I trust that will be okay with you?"

"Yes, yes, yes, can I see her?"

"No. We don't allow anyone in the back."

"Okay, I get it, she doesn't like me anyway."

Dr. Schiller smiled. "I'm sure that's not true."

"It is, but I love her. Will you tell her I love her and that I'm very, very sorry?"

"I'll tell her, personally. Bye now." Then Dr. Schiller quickly backed out of the room before I could hug him again.

Later, I waited at the counter to pay the bill, and a thick white candle was burning at the other end, next to a pastel sign that read PLEASE BE RESPECTFUL. SOMEONE IS LOSING THEIR BEST FRIEND.

My throat thickened. It could have been Mango, it could have been me. It could have been Emily. One day, it was Jesse.

It was over.

I was going to stay sober and get myself out of trouble, or whatever trouble John had gotten me into with the police. I had questions for my brother, but I couldn't ask him.

I had only one other option, and I had to give it a try.

All I needed was a fast car.

Luckily, I owned one.

CHAPTER FORTY-FIVE

I had coffee and a Wawa hoagie on the road, so my brain was returning to normal function as I drove into Bay Head, one of the old-money beach towns on the Jersey Shore. I'd been here once for John and Nancy's engagement party, thrown by her parents at their magnificent waterfront home. I was coming for a very different reason today.

I'd driven with one eye on the rearview mirror, worried I'd be spotted by a cop or whoever was following me before. I was coming today unannounced because I didn't want to give my sister-in-law the chance to call the cops. It had taken me only two hours to get here, with the sun climbing in a beautiful, cloudless sky.

The road approaching the house was from the back, since its front faced the beach, and it was a large traditional with two wings and white shutters that looked classic with grayish shakes. The lot size was among the biggest on the street, and an American flag flapped over a verdant patch of short lawn in the back.

I parked on the street and got out of the car to the cawing of seagulls. I always associated the beach with beer, cold six-packs from Styrofoam coolers in Wildwood, boozy nights on back decks in Avalon, and party houses in Ventnor with my frat brothers. I pushed the thoughts away. If I was triggered by the Atlantic Ocean, I was in bigger trouble than I thought.

A footpath of wooden slats led to the beach, and I started up the path, spotting Nancy up ahead, sitting at the water's edge with Connor. I made a beeline for them, passing dune grass planted like hair plugs. The beach was mostly empty, effectively private for the lucky few. Someday I would understand how the American coastline could be bought and sold.

I made my way toward them, and Connor was digging a hole with a bright orange shovel. Nancy was laughing, looking beautiful in a wide-brimmed straw hat and a loose white muslin shirt over a one-piece bathing suit. She had a blue shovel, helping Connor dig, a devoted mother. I gave her credit for that, even though we'd never been close. My brother didn't deserve either of them.

"Uncle TJ!" Connor spotted me first, scrambling to his feet and running toward me in a way that lifted my heart.

"Vroom, vroom!" I called to him, our motorhead call-and-response.

"Vroom, vroom!" Connor called back, opening his little arms, and I jogged to him, caught him, and swung him in the fresh, salty air.

"Look at you fly!"

"Uncle TJ, I made a hole! It's so big!"

"Show me!" I carried Connor to Nancy, who turned up the brim of her hat, which shaded a puzzled smile and lips slick with whitish balm.

"TJ, what a surprise."

"Great to see you." I set Connor down, stalling until he was out of earshot.

"Mommy, Uncle TJ wants to see what I made!" Connor scampered over to his hole, sloshing with greenish water from a foamy wavelet. "Look, look!"

"Wow, I see, that's great!" I told him, meaning it. He was so cute, happy and energized at the beach with the big waves crashing behind him. The sea was a perfect greenish blue, churning with seaweed and smelling briny and fresh. The wind off the water rejuvenated me, renewing my sense of purpose.

Nancy handed Connor his orange pail. "Honey, why don't you rinse this off in the water? But don't go in."

"Okay, Mommy!" Connor scurried off with the pail.

Nancy turned to me. "TJ, are you drunk?"

"No," I said, taken aback.

Nancy's eyes turned flinty. "I smell it on you. It's coming out of your pores."

I flushed, embarrassed. "Okay, I did drink last night but I'm okay now. Leave that aside for a moment, I want to talk to you about what's going on. I need to know what John's up to."

"What do you mean?"

"I need to know what he told the police about me. He must have called you."

"Um, he hasn't said anything." Nancy blinked. "Why don't you tell me what you're talking about? Why would he talk to the police about you? What did you do now?"

I let it go. "He gave the police a statement in connection with Lemaire's death."

"Who?" Nancy glanced at Connor, running along the water's edge.

"Neil Lemaire, the accountant who died. Runstan's accountant."

"I don't know anything about that."

Come on. "Level with me, will you? Did John tell you not to talk to me? I have a right to know what he said."

"Wait a sec." Nancy rose, brushing sand off her muslin shirt. "Let's walk and talk." She turned to Connor, waving. "Connor, let's go for a beach walk!"

"Yay!" Connor ran ahead of us, swinging the pail.

I called out, "Connor, find some shells! I need shells!"

"Okay!"

"TJ, why are you here?" Nancy looked at me with a frown, and I fell into step beside her.

"I want to know why John's framing me for murder."

"What?" Nancy recoiled. "Are you serious?"

"You really don't know what I'm talking about?"

"No, I don't." Nancy cocked her head in a way that told me she was genuinely puzzled.

"Neil Lemaire was an accountant at Runstan and he was found dead in his car last week. The police ruled it was suicide, but now they're thinking it's murder because John gave them a statement about me."

"Are you serious?" Nancy's blue eyes flared, and her mouth formed an astonished circle. "You mean he *implicated* you?"

"Yes. Cops came to my house."

"Why would he do that?"

"I don't know, that's what I came to find out." I didn't want to tell her more if she didn't know it.

Nancy stopped walking. "TJ, you might as well know the truth. John and I broke up. Connor and I live here, at my parents'."

What? "What?" This time *I* was shocked. Waves crashed behind me, but I didn't hear them for a moment. "For real?"

"Yes."

"Is this, like, a separation?"

"No, a divorce. We're negotiating the settlement now. The marriage is over."

"My God." I felt stunned. "When did this happen?"

"Six months ago."

"Wait, what? You were just at my father's birthday."

"We're keeping it from your parents. Please don't tell them. I drove back after your father's birthday dinner. I don't live there anymore."

"My God." I didn't know what to say. "I feel terrible."

"Do you?" Nancy eyed me directly under her hat. "We're not exactly buds, TJ. You know I didn't like you drinking around Connor, then you went to prison."

Ouch. "Okay, but still. You're family, and Connor is such a great kid, I would really miss . . ." I felt my throat catch, unable to finish the sentence. I couldn't get my bearings. I hadn't seen this coming. I really thought they were happily married.

"I'm sorry." Nancy's expression softened, her lower lip puckering. "I didn't mean to be glib. I've lived with this longer than you have."

"So." I swallowed hard. "Is this your choice or his? Can I ask?"

"Mine. I left him."

"When I was in prison?"

"Yes, you were about to get out." Nancy shook her head, and we resumed walking along. Connor was running ahead of us, leaving little footprints that filled quickly with water.

"So why did you break up? What's going on?"

"Simply put, I don't know your brother anymore." Nancy looked away, toward the water. "We were happy in the beginning. Really happy. We worked hard and we got along great. We married late, so I was ready for a baby. I loved my job but I quit to stay home with Connor."

I remembered. Nancy had been a corporate event planner and used to organize parties at high-end restaurants and bars. I'd gone to one when she needed to fill a guest list. I drank too much that night, and she never asked me back.

"But after Connor was born, your brother got so selfish and distant. He's obsessed with work and getting new business. He was always taking clients to dinners and games. I got sick of being ignored. Sick of him ignoring Connor." Nancy shook her head. "I thought to myself, if I'm going to be a single mother, I might as well be single. He didn't want to go to marriage counseling. So I left him."

"How long has this been going on?"

"Over the past two years. I think it's getting worse as we get close to your dad's retirement. It all went downhill after he renovated the basement for a home office. He's down there all the time, working."

"His man cave."

Nancy scoffed. "Man caves are for men to have friends over. His is a bunker. He never sees his friends. He ditched them to entertain clients, trying to get new business in mergers and acquisitions. He says he has to."

"Why did you go to the birthday dinner with him? Why doesn't he want my parents to know you split up? They're going to find out sooner or later."

"John thinks if your dad finds out, he'll never retire."

"Why are *you* faking it? I mean, why agree?"

"He's holding Connor over my head. He says he's going to ask for full custody if I don't play ball."

"*John's* doing that? That's not like him. It doesn't even make any sense. How would he take care of Connor, if he's working that hard?"

"He'd hire a nanny on his weeks. He'd be fine with Connor going back and forth every week. Meanwhile I've been home all this time and I love it. I would go for the standard custody agreement, but he won't do that. I know some kids alternate weeks between parents, but Connor needs routine." Nancy sighed. "So I made the deal. It's not long until your dad steps down, and I can wait. Besides, a lot of divorced parents make a good showing in public, and I'll probably still go to Christmases at your parents'. Connor loves them and you. He'd hate never seeing you again."

"I'd hate never seeing him again." I watched Connor running along the waterline, his little legs chugging, his hair flying off his adorable face and a smile from ear to ear. The sight was so charming that we both fell quiet for a moment and took it in.

"John's been a bastard in the divorce, too. He drained our accounts. He shut down our credit cards. He used every financial lever he has against me. He won't even pay for Connor's support."

"Wait, what?" I looked over, horrified. "That's not possible."

"It's true." Nancy met my eye, her resentment plain.

"You're telling me my brother won't support his son?" It was inconceivable to me. "That doesn't sound like him."

"Well, it is," Nancy shot back. "He counts on my parents picking up the tab, and they are, but it drives me crazy. I'm not even asking for alimony."

I'd never felt so dark about John. This was a new low.

Nancy sighed. "I never thought he'd jerk me around on money, especially when we have it. How do you explain a rich man who won't support his own child? How does he live with himself? That's why I say I don't know who he is anymore."

"Do you think he's having some kind of breakdown?"

"John? Not likely. Anyway, I don't care. He's a big boy, he can take care of himself. Connor's my priority." Nancy looked out to the sea and I followed her sight line, watching the waves in constant motion, the shifting shards of light and dark. The ocean was a vast set of variables, possibilities, and forces, unseen and ephemeral, yet strong enough to pound rock and change the very face of the planet.

I turned to her. "My brother doesn't know how lucky he is."

"Thanks." Nancy looked over with a bittersweet smile. "Now, what did he go to the police for? To somehow suggest you were involved with this Lemaire's murder? That's ridiculous. You'd never kill anybody."

"Thank you for that." I felt a surge of validation, and I was starting to change my opinion about Nancy. "My father told the cops, 'My son didn't commit murder to the best of my knowledge, information, and belief.'"

Nancy smiled. "I could've told them you didn't do it, and I don't even *like* you."

I smiled back. "But now you do?"

"Yes, you won me over on my way out the door." Nancy's smile faded. "Don't take it so hard, TJ. Your dad loves you. He's just worried about the firm."

"I know and I get it, I do. He's calling a PR firm for crisis management. The police are looking for me. My mother's calling my lawyer. Nobody knows where John is. We're falling apart."

"The Devlins? Never." Nancy waved me off. "You're not a family, you're a *force*."

"Not anymore." Part of this tore me apart, and the other part made me feel strangely free. "All along I've been thinking I have to change, and I do, for good. But really, *we* all have to change. My *family* has to change." I met her eye. "I want to tell my parents about you two. Can I?"

"Why?"

"Because all roads lead to John and the Runstan deal. Dad won't retire after all this anyway, it's too far gone. He'll have to rehab our image, and Runstan's acquisition is foundering. If the cops have reason to believe Lemaire was murdered, by me or by anybody else, Vuarnex will bounce. It's game over."

"So what are you going to do?"

"My job. Investigate."

"Investigate what?"

"John."

"Oh boy." Nancy looked away at Connor, thinking it over. "Okay. You can tell your parents about us. I'm sick of faking it anyway."

"Thanks. The truth shall set you free, right?"

"In theory." Nancy waved at Connor, who waved back, a shell in his hand. "I should get Connor. It's time for dinner."

It was getting dark on the beach, and there wasn't another soul out except for me, hands on hips, looking out to sea. A dusky periwinkle streaked the sky, shading to gray at the horizon and vanishing into the water. The sea was dead calm in the distance, churning as it got closer and closer to shore, the big waves spewing seaweed, shards of shells, and stones smoothed by centuries.

The wind picked up, and I breathed in the salty air, cooler and lighter since the haze had been swept away. I couldn't bring myself to leave yet, though Nancy and Connor had gone back up to the house. I'd kissed Connor goodbye, hurting at the realization that he wouldn't be in my life the way he had been.

Vroom vroom.

My little nephew had gotten under my skin from day one, and I flashed on visiting him in the hospital, sober for the occasion. I'd been suffused with wonder at his delicate features, filmy hair, and little body swathed in a soft white blanket. He'd wrapped his tiny hand around my index finger, his grip surprisingly tight.

I wiped my eyes, suddenly overwhelmed by the sensation of losing him, Nancy, Carrie and Emily, and Jesse. There'd been so much loss, my brother and my father, even Rigel and Lemaire. I'd lost so much of my own life to drinking, to mistakes, to bad impulses, to cleaning up after myself, all of it leaving me filthy and reeking *through my pores*.

On impulse, I tore off my jean jacket, T-shirt, and jeans, stripping down to my boxers. I kicked off my sneakers and jogged into the water, running on sharp shells, then diving into the first bracing wave. I popped up on the wave's other side, the cold water forcing a half agonized shout and a half war cry, my body reacting to all of the pain and the heartache and the love.

I yelled again and again, diving under the next wave and the next, plunging in again and again, feeling the bracing cold and the tart salt and the clinging seaweed and the gritty silt swirling everywhere, then I rubbed my face and my chest and my underarms and my head with seawater, scrubbing away the pain, washing off the impurities, cleansing myself of the past.

I started swimming parallel to shore, the waves pounding powerfully around me, and I felt surprised when my body served me, my heart pumping and my lungs filling with air. I'd gotten in the best shape of my life in recovery, lean and cut, and I felt my own strength with every stroke. I didn't feel the chill of the water anymore and kept going, fighting the current, the waves, and the whitecaps.

I felt more and more power with every hard stroke, giving me the will to know that I had a power of my own, that I could get through these waves, that I really would get through this mess of my life, and maybe I could even get my family through it, too.

I turned around and swam back in the opposite direction, but the undertow kept tugging me backward. Still I took one stroke and the next, fighting the waves to get back, my lungs beginning to burn, my thighs beginning to ache, my shoulders begging for a break, but I kept going.

I made my way toward the beach and was finally able to stand, my feet newly immune to the shell shards as I jogged onto the shore, wiping my eyes clear and feeling wonderfully elemental, a part of everything around me, the water, the beach, the sky, even the sinking sun, and I knew I was a different man than when I walked in.

I was better, I was stronger, and I was finally myself. I was returning to my life, but this time, I had closure. I realized that I'd needed to talk to Carrie and face up to Jesse's death. I'd had unfinished business all along. But now, something clicked in my brain, like a mental switch. I was going to get back to meetings and stay sober one day at a time. I could *feel* it inside.

And I was going to save the Devlins, too.

I just had to figure out how.

CHAPTER FORTY-SIX

It was dark by the time I crossed the border into Pennsylvania and reached the Main Line in Sunday night traffic, typically light. Shops and businesses were closed along the route, but I kept checking the rearview. I felt edgy being back, but first things first, I called my mother.

"Mom, hi, where are you guys?"

"Still at the office. We'll be here until late. We're getting ready for the start of business tomorrow. How are you, honey?"

"Fine. Sorry I wasn't there to help. Did you hear from John?"

"No. Your dad's not happy."

"How about the detectives?" I realized she didn't know about my real relapse. I'd have to get my other car later, in front of Ellen's Eatery. "Did they call or anything?"

"No. Angela got back to me, though. She's available to meet with you tomorrow morning."

"Terrific, thanks. I'll speak to her directly from now on. You don't have to be in the middle."

"I don't mind, I want to help. Where have you been?"

"I'll tell you when I see you. I'll be there in half an hour. Gabby there?"

"Yes, and Martin."

"Good, see you soon. Love you."

"Love you, too." I hung up as I approached the garage where I kept my other cars, scanning the scene. The office buildings that flanked it were dark and the only activity was across the street at the entrance to Paoli Hospital. I took a left up the steep drive and could see the lights on in the garage. My buddy Billy Riordan owned the business and lived in the apartment above, a terrific mechanic who worked all the time, like most of the self-employed.

I parked the Maserati in the back next to my Toyota RAV4 and cut the ignition. It might be my last time in the driver's seat, but there was no time for long goodbyes. I got out of the car, chirped it locked, and headed for the side door of the garage.

"Billy!" I called out, walking through his cluttered office to the garage, where he was digging in his tool chest next to a Ford F-150 on the lift. The garage was reasonably clean, with tall rolling tool chests, a Shop-Vac, a generator, a compressor, and trash cans. Gray cinder-block walls were covered with grimy signs for Pennzoil, Interstate Batteries, and Mopar parts. The air smelled like oil, which I loved.

"TJ, good to see you." Billy glanced over his reading glasses, a surprisingly cool look with his Maori tribal tattoos. He was in his fifties but looked younger, which he attributed to daily Krav Maga and permanent bachelorhood.

"You, too. Billy, I'm gonna make your night. I want to sell the Maserati. It's time to put away childish things."

Billy smiled. "You're going to make bank, son."

"We both are. I'll pay you a finder's fee if you sell it for me right away. Talk to one of those suits who keep asking. See if you can get them bidding against each other."

"Sweet, thanks. Will do."

"One other thing. Can you lend me something to drive?"

"Sure, but why not the RAV4?"

"It's a long story."

"Where's the Subaru?"

"Left it in Delco."

"Okay. Take the Altima, no problem."

I reached the Devlin & Devlin office and glanced around before I parked at the entrance. It felt good to be in a car that nobody could recognize as mine, without the cops or anyone following me. There were no cruisers in sight.

I got out of the car, hurried inside the building, and opened the door onto our offices, where modern rental furniture had replaced Merrie Old England. Andre was helping Sabrina with her new desktop, bent over her desk. Sabrina looked tired, her graying hair slipping from its ponytail, but Andre was only in his twenties. He was skinny and Black and wore artsy glasses and a light blue T-shirt with jeans.

"Hey, guys," I said, crossing to them. "Good to see you. Can you meet me in the conference room? We need to talk."

"Sure," Sabrina answered, and Andre nodded.

"Thanks." I could hear talking coming from down the hall and I hurried that way. I was going to call a meeting, though I never had before. I'd planned it on the drive home.

"All hands on deck!" I clapped my hands, sticking my head in my father's office, who looked up, startled. His fussy furnishings had been restored, and he was arranging files on his imposing mahogany desk.

"TJ, where the hell have you been?"

"Dad, can you come into the conference room? We need to put our heads together."

"Answer my question."

"Tell you in the conference room." I kept going down the hall, stopping in my mother's office, which looked perfect again, all the family photos and Dante books back in place.

"TJ, what's going on?" My mother looked up from her new laptop with a weary smile, pretty in her nice black sweater and khaki slacks.

"Can you come in the conference room, Mom?"

"Sure."

"Thanks." I left the office and went to Gabby's, where she and Martin were at her desk. "Hey, guys, can you come in the conference room?"

Gabby cocked her head. "What's gotten into you?"

"I'm new and improved. We need to talk."

Martin rose. "Fine with us."

I headed back down the hall and into the conference room, pulled down the sliding whiteboard, and grabbed a black marker from its metal well, feeling like Dry-Erase Virgin.

Everyone filed into the conference room and took seats at the table, and my father started in, "TJ, you owe us an explanation for where—"

"Dad," I interrupted. "I'm about to explain everything. We have to stage an investigation."

"What kind of—"

"Dad, let me finish. I have a lot to say, and we have to get busy."

My father simmered. My mother smiled but didn't reply. Gabby and Martin exchanged glances. Sabrina and Andre listened politely, since employees didn't laugh at Devlin family members. At least not to our faces.

I launched in. "This afternoon I was in Bay Head seeing Nancy, and she told me that she and John split up six months ago. She gave me an earful, and I think he's spiraling down, hiding something, and it has to do with Runstan."

They all looked shocked, and my mother's eyes filmed. My father was about to start talking again, but I raised an index finger and he clammed up. If I'd known it was that easy, I'd have done it a long time ago.

"I think John is mixed up with something, with some bad actors like you say, Dad. If that's true, then he's in trouble and he needs our help. The other theory is a darker one, that he's up to no good. We have to know either way, and the answers have to be in this office, with us. After all, it's about Runstan, and Runstan—"

"Is my client," my father supplied.

I let it go. "Right. So here's what we need to do. Dad, do you know how Runstan's operation works and generally about its finances?"

"Of course."

"Then get all the Runstan files we have, from your office and from John's, and I want you to look them over." I wrote on the board *DAD—RUNSTAN* to keep my thoughts in order. "John told me that he found irregularities in their accounting, which was why he was meeting with Lemaire on your birthday. There has to be some kernel of truth in that story. It might be that it's the other way around, as in maybe Lemaire found irregularities in Runstan's accounting and wanted to meet with John about it. Either way, we need to know about Runstan's finances."

My father nodded slowly. "Okay, I can do that."

My mother recovered her composure. "TJ, do you know where John is? We've been calling him."

"No, I have no idea. I've been wondering if he's with Stan."

My father interrupted. "He's not. Stan doesn't know where he is, either. It's not like John to go AWOL."

My mother seemed to lose focus. "I'm worried about him. He always returns my calls."

Gabby patted her hand. "I'm sure he's fine. It's the weekend, and he'll be in tomorrow morning."

I had to get the meeting back on track. "Dad, did Stan say anything about the fight at the wake? Was there any fallout from Vuarnex?"

"He didn't say. Maybe that's where he is, meeting with Vuarnex and trying to save the acquisition."

"No, Stan would know if he were there, if Stan was telling you the truth." I turned to Andre. "You're our IT genius, and we need you now. First, it looks like everybody's got new computers, huh?"

"Yes, and I set them up."

"All our documents are stored in the cloud, right? So we didn't lose anything as a result of the burglary?"

"Right."

"Can you get into John's computer files, even if they're under password?"

Andre hesitated. "Yes, the system saves the passwords, so I can get them to plug in, even if they don't reveal themselves to me. That's all you need, right? To see what's in the files?"

"Exactly, thanks." I turned to my mother. "Mom, the way billing works is that each individual lawyer sends out his own bills, isn't that right?"

"We draft the bill. The bookkeeper actually sends them. You know Brigitte."

"Okay, I want you to look at John's billing practices, specifically with respect to Runstan." I wrote on the dry-erase board, *MOM & ANDRE—JOHN'S BILLING.* "We know that he was charging them a premium, and I want to understand more, in detail. I also want to understand if there's any other clients he was charging on a premium basis. He had business clients with smaller deals, didn't he?"

"Yes, he was building his book of business."

"Perfect. Then you and Andre work together, okay? We need to generate a list of John's clients and the bills he sent for each, over the past two years, let's say. I'm sure that's in digital files, if not paper, right?"

Andre nodded. "It's digital."

My father frowned. "But what if it's encrypted? Or hidden? I mean, can you do that, Andre? Do you have to hack in?"

"No." Andre shook his head. "I wrote the software. I use it for all my law firm clients. It organizes case files, administrative, and billing."

"Now for Gabby and Martin." I turned to them, sliding my phone from my pocket, scrolling through my photos, and finding Fake Elliott Thompson's driver's license. "Guys, see this man? He's posing as an Elliott Thompson, but it's a fake ID. He's one of the men who broke into our office."

My father gasped. "How do you know?"

"He pawned Mom's coral earrings. I found them and I'll buy them after the holding period."

"Oh my God!" My mother lit up. "TJ, that's wonderful!"

"Good." My father looked impressed, which had to be a first.

"Now, guys." I scrolled to the photo that Mike Dedham had given me and held it up. "This man is named Ryan Martell, and he might be Fake Elliott Thompson. You can see the photo's blurry and his face is half out of the frame. I think he looks like Fake Elliott Thompson, but I can't be sure. Now, Ryan Martell was a union steward for IBEW, Local 98, the local electrical workers union in Philly, a friend of Stan's from way back."

Gabby craned forward at the picture. "It's not much to go on with half a face."

Martin looked over with a smile. "Darling, I repair cleft palates for a living. I'm pretty good with faces."

"Gabby and Martin, the question you have to answer is whether the man in the driver's license is Ryan Martell." I wrote on the dry-erase board, *GABBY AND MARTIN—IS FAKE ELLIOTT THOMPSON REALLY RYAN MARTELL?* "The IBEW, Local 98, has to have a website. You should be able to drill down to find a list of the union stewards in the past. Or there has to be some calls you can make. This should be public information. By the way, their former business manager is in prison."

Gabby nodded. "How does Ryan Martell fit in?"

"If the man is Martell, then I think he was in a conspiracy with Barry Rigel. I think they've been following John and me, and I think they have something to do with Lemaire's death, which I believe was murder." Everyone fell silent at the word, which had a weight of its own. "I think Martell poses a danger to us and I don't know if it's a two-person conspiracy or more. I don't know why they're doing what they're doing or how John is mixed up with them."

My father's face fell, and my mother reached for his hand.

I turned to Sabrina. "I know that John keeps his own calendar but when he goes out, he tells you where he's going, like I do."

"Yes, and often I'll mark it down."

Fantastic. "I'd love it if you could get your calendars together for the past year or so and generally give me a sense of who he's been meeting with and where he's been going. I'm hoping that we can see how that jibes with his billing and understand more about what he's been up to. Do you think that's possible?"

"Yes."

Suddenly we heard a commotion in the reception room, and I realized with a bolt of fear that the front door hadn't been locked when I came in tonight.

Everyone startled, and my father jumped up in alarm. I hustled from the conference room as someone called out:

"Hello? This is Detectives Willoughby and Balleu, looking for TJ Devlin!"

CHAPTER FORTY-SEVEN

My father hustled past me, heading into the hallway. "Detectives, how can I help you?" he asked in his Chamber of Commerce voice.

"Paul, good to see you again. Do you know where TJ is, by any chance?"

"Yes, he's here."

I went down the hall, my mind racing. "Detectives, yes, what do you want?"

"TJ, hello." Detective Willoughby eyed me hard. "A blue Subaru Forester registered to you was stolen last night from outside a restaurant in Delco. Couple of kids took it for a joyride. The keys were left inside, and they found the door hanging open. We picked them up this afternoon. Is that where you left your car?"

Oh shit.

My father jumped in. "Detective Willoughby, if TJ's car was stolen, why does it matter where it was left or if the keys were inside? Are you pressing charges?"

I masked my surprise. No More Mr. Nice Lawyer.

Detective Willoughby frowned. "They're two skateboarders from nice families in the neighborhood. The parents came forward and called us. They're minors, and it was a first offense. Unless you feel strongly otherwise, the DA's willing to let it go."

"It's up to TJ. I hope they didn't do any damage."

"Not that I know." Detective Willoughby turned to me. "TJ, what do you say? You can inspect the car before the DA makes a final charging decision. It's at the impound lot. I'll let you know when you can come down."

"Fine with me."

"I'd like to know why you left it with the keys in and the door open. Were you drinking? If so, that's a violation of your parole conditions."

"No," I lied, remembering that the bartender had said today was his day off, so they probably hadn't been able to ask him.

"Then why did you leave the car?"

My father interjected, "You don't know he was the one who left it. You're making an assumption."

"I'm only asking." Detective Willoughby produced my keys from his pocket and held them up. "These were in the ignition. We went to TJ's house this afternoon, but he wasn't home. We tried a key in his front door. It fit."

My mouth went dry.

My father replied, "I hope you didn't enter without a warrant."

"We didn't." Detective Willoughby pursed his lips. "But the fact that TJ's keys were in the ignition suggests he was the driver."

Suddenly my mother came forward, waving her manicured hand. "Oh my goodness, if you must know, I was driving."

What?

Detective Willoughby turned to her. "*You* were? Why did you leave the car?"

My mother laughed lightly. "I ate at Ellen's, but I don't see so well at night anymore. I hate to admit it, it's an age thing, you know.

Anyway, I called Paul and he came to pick me up. I must have left the keys in the car and the door open. Silly me." She snatched the keys from Detective Willoughby's hand. "Thank you."

"Why didn't you go back for the car today, Ms. Devlin?"

"I haven't had a chance yet. We've been working to get back up and running for tomorrow morning. Any progress on who burglarized us?"

"We're on it. We'll keep you posted."

My mother went to the door and opened it wide. "Detectives, I'd appreciate it if you would prioritize protecting our business over harassing our son. Now, please, let us get back to work."

Detectives Willoughby and Balleu followed her to the door. "Thank you for your time."

"You're welcome," my mother said, letting them out and closing the door behind them.

I clammed up while the detectives were within earshot, wondering what had come over my parents. I had never seen a couple work so smoothly together, like the Astaire and Rogers of the Pennsylvania Bar Association.

"Thanks, Mom, Dad," I said, grateful. "I did drink, that's why I left the car, but that's all over now. Believe me, it will never ever happen again. I know you've heard that before, but now isn't the time to convince you. I'll show you from now on, and you'll know."

My mother shot me a stern look. "I backed you only because it sounded like you didn't drive."

My father brushed past me, his gaze averted. "Let's get back to work."

We worked together in the conference room for the next several hours, my father and Sabrina at the head of the table, my mother and

Andre on one side, and Gabby and Martin on the other. Everyone had his laptop, and in the middle of the table were twelve accordion files that contained Runstan's legal matters in chronological order, spanning my father's and my brother's time as their lawyers.

Everybody worked on their assignments, and I circulated among them, seeing if they were learning anything and trying to put it together. We ate bad pizza and drank worse coffee. My mother took breaks to call John but he didn't call back.

I knew my father was worried, but he reviewed the Runstan files quietly. I continued to worry about John, too, and at the same time sensed that nobody was learning anything new in the files.

My investigation was failing.

Sabrina sighed. "Well, TJ, I've gone through my calendar for the past year and I made a list of every time John told me where he's going. Here it is." She pushed forward a list of dates and times, which covered only a single page.

I read off the first few entries, "Gym, Phillies game with Petersen Concrete, Dr. Himmel—dentist, Dr. Rubin—mole check. That's not a lot of entries. Does it jibe with his online calendar?"

"Yes. Andre will fill you in on that."

"Here," Andre said, coming to her side. "Those entries are in his online calendar, too. The only significant conclusion we could draw is that if you look at Sabrina's past calendars—that is, years previous to this last one or two—he used to be better about telling her where he was going and used his online calendar less. Now he uses his online calendar exclusively."

"So he's keeping more to himself."

Andre nodded. "Yes, but many of my clients are slow to adapt to the digital calendar. People still have loyalty to Filofaxes and Covey. Artists like the Hobonichi planners from Japan. Apple's calendar isn't the best of its apps."

"And there was nothing unusual with respect to his Runstan meetings?"

"No, not at all. There were regular meetings with Neil Lemaire and the previous accountant." Andre flipped through some pages and slid one across to me. "Here's a list of all of his meetings from the digital calendar."

"Thanks." I skimmed it, and the entries didn't seem odd to me, either. "The only thing new is the name of Runstan's previous accountant, Warren Clemons."

My father interjected, "I knew Warren."

"What happened to him?"

"He died suddenly of a heart attack. That was when Stan hired Lemaire."

Everyone went back to work.

I started praying.

An hour later, Gabby looked up. "Okay, I think we have an answer, but you're not going to like it, TJ."

"Give it to me straight," I said, my heart sinking, and everybody stopped working to listen.

"It took some doing, but we found a list of the union stewards. Ryan Martell was a union steward in the eighties. Here's his picture from his sixty-fourth birthday party, which we got from his wife's social media. It took us a long time to find because he has no social media and he's had two wives since then." Gabby set down an enlarged photo.

I recognized Martell as the man in Mike Dedham's photo, but he looked older.

Martin pointed. "This is the man in the driver's license photo, but this one was blurry and had only half a face. I constructed the full face by taking the half face and flipping it over." He set down another picture of a man's face, enlarged. "Then I used software from my office, which helps our patients visualize what they'll look like after their procedures. It even corrects details and extends fine lines, if necessary."

I compared the photos. "They're not the same man."

"No, they're not. They look very much alike, but they're not the same. Their eyes are similar, which is what threw you off. We tend to look first at the eyes. We notice shape, color, and symmetry. It's where we see familial similarities first. That's a product of our DNA, but also a reflection of how we relate to one another. After we have an answer in the eyes, we tend not to look for other facial similarities or differences." Martin gestured at the forehead of the second photograph. "The man in the driver's license photo has a more prominent forehead than Ryan Martell's."

"So Fake Elliott Thompson is not Ryan Martell. That means we still don't know the name of the man in the driver's license."

Martin nodded, puckering his lower lip. "Someone with facial recognition software could probably run a search based on the image in the driver's license, but I don't have such software."

"I understand, thanks."

"So how else can I help?"

"You're not too tired?"

"For family? Never." Martin smiled.

Gabby kissed him on the cheek.

• • •

"Okay, TJ." My father pushed his laptop away, rubbing his eyes. Stacks of manila folders and Runstan documents surrounded him, Gabby, Martin, Sabrina, and Andre.

"What do you have?"

"Nothing." My father met my eye, his gaze weary. "We've gone over these financials. Some are from when I was their lawyer, others are from John. I don't see anything out of order. I don't know what financial irregularities John or Lemaire could have found. I don't have their tax returns, by the way."

"Who does their tax prep?"

"They use Ryder Bates, one of the small indies."

"I guess we can't get them?"

"Not now, not without telling Stan."

I let it go. "Okay, thanks, Dad. All of you."

"This is driving me crazy. I'm not giving up."

"Neither am I."

"I'm exhausted." My mother put her face in her hands, and I looked over, concerned.

"Mom, you want to go home? You can."

"No." My mother shook it off. "But we're not finding anything. John's bills to Runstan look normal."

"How so?" I sank into the chair on the other side of the table, facing a row of somber expressions on my mother, Gabby, Martin, Andre, and Sabrina.

"Here." My mother looked up from her notes. "He hasn't billed for the acquisition yet. But before that, he was billing them on an hourly basis, four hundred dollars an hour. He billed about thirty thousand a year from 2017 to 2022, for routine business advice. It's all in order."

My father frowned, looking over at her. "Marie, what did you say? How much a year?"

"Thirty grand."

"That's strange."

"Why?"

"It sounds high. I doubt I ever billed Runstan that much in a year."

"Were you as active?"

"Certainly, more so in the early days."

My mother blinked. "Then your rate must have been lower."

"Not really. I didn't charge Stan much because I knew he couldn't afford it."

I tried to follow. "But, Dad, you said there was nothing irregular in the Runstan finances."

"There wasn't, but I didn't look at my bills to Runstan. I was looking at Runstan financials. Their statements show that they expensed us as a deduction, and that's proper. But I didn't compare what I billed them to what John billed them. I don't have John's bills."

My mother interjected, "I do. Paul, get your bills, and we can compare."

I rose, encouraged. "I'll help."

An hour later, I was back at the dry-erase board, finishing a chart of my findings. On the left side were the years since 2000, which was the date of Runstan's incorporation. There had been three different accountants during that time, and my father and I constructed a timeline: 2000 to 2012, Joseph Beck, deceased, aneurysm; 2012 to 2022, Warren Clemons, deceased, heart attack; 2022 to 2023, Neil Lemaire, deceased, gunshot wound.

The middle column showed the years in which my father had been Runstan's lawyer, from 1996 to roughly 2019. There was no overlap of their tenures, and my father stopped doing work for them in 2019, when John started with Warren Clemons. Warren died in 2022, when Lemaire took over. My father's billing rate was $500 an hour, and John's was $400.

The far right column on the chart showed annual billings during the entire chronology, and my father's earlier thought had been correct. He billed approximately 18K a year from 2002 until 2019. But when John took over in 2019, the billings increased to 30K and that followed every year until Warren passed, in 2022. Bills to date to Lemaire were approximately $15,000 and it was only May. Projected out at that rate, the annual rate would reach 30K again.

The bottom half of the chart was devoted to a comparison of the time spent on a typical task, as recorded by my father's and by John's bills. Our firm used specialized software called Timeslips, in which individual lawyers recorded the time they spent on various matters in six-minute increments, which was standard in the profession. Lawyers were required to fill in a box that described the task briefly, so we'd compared recurring tasks like Review of Labor Contract, Union Negotiations, Advice Letter Regarding Hydraulic System Purchase, and such. In every case, John spent two-thirds more time on the task than my father.

I capped my marker, having lost my Dry-Erase Virginity. The pattern was clear; when John took over the billing under Warren Clemons, the billing was two-thirds more. It didn't make sense because

John was unbelievably efficient, to the point of being impatient. The notion that he would belabor something compared to my father was absurd, but I still needed an explanation of what I was seeing.

My father stood staring at the chart, slightly stooped over as if he'd been punched in the gut. My mother was pale, and Gabby eased into a chair next to Martin.

Sabrina and Andre exchanged uncomfortable glances.

My father cleared his throat. "Sabrina, Andre, we can handle this from here. You guys go home and get some rest. Thank you for your hard work. Andre, bill me as soon as possible. Sabrina, you don't need to come in tomorrow. Take the day off. Please cancel my meeting with Grant Albertson. It's the only one. Marie, how about you?"

"I'm clear tomorrow," my mother answered, hushed.

"Okay." Sabrina managed a shaky smile. "Thanks. See you Tuesday."

"Yes, thanks." Andre picked up his backpack and laptop, closing it hastily. "Bye now."

I watched them leave, heartsick, exhausted, and a little confused. Dismissing them struck an ominous note, as if whatever came next was something only family should hear.

Instinctively, I closed the door.

CHAPTER FORTY-EIGHT

I turned to my father. "Dad, was John doing what I think he was doing?"

"I really hope we're wrong." My father sighed heavily, his big chest going up and down in his wrinkled oxford shirt, his tie long gone. We stood side by side opposite the chart. "I think he was intentionally overcharging Runstan by two-thirds, across the board. If I'm right, it's fraud."

Whoa. I remembered John saying, *I'm in a fiduciary relationship to Runstan.*

"Mind you, as a legal matter, it's Devlin & Devlin, not John. Devlin & Devlin is defrauding Runstan." My father straightened. "Your mother and I, and Gabby, are scrupulous about our bills. It's a point of pride. We can justify the time and costs on each and every bill that leaves this office."

"Exactly," my mother said quietly.

"Amen." Gabby folded her arms.

I tried to process it. "So now what? Is the firm in trouble?"

"Civilly, yes, we're liable. The firm is civilly responsible for the acts of our employees. We're not liable criminally because we didn't know what he was doing."

"Is there any way you could have known?"

"No." My father shook his head. "We don't see the bills John sends out. Every two weeks we get a report on how much time we've billed and earned to date. I just thought your brother was working hard. He had a 2,300-hour year last year, and that's only billable time, so it means he's working around the clock. I'm sure your mother thought the same thing."

My mother nodded sadly. "Totally. He's in all the time and he works at home, too. He's always meeting with clients or on the phone."

I thought John was a workaholic, too. I should know, as an alcoholic.

My father gestured at the chart. "But this? This shows that something else could be going on, even worse."

"Much worse," my mother added gravely.

"Try criminal," Gabby snapped.

"What?" Martin blinked in confusion, which was exactly how I felt.

"Dad, again, please explain to those of us without a law degree."

"Look." My father pointed at the chronology. "As you see, I worked with Warren before John. John increased the fee when he took over because even though his hourly rate was lower, he billed more time, and Warren had to know the increase was unusual. I just read the Runstan correspondence file and I didn't see any email from him objecting to any increase or raising a question. That gives me reason to believe Warren was complicit."

"How complicit?"

"Warren approved the inflated fee knowingly."

"Why would he?"

My father's lined face fell. "If there was something in it for him."

Yikes. "So John was overcharging Runstan and he and Warren shared in the difference? Was John paying Warren to accept the inflated bill?"

"Yes, that's one way to think of it. Essentially, it's a kickback scheme."

"Does that sound like Warren?" I couldn't begin to deal with whether it sounded like John. I just wanted to know what my father knew.

"Yes, Warren was a sleazebag, one of Stan's cronies from the old days. He was the accountant you have when you start a business, when you play fast and loose, not when you take off." My father's shoulders sagged. "I never would have believed John would do this." He turned to my mother. "Honey, did you see this coming?"

"Never," my mother answered, hushed, and Gabby placed an arm around her shoulders.

"Mom, it's going to be okay."

I asked, "Dad, how do you think it works? John sends the bill, Warren pays it, and John kicks back to Warren in cash?"

"Yes, but not half, a percentage. It wouldn't be worth it otherwise because John has to pay taxes on the income. If he kicks back too much, it's not worth the risk." My father grimaced with disgust. "I can't believe he would do this to Stan. I've been calling Stan, and he's not returning the calls. I wonder how much he knows. John jeopardized the relationship, and my *integrity*."

"But I don't get it, Dad," I said, mystified. "John has money, so why rip off Runstan? Nancy told me he took the money out of their bank accounts, too."

My mother gasped. "You've *got* to be kidding."

"This is too much." My father looked down, hands on hips, then met my eye directly. "TJ, you might be right, and here's what worries me. Runstan might not be the only client he's stealing from. He's working for almost all of my clients now. A kickback scheme makes sense only if he's doing it at scale."

Oh man. "You mean he's padding bills with all the clients?"

"It's possible."

"But would they all take kickbacks?"

"No, not all, but some will, the ones who don't mind stealing from the company." My father sighed. "You have to understand, the people who approve our bills at my clients' aren't usually accountants. They're bookkeepers or clerks and they don't earn much. For the others, John could be padding the bills. He could get away with a minor increase. I've worked with them for years, and they trust me. They'd never question a bill." My father's faced looked pinched. "If I'm right, it's massive wire fraud, mail fraud, and conspiracy. Federal crimes, state crimes. People go to prison for this."

"John, in *prison*?" I blurted out, only because it was unthinkable.

"No," my father shot back. "Over my dead body."

"Everybody, stop." My mother stood up, setting her jaw. "It's almost morning, and John gets in at seven, if he's coming in. I think we need to get the facts. I think we should go through *all* of John's bills. We need to understand the scope of the fraud and give him a chance to explain."

"Right, I'm going to his office." My father started for the door, but I touched his arm.

"Dad, can you explain one thing? Why does John need the money? He makes a fortune."

"You think the only people who steal are ones who need the money? If that were true, there'd be no such thing as white-collar crime." My father whirled around to my mother. "Marie, I'm getting his files. Can you get that PR lady and give her the heads-up we're going to need her? And can you call Angela and get us a list of white-collar criminal lawyers?"

"You mean now?" my mother asked, astonished. "It's not even dawn—"

"Yes. Today we need a lawyer and so does John, and they can't be the same. He has criminal exposure, and the firm has civil exposure. I don't even think we should meet with him without counsel."

"Paul, he's our son." My mother's dark eyes began to glisten, and my father put a gentle hand on her arm, drew her close, and gave her a hug.

"Honey, you know it, too, you're just upset. Don't worry. We'll take care of him and the firm, too. We'll fix this."

"How?" My mother pulled away, anguished. "What are we going to do?"

"We're going to figure out how much he stole and we're going to pay back every penny. We'll say it was an accounting error. The clients won't question it. Nobody complains about a bank error in their favor."

My mother wiped her eyes. "Right, that's the way to go. We'll make the clients whole. We can cover it if we don't get hit with lawsuits."

"That's the problem. We don't know how many clients, how much money, or what we owe, and if we get sued, we could be very exposed. We have insurance but it may not cover in case of fraud. So I won't retire next year, I didn't want to anyway. Everything will be all right. We'll keep going."

My mother nodded. "I can keep working, too. John will have to take a leave, though. Nobody has to know why but us."

I realized I was engaging in a conspiracy, but I had no cause to complain. My parents would lie for John the same way they'd lied for me. But it had just become more likely that John had killed Lemaire, maybe because Lemaire wouldn't go along with his kickback scheme.

Gabby shifted in her seat. "Mom, Dad, I know you love John, and so do I, but should we tell the cops? This is illegal—"

“No.” My father shook his head. “Billing fraud could take down the firm. We’d never recover. You’d be out of a job, too.”

My mother lifted an eyebrow. “Gabby, that boy will be punished enough after *I* get through with him.”

I saw an opening. And I had a plan. “You know, I should go to his house right now, and see if he’s there. He’s not taking your calls, and this is too important to wait. I want to get to the bottom of this. I’ll tell him what’s going on and give him a chance to explain. I can talk to him, I’m not a partner or even an associate.”

My parents exchanged glances.

“Go get him, TJ,” my father said grimly.

CHAPTER FORTY-NINE

I pulled into John's driveway behind his Range Rover. I couldn't wait to confront him, now that I'd have him alone. I had to know if he put me on the hook for Lemaire's murder. I also had to know if he killed Lemaire himself.

I got out of the car and stalked to the front steps. There was a fancy gaslight mounted on the wall at the entrance, and when I got closer, I could see the front door was splintered and hung ajar, as if the house had been broken into.

Jesus. "John!" I pushed through the door and ran inside, terrified. The entrance hall was dark and still.

"John!" I heard an agonized moan from the kitchen. I ran in and turned on the light.

John was lying on the floor, beaten. Blood covered the left side of his face, spattering onto his white shirt. His eyebrow looked split. Reddish bruises swelled on his forehead.

Oh my God. "John!" I rushed to his side, shocked.

"TJ?" He squinted up at me.

"My God, what happened? I'm calling 911."

"No, no . . . don't." John's voice was hoarse.

"Yes."

"No . . . please."

"John, who beat you up? Was it those guys following us? Did they follow you home?"

"No, it . . . wasn't them."

"How do you know? Was there a fight? Were you robbed?" Horrified, I looked around at the mess in the fancy kitchen. Chairs had been knocked over. A big crystal bowl shattered into shards. A chrome Cuisinart and a lime-green Vitamix had been dumped, trailing electrical cords. Spatulas, serving spoons, and utensil jars lay strewn on the Mexican tile floor.

"I'm . . . fine," John croaked.

"No, you're not." I squinted at the cut on his eyebrow. "You need stitches. I'm calling 911."

"No, don't." John cleared his throat. "No cops."

No cops? "What are you talking about?" I asked, bewildered. "What's going on?"

"Help me up."

"John, what happened? Who did it?"

"I don't . . . know." John moaned.

"So then how do you know it's not the guys following us? How do you know it's not whoever killed Lemaire? Unless *you* killed Lemaire." I tried to collect my thoughts. "John, you have to tell me what's going on. What are you up to? It stinks to high heaven."

"Calm down." John snorted. Fresh red blood bubbled from his left nostril. "You're giving me . . . a headache."

Asshole. "Did you frame me for Lemaire's murder? If you did, I'll beat the shit out of you myself."

"Help me up." John raised his arm, with effort. "Ow . . . my ribs."

"Do they hurt?"

"Yes, I think one's . . . broken."

"Excellent," I said, wrenching him to a sitting position.

• • •

I poured John a Macallan, having gone from wanting to kill him to being grateful he was alive. I'd helped him upstairs and into the shower, and he'd changed into a T-shirt and jeans while I'd cleaned up the kitchen and texted our parents that we'd be back soon. He sat at the kitchen table across from me with wet hair, holding a blue ice pack over his left eye.

I set the whiskey in front of him. "Here."

"Are you drinking again?"

"No. 'At the beginning, nothing comes, in the middle, nothing stays, and in the end, nothing goes.'"

"Whatever." John took a sip with difficulty, through a swollen lip.

"Tell me who beat you up. I'm trying to identify one guy, I can show you his picture on a driver's license—"

"TJ, it was guys I owe money to."

"What? What guys?"

"Bookies."

"*Bookies?* You mean like bookies that you gamble with? They came and beat you up?" I felt like I was talking to anyone but my brother. "What the hell are you saying?"

"What part of 'I owe money to bookies' don't you understand, TJ?"

"Are you kidding me?" I asked, astonished. "You gamble with *bookies*? You owe them money?"

"You said that already."

I tried to gather my thoughts. "So you were lying when you said you didn't know them?"

"No. I don't know them. I only know who they work for."

Sweet Jesus. "What is it with lawyers and meaningless distinctions?"

"It's the truth." John shrugged.

"For real? You gamble *that much*?"

"I gamble."

"Enough that bookies *beat you up*?"

"It happens."

"Not to you, dude. What do you gamble on?"

"Sportsbook. Mostly on the apps. I have a PO box where I send the credit card bills. It's a system. It works great."

My mouth dropped open. Suddenly it all made sense. John always had a game on, and he was on the phone constantly. I thought he was working, but he could have been gambling. I thought of the sports memorabilia lining his man cave. I would have guessed he gambled a little, but never that he'd go this far.

"TJ, it's not that big a deal."

"What do you bet on?"

"What do you think? Games, the next field goal, the next play, the next shot. A lot of people gamble."

"Not like *this*, bro," I shot back, incredulous. "You got beat up. They trashed your kitchen."

"It won't happen again."

"Did it ever happen before?"

"No, and I'll pay up next week. I'll have the cash then. They'll come back. They don't speak wire transfer."

Dumb smart guy. "When did you start all this?"

John sipped his drink. "When the apps came. 2019? 2020?"

"Why?"

"The *money*, what else?" John chuckled, then winced. He took off his ice pack, leaving a pinkish swath on his face. "It's fun, too—it's a rush, a release. I have a lot of responsibilities, TJ."

"So, pressure. Discomfort. Suffering."

"Are you just saying words?"

"It's Buddhism. I'm a drunk monk." I'd read some Buddhist philosophy on my phone the other night, and it talked about cultivating compassion. Maybe that's why I didn't want to yell at John. "I can't believe this. I thought *I* was the only problem child. How much money have you lost?"

"What's the difference?"

"Tell me. We're talking."

"About a million," John said irritably.

I gasped. "A *million* bucks? John, it's out of control. That's a gambling addiction."

"I'm not an addict."

"Yes you are. You're pissing away a *fortune*."

"I have it in control."

"No, you don't." I put it together. "Dude, you're stealing to support your habit. You're running a kickback scheme with our clients."

John hesitated, then frowned in fake indignation. "What are you talking about?"

"Please, don't bullshit a bullshitter. You're padding your bills. You're scamming the clients. You're kicking back a percentage. Tell me again about fiduciary duty, bro."

John set his glass down with a *clunk*. "So you know?"

"We all do."

John grimaced. "Mom and Dad? They know, too?"

"Yes."

"Shit." John sighed heavily. "Pass me the bottle." I slid it over, and John poured himself another drink.

"You closed your joint account with Nancy?"

John's swollen eyes flared, as much as they could. "You talked to her, too?"

"I'm an investigator, remember?" *Sinecure, my ass.*

"What did she tell you?"

"That you guys broke up. Why aren't you supporting Connor? Why are you giving her such a hard time?"

John pursed his lips. "Look, it's leverage. I need her to play ball. I want Dad to retire."

"John, really?" I could see he was desperate, and that it was the-end-justifies-the-means time. Addicts and drunks were horribly selfish: God knows I'd been. "How can you do that? You love Connor."

"Of course I do. Connor's fine."

I let that go, since it was moot now. "You're screwing up your family and mine."

"Listen, TJ, everything is going to be fine after the acquisition. The fee gets me out of the hole, and the deal establishes me as a player in mergers and acquisitions in Philly." John's eyes lit up, newly animated. "Every single deal will be as big as Runstan, even bigger, with an upside *through the roof*—"

"You're chasing the high, John. You'll never get out of the hole."

"Yes, I will. I have a cash flow issue but it's temporary. I have money in Berwyn Trust but I didn't want to take it out in a down market. That's why I liquidated my joint checking with Nancy. It's non-interest bearing."

"You're robbing Peter to pay Paul."

"I know what I'm doing. I can handle it. Enough with the lecture." John poured another whiskey. "What happens now?"

"We go to the office and tell them everything."

John groaned. "They're at the office?"

"Yes, they've been there all night. Mom's been calling you. They're trying to get you out of this. They're lawyering up. They want to make the clients whole. They were going to use their money, but you'd better use yours first. You better say you're sorry for what you're putting them through. You'd better *grovel*."

"Dad's still on track to retire, isn't he?"

"No, of course not." I could see he wasn't getting it. "They're going to keep working. They're not going to hand you the reins now."

"But Dad *has* to retire." John shifted forward in the chair. "This doesn't change anything. This is nothing. I'm going to buy the firm."

I sensed he was in magical-thinking territory. "John, wake up. You cheated our clients. You got the firm in major legal trouble. Mom and Dad can't even use the same lawyer as you. You've got to go to rehab."

"Hell no!" John smacked the table. "I don't need rehab."

"I'm not going to fight with you. Tell me what you told the cops about me."

John hesitated. "Oh man."

"Just say it. What did you tell the cops?"

"TJ, I had to." John took another sip, cringing.

"No, you didn't."

"Yes, I—"

"Tell me."

John sighed. "I told them that you told me you and Lemaire were stealing money from Runstan. That you went to meet Lemaire on Dad's birthday and confronted him that he was shorting you. You hit him with a rock, you were worried you killed him. Then the stuff you did after that, like looking for his car and all that."

Jesus. "So, you *did* put me on the hook. You *framed* me."

"I'm sorry."

"*Now* you apologize?" I felt my anger resurge. "What a guy."

John frowned. "For what it's worth, I didn't tell them I thought you did it. I said I didn't know."

"What really happened with Lemaire? Did you kill him?"

"No, I didn't."

"Then why put me on the hook?"

"I had to do *something* after the fight at the wake. I wanted the Runstan acquisition to go through."

"How does putting me on the hook for Lemaire's murder make it more likely the acquisition goes through?"

"If you're being investigated for killing Lemaire, nobody's looking to find kickbacks. I figured eventually you'd be cleared. They'd hire Angela to get you off, but I needed that deal. It's going to save my ass—"

"John, you're in denial."

"TJ, you don't know anything about it. I have this all planned. Mergers and acquisitions is huge. I can premium-bill on every deal, it's all high stakes."

"You're gambling, only with cases."

"I can make a killing."

"You already did. Remember Lemaire?"

John pursed his lips.

"What happened to him?"

"I didn't kill him."

"Tell me who did, and it better be the truth."

"I don't know. Lemaire figured out I had a deal with Warren. I offered him the same deal, and he took it. He'd approved one of the bills, and I kicked back to him, but then he got cold feet. He didn't want to keep going. He called and said he wanted to talk, so I said we should meet. We did, where I said, at the quarry. He said he wanted to stop, he threatened to bust me. I told him he'd be taking both of us down. We had a fight, and I threw the rock at him and hit him in the head. He lost consciousness, like I said. I was scared I killed him. I panicked and drove to Mom and Dad's."

"Did you really think you killed him?"

"I didn't know, I wasn't sure."

"But why involve me at all? Why tell me anything that night?"

"I was scared, I was panicky and I thought . . ." John didn't finish the sentence, and I realized the words were too awful to say.

"You thought you might pin it on me? Like, if you really killed Lemaire?" My chest tightened. "I'm your get-out-of-jail-free card? Your drunk ex-con brother with zero credibility?"

"No, no, no, it's not like I planned it that way from the outset. It was more like I was . . . well, improvising. The night of Dad's birthday, I needed your help, I really did, but then realized I could pin it on you if I had to. I'm sorry, TJ."

"So many apologies, dude. Honestly, you're too kind." I stuffed it to stay on point. "So what happened the next night, when Lemaire was found dead in the Mercedes?"

"Okay so that day, after the night I hit him with the rock, he called in sick to work. He called me at the end of the day. He said he drove around, trying to figure out what to do. He couldn't take the pressure. He was losing it." John shook his head. "So I convinced him to meet me at Dutton Run Park that night."

"Why would he agree to that? Why wasn't he afraid you'd try to hurt him again?"

"He was, but I threatened him. I told him if he didn't show up, I'd go to the cops about him. We had a gun to each other's head, and he scared easy."

I felt a pang for Lemaire. "So that night, how did he die if you didn't kill him?"

"I didn't do it." John hesitated, newly grave. "I drove to meet him at Dutton Run Park. It was pouring, you remember. When I pulled into the lot, he was already there, parked and waiting. Just then I realized there was a car behind me. I hadn't seen it before, maybe because of the rain. I was being followed."

Whoa. "What kind of car?"

"I don't know, I'm not a car freak and I couldn't see in the rain. The car followed me into the lot and all of a sudden the driver shot at me. I kept driving and got away. Lemaire couldn't start his car."

"Oh no." I remembered that Daniel had told me that Lemaire's car had just gotten out of the shop. It must not have been fixed properly. "So you got away, but he didn't?"

"Correct. If I didn't keep going, I'd be dead. I didn't call the cops because it would all come tumbling down."

"Like it is now, anyway. Did you see the driver's face?"

"No, I couldn't. I didn't look back."

"If I showed you a picture, could you identify the driver?" I started scrolling on my phone, found a picture of Fake Elliott Thompson, and held it up. "Is this him?"

John leaned over, squinting. "I don't know, TJ. Like I said, I couldn't see in the rain."

"It wasn't Barry Rigel, was it?"

"I don't know."

I had another thought. "Maybe the driver was one of your bookies. Maybe it wasn't related to Runstan."

"It's not a bookie. Bookies don't kill people they want money from."

"So then what happened?"

"I saw on TV that Lemaire was dead. The driver must have shot him and made it look like a suicide. He wouldn't want Lemaire to identify him."

"So it really wasn't you? You swear to me?"

"I swear it on Connor's life." John shifted to get up, wincing. "Let's go get this over with. I'll explain to Mom and Dad. Everything will be fine after we pay the clients. Come on, get up." John motioned me up. "I have everything in control."

"You can't even walk."

"I can *walk*, TJ." John shuffled from the table in his Adidas slides, and I got up, took his elbow, and walked him down the hall. It was almost dawn, and daylight slipped through the cracks in the door.

"You need a locksmith and a carpenter."

"I'll call from the car." John opened the broken door, and the knob came off in his hand. "Damn."

"Give me that." I took the knob, set it on the console table, and tried to close the broken door behind us. "Let me help you down the steps."

"No, I'm fine." John made his way down, his hand on the wrought-iron rail.

"Mom will want you to go to the hospital."

"I don't need to. I'll call my concierge doc."

"Good. Tell him you got beat up by your concierge bookie."

Suddenly we heard traffic on the street, and in the next moment, a gleaming black Tahoe bounced into John's driveway, its massive engine rumbling. Another Tahoe drove on its bumper, and another one after that, then two black SUVs. They seemed like official vehicles, swarming all over the driveway, jumping its border of Belgian block, and lurching to a stop on the manicured grass.

John gasped. "What the hell?"

The sight sent a bolt of terror through me. The Tahoe doors all flew open at the same time, as if on cue. Men in navy-blue windbreakers and bulletproof vests jumped out of the cars, converging on us with long guns.

This is it. I put my hands up reflexively.

CHAPTER FIFTY

Don't shoot!" I shouted, my knees weak.

"FBI! Get on the ground!" the agents yelled. "Down on the ground!"

"Okay!" I hit the deck, my hands still raised. My chin grazed the pebbles of the driveway.

"I'm doing it!" John grunted, lowering himself.

A cadre of FBI agents swarmed us. "Either of you John Devlin?"

"I am," John answered from his knees.

"We have a warrant for your arrest!" one of the FBI agents shouted. They surged to John and hoisted him to his feet. One agent patted him down, the other wrenched his arms behind his back and handcuffed him.

"What for?" John asked, gasping. "What are the charges?"

My thoughts fled. I felt panicked. I didn't know what was going on. I'd thought they'd come to arrest me. It hadn't registered they were FBI, not local. I had no idea why they were arresting John. They couldn't have known about the billing fraud this fast.

"We have a search warrant for the premises!" shouted another FBI agent, brandishing a flurry of paper. FBI agents thundered past me and streamed into the house. I could hear their heavy footfalls inside, their shouted directions to each other.

"TJ, call Dad!" John yelled as FBI agents pressed him into the back seat of one of the Tahoes.

Still stunned, I stood on John's front lawn, my phone to my ear, listening to it ring. John had been taken away, and FBI agents were searching his house. I could see them through the windows hustling this way and that, carrying boxes.

"Dad?" I said, when the call connected. "Listen, I have bad news. I'm at John's. The FBI arrested him and they're here—"

"They're there, *too*?" my father asked, aghast.

FBI agents were swarming all over Devlin & Devlin, searching John's office, as well as my parents', Gabby's, and the file room. They carted in empty cardboard boxes, and I could hear conversation and rustling as they riffled through file drawers and packed documents. They seized the new laptops and my father's phone, but no one else's. We still didn't know the charges against John. I'd filled my parents in about the arrest and the beating he'd taken.

We were confined to the waiting room, and I stood next to my mother, my arm around her shoulders. She had reached Angela, who had sent a lawyer to us and another one to John. Surprisingly, my mother was doing better than my father, who'd gone silent, sitting in a wing chair flanked by Gabby and Martin.

We all watched wordlessly, knowing that we couldn't talk in front of the FBI agents. No one had anything to say anyway. We were collectively horrified, and I was worried about my parents, who'd been up all night. Luckily Mango was at the vet's, so I didn't have to run home.

I felt everything turning upside down, my own personal bizarro world. John was behind bars, not me. He'd become the Bad Son, and I was the Good Son, or at least the Not-As-Bad Son. My father was quiet, and my mother was in charge. Our offices were being upended, and so were our lives.

I had to believe this was the demise of Devlin & Devlin. It was too much for my father, the reason he'd emotionally imploded. He couldn't bear to witness the end of the family firm.

I was just hoping it wasn't the end of the family.

Five hours later, the FBI was almost finished with its search, and the office felt like a hollow shell. We'd been allowed back into the conference room, where we spent the day wondering, whispering, and ordering takeout. Styrofoam clamshells filled the trash, and the aroma of leftover French fries permeated the air. Our new lawyer, John "Jack" Lynch III, had arrived half an hour ago, having taken the shuttle from Washington, D.C. He headed the White Collar litigation team at Contro & Lynch in Philly and was meeting with the FBI in the reception area. We awaited his return on tenterhooks.

Finally the door opened, and Lynch entered the room. His expression was no-nonsense on a handsome face, with sharp blue eyes and graying hair, and his build, in a boxy khaki suit, was similar to my father's.

"How bad is it?" my father asked, having regained his footing after

Lynch had been hired. They knew each other from Aronimink Golf Club, and Lynch had been club champ three years ago, which presumably made him a better lawyer.

"I have some preliminary information for you." Lynch set down his legal pad and a gleaming black Montblanc. "John is in custody and has already consulted with his lawyer, Natalie Christiano. He'll be arraigned before a magistrate judge in federal court tomorrow in Philadelphia. We'll get a copy of the indictment then."

"Okay," my father said, and my mother exhaled a shuddering sigh. Gabby shifted closer to Martin.

I felt sorry for all of them. My parents were witnessing the downfall of their firstborn son and the destruction of everything they'd worked for. The firm they'd built to guarantee our future was devolving in disgrace. Gabby had been teary off and on, and I knew she was upset and ashamed. The media called all day until I unplugged the phone. Employees at our office complex gawked at the FBI raid, with agents in black SUVs.

Lynch continued, "They'll give us an approximate time so you can be present at the arraignment. I assume you all want to go."

"Yes, of course," my father answered. My mother nodded.

"Okay, I'll meet you there, and we'll go together. It's vital to show the court that John has the support of his family, especially in a situation like this one."

"You mean because the firm has liability now, for his bad acts?"

"Yes. If family is present, it sends a signal to the judge and sets the tone for the rest of the case. Natalie tells me she will argue that John's gambling addiction motivated his misconduct. She'll find a way to introduce John to the court as someone who needs treatment."

"Good point," my father said, straightening.

"I've confirmed that the FBI search here was to obtain evidence in support of an indictment for wire fraud, mail fraud, theft of honest services, and conspiracy in connection with a fraudulent billing and kickback scheme."

My father looked sick. "So, it's what we thought."

"As bad as it gets," my mother added.

Lynch's expression softened. "Marie, allow me to suggest that it could be worse. This is white-collar crime, not a crime of violence. John's misconduct was related to a gambling addiction disorder, which is mitigating. He's in a position to make restitution to the clients, and so are you. So no, it's not the worst thing in the world."

My father asked, "Will they offer him a deal?"

"I suspect they will down the line, but I can't guarantee anything. His hand isn't strong. To the best of my knowledge, he has nothing to offer the government except for saving them the time and expense of a trial." Lynch eyed my parents. "We have to leave the decision about whether John should plead guilty to him and his lawyer. I won't be privy to those conversations, and you must avoid them with John. I was able to talk to Natalie today only because his arrest has just taken place. Going forward, we need to shut down communication, for John's welfare and yours."

My father nodded. "What about jurisdiction? This is federal, but does the state have jurisdiction, too?"

"Yes, but the feds take priority."

"What I don't get is how the FBI knew. We just discovered it last night."

"Natalie said there was an undercover operation. The FBI set up a shell corporation, and agents pretended to be principals needing representation in a merger with another company. They hired John and introduced him to their accountant. Thereafter, John proposed a kickback."

My father's eyes flared. My mother's hand went to her mouth. Gabby's eyes filmed, and Martin put his arm around her.

"They have a strong case. The agents were wired and the meetings recorded. They have wiretaps of John's phone, too." Lynch paused. "Kickback schemes are risky because they depend on the complicity of regular people, not hardened criminals. Any one of them could have told their spouses or friends, or changed their mind and tipped off the FBI."

My God. It rang true because it was what happened with Lemaire. I wondered if the FBI would link John or me to the murder, or liaise with the Chester County police. I also wondered if I should tell the FBI everything I knew about Lemaire's murder, but I didn't want to compromise John's defense. My only choice was to sit tight for now. It would take time for the two jurisdictions to begin to cooperate, but I didn't know how much time. I had to find Fake Elliott Thompson before he found me.

My father raised a finger. "I have one last question. What do you think we're talking about in terms of sentence, if John is found guilty?"

"If I were his lawyer, I would advise him to plead guilty, and most white-collar indictments end in a plea bargain. Otherwise, for John, it's from five to twenty years in prison."

My father fell silent, stricken.

My mother looked down.

I caught Gabby's eye, and we exchanged solemn looks.

"Folks, I think I'm finished here." Lynch picked up his pen and tucked it inside his jacket. "This will be a long haul, and it's only the beginning. This will be a difficult experience for you, having John face the loss of his liberty. If you think civil litigation keeps you up at night, criminal charges turn you into a basket case. But perhaps you know that." Lynch's gaze flickered to me. "Sorry, TJ."

"It's okay." I nodded, my face going hot.

"In any event, I advise you to go home and get some rest. I know you're worried about John, but he's in capable hands." Lynch picked up his pad and slid it into a leather envelope. "Any other questions, please feel free to call."

"Thanks." My father began to rise, but Lynch waved him back into the chair.

"I'll see myself out, Paul. Marie, Gabby, Martin, TJ, it was good meeting you. Stay strong."

"We will," my father said, and everybody said their goodbyes. Lynch left, closing the door behind him.

I glanced at my mother, worried she would start to cry. "Mom, somebody once said, 'When you're going through hell, keep going.' Maybe we should put that on our family crest?"

My father forced a smile.

My mother cocked her head, sad but thoughtful. "We always talk about that quote, but Churchill doesn't say how to get through hell. Dante does, in *Inferno*. He devotes a lot of the poem to the fraudsters he finds in hell. In his view, the sinners who are the worst." She sighed, thinking aloud. "Ugolino the politician manipulates everyone and spends eternity in hell, watching his children die of starvation, even cannibalizing them. That's what Dante thinks fraudsters deserve. He loathed men who manipulate, steal, and lie—all the things my own son did."

I had no idea what to say, but my mother had the floor anyway.

"Dante says that the way to get through hell is with love and with compassion. That's how we'll get through this, with love and compassion for John." My mother's dark gaze shifted to us. "Dante doesn't feel scorn for sinners. He sees how they suffer and knows they're human beings who make mistakes. John is a sinner, and this isn't what any of us wanted for him, but we'll get through this together, as a family."

"You're absolutely right." My father looked at her with shining eyes, and I could see the love he had for her, which touched me.

"We will," I said, feeling new gratitude for them. "I know you all pulled for me, and I'll pull for John."

Gabby cleared her throat. "Mom and Dad, there's something I have to say."

CHAPTER FIFTY-ONE

Gabby stood up, resting her hand on Martin's shoulder. "There's something I need to say. I was the one who told the FBI about John."

I felt my mouth drop open.

My father recoiled.

My mother looked thunderstruck.

Martin turned to Gabby, shocked. "Gabs, *what* did you say?"

"I turned John in. I tipped off the FBI." Gabby put up her hands, like a traffic cop. "Mom and Dad, before you start yelling, let me explain. It started when—"

"Gabby!" My father jumped to his feet. "What were you thinking? You ruined John's life! You destroyed the firm!"

"Gabby?" My mother rose, her eyes flying open. "He's your brother, your own brother!"

"Now, let's stay calm." Martin rose. "Mom, Dad, hear her out. She didn't do anything wrong. John did."

"What?" my father shot back. "Martin, you don't think it's wrong to betray your own brother?"

"Dad, really?" I stood up before a fight broke out. "Martin's right, calm down. Gabby wants to speak. Everybody, sit down, please. Chill." I met my sister's stricken eye from across the table. "Gabby, you sit down, too. You're not in court and you don't have to argue a case. Let's just talk, like a family. We're a family. Remember, everybody?"

"*We* remember," my father said pointedly.

Gabby swallowed hard. "I knew you'd be mad, but I can explain."

Martin placed a comforting hand on her arm. "Go ahead, love."

"Okay. Just know this wasn't easy for me, and I didn't want to do it. But I had to, and I did try to talk to John, but he blew me off." She paused. "About a year ago, I referred a friend of mine from law school to him. Ted Lee, if you remember that name. Ted had a software start-up and needed a business lawyer. John incorporated him, but the bill was high and John told him it was normal. But Ted showed me the bill, and I could see it was padded. Every task took way too much time. It didn't make any sense. You all know John, he's efficient."

My parents seemed to settle in to listen.

"As I said, I raised it with him because I felt bad for Ted. He didn't have the money and it just seemed strange. It didn't even seem like John. But he didn't take it seriously. He was always in a rush, always moving so fast, and he wouldn't talk to me." Gabby's voice strengthened, and she sat taller. "Then, just out of curiosity, I looked at the files of two other clients that I had referred to him, who *hadn't* complained to me. I went to his office when he wasn't there, and I could see in both cases, the bills were padded. I tried to talk to him about it again, but he blew me off." Gabby ran a tongue over dry lips. "I'm sorry I did what I did, but I had to, and it was the right thing to do. These are my friends, I referred them to this firm, and they trusted me. John was cheating them, and that's *wrong*. It shouldn't even matter if they were friends because it's just plain *wrong*. Justice is blind, remember? Supposedly? Allegedly?"

I couldn't begin to think about whether Gabby was right. I was trying to process the information. My father and mother sat in stunned silence. Martin reached for Gabby's hand, his expression tender, his lips sealed.

"So that's why I did it, that's it. I didn't want to and I'm sad that I had to. I feel horrible that John got arrested. But somebody had to do the hard thing, and if it had to be me, so be it." Tears filmed Gabby's eyes. "I knew you guys were going to be mad, but I matter, too, and I'm in the right. I'm *not* the one who sent John to prison. I'm *not* the one who ruined the firm. *He* is." Gabby finished speaking, as if awaiting judgment.

My father leaned forward, gritting his teeth. "Why didn't you come to us?"

"Why? What would you have done? What you've always done? What I saw you do when you found out what he was up to?" Gabby threw up her hands. "You'd cover it up, that's what you'd do. You pay people off and you hire lawyers and you think you make it better, but you just make it *smooth*. You don't make it *right*. Smooth isn't *right*." She blinked her eyes clear. "My whole life, I've watched you bail out TJ and now John. It's not TJ's or John's pattern, it's yours. The more you let it go, the higher the stakes. Now it cost us the firm. I mean, this has to end somewhere. You guys keep looking the other way. Where does it end?" Gabby turned to me, pointing. "TJ, that's why I give you so much credit."

"Me?" I asked, astonished.

"Yes, you took responsibility for what you did. When you pleaded guilty, you *accounted*. You weren't trying to get away from the consequences. Mom and Dad hired Angela for you, and they all wanted you to fight the charge. You're the one who said no. You're the one who wanted to plead guilty, and I watched you in that courtroom. I could see you felt terrible. You thought it was your worst day, but I thought it was your best."

Whoa. I'd never thought of it that way. I couldn't speak for a moment.

Gabby heaved a sigh, facing my parents. "So I tipped off the FBI. They told me not to tell anybody and I didn't, not even Martin. Sorry, babe." She glanced at him, then faced us again. "I didn't know what they were doing or about the undercover operation. I assume they've been investigating since then, and they must have been ready to go because yesterday, when you guys figured out John was padding the Runstan bills, I called them. I told them I found more evidence."

"*What?*" my father asked, shocked. "Is *that* why they raided us today?"

"Yes, Dad, and I had to do it. That's why I didn't say anything when you were going through John's bills. I knew it was in the government's hands and I couldn't interfere. I didn't know if I could stop you, but I knew that they could. I was left with no choice. It was either my brother goes down or my whole family goes down—for *his* actions." Gabby frowned. "Dad, if you guys did what you intended—paying off the clients, lying to them that it was an accounting error, covering the whole thing up—then *you'd* be guilty of wire fraud, mail fraud, conspiracy, all the things they're charging John with. You would have put yourself in worse legal jeopardy. You would have made yourselves criminally liable, not just civilly. *You* would have been the fraudsters, Mom and Dad. If TJ helped you, he would be, too. *You'd all be behind bars.*"

I felt stunned, realizing she was right. I loved my sister and I'd never admired her more. "Gabby, you saved us from ourselves."

My father blinked, dumbfounded.

My mother looked down, beginning to cry.

"I'm sorry, Mom." Gabby bit her lower lip, trying not to cry, too. "I hope later you'll realize I did the right thing. But for now, I'm going home. I have work to do." She rose and looked at me. "TJ, the press conference in the Holmesburg case is tomorrow at eleven o'clock, at Hessian Post Plaza. I got the Complaint and a press packet copied, but they aren't collated. It's busywork, but can you do it? They're in boxes, and you can do it at home. I have to prepare Tony Bales to give a statement. I got the community involved, and there's going to be a lot of media."

"Of course I'll help," I said, rising.

I was ready to go home, too.

Right after I picked up Mango.

CHAPTER FIFTY-TWO

Traffic was light since rush hour hadn't started yet, and I felt nervous and exposed outside. I scanned the passing cars and checked my rearview mirror, but I didn't think anybody was following me. I hated not knowing who or where Fake Elliott Thompson was. The guy was somehow connected with John, Stan, and Runstan, which meant he was also connected to me. I felt like a moving target, so I kept moving.

I thought of my parents in the conference room, trying to come to terms with what Gabby had said. Devlin & Devlin was in shambles, and I'd taken the boxes of her documents and packed them in my trunk, trying to hold my head high in the parking lot. Employees had stood around gawking, taking photos and videos. The FBI had been finishing up, their agents stowing boxes in their Tahoes.

I'd picked up Mango and drove home through my neighborhood with her in the cardboard carrier the vet had given me. She was healthy again, meowing at the top of her lungs, but I didn't mind. The vet bill had been a small fortune, but I would have paid more, gratefully. I had my furbaby back.

I turned down my street, my senses on high alert. I scanned for suspicious cars but didn't see any, and the street was quiet. I cruised ahead and pulled into my driveway, satisfied I hadn't been followed.

I cut the ignition and got out of the car with the cat carrier, relieved that my neighbor Susanne's car wasn't in the driveway. The last time I'd seen her, the Chester County detectives had been looking for me, and I didn't want to have to explain anything. I dreaded to think what she was reading about the FBI raid at Devlin & Devlin. The Devlins had gone from legal royalty to crime family.

I unlocked the front door, carried Mango inside the house, and opened her cat carrier on the couch. She popped out like a jack-in-the-box and scooted under the couch, but stopped meowing.

"Be right back," I told her, then went out to fetch Gabby's boxes.

I made quick work of bringing them in and setting them on the floor. There were fourteen boxes, and I knelt and took the lid off the first one. My genius sister had packed me a big stapler, which rested on top of the papers.

You thought it was your worst day, but I thought it was your best.

I felt a rush of gratitude for Gabby and got busy on my busywork. I took the first Complaint out of the box and looked it over. COMPLAINT, it read at the top, and on the left: GABRIELLA DEVLIN, ESQUIRE, DEVLIN & DEVLIN, ATTORNEY FOR PLAINTIFFS, with her attorney identification number, our office address, and phone number.

I eyed it for a bittersweet moment. I was so proud of her for bringing this lawsuit, but at the same time, it hurt to think there was probably no more Devlin & Devlin. I felt the loss for her, my parents, John, and even for me. I wished for the umpteenth time that I had graduated and hadn't screwed things up so badly. Maybe I could have become a lawyer and joined the firm. Now that could never happen.

Dad's still on track to retire, isn't he?

My thoughts strayed to my brother, and surprisingly, my heart followed. I knew how terrified he would feel, hearing the evidence the government had against him. I didn't know if he would plead guilty, and I couldn't figure it out now. All I could do was feel for him, since I knew how awful it was to be a human being in a cage.

Exhaustion washed over me. I realized I hadn't slept for hours and I'd barely eaten. My brain was foggy, and I remembered that the bug was still in place. I wondered idly if the FBI had installed it.

I was too tired to figure it out, but I wanted to get this job done and it required a brain. I got up to make a sandwich.

After I ate, I gave Mango her evening shot, then returned to collating. It was dark out by the time I finished, and it turned out that the last two boxes only contained Gabby's notes and papers, so the task took less time.

I closed the last box and placed the lid on top, feeling a wave of fatigue. I stretched out on the floor, slid my phone out of my pocket, and set my alarm to wake me up at seven o'clock in the morning, in case I slept through the night. That would give me plenty of time to shower, get dressed, and give Mango her morning shot.

Sober Daddy was home.

I closed my eyes and fell into an exhausted sleep.

When I woke up, it was morning and Mango was sleeping curled against my side, her fuzzy chin resting on my arm.

Aw.

But it was oddly sunny in the living room. I felt around for my phone and found it on the rug.

The home screen had gone black. I touched it to turn it on. It didn't light up. The battery must be dead.

I checked my watch, beginning to panic. It was 10:07 A.M. I'd overslept.

"No!" I shouted. I had a slim-to-none chance of making the press conference on time.

Mango woke up and tore away.

I jumped up, frantic. I couldn't be late. I had the Complaints and press packets. I couldn't screw this up. I wasn't even drunk.

I flew into my bedroom.

CHAPTER FIFTY-THREE

I dressed and raced out of my bedroom, my tie undone. There was no time to shower or shave. There was only time to medicate the cat. I couldn't leave without giving her a shot. I wouldn't be back until midday. I refused to take another chance with her life. Unfortunately, she wasn't cooperating.

"Mango, please, you love me now!" I begged, but she raced under the couch, then under the bed, then under a chair.

"You slept with me!" I told her, unsure whether I was talking to Mango or Carrie. I took a flying leap and tackled her just as she ran out from under the chair.

I scooped her up, hustled back to the kitchen, and set her on the counter to give her her shot. She had dry food and I'd give her wet later. I had to load the boxes with the Complaints and press packets.

I grabbed a box, ran with it out to the car, and threw it in the trunk. I went back for the next, carrying two this time. I ran back to the car again and again and again, sweating in my suit.

I was down to three boxes. I didn't need to load the ones with Gabby's notes, but I didn't know which ones they were and didn't have time to look. I loaded boxes until there was only one left and raced out with it, locking the door behind me and scanning the street. I didn't see anything suspicious.

I ran to the driveway, but suddenly tripped, dumping the box. The lid came off and the papers flew all over the driveway.

I got up, gathered the papers, and started stuffing them in the box. There was a Johnson & Johnson prospectus, printed web pages about Penn's endowment, financial reporting from Rhone Pharma, and an old newspaper clipping about Fournette Laboratories.

I was about to put the clipping in the box, but a photo caught my eye. It showed a man at a podium, and behind him was a line of men. The one on the end was a man in a corporate blazer with a security patch on the pocket.

What the hell?

I recognized the face of the man in the photo. It was Fake Elliott Thompson.

I picked up the newspaper and stared at the photo in astonishment. The headline read FOURNETTE LABS PICKS NEW CEO, and the clipping was dated September 27, 1998. The caption identified the man at the end as Denver Mortensen, head of security at Fournette Laboratories.

Fake Elliott Thompson is Denver Mortensen?

I put the puzzle pieces together, filling in the picture. I had thought Fake Elliott Thompson/Denver Mortensen was connected to Runstan, but he must have been connected to Fournette Laboratories. The thugs hadn't been hired by Stan, but by the *drug company*. They hadn't been after me because of John, they'd been after me because of *Gabby*.

My God. My mind raced. My chest went tight. I realized that somebody at Fournette Labs must have wanted to stop Gabby and me because of the Holmesburg lawsuit.

My thoughts flew ahead in horror. Mortensen had tried to kill

John when he met Lemaire at Dutton Run Park. Mortensen must have mistaken John for Gabby. Both drove black Range Rovers. It had been hard to see in the dark and the downpour.

Mortensen was still out there. He would want to finish the job. Gabby was in mortal peril. Mortensen's last chance was the press conference.

I jumped in the car and hit the gas.

CHAPTER FIFTY-FOUR

I zoomed out of the driveway. I had to call Gabby and warn her. I reached for my phone. I remembered it was out of battery.

I plugged it in the charger at speed, almost swerving out of the lane. But traffic was light and I knew I wouldn't hurt anybody. If a cop tried to pull me over, he'd have to chase me to the press conference. I wasn't stopping for anybody.

I kept a hand on the steering wheel. My speed went to sixty, then seventy on streets with a forty-miles-per-hour limit. I steered around cars, vans, and SUVs.

I pressed the button to call Gabby and held the phone to my ear.

The phone rang and rang. She didn't pick up.

I scrolled to the text function, hit DICTATE, and sent her a text. **CALL ME EMERGENCY**

A blue text bubble popped onto the screen: **I'M DRIVING WITH MY NOTIFICATIONS SILENCED . . .**

No! I hit Route 202 and accelerated to eighty, then eighty-five. The road rumbled. The asphalt was smooth. My hand gripped the wheel, steady.

I tried to think who else to contact. Martin. I scrolled to his number and called. I let it ring and ring, then hung up. He must have been in surgery. He wasn't easy to reach but he always called back. But I knew it would be too late.

I zoomed ahead on Route 202, weaving in and out of lanes. I tried to accelerate but the car shuddered, underpowered. If I were in the Maserati, I'd have been there yesterday.

I called my mother. She could reach Gabby. I held the phone to my ear. It rang and rang, then went to voicemail.

I called my father. It rang, then I remembered the FBI had seized his phone.

I thought fast. My parents would be at the office. I started to call the main number, then remembered I unplugged the phone yesterday.

I called 911, a Hail Mary pass. As soon as the call connected, I said, "Hello, emergency, I'm calling because my sister's life is in danger and—"

"Sir," the dispatcher said calmly. "Please let me have your name and address."

I told her. "But it's not about me, it's about my sister, she's at Hessian Post Plaza off of Route 202, giving a press conference. I'm on my way there—"

"Excuse me, sir. Are you with your sister at this time?"

"No, but someone's going to kill her. It's part of a conspiracy and this guy is a killer—"

"Sir, if this is a joke and—"

"It's not, I swear. You have to believe me. Send the cops to Hessian Post Plaza."

"Sir, please speak more slowly—"

I hung up, knowing I couldn't explain. I'd be there in seven minutes, faster than any cop anyway. I whizzed past corporate centers and shopping centers. I could see Hessian Post Plaza in the distance on the right.

I checked the clock. It was eleven o'clock.

I could only pray they were running late.

I spotted an old brown Honda behind me and felt like I had seen it before, but I couldn't be sure.

I accelerated, clenching my teeth.

CHAPTER FIFTY-FIVE

I reached Hessian Post Plaza, veered into the parking lot, and slammed on the brakes at the hubbub. Gabby had said she was going to engage the community, but I had never expected a crowd this large. Hundreds of demonstrators thronged in front of the buildings, all races, ages, and sizes walking in a circle, chanting, "No justice, no peace," and carrying signs, JUSTICE FOR THE HOLMESBURG SEVEN, TUSKEGEE TODAY, and PHILLY, PAY UP! They massed over the east end of the plaza, blocked the entrance, and overflowed the sidewalk. Cars and news vans congested the parking lot. I didn't see the brown Honda anymore.

I double-parked, jumped out of the car, and ran to the building, scanning frantically for Gabby or Mortensen. The media was everywhere, reporters interviewing activists and video camera operators filming the demonstration. The noise was deafening, and many of the protesters had bullhorns. I spotted my parents on the far side of the throng, my father head and shoulders above the crowd. I hadn't expected them here and it was too loud to call to them. Employees filled the office windows, watching what was going on. Uniformed security guards stood in groups, nervously eyeing the situation.

"Excuse me, it's an emergency," I shouted, threading my way through the noisy crowd to the building. Gabby had to be inside already. I had to get to her. The press conference would soon be underway. I couldn't call her because I'd left my phone in the car in my panic.

I made my way to the propped-open door and ran down a large hallway. The outside noise reverberated throughout the building. The press conference was being held in the conference room where we'd met with defense counsel to present the Complaint.

I ran there and flung open the door. The conference room was empty. They must have changed the room. Gabby must have been surprised by the crowd size, too.

I ran back down the hall. I didn't know my way around. The entire first floor was spaces for rent, a warren of empty offices and unsigned halls. I ran down one hallway, then the next, but there was no one around. Finally I spotted our lead plaintiff, Chuck Whitman, sitting alone in a folding chair.

"Chuck, where's Gabby?" I asked, reaching him, breathless.

"Hey, TJ, calm down. She's looking for you. We got time. They put a delay on the press conference. Everybody turned out, and they gotta find us a bigger room." He chuckled. "They never *saw* so many Black people out here. They called the cops."

"But where's Gabby? It's an emergency."

Chuck's smile vanished. "She's gonna make an announcement about the delay. She's outside. That way." He pointed to the left.

I ran down the hall toward another exit door on the west side of the building. It was glass, and I could see the crowd outside, facing the building and flooding the sidewalk. Everybody held up phones. Reporters raised cameras.

Gabby had to be right outside. I raced to the door and pressed the handle, but it was locked.

"Open the door!" I shouted, but nobody heard. I jiggled the door again and again. Nobody noticed. There had to be another way out. There was a hallway to my right and to my left. I sensed the one on the right led to an exit.

I turned around just in time to see a man in a black ball cap and sunglasses.

Aiming a gun with a silencer at me.

CHAPTER FIFTY-SIX

Crak! The man fired the gun, the suppressed shot too quiet to be heard over the roar.

I sprang aside. The bullet whizzed hot past my head.

I felt a bolt of sheer terror. I took off racing down the hall. There was nothing except a line of closed doors. I ran to the first one on the right. I tried the door. It was locked.

Crak! The man fired as he reached the hall. I flattened against the door, which was recessed. He missed again.

The door across the hall was frosted glass. I launched myself at the glass, breaking through. Shards flew everywhere.

Crak! The bullet whizzed by the room.

I fell inside amid the shards. It was a break room with vending machines but no cover. I grabbed a shard, scrambled to my feet, and flattened against the wall out of view.

I tried to think despite my fear. The man didn't look like Mortensen. He must've been a third guy in the conspiracy. The guy in the brown Honda. That meant Gabby was still in danger. Mortensen would kill her.

Crak! The man shot inside the room at an angle.

"Ahh!" I cried out like he'd hit me. In the next moment, the man began walking toward the room to finish me off. The suppressed muzzle of the gun inched into my view. His right hand was wrapped around the handle.

Now.

I lunged and brought the glass shard down hard on his hand, slicing across the row of bones. The man shouted in pain. Blood squirted from the gash in a gruesome fan.

He dropped the gun. I dropped the bloody shard.

I barreled into him with all of my strength, tackling him. I landed the first punch, then the second. He connected with a right that rattled my skull, but I jabbed him under the jaw, again and again until he lost consciousness.

I staggered to my feet, my chest heaving. The gun lay on the floor. I couldn't kill him, but I had to immobilize him.

I picked up the gun and shot him in the lower leg.

I ran down the hall to the exit, pocketing the gun.

CHAPTER FIFTY-SEVEN

I flew through the doors, my hand bleeding. I looked wildly around for Gabby. I didn't see her. The demonstrators had migrated to the east side, shouting, chanting, and pumping signs. Media jostled them with video cameras and boom mics. My father and mother were in the crowd, with him a head taller.

Suddenly the crowd surged to the building. I looked to my left and saw Gabby far from me, at the other side of the crowd. She was climbing up on a raised platform with a bullhorn.

I scanned the crowd for Mortensen. I spotted him, moving around the back of the crowd. I had a gun, but I couldn't shoot safely.

"Gabby, get down!" I shouted, frantic, but she couldn't hear me.

Mortensen stopped. I sensed he was in position to shoot. He was too far from me, but not from my father.

"Dad, behind you!" I screamed, waving my hands to get his attention.

My father spotted me, pivoted, and suddenly plowed into Mortensen like the power forward he used to be. He took Mortensen to the ground. A gun went off with a deafening report and flew into the air.

"Active shooter!" "It's a shooter!" "He has a gun!" The crowd erupted into terrified chaos. People ran in all directions for their lives. Cameras and phones hit the ground. A young woman was almost trampled. My mother started screaming, almost knocked over in the melee.

I weaved to her, scooped her up, and shielded her with my body. The frantic crowd buffeted us. We fought our way toward my father. The crowd was clearing fast. A police cruiser veered around the corner, its siren bursting into sound.

My father was on top of Mortensen, punching him. The two men grappled. Mortensen punched back, hitting my father in the head, then scrambled out from under him, and ran. Men in the crowd chased him into the parking lot. Cops leapt from cruisers and followed on their heels.

"Dad!" I reached my father, my heart pounding. I threw myself on the ground. "Dad, are you okay?"

"I got him," my father said, smiling. He turned over, dazed and sweaty.

I looked down in horror. His white shirt was in tatters. Dark red blood oozed from his gut, spreading on his chest. His breathing was ragged.

"Paul!" my mother screamed, kneeling at his side.

"Dad!" Gabby cried.

My father's eyes rolled back in his head.

In the next moment, he lost consciousness.

CHAPTER FIFTY-EIGHT

My mother, Gabby, and I sat huddled together, numb and stricken in the ER waiting room while my father was in surgery. Everything that happened after he got shot had blurred into a single horror. He'd bled so profusely that I'd used my jacket as a compress. An ambulance arrived quickly, and EMTs intubated him in the parking lot, then whisked him to the hospital with my mother. Cops had arrested Mortensen and the guy I shot, then I'd taken a distraught Gabby to my car. We'd raced to the hospital, where they dressed the cut on my hand.

Luckily there was nobody else in our section of the waiting room. Its walls were a blue pastel, lined with framed prints of native wildflowers. A flat-screen TV played on closed-captioning, and the end tables held outdated magazines. A wall clock told me that we hadn't been here that long, and the ER doctor had said that my father's surgery was expected to take several hours. The doctor had declined to speculate on the prognosis, offering only that his condition was critical, and we'd called John's lawyer to let him know what was going on. Gabby had called Martin, and he was on his way from a medical conference in Baltimore.

I had one arm around my mother and the other around Gabby. My hands were stained with my father's blood, which dried in nightmare crescents in my fingernails. My clothes were spattered, and so were my mother's and Gabby's. They talked and cried, clutching Kleenexes, and I listened to their mother-daughter echoes.

Thank God the ambulance came so fast. That has to help.

It will, Mom. It has to.

There was so much blood.

So much blood.

He didn't know he was shot.

He was in shock.

The gunshot was so loud.

The crowd thought it was an active shooter.

Suddenly my attention was drawn to the far side of the waiting room, where Detective Willoughby was entering with his partner, Detective Balleu. I'd assumed they'd show up sooner or later. Their expressions were grim and professional as they made a beeline for us, and I remembered that the last time I'd seen them, they'd questioned me as a suspect in Lemaire's death.

I shifted position and got ready to meet them, come what may.

Detective Willoughby sat opposite us with his plastic folder and fresh legal pad open on his lap. Detective Balleu was in the chair next to him, legs crossed, with a skinny notepad.

"Marie and Gabby, good to see you." Detective Willoughby slid out his Cross pen from its holder. "Please accept our apologies for having to intrude at this difficult time. We have some preliminary questions. The rest can wait until later."

"Thank you," I answered for us.

"We understand that John is in federal custody. That's not our jurisdiction, nor is it why we're here." Detective Willoughby glanced at my mother, then Gabby. "We're all pulling for Paul. He has so many friends on the force. Your family's been a supporter for a long time."

"Thank you." My mother dabbed her eye with a Kleenex.

"We're beginning our investigation into what happened to Paul." Detective Willoughby turned to Gabby and me, nodding solemnly. "Of course we'll investigate the assaults on both of you. We have uniformed officers at the scene right now, taking statements from eyewitnesses and collecting film and other evidence. The district attorney and his office are committed to getting to the bottom of what happened today at Hessian Post Plaza."

"Good." My mother sniffled. "Thank you."

Detective Willoughby faced me. "TJ, my first questions are for you. We can discuss it here or elsewhere in private. Your choice."

"Here is fine," I told him. My mother nodded, and so did Gabby.

"We have Denver Mortensen and Viktor Solkov in custody."

"Is that the man who tried to kill me? Viktor Solkov? I shot him in the leg."

Detective Willoughby hesitated. "Yes, but that's confidential information—"

"Well, I was there, so it's not confidential from me. I gave his gun to a uniformed officer at the scene. Did you get it?"

"Yes, it's in our custody, bagged as evidence."

"Is Solkov talking? I assume he was working with Mortensen, but who were they working for at Fournette Labs? Why did they want us dead? It had to be because of the lawsuit. It has to go high up."

Detective Willoughby pursed his lips. "I'm sorry, I'm not at liberty to discuss the matter with you. We've just begun our investigation.

As soon as we're able to let you know, we will. We're aware that you've all been through the mill, and I apologize for adding to your burden at this difficult time." Detective Willoughby frowned. "Can you explain briefly to us what happened? If you outline the basics, we can take a more detailed statement later."

I launched into an explanation, telling as much as I could without compromising John's defense. My mother and Gabby listened raptly, and I made quick work of the summary. It was hard to function normally with my father in surgery. Detective Willoughby and Balleu took notes as I spoke, putting me in the bizarro-world position of being an authority to the authorities.

"My God," Gabby said, hushed, when we were alone.

"That's just what I was thinking." My mother rose stiffly, brushing down her bloodstained sweater and slacks. "Come on, get up, you two. Now let's go."

"Where do you want to go?" I asked, confused.

"This hospital must have a chapel. Your father needs our prayers."

CHAPTER FIFTY-NINE

I made the sign of the cross on my chest, kneeling on the kneepad next to Gabby and my mother. The chapel was small, generic, and devoid of any spirituality whatsoever. The front was like a stage and the pews were modern. The overhead lights were soft, and we were the only people here. The air smelled musty.

Gabby and my mother bent their heads in prayer, but my mind wandered. I flashed on the horror of my father, bleeding out under my palms and soaking my suit jacket. Then John, lying beaten on his kitchen floor and soon to be sitting in a cell, trying to keep his sanity amid the noise, brutality, and cruelty of prison. I worried that, unlike me, he'd go deeper within and shut down, which would only make doing time harder.

I sighed inwardly, mentally reviewing what I'd told the detectives and hoping I hadn't hurt John's defense. I didn't know when I would get to talk to him again, but I'd beg him to plead guilty. He would serve less time and in the long run, maybe it would make him feel better, as it did me. I'd never thought about it the way Gabby had the other day, but now I saw it with new eyes. I had taken the punishment I deserved for what I did to Emily that night, and now I had apologized to Carrie, which lightened my load somewhat. I had to come to terms with the fact that she had moved on. Maybe we just weren't to be.

I could hear my mother in whispered prayer, and I loved her for it, knowing that her faith was as much a part of her identity as being Italian. She had grown up in a Catholic tradition of service and imbued it in Gabby, which was why my sister worked so hard for the public good. My mother used to drag us to church every Sunday, where I'd been intimidated by the grand marble altar with its life-size statue of Jesus Christ, hammered to a massive crucifix through his wrists and crossed feet, his head bleeding under a crown of thorns.

The guilt and shame in my religion became as familiar as old friends in my drinking days. But I had changed, believing in God as I understood, and now loved him. I believed in the program, too. It struck me that I hadn't thought about drinking for another whole day. My new sobriety date was May 22.

I sent up another prayer for my father.

The three of us sat in the pew, and my mother dried her eyes after another crying jag. "Gabby, TJ, there's something I want to say before we go back upstairs. I'm sorry if I let you guys down as a mother. I really think—"

"What?" I interrupted her. "Don't be ridiculous."

Gabby added, "Mom, you're a great mother, and Dad's a great father. You guys have been amazing to us. John would say the same thing."

My mother pursed her lips. "Gabby, I have a lot of soul-searching to do about John. I made mistakes with him, but I'm talking to you two now. I want you to know that I love you both and I'm sorry for any mistakes I made, and your father, too."

I started to protest, but my mother raised her hand to silence me, then turned to Gabby.

"Honey, Dad and I went to your press conference today because we wanted to show our support. We haven't been respectful enough of your pro bono cases. That stops now. We're very proud of you for the work you do." My mother swallowed hard. "I'm sorry we reacted badly when you told us you went to the FBI, too. You were right. Somebody had to do the hard thing, and you did. It was unfair of your father and me to ask you to cover for John."

Gabby's eyes welled up. "I didn't mean to be so harsh."

"You weren't harsh." My mother patted her hand. "You told the truth about us. It's the truth that's harsh." She turned to me, trying not to cry. "And, TJ, you've been through hell, but I swear to God I see a new strength in you. I listened to what you told the detectives and I'm amazed by this investigation you've done. Son, you saved your sister's life today."

My chest went tight. It was impossible for me to see it that way. "Mom, I sent Dad into harm's way."

"No, you didn't, TJ." My mother grabbed my arm and squeezed it hard, her dark eyes flaring with maternal ferocity. "Listen to me. You know your father. Paul Devlin doesn't do a single thing he doesn't want to. I pray to God he lives through this, but if he doesn't, know that he did *exactly* what he wanted to do." A tear rolled down her cheek, but she ignored it, trembling with emotion. "The truth is, your father loves his children more than his own life, and today, he proved it."

Gabby burst into tears, and I hugged her and my mother, holding them close while they began to cry, and in time, the three of us shared our sorrow, fear, and love in a generic chapel that somehow became a sacred place.

Through the miracle of family.

Suddenly we heard the door opening, and a nurse peeked inside the chapel. "Ms. Devlin? The doctor would like to see you."

CHAPTER SIXTY

My mother sat by my father's bed in the ICU, holding his hand. He looked pale and weak, hooked up to an IV and monitors that blinked his vital signs in green and blue. We had a private room, and the late-day sun waned through the window. His surgery had taken five hours, during which he'd been transfused. Doctors had repaired the damage done by the bullet, which had lacerated his abdomen. No major organ had been hit, so he was expected to recover.

Gabby sat next to my mother, and I sat on the opposite side of the bed, holding my father's other hand, which felt warm and surprisingly heavy in mine. I couldn't remember the last time I'd held his hand or even touched him for this long.

My father's eyelids fluttered open. "Marie?"

"Honey?" My mother startled with relief, leaning over him. "How are you doing, sweetheart?"

"You . . . tell me." My father spoke with effort, managing a shaky smile, and my mother smiled back.

"You're doing great. Your surgery was a success, and you're going to be okay."

My father paused. "Did you . . . pray a novena?"

"You know I did. You can thank me anytime."

My father's face softened. "Thank you . . . I love you."

"I love you, too." My mother kissed him on the cheek and smoothed back his hair. "How do you feel? Are you in pain?"

"Not . . . much." My father shifted his weary gaze to Gabby. "Love you . . . honey. I picked a good day . . . to see you at work, huh?"

"Or a bad day." Gabby's eyes began to glisten. "I'm so sorry—"

"No . . . hush," my father interrupted, speaking with effort. "I'm . . . sorry. You were right . . . about John."

My mother interjected, "Paul, I told her already. We can talk about it later when you feel better. The doctor said you need to rest. This isn't the time."

"Yes . . . it is." My father lifted an eyebrow, amused. "I gotta tell these kids . . . how I feel . . . What if I . . . throw a clot, Marie? I could check out . . . any minute."

"That's not funny." My mother chuckled, and so did Gabby, but I sensed he wasn't kidding.

My father squeezed my hand feebly, turning to me. "TJ . . . nice work . . . today."

My throat caught. "Hardly. I almost got you killed."

"Nah . . . just the opposite." My father smiled, shaking his head. "You passed me . . . the ball. You made the . . . mother of all assists. It was . . . a total MVP move."

MVP, me? My heart eased, and I felt tears in my eyes. "I love you, Dad."

"I love you . . . too." My father paused. "Who was . . . that guy anyway? Why did he . . . wanna kill Gabby?"

My mother interjected again, "We'll talk about it later. TJ cracked the case."

My father smiled again, his eyelids fluttering. "That's . . . my boy."

Wow. I squeezed his hand, and he held mine.

Neither of us let go.

CHAPTER SIXTY-ONE

I sat in the gallery of the courtroom with my mother, father, Gabby, Martin, and Nancy, who'd left Connor at home with her parents. We were dressed like we were going to a funeral, and it was hard not to feel that way. John was pleading guilty today and was due here any minute. We'd come separately on the advice of both lawyers.

My family and I sat in silence, cowed by the size and grandeur of the federal courtroom. Wood panels encased us on all four sides, and the jury box and the witness stand were monoliths of dense, indeterminate wood. The judge wasn't in the courtroom yet, and the dais was the biggest monolith of all. It was flanked by flags of the United States and the Commonwealth of Pennsylvania, and between them hung the massive, round seal of the federal district court, as bronze as a burnished sun.

The assistant U.S. attorneys weren't here, and we were the only people in the courtroom except for two lawyers talking in the back, their occasional laughter echoing in the cavernous space. I couldn't imagine being that relaxed in a courtroom. I still had my knee-jerk reaction to authority, as nervous as if I were the one under federal criminal indictment. Even the air-conditioning was powerful, setting my teeth on edge.

Our lives had turned upside down since John's indictment, but we were getting used to the new normal. My father had required additional surgery and was still in rehab. His brush with death had become a de facto retirement, and the scandal that broke after John's arrest had made staying in business impossible. Devlin & Devlin was defunct. The Runstan acquisition had gone through, since Stan had committed no wrongdoing. John had been covering for himself when he'd lied to me about telling Stan about Lemaire.

Surprisingly, my father hadn't taken the emotional nosedive we'd all feared when the office closed. The media reported that he'd saved Gabby at Hessian Post Plaza, which salvaged his reputation. It also made me see him with new eyes. He wanted to be the family hero, and in a way, he was. He sold the practice and made sure that the clients John had cheated were made whole, with interest.

My mother took him to his various doctor appointments, and despite their troubles, she seemed less burdened, too. She was taking a Dante class online with a famous professor, and her nose was always buried in the *Divine Comedy*. Today she sat silently next to me, and I worried about her.

I leaned over. "Mom, what would Dante tell us about today?"

"That we're entering purgatory."

"Is that good?"

"It's better than hell," she answered flatly. "In *Purgatorio*, there's movement and light because the penitent souls have admitted their sin. So they're not sinners, they're purging themselves. It takes work. They have to use free will to 'winnow good from evil.' I have hope for John, and all of us."

"Good, Mom." I took her hand, strangely comforted.

"We were in hell before, honey. We just didn't know it."

Suddenly, we heard the door open in the back of the courtroom, and I turned to see John enter with his lawyer, Natalie Christiano. My brother's expression was impassive, which was trademark John in the clutch. He had on a silk tie and his best Brioni suit, and we joked yesterday that white-collar criminals dressed better than schlubs like me. He'd entered Gamblers Anonymous as a condition of bail and was in a better place since his arrest. We'd compared notes, since AA and GA were companion programs, and I told him he was the next Relapse Virgin.

My mother squeezed my hand as John reached us, and Natalie went ahead to counsel table. John paused to say goodbye, kissing Nancy on the cheek, shaking my father's hand and Martin's, and kissing my mother and finally Gabby, whose lower lip trembled. His dry eye met her weepy one with a brave smile. He'd forgiven her for turning him in, and I was proud of him.

I eyed John, and we shook hands, saying nothing. We'd talked more since his arrest than we ever had before and we'd said everything we had to say. We'd resolved some old hurts, and I told him I loved him. He told me he loved me, too, and yesterday, he'd managed to find some dark humor in going to prison for three years.

TJ, I got three years, and you only got one. I win.

CHAPTER SIXTY-TWO

I never expected to be in another courtroom so soon, especially not with the man who tried to kill me, but I was learning to expect the unexpected. This time we were at the Chester County Justice Center, and sitting in the witness stand was Viktor Solkov, a fortysomething thug whose entire face I was seeing for the first time. He had light eyes, angular cheekbones, and a scar on his chin. The last time I'd seen him, he had on a ball cap and sunglasses and was chasing me down a hallway at Hessian Post Plaza with a gun.

I couldn't take my eyes off Solkov, and he avoided my gaze from behind the black stem microphone. He looked freshly shaved, and his blond hair was newly cut. He was dressed in a cheap suit bought for court. I wanted him to pay for what he tried to do to me, along with Mortensen and the man at the top, who masterminded the conspiracy.

Solkov had pleaded guilty to criminal conspiracy and attempted first-degree murder, as had Mortensen, who had testified yesterday, also charged with criminal solicitation. Both men were serving seven-year sentences on three counts of the crimes, for me, Gabby, and my father. The two had gotten a lenient sentence in return for testifying today against the man who had hired them, the CEO of Fournette Labs himself, Dr. Carl Bostwick.

Dr. Bostwick sat at the defense table in a well-tailored gray suit that coordinated with his steely gray hair and wire-rimmed bifocals. He had been Fournette CEO for the past eleven years, so he was wealthy enough to hire Deidre Yler, a well-known Philadelphia lawyer who sat stiffly next to him in a no-nonsense dark suit. Bostwick had chosen to go to trial, a savvy move given that the only evidence linking him to the crimes was the testimony of Mortensen and Solkov, plus a security-camera video of him meeting Mortensen in a public parking garage. Mortensen testified that the video showed the conversation in which Bostwick had hired him to kill Gabby and me, but his testimony couldn't be verified without audio.

"May I approach the witness, Your Honor?" Assistant District Attorney Matthew Nolan was tall and thin in a pin-striped suit, with a nimbleness in the courtroom that made it look easy.

"Yes," answered Judge Rati-Jio, who had presided over my guilty plea, back in the day. If she was surprised to see me return as a crime victim instead of a criminal, it didn't show.

"Now, Mr. Solkov, you've testified that you went to Hessian Post Plaza on the day in question with instructions. Who gave you these instructions?"

"My cousin Denver Mortensen."

"Did he do this in person or by phone?"

"In person."

"Where did this conversation take place?"

"At home, in my apartment over the garage. It's his garage apartment, really. I live with him."

"Was anyone else present during this conversation?"

"No."

"When did this conversation take place?"

"Sometime last May, mid-May, I forget exactly. Denver, uh, Mr. Mortensen said they needed me to replace some guy that got killed by a truck."

Yler shot to her pumps. "Objection, Your Honor. That statement should be stricken as hearsay."

Nolan pivoted smoothly to the bench. "Your Honor, it falls within the hearsay exception for out-of-court declarations of one co-conspirator against another, made during the conspiracy and in furtherance of the common design."

Judge Rati-Jio nodded. "The objection's overruled. Go ahead, Mr. Nolan."

Nolan faced Solkov. "You may answer. Do you know the name of the man you replaced?"

"Yeah, Barry Rigel."

"Did you know Mr. Rigel?"

"No, but Mr. Mortensen said he was a screwup. He was following Gabby Devlin but she drives the same car as her brother. Rigel took a shot at the brother and missed, then he had to kill some random guy who made him."

"Do you know the name of this so-called random guy?"

"Neil Lemaire. Wrong place, wrong time."

Dear God. I already knew what had happened, but hearing it aloud made me sick to my stomach. After the police had told me, I'd reached out to Neil's boyfriend, Daniel, and he mourned Neil all over again.

"And what did Mr. Mortensen tell you to do?"

"He told me to take out the brother. Thomas Devlin."

"And did you understand what Mr. Mortensen meant by 'take out'?"

"Yes."

"What did you understand?"

"He meant kill, and he gave me a gun with a silencer."

I shuddered, and my mother's face drained of color. I patted her hand, and she straightened. We Devlins were battle-hardened, having testified already and watched the proceedings every day. My father, who was slowly recovering from his gunshot wound, had crushed it on the witness stand. The media dogged us, but Gabby used every interview to raise awareness of the Holmesburg lawsuit. Chuck Whitman and Tony Bales sat with us in court, plaintiffs who had become friends, and the community packed the gallery, too. We were turning into a media sensation, reported as the lawsuit that corporations would kill to stop.

Nolan faced Solkov. "Now, did Mr. Mortensen offer you money to kill Thomas Devlin?"

"Yes."

"How much money?"

"Five grand."

"And did Mr. Mortensen tell you where he was getting the money that he was going to give you to kill Thomas Devlin?"

"Yes."

"And where did Mr. Mortensen say he was getting that money?"

"Mr. Mortensen said Dr. Bostwick was going to pay him ten grand to kill the woman lawyer, Gabby Devlin, and Dr. Bostwick would pay me five grand to kill her brother."

The gallery reacted with gasps. Shocked faces wheeled to one another. The courtroom artist sketched madly, and Gabby and I exchanged knowing glances. We'd heard all this during Mortensen's testimony, and we shared a dark laugh over my life being worth half of hers.

Nolan stood tall, finishing up. "And did Mr. Mortensen tell you why Dr. Bostwick wanted Gabby Devlin and Thomas Devlin dead?"

"Yes."

"And what did he say?"

"Dr. Bostwick said the lawyer and her brother had a lawsuit that would have made Fournette look bad and hurt the stock price. Dr. Bostwick had a lot of stock and he didn't wanna lose any money he was gonna make when the company went public."

"Did Mr. Mortensen tell you how much money Dr. Bostwick would have lost if the stock price went down?"

"He said millions. He didn't say how many millions." Solkov smirked. "If it's millions, it don't matter how many."

The jurors smiled, and two nodded in agreement. I took heart, hoping they believed his testimony. I sure did.

Nolan nodded. "Your Honor, I have no further questions."

Judge Rati-Jio motioned to the defense counsel. "Ms. Yler, your witness."

Yler shot up in front of her chair. "Mr. Solkov, you never spoke with Dr. Bostwick in connection with these alleged crimes, isn't that correct?"

"Yes. Correct."

"You were never given any audio recording of Dr. Bostwick in connection with these alleged crimes, isn't *that* correct?"

"Yes."

"Finally, you were never given a video recording of Dr. Bostwick in connection with these crimes, isn't that correct?"

"Yes."

"So isn't it fair to say that, even if the jury were to believe your testimony, the only thing you know about Dr. Bostwick's alleged connection to your crimes is what Mr. Mortensen told you?"

"Yes."

"Let's switch gears, Mr. Solkov. You were dishonorably discharged from the U.S. Army, were you not?"

Nolan half rose. "Objection as to relevance, Your Honor."

Yler sniffed. "Your Honor, it goes to credibility, which I'm certainly entitled to explore on cross."

"Agreed, the objection is overruled."

Yler nodded at Solkov. "You were dishonorably discharged, were you not?"

"Yes."

"And two years subsequent to your dishonorable discharge, you served two years in Delaware County prison for spousal abuse on your then-wife, isn't that correct?"

"Yes."

"Upon your release, you were found in violation of parole for possessing an unregistered firearm and sent back to Delaware County prison, isn't that correct?"

"Yes." Solkov shifted in his seat and I glanced at the jury, who had begun to collectively frown.

"Mr. Solkov, upon your release from Delaware County prison, is it true that you were convicted again of aggravated assault on your then-wife?"

"Yes."

Yler's upper lip curled with contempt. "And upon conviction, you were resentenced to Delaware County prison for an additional two years, isn't that correct?"

"Yes."

"Isn't it also true that since your release you have been the subject of eight protection-from-abuse orders applied for by your ex-wife?"

"Yes."

"Mr. Solkov, you are unemployed, isn't that correct?"

"Yes."

"You have been unemployed since you were last released from Delaware County prison, isn't that correct?"

"Well, officially, yes."

Yler sat down, her disdain plain. "I have no further questions of this witness."

I sneaked a peek at the jury, and I saw plenty of outraged looks and disgusted expressions. They didn't like Solkov, and they hadn't liked Mortensen, either. It was going to come down to the word of two thugs against a CEO, whom nobody expected to testify. I didn't know how much doubt was qualified as reasonable, but we were going to find out.

Very soon.

CHAPTER SIXTY-THREE

I sat in the front row of the gallery, next to my mother, my father, Gabby, and Martin. On my left sat Chuck Whitman, and next to him, Tony Bales, plaintiffs from the Holmesburg case. On the other side of Gabby were the other plaintiffs and members of the community who had dedicated themselves to bringing to light what happened at Holmesburg. We awaited the jury in silence, having been told that they had reached a verdict. The suspense had been excruciating, lasting three days.

I glued my gaze to the paneled door, and the jury was about to file in. I reviewed the evidence in my mind, because I replayed it at night when I got home, wondering whether Bostwick would get convicted. He hadn't taken the stand, but the defense lawyer had put up two expert witnesses who testified that the lawsuit wouldn't necessarily have affected the stock price of the company. It went against common sense, an argument that Assistant District Attorney Nolan made in his closing to the jury. They had listened carefully to both sides, and by the time they'd filed out of the courtroom to deliberate, I had no idea which way they would go.

My gaze settled on Bostwick, of whom I had a view in semi-profile.

The CEO kept his gaze trained on the judge, looking neither right nor left. My eyes bored into the side of his head, and I realized that's where he would've drilled a bullet into mine.

I tried to understand the depth of depravity that would cause one man to order the killing of another, but it was beyond me. All I knew was that I wanted to see this doctor go to prison for what he had done, like Mortensen and Solkov. I didn't know if we'd get justice, but I prayed for it every night. If Solkov and Mortensen were in jail, then there better be a cell for Dr. Bostwick, too.

Suddenly the courtroom side door opened and the jury began to file in, twelve residents of Chester County, male and female, each looking solemn and grave, each dressed like everybody else because they were everybody else, except today they had been charged with the awesome responsibility of delivering a verdict. In other words, upholding American law.

I craned my neck to see them, and so did everybody else in the row. My mother took my hand, and I heard my father grunt, shifting uncomfortably on the pew since he still hadn't healed fully from his surgery. Gabby perched on the edge of her seat, on point as a bird dog as she watched the jurors settle into their chairs and scrutinized their expressions. She had told me that if they were smiling, it was good for us, but I didn't see any smiles now.

Everyone shifted in the gallery, and Chuck caught my eye with a tense smile. I wanted this verdict for him and all of the other plaintiffs as much as I wanted it for us, and Gabby felt exactly the same way. Today wasn't about her and me at all, but about whether you could stop justice with a bullet. I knew it happened in other parts of the world, but it wasn't supposed to happen here.

Judge Rati-Jio turned to the jury. "Ladies and gentlemen, I understand that you've reached a verdict?"

"Yes, Your Honor." The forewoman stood up, an impassive expression on her lined face. She must've been in her sixties, and on the short side in a plain denim dress, but there was a strength in her frame that I could almost feel, like my mother's.

"I'll have the clerk take the verdict."

The uniformed clerk, whom I remembered as Mack, faced the jury. "Has the jury reached a verdict?"

"Yes," the forewoman answered again.

"Do you find the defendant, Dr. Carl C. Bostwick, guilty or not guilty of the crime of criminal conspiracy regarding the attempted shooting of Thomas Devlin?"

"Guilty."

My God. Tears filled my eyes. I wanted to shout for joy, burst into tears, and jump up and down.

My mother covered her mouth, and my father grinned from ear to ear. Gabby gasped, her hand flying to her chest, and Martin quietly put an arm around her.

The clerk asked the forewoman each of the questions and each of the counts as to me, Gabby, and my father, and the answers came back "yes," "yes," "yes."

"Hot damn," Chuck said under his breath.

"We did it." I squeezed his arm.

"We sure as hell did. Justice was served." Chuck's cloudy eyes rimmed with tears, and I tried to keep it together.

"They couldn't stop us."

"No, they couldn't. They can't. They can slow us down, but they can't stop us."

"That's right," I told him, then my throat caught. I realized that he was saying something profound, something more than what was happening in this courtroom or this lawsuit. Something that had been happening in this country and every other country from the beginning of time. Some men would struggle to be considered equal, and other men would try to keep them down. Nobody knew that better than Chuck, Tony, our other plaintiffs, and the rest of the community, filling the gallery and unable to stifle tears of joy and relief.

Judge Rati-Jio was saying something on the dais, then defense attorney Yler asked the judge to poll the jury, a common practice. We composed ourselves as every single juror called out "guilty," "guilty," "guilty," one after the next, twelve in all, a collective judgment of humanity on those who would seek its destruction.

"Wow," I said to myself, wiping my eyes.

"TJ," Chuck whispered. "You should go to law school."

"I didn't even graduate college," I whispered back, like a confession.

Chuck smiled. "What're you waitin' for? I think they're still open."

CHAPTER SIXTY-FOUR

It was the day of Gabby's press conference, and everything was bigger and better than ever. It was being held in the glistening National Constitution Center at the historic center of Philadelphia, across from the Liberty Bell and Independence Hall, where the Declaration of Independence was signed and our country born. The United States Courthouse was next door, where John had pleaded guilty. But today, Gabby was fighting for justice in the Holmesburg lawsuit.

We had rented the Grand Hall, a vast open space that comprised the entire first floor of the building, and it had a soaring sixty-foot ceiling with flags from every state and a sweep of windows overlooking Independence National Historical Park. The walls were adorned with wraparound excerpts from the United States Constitution, which was about to come to life. The Grand Hall usually hosted cocktail parties for the Philadelphia Bar Association and various corporations, but today had a higher purpose. The vast empty room awaited the media, and they would be let in any minute.

We had set up a long table on a dais, and our clients Chuck Whitman, Tony Bales, Joaquin Hernandez, and Walter Melendez were seated. They were the plaintiffs who felt well enough to come, and each would be speaking today, so I busied myself checking on them and making sure they had water, a notepad, and a pen. There was an empty chair for the late Joe Ferguson, the plaintiff who had shown such humor in the face of his own death. The only other people present so far were the plaintiffs' families, who sat with my mother and father in the front row.

Three hundred chairs had been set up and on each seat was a Complaint, a set of medical and expert exhibits, and a thick press packet that contained bios of each of the speakers, including me. The recent developments in the case had gotten national attention. Dr. Bostwick, Mortensen, and Solkov were in prison, serving time for conspiracy to commit murder in order to stop the litigation. Their convictions had been splashed across the media and the cases were only helping us, shining a searing spotlight on our Holmesburg case. All major networks, cable, radio, and online news would be here today.

The community had showed up in triple the numbers, and they were demonstrating outside, coordinating with representatives from the clergy, various prison projects, medical organizations, law students, and an array of other public-interest groups. The story was blowing up, which would only intensify pressure on the defendants to settle.

Gabby bustled into the room from the double doors in the back, looking professional in her navy-blue suit, clapping her hands like a coach. "Okay, gentlemen, let's do a last run-through before we let them in. It's showtime!"

I'd never seen so many cameras and phones in my life, all pointed at the dais, where I sat at the end. Gabby started the presentation, outlined the Complaint, and introduced each of the plaintiffs. Chuck

Whitman, Tony Bales, Joaquin Hernandez, and Walter Melendez each told his own story about how he came to Holmesburg, the medical experiments that had been performed on him, and the terrible consequences on his health, suffered for decades. The media reacted instantly, murmuring among themselves, and even hardened reporters looked moved, appalled, and outraged. The plaintiffs' families wiped their eyes, and so did my mother.

When the plaintiffs were finished, Gabby retook the floor. "As you may know, Fournette Labs' former CEO, Dr. Carl Bostwick, has been convicted of conspiracy to murder my brother TJ Devlin and me, having hired killers to stop the lawsuit you're going to hear about today. But he failed, and we're here. So is my father, Paul Devlin, who was injured saving my life. My dad's in the front row, recovering from his injuries."

"Hear, hear!" my father shouted, grinning.

The media reacted with spontaneous applause, and there was hooting and hollering from the back, where the demonstrators had filled in.

Gabby gestured to me. "And now, I would like to turn the program over to my brother TJ Devlin, who was at Hessian Post Plaza that day. An investigator, he figured out Dr. Bostwick's murder-for-hire plot in time to thwart it and save both our lives." Gabby flashed me a smile. "Obviously, I'm grateful to TJ and my father. But what matters today is that Dr. Bostwick and his henchmen were willing to kill to prevent justice from being done in this case. You, as members of the press, know how vital your function is, as we sit here across from the Liberty Bell itself."

Gabby gestured to me. "I'd like TJ to tell you exactly what happened to us at Hessian Post Plaza, so you can hear firsthand what it's like when violence assaults justice. TJ?"

I stuffed my jitters and launched into a retelling of that day, as briefly as I could. Gabby had thought the story would get us extra media attention and shame the other defendants into making the offers we wanted. The media reacted, talking among themselves, and my parents beamed like I was the lead in the high school play.

Gabby looked over. "Thank you, TJ. Thank you to all of the plaintiffs, among them Chuck Whitman, Tony Bales, Joaquin Hernandez, and Walter Melendez, who spoke today. Special thanks to Joe Ferguson—and the empty chair at the end represents him. He passed away during this lawsuit, and I hope that his empty chair reminds you that there were countless men who were incarcerated throughout the Philadelphia prison system and died before they could get the justice they deserve. In criminal law, justice is served by going to jail, but in civil law, justice is served by financial compensation. I hope that today's presentation will encourage the defendants to compensate the plaintiffs for what they have gone through, in a horrendous situation that never should have happened in our historic city." Gabby paused. "Now I'd like to open the floor to questions."

Hands shot up, and everyone shouted at once. Gabby fielded questions and so did each of the plaintiffs. Finally she said, "We have time for one last question."

A male reporter raised his hand. "I have one for TJ Devlin. Mr. Devlin, your bio in the press packet neglects to mention you served time in Chester County Prison. Would you like to elaborate?"

My mouth went dry. I didn't relish exposing my criminal record to the public.

Gabby interjected, "I don't see how that's relevant."

"Why not?" The reporter scoffed. "You just said the press has the right to know the truth. Why withhold it from us with respect to your brother?"

Gabby started to answer, but I waved her off.

"Gabby, I'll answer that." I turned to the reporter, bracing myself. "Yes, I'm a recovering alcoholic and I served time for my crime, which was leaving a toddler in a car while I went drinking. It was a terrible mistake, but I've turned my life around since then." The words left my lips, and though the reporters chattered among themselves, I realized the world didn't end. Suddenly I felt a load lifted, one that I hadn't known I'd still been carrying. "So yes, I have a record, I served time, and I paid the price. My crime was more heinous than anyone else's on this panel, and we all paid our proverbial debt to society." I continued, speaking from my heart, "But here's the thing. We're here today because we're suing corporations and institutions that have *not* served a single day for their bad acts, nor have they paid these men, even though they *know* they caused untold suffering to them and their families. We're all human and we all make mistakes. Some of us pay for them, but not all of us. We sit here in Philadelphia at the epicenter of equal justice, and I hope that one day, there will truly be equal justice for us all. Thank you."

Gabby smiled, delighted. My mother jumped to her feet, clapping wildly.

My father looked positively teary, and the demonstrators cheered, hooted, and hollered. Some of the media even got up, clapping.

Chuck looked over at me, with a smile. "TJ, did you apply yet?"

"To what?"

"College. You gettin' younger?"

CHAPTER SIXTY-FIVE

I walked into Petco for the first time, dazzled by its gigantic size, superbright lights, and primary-color signage. I was a Petco Virgin because I bought my cat food online, but I needed emergency salmon-and-rice. Mango still wanted nothing to do with me during the day but slept with me every night. I settled for that deal since I wasn't getting any better offers anyway.

I tried to orient myself in Petco, but the layout bewildered me. There were aisles upon aisles of cans, bags, leashes, and toys for dogs, cats, fish, ferrets, and even turtles. The air smelled carnal from end-caps with rawhide rolls, sticks, and balls, next to a display of dried pig ears, elk antlers, and cow hooves, which I found horrifying.

I wandered into the nearest aisle and spotted a pretty brunette with a little black-and-white dog at the other end. I realized it was Maya Vitelli, my old almost-flame, Patrick's niece. She looked even better off duty, with no makeup and her thick black hair down. She had on an oversize T-shirt, gym shorts, and flip-flops.

I didn't know whether to say hello. The last time I'd seen her had been mortifying, apologizing in front of her friends for standing her up. Plus my flirting skills were rusty. Okay, covered in cobwebs. Maybe even barnacles.

"TJ?" Maya asked, turning.

She remembers my name? "Oh, hi, Maya." I took a few steps closer. "How's the calculus business?"

"Selling like hotcakes." Maya smiled, and her eyes were that amazing light brown.

"Your dog's cute."

"Thanks. Her name's S'mores."

"What breed is she?" *Flirt, TJ, flirt!*

"Havanese. I always take her here on her birthday and let her pick out a toy."

Aw. "Happy Birthday, S'mores." I bent down and the dog trotted over, her round eyes rolling and her pink tongue lolling out of her mouth. I scratched her soft ear. "She's adorable. How old is she?"

"Three."

Nothing. I got nothing.

"TJ, do you have a dog?"

"No. I have a cat who barely likes me."

"That's hard to believe."

Is she flirting? I didn't know what to say. I tried not to think of Carrie anymore, though I did think of beer. But I'd stayed sober by working the program, and home group welcomed me with open arms.

"If you don't have a dog, why are you in this aisle?"

Be funny, TJ. "I'm fleeing the scary pig's ears."

Maya's eyes flared. "I know, right? Who wants *those* on the living room floor?"

"Not me. That's where my socks go."

Maya chuckled. "I'm a vegetarian. Are you?"

"No, but I think about it." *I'll give up bacon for you. Say the word.*

Maya's smile faded. "I'd ask how you are but I kind of know. I was at work the day of the shooting. I heard they tried to kill you and your family. Is your dad okay? I read he was shot."

"He's fine, thanks." *Nice.*

"So a crooked drug company was behind it, and you brought them down?"

"Totally. I'm a hero now."

"I knew you had it in you."

"You did?" I asked, surprised. "How?"

"You're funny. Funny people are smart."

"Thanks." It struck me as something my mother would say, and I liked it. Maybe our attraction was mutual, after all. "My big news is I'm going back to school, so I'll be a hero with a college degree."

"For real?" Maya cocked her head, pleased.

"For real. They'll transfer my credits, so I only have two more classes." I'd paid my tuition with proceeds from the sale of the Maserati, proof that my values had gone down the tubes.

"You must be excited."

"I am. I already have my pencil case and Lisa Frank notebook."

Maya laughed. "I had one of those!"

"Of course you did. You're a cool girl."

"Oh really?"

"The coolest." *Are we vibing or what?*

"So what's up with your cat? Why doesn't she like you?"

"She thinks she's out of my league, but I'm pretty sure I could make her happy and I'm crazy about her eyes."

Maya burst into laughter. "Oh, I got you!"

"Do you?" Then I went for it. "I mean, can I get a second chance? How about I take you and S'mores to lunch for her birthday?"

Maya smiled slyly. “Well, you *are* a hero now . . .”

“Totally.”

“Okay.” Maya chuckled, turning away. “But first let’s get your cat a toy.”

S’mores trotted after her.

And so did I.

EPILOGUE

It was a cool and beautiful night, and a string of twinkly white lights festooned the deck, swaying in the breeze off the water. I was standing outside with Maya, and we were making out like teenagers. The party was inside, and the air was filled with the smooth-sailing sounds of my father's Yacht Rock playlist.

We were at my parents' new house in Point Pleasant Beach, a charming three-bedroom. It wasn't the big McMansion they used to have, but they moved here to be near Connor, having retired after the firm closed. They'd been humbled by what they'd gone through and it had changed their lives. They put their love and time where it belonged, with each other and the family.

John was still in prison, and Nancy had gone back to work, so all four grandparents took turns babysitting Connor, the sun in our family solar system. I still brought him Matchbox cars because he hadn't outgrown them. Okay, *I* hadn't outgrown them.

Maya smiled, gorgeous in a black dress. "Are you going to wear that all night?"

I looked handsome as hell in my mortarboard and gown. "Of course. It's my graduation party."

"Right, but it's not a costume party."

"So? I'm wearing it to bed later. Get ready for college-educated sex."

Maya burst into laughter. "You're silly, Thomas."

"I love that you call me that. It's like you're reading my diploma." I readjusted my mortarboard. "I think I need another bobby pin."

"That's not sexy."

"Just wait until later." I leaned over and kissed her. "I love you."

"I love you, too." Maya touched my cheek.

I breathed in, feeling a happiness I'd never known. Maya was a woman who wouldn't settle for less than the best in me, and I was a better man these days, for the both of us. We'd moved in together, and Mango loved her, S'mores, and me, in that order. I'd stayed sober and would start at Temple Law after a summer job at a West Chester law firm. Gabby was at Community Legal Services in Philly, working full-time in the public interest. She still represented the Holmesburg plaintiffs, and the lawsuit was making its way through the courts. None of the other defendants had settled, which broke her heart, and mine.

I put an arm around Maya, and we looked up at a beautifully starry sky, a sight that money couldn't buy or reserve for the rich. I thought that justice should be the same way, free and available to everyone. I knew it was far from that yet, but I prayed that it would be, someday. Hell, I'd gone from ex-con to soon-to-be-lawyer, so yes, I believed in the impossible.

I just had to have faith, and work for justice.

I couldn't wait to start.

ACKNOWLEDGMENTS AND AUTHOR'S NOTE

First, thank you very much to each and every one of my readers. I've written thirty-six novels in almost as many years, and I'm grateful every day of my life that I make a living writing books. I've been blessed to see my readership grow over decades, and with every sentence, I think how my reader will react. So I'd love to hear your reactions to this novel, both good and bad, and I read all of the reviews that people post online. I'm grateful for every one because no story is complete unless it is told and heard by another person, namely you.

That said, thank you to the experts who helped me with the research of this novel, and any mistakes herein are my own.

TJ's recovery story is completely fictional, but I did research aplenty to inform his character and his journey. I read most of the major publications from Alcoholics Anonymous, like the seminal Big Book and *Twelve Steps and Twelve Traditions*. They were vital resources for me, as they would be for anyone struggling with alcoholism or drug addiction. The fundamentals of the program resonated for me in many ways, and Alcoholics Anonymous is a living example of people helping one another and serving the community as a whole.

I also attended a slew of AA meetings via Zoom, anonymously, since there are open meetings that the public may attend, but confidentialities must be maintained. I have kept confidential everything

I've heard in those meetings, and none of it appears in this novel in any way, shape, or form. I was so moved by the bravery and the honesty of group members in each and every meeting, stepping up to share his or her stories, and I hope TJ's struggle pays them the honor they so richly deserve.

I also read a number of memoirs written by recovering alcoholics, and I would recommend any one of them, including Erica Barnett, *Quitter: A Memoir of Drinking, Relapse, and Recovery*; Mary Karr, *Lit*; J. R. Moehringer, *The Tender Bar*; and David Carr, *The Night of the Gun*.

Finally, thank you to Marge Figun, a dear friend of mine in recovery, for reading the manuscript and making suggestions, for which I am very grateful. I want to acknowledge those of you who are in recovery from alcohol or drug addiction, or who have family or friends in that position. If you or someone you love is struggling with alcohol or drug issues, please visit aa.org, al-anon.org, or na.org.

This is a work of fiction, but the elements of the law and justice are true. This matters a great deal to me, because I'm a former trial lawyer and adjunct law professor, and I've taught Justice & Fiction at the University of Pennsylvania Law School, a course I developed to illustrate how popular fiction can convey needed information about our systems of civil and criminal justice. For that reason, I hew as close to the law when there are legal situations in the novels, and Gabriella Devlin's lawsuit on behalf of the former inmates at Holmesburg Prison in Philadelphia is a case in point.

It is horrifying but true that inmates at some of Philadelphia's prisons were used as human subjects of medical experimentation from the early fifties to the early seventies, the era before informed consent. The inmates tested an array of products under the auspices of the late Dr. Albert Kligman, who was then a professor in the medical school at Penn. Thus, while the plaintiffs in the novel are fictional, the case they brought is founded on true historical facts as described herein. I can only hope that if the public becomes aware that such misconduct took place, it will help ensure that nothing like it ever happens again. For those wishing to learn more about the horrific medical experiments at Holmesburg, I would recommend Allen M. Hornblum's excellent *Acres of Skin* and *Sentenced to Science*. Professor Hornblum was a volunteer at Holmesburg Prison during the time in question, and his books include his eyewitness reports of the skin-patch and other tests.

Huge thanks to Nick Casenta, Esq., the recently-retired chief deputy district attorney of the Chester County District Attorney's Office, one of the best lawyers in the Commonwealth and a man I'm proud to call my friend. Nick still gets his brain picked daily by his colleagues and me. He helped so much with the legal procedure and law in this book, as well as every one of my novels set in my home state of Pennsylvania.

I loved learning about Buddhism, and I recommend Matthieu Ricard's *On the Path to Enlightenment* as well as Thich Nhat Hanh's *Taming the Tiger Within* and *The Heart of Understanding*, both of which I listened to on audiobook narrated by the incomparable "Golden Voice" Edoardo Ballerini.

Thanks to Adam Kelly of Phoenixville Coin and Jewelry Exchange and Brandon Shim of Phoenixville Gold Buyers. Big thanks to Young King Mike Juliana at Maserati of the Main Line, who taught me everything about those amazing cars. Thanks to Natalie Christiano and John "Jack" Lynch III.

Thank you to my amazing team at G. P. Putnam's Sons, led by the great Ivan Held, who inspires and supports me at every step. Thank you to my wonderful editors, first Mark Tavani and then Sally Kim, both of whom improved this manuscript and guided it into publication. Thank you, too, to Aranya Jain and Tarini Sipahimalani for their great support.

Thanks to Alexis Welby and Katie Grinch for their hard work in publicity and to genius marketers Ashley McClay and Molly Pieper. Thanks to Anthony Ramondo and Tal Goretsky for topping themselves yet again with a sensational cover, and thanks to audiobook mavens Karen Dziekonski and Scott Sherratt. Lots of gratitude and love to the reps and everyone else at Putnam who works so hard on my behalf.

Thanks and love to my terrific agents, Robert Gottlieb and Erica Silverman of Trident Media Group. Finally, thanks to their assistant, Aurora Fernandez, who has been so helpful. Thanks for their hard work in Hollywood to Debbie Deuble-Hill and Kyle Loftus of Independent Artist Group. And thanks to the greatest speakers' agent ever, Trinity Ray of the Tuesday Agency.

Finally, lots of love and thanks to my beloved Laura Leonard, who supports me every day in every conceivable way. Thanks and love to Nan Daley and Katie Rinda, who help with research, marketing, and every other kind of support.

Thanks and big love to my amazing daughter, Francesca Serritella, a novelist in her own right. I've been writing about family all my life, because that's what matters most to me, and I'm blessed to have an amazing daughter, who's also my best friend.

Love you, honey.

HOW I WROTE THIS NOVEL

I'm so happy to have *The Truth about the Devlins* published as an exclusive edition for Barnes & Noble, and I thought I would write something really special. Here, I'm going to lift the curtain on my creative process and show you how I go about writing a novel—in particular, this one. This requires me to divulge my trade secrets: what goes on behind the scenes, especially at the beginning, when the most important decisions get made.

I'm also guessing that some of you may be thinking about writing yourselves, and you might find this encouraging and handy. I truly think every one of us has a novel inside, or maybe several, maybe even a series. I feel so lucky to be published, and when I think back to my first novel, I didn't have an idea for a second one or any sense of what was to come in my career. But here we are, more than thirty years later, during which time I've written thirty-six novels, including this one. To tell you the truth, I have no idea how that happened. I just started writing and didn't stop, and my profession is one of the greatest blessings of my life, aside from my beloved daughter.

If you are thinking about writing, let me say one thing at the outset. There is no right way to write. However you do it and however it suits you is what's right for you, and that's all that matters. So what follows is how *I* write.

First, be not afraid.

Before I get into the nitty-gritty, I just want to say a word about any fear or anxiety you may have about starting a novel. If you feel nervous, it's okay. God knows, it's a daunting task. No one teaches you how to do it in school, and even if they had, you'd still be on your own when you face not only one blank page, but about four hundred of them. Worry is part of the process. Just accept that. I feel nervous every time I start a new book and I've been doing it since forever.

So what do I do about my case of nerves?

You press on regardless. Don't let worry stop you. Just do the best you can and go forward and give it a try. No one ever sees your first draft. No one has to even know you're writing a novel. You can keep that to yourself. You don't have to tell everybody everything. This could just be your thing you do for yourself. Your dream, even.

We always ask kids what they want to be when they grow up, but we never ask adults. And if you're like me, you change over time, you grow. Maybe you get married, maybe you get divorced. Maybe you try this job, maybe you try that one. Maybe you move, change your mind, and move back. Reverse is a legit gear. In my opinion, all of these things are good. That's the life part.

I believe that adults are allowed to have dreams. So if you decide that you want to become a writer, at any stage, you should just start writing. Set some time aside to do it and do it regularly. Write whatever comes. The late Stephen Sondheim wrote the great musical *Sunday in the Park with George*, which is about the creative process, and in one of its songs, "Move On," he says, "Stop worrying if your vision is new, let others make that decision, they usually do, you keep moving on." I think what he means is that the job of the artist is to create, and the rest is beside the point.

So if you want to write a novel, give it a try. Protect the time in which you write as if it were a candle and you were one of those people wandering around a dark Victorian house in a scary movie, cupping the flame with your hand. Protect your candle. The candle is you and your dream.

How do I even begin?

Let's go back to Sondheim. In another of his songs, "Putting it Together," he writes, "Art isn't easy, every minor detail is a major decision." I remember those words every time I face a blank page. Self-doubt creeps in, which is completely predictable because I don't write with an outline. My method, such as it is, is to start writing and keep writing, at least two thousand words a day, allowing the characters to emerge and act in ways that reveal themselves to me and the reader at the same time. It's the most anxiety-producing way to write, but I believe that it keeps readers turning the pages. If I don't know what's going to happen next, how can you? We're both in suspense. And the surprise ending comes as a surprise to me, too.

But whatever the method, there are decisions I make at the beginning, and I will spotlight a few that led to *The Truth about the Devlins.*

What's this book about?

One day I knew I wanted to write about a family in close-up, burrow deep into characters, and explore their relationships in depth. I think this was in reaction to just having finished writing *Loyalty*, a historical novel that had five main characters, several different families, and was wide in scope. I found myself wanting to change things up and narrow my focus. It's how I felt, but it's also how a reader who follows me from book to book might feel, and I am always very mindful of my readers because I'm grateful for every single one of you. I want you to get a variety of stories from me, and I want to write a variety to keep it fresh for me, so that it's fresh for us both.

So who's your hero?

This is one of the most important decisions you will have to make, and one of the most fun. It's a question of whom you want to write about, and since it takes a long time to write a novel, it's a question of whom you want to be in your mind for that time. I basically write a novel a year, which means that I am writing a first draft for about seven months. So my main character has to be someone I want to spend a lot of time with, and more importantly, it has to be someone whom the reader wants to spend a lot of time with.

I feel about my main characters the way I feel about my friends. I like heroes who are likable, but have flaws. I want them to feel real, and to create a character like that, you have to draw upon your imagination. And since my focus here was going to be on the Devlins, and story was going to go deep, I realized that this novel would be carried on the strength of the hero. So I knew that he would have to be voicey. Enter TJ Devlin.

Wait. What's voicey mean?

To me, voice is *how* the character tells a story. People in your life tell you stories, and everybody tells a story a different way. Sometimes they use long sentences and sometimes short ones. Sometimes they tell it funny, but sometimes they're serious. The way you tell a story reflects who you are, and that's why voice and character are, in my mind, not just closely aligned but the same thing.

And while we're on the subject, I'll throw in my other trade secret, which is that I believe the voice and character and *plot* are the same thing. In other words, a certain type of character will tell the story in a certain way, and he will also find himself in a certain type of situation, and he will handle it in a way that would be consistent with his character. His actions will inform who his character is at the same time they reveal *who* his character is to the reader, and even to the writer, if the writer is me.

So voice really matters, and if a person can tell the story really well, you might be carried along by the way they tell it. That was the kind of hero I wanted for *The Truth about the Devlins*, and as soon as I thought that, I thought of one thing.

You want to make him funny, don't you, Lisa?

Because I knew *The Truth about the Devlins* would be carried on the voice of the main character, I felt he should be witty. The phrase "charming disappointment" popped into my mind. I don't know why, and I can't explain it, nor do I want to try. It doesn't matter. You could just have some crazy idea like that if you're writing, too, and you get to go with it because this is America and you get to write whatever you want.

So I knew my hero had to be "charming," and for me, charming is wonderful. I love charming people, and one of the aspects of charm is humor. I wanted to make him funny. Now that's daunting because it's not always easy to be funny, but I thought I could be funny if I had thirty-seven tries, which is probably the number of drafts I go through before anybody sees anything I write.

So I said, Let him be funny, because humor is a great way to deal with trouble. It's endearing. Plus, it's better than whining. Nobody wants to read about a guy who's complaining. I'd much rather have a guy who's in a heap of trouble and dealing with it in a way that's entertaining, and even admirable.

As for the "disappointment" part, I was feeling like I wanted to write about a hero who has made mistakes, and I mean really big ones. I don't want to spoil anything if you haven't read the novel yet, but TJ Devlin makes king-size, holy-crap, no-joke mistakes. I don't mean to make light of it, but he really drives his life into a ditch. I don't judge him, because I have great respect for the fact that your life can take a wrong turn. I empathize with the mistake-makers of the world. A lot of us make trouble for ourselves that we have to get out of. I'm divorced twice for a reason.

I wanted a character who had gotten himself into a ditch because I was curious about how far down you could go and still get out. I'm realizing now, for the first time, this is what I meant when I said going deep. TJ Devlin had put himself into a very deep hole, and I thought that if he could get himself out, we would really admire that, and that would be a story well worth telling, and reading.

So I had the "charm" and I had the "disappointment," and that would mean that TJ Devlin would be the black sheep of the family. It made me think about how we all have roles in our family, and how those roles define us, whether for good or ill. You probably know families where one is "the smart one" and one is "the cute one" and one is "the problem child." These roles may be true when you're six years old, but a child labeled "the dumb one" will start to think he's dumb, and it becomes a self-fulfilling prophecy.

I think we change and grow throughout life, and that's why as you get older, you can go back to your family of origin or visit for Thanksgiving and all of a sudden things aren't great because you're trying to fit into a role that doesn't work anymore, like putting on a pair of jeans after you've gained some weight—not that I know anything about that.

By the way, why did you make the main character male?

Bottom line, I started writing a long time ago, and part of the reason I started writing was because I wanted to see strong, independent female main characters in crime fiction. Back in the 1990s, I felt like women were still second banana in a lot of thrillers. I'd been a trial lawyer, and even legal thrillers of the time never showed women standing up in front of a jury. I thought this really had to change, and that I might as well try and change it myself.

That's when I got the aforementioned divorce, then decided to change my life because I had the aforementioned child and I realized I wanted to stay at home and raise her. So I had to find a new way to make a living. I always thought I had a novel in me, and it turned out it was true. And when I started writing, I wrote only female main characters because that was what I thought the world needed more of, and what I wanted to do the most. I wrote so many female characters that I wrote seventeen books in a series about an all-female law firm, Rosato & DiNunzio. I was really leaning into the estrogen.

But at some point in my career, I started to wonder if I *could* write a male main character. I think fear built up that I couldn't. So I tried it. And luckily, it worked out, and I said, Okay, you can write men or women and not sweat it. You just have to have an imagination and a heart and a soul, which I'm pretty sure that both genders have.

So when it came to Devlins, I wanted to write a male main character because I wanted to write about the "charming disappointment" and also wanted to explore the subtle forms of sexism in a family like the Devlins. That would mean that the most disappointment would come from a male child, because one sad-but-true truth about the Devlins is that they don't expect as much from their daughter as from their sons. (Odd, even though the mom is a lawyer, too.) Somehow it's okay for Gabrielle to go off on her own, travel, and do pro bono work in a way that might not be acceptable for John or TJ. I'm always interested in how stale gender traditions hurt men and women alike.

So that meant that I would write a male main character where more would be expected from him by his father and even by his mother, who favors him in many respects. They have a very special relationship, but at the same time, even she has learned not to expect much from him, as much as she loves him. And so TJ doesn't expect much for himself. Ultimately, he is a charming disappointment even to himself.

What's with TJ and cars?

There are lots of ways to create a character, but my favorite way is to explore all different facets of them. Like that TJ's a charming disappointment or that he's clever. But what does he look like? What does he eat? How does he dress? Who are his heroes? What are his hobbies? What defines him, to himself?

For TJ, it became cars. It occurred to me that he would be a car guy, and I like that he would even think of himself that way. It's something that we all do, almost the same way that we assign roles in families. We say, I'm a dog person, I'm a horse girl, I'm an Eagles fan. We have ways of defining ourselves to ourselves, and sometimes they're even accurate.

And if a character has a hobby like fixing cars, what does it show you about him? I think it shows you that TJ is really smart, even though he didn't finish school. Anybody who can take a car apart and put it back together again is smart. And not only are they smart, they're tenacious. Also, he's flipping cars. He's going to the auctions, he's finding the right cars, he's putting the money together to buy cars, he's going to fix them and sell them to turn a profit over time. He has an entrepreneurial spirit. In a way, he's his father, writ smaller. He's a good businessman, and he's his own boss, but he's held himself back in so many ways.

And the fact that he loves cars tells you even more. He loves his Maserati—who wouldn't? He likes to go fast, and what does that tell you about him as a character? He likes action. He's confident when he steers. He's bold. He takes chances. I wanted him to be a guy in motion, and in this book, he's chasing people and doing things all the time. He's different and kinda cool. A Maserati.

And by the way, it makes an interesting contrast with his father. When you're talking about creating a character, you think about the major characters, but also minor characters, like the father. He's not the star of the book, but he really matters. What is Paul Devlin's hobby? I didn't set it up this way, but when I started to think about it, I thought the father should collect watches. He's a watch guy.

Look how different that is from what TJ does. Paul Devlin collects fancy, expensive watches. A watch is a small but beautiful piece of machinery, like the car engine is a big but beautiful piece of machinery. So father and son are a lot alike, more alike than they know.

Also, while we're on the subject of Paul Devlin, he's a good example of a character that I assigned a hero to. He's a big fan of Winston Churchill. Who someone chooses as a hero tells you a lot about them. I'm interested in Winston Churchill myself and I admire his qualities of leadership, just like Paul Devlin does. He tries to get his kids interested in his hero, he propagandizes. He wants them to grow up to be leaders, so he tells them a leader to admire. We all know people like that, maybe we *are* people like that. But that's another way you can delineate character.

Interestingly, TJ doesn't really have a hero. There's no one he really admires outside of his brother and his father. In a way, he's self-actualized, which might even be better than admiring someone else and trying to be like them. I'll leave that to you.

Now that you have main character, who else is in the story?

So TJ Devlin grows up being the baby of the family, not expecting much from himself and no one else does either. Still, they're charmed by him. He's fun. But after a while, he's a permanent man baby, and ultimately, he can't feel good about himself. Then that made me realize that he needed a foil, a contrast, so he should have an older brother who is the firstborn child, the responsible one, and the high achiever. TJ would naturally idolize that brother, but at the same time would be forever defining himself in relationship to his older brother and coming up short. So I knew I'd have good stuff between the brothers to deal with, and that would be part of TJ's struggle.

As for the big brother, John Devlin, I wanted him to be the responsible one, and while that has its advantages, it can be a burden. And then I wanted to intensify John's struggle, so I gave him a double whammy in placing the family in family business. The future of the family *and* the firm are on his shoulders. A family business has its own unique set of problems—if you mess up, you mess up your family life *and* your family's livelihood. That's what TJ does when he screws up, and it's a luxury that only the baby of the family has. The one who is supposed to achieve *has to* come through, and John knows that.

Then I knew I wanted a sister, Gabrielle, and she's at least the equal of these boys, though she isn't given credit within the family. I like that she does what some middle children do, which is be a peacemaker between the older brother and younger brother, and even between the kids and the parents. That has to be an impossible position, but I love it for her characterization because it really underscores what Gabrielle does as a lawyer. In her pro bono case for the former Holmesburg inmates, she puts together different plaintiffs and sues an array of defendants. That's a skill set that she developed in her family, whether she knows it or not. She sees the big picture, in so many different ways.

She also has a very happy marriage, and she and her husband share a broad-minded and open-hearted approach to life and the world, which contrasts with her father. I like Paul Devlin, too, but his world is confined to the firm, his clients, his Chamber of Commerce pals, and the golf course.

Last but not least is the mother, and I kind of adore her, and that's not me taking credit for her. She just came to me partly because I'm Italian American and I felt the family needed a little flavor, but also because she's feisty in her own way. I'm a single mother and I adored my mother, and I really have such a true admiration for mothers of all kinds and what it takes to keep a family together. Marie Devlin wields power in a subtle way, but only because her husband is dominant. They are equals because she has a completely different sphere of practice than he does, and they earn money together. And they've worked out the marriage they have and their affection abides over time, and I wanted that to come through in the novel.

Marie Devlin is very important to TJ, and their relationship is unique. I think this does happen between the baby of the family and the mother, and I can understand how it comes about. She's such a good mother that she gives him the deep and unconditional love that he needs, and he is grateful to her. There's a scene in the book that I won't recount here because you may not have read it yet, but I like when she confronts TJ with how she feels. She allows herself that moment only *in* that moment, and I think we understand the dynamic between the two of them in that chapter. The reader will know how she feels, maybe we all feel the same way about him at this point. That, to me, is what makes TJ so interesting as a main character, in that his charm is abundant, but his flaws are really clear, and as the novel goes on, they are possibly getting worse. Which brings me to the next big decision:

What does your hero want?

I did not know about this question when I first started writing novels for a living, but I eventually found out that this was the most important decision that you're supposed to make. This is when they start talking about the character's motivation, but I honestly think it's much more than that, now that I've done this thirty-six times.

Your character has to want something, and the reader has to know what that is right away. Now, you might wonder why that's so, and I'll tell you. The reason is so that the reader will identify with your hero. The reader will root for him, but we have to know *what* he wants.

I think that's because any novel is a story that goes from point A to point B. The story begins when we know what he wants and it ends when we see whether he gets it. I think that happens subliminally in people's thinking because we were raised to think of stories that way with beginnings, middles, and ends. It's a logical way to think, and I think the key to writing a believable character as well as a smooth narrative is sometimes as simple as logic.

In *The Truth about the Devlins*, what's interesting is that TJ is a character who isn't completely sure of all the things he wants, which is a great situation because it's complex to think about and for me to write about and for you to read about.

For example, he's in recovery so he wants to stay sober, but that isn't all he wants, is it? He might want to grow up. He might want to change his life. He wants to be in love. He wants to have a child. He wants a family. His heart is telling him he wants to be an adult. He doesn't want to be like his big brother anymore, he wants to be himself, but he isn't quite sure who that is. He's got to figure it all out, and that's a perfect example of how going deep in the character will be so interesting, because ultimately he's having a huge identity crisis, and that will be a layered underpinning to the story that will live underneath and enrich the topline plot and action. If he can really grow up during the course of the novel, in addition to solving whatever the topline problem is, then I could have a really satisfying story. That was my hope.

What's the setting?

This decision is also an important one. I've set many thrillers in my hometown of Philadelphia, and an urban setting gives a novel grit, tension, and urgency. I've also written historical novels set in Rome and Palermo and used the ancient and dramatic geography of those places. Reviewers often say that my settings become a character, and that makes me happy. Bottom line, setting anchors characters.

Or it doesn't.

I decided to turn that rule on its head in *The Truth about the Devlins*. I did *not* want setting to be a character at all. I wanted the setting to recede and allow TJ to take the stage, since he's having the crisis of his life. So I decided to set the novel in the suburbs, neither city nor country, and it could be anywhere, because I wanted the setting to provide TJ as little anchor as possible. You'll see throughout the book that there are corporate parks, strip malls, and anonymous housing developments, and they intensify TJ's sensation of not knowing where he belongs. His apartment is new, and he didn't grow up where his parents live. He literally has no roots or foundation, which mirrors his instability. If where we're from helps us define who we are, then TJ has to come up with that answer on his own, intensifying his struggle.

You have characters and setting, so what happens now?

This is just a way of saying, "What's your idea?" and I had this idea almost the minute that I knew that I wanted to write about charming disappointment. The idea was the older brother would tell the younger brother that he killed someone. I really wanted something that would surprise my main character, and this was the most surprising thing that came to me. For the black sheep to hear that his adored and anointed older brother had done something so heinous would be upside-down, especially in the world of the Devlin family. So when the good son does the worst thing that you could possibly do, it's going to freak out the bad son. And that worst thing is murder.

So how did you write the rest of the book?

Again, it's decision after decision after decision. The first chapter is the good brother telling the bad brother that he committed a murder, so the second chapter is, what happens next? And basically every day, when I start a new chapter, I ask myself, What would they do next? What would TJ do next? What would the people around him be doing next, and how would that affect him?

If you just ask yourself that question, chapter after chapter, believe it or not, you will have a finished novel at the end. It's kind of a miracle. I have found that if I keep going this way, what really is happening is that I'm constructing a novel bit by bit, and as such, it will have that realistic characterization and logical narrative flow that I mentioned earlier.

Sometimes people ask me if I have to go back and put in a clue or something like that, and the answer is always no. Because when a novel is constructed organically, the character is given free rein to take over, and he does. He behaves in accordance with who he is, and in *The Truth about the Devlins*, TJ gets setback after setback, and at the same time, he gives himself setback after setback.

So he gets in a deeper and deeper hole, and as I was writing the book, I didn't know if he would ever be able to get out. And as I said earlier, if I was wondering if he'd get out of it, you would be, too. And you can really write a novel that way, and for me, that's enormously satisfying. It means that you invented the whole thing, or rather, your characters did, which will make a fictional person in a fictional struggle come to life, even though none of it is true.

I can't even write that last sentence without cringing, because to me everything that happened in *The Truth about the Devlins* is true. It reminds me of a wonderful quote from the great director Francis Ford Coppola, something like, "Nothing in my movies happened, but all of it is true." And that's how I feel about what I write, and certainly about the Devlins.

For me, a novel like *The Truth about the Devlins*, and all of my books, come down to a story of what it is to be a human being, to live life, to love and lose, to try and fail, and hopefully, ultimately to succeed. I always feel better after I finish writing one of my books because my hero got himself out of the colossal bind he got himself into.

And it inspires me. I know that sounds crazy, but I feel very inspired by the books I write, and every book I read, and every movie and TV show or play I see. All of the arts magnify each other, and all of the arts inform each other. That's why when I look back on this piece, it quotes novelists and playwrights and film directors.

The arts matter because they teach us about ourselves, and they connect us, not only to each other but to ourselves. That's why I feel so lucky to be able to write and read books, and I am so grateful to Barnes & Noble for allowing me to write this piece, and I'm so grateful to all of you for taking the time to read it, and my novel.

I cherish each and every one of you. You have supported me, literally and figuratively, my whole entire life.

You have my gratitude and my love.

Lisa Scottoline
Philadelphia, 2023